BHUMIKA

*To my younger self and all those out there who look for a
rainbow beyond the storm of their minds.
This one's for you.*

Playlist

Perfect by Ed Sheeran

I Like Me Better by Lauv

Rolling in the Deep by Adele

A Thousand Years by Christina Perri

Hass Hass by Diljit Dosanjh feat. Sia

Heaven by Julia Michaels

Still With You by Jungkook of BTS

Grenade by Bruno Mars

I Found by Amber Run

Under Your Influence by Chris Brown

Die With a Smile by Bruno Mars & Lady Gaga

If the World was Ending by JP Saxe & Julia Michaels

Author Note

Dear Reader Friend,

This is my first ever creative endeavour, and I hope from every corner of my heart that I've done justice and brought a story to you that holds meaning. Thank you for giving your time for *Healing Love*.

As I write this, I understand how phenomenal everything feels. Never in my wildest dreams I thought I would've written a book let alone have such wonderful people read it.

Healing Love is the first instalment in The Healing Phoenix series, following the story of Bianca and Jason.

It is set in Australia and is written in British English.

In saying everything, I would like to bring your attention to the trigger warnings that come with reading *Healing Love*.

Healing Love contains parental cheating, suicidal ideation and attempt, self-harm, grief, strong sexual context and scenes, profanity, panic attacks, mentions of arson and violence, and murder. Therefore, reader discretion is advised as your mental health is important to me, and it is suitable for readers of 18+.

In all, *Healing Love* is full of love from the many relationships we may have in our lives and also those who we meet randomly. *Love can be found everywhere we look.*

Happy reading!

Bhumika

The Series Statement

The process of living is an ongoing attempt to heal. No matter how much composure we get, one is still healing; coming to terms with their world and the changes it brings with it. The healing process of emotionality, spirituality, mentality, and physicality is both universal and infinite.

The symphony of growing and healing is carefully constructed to leave behind lessons—not ones with a finite end.

CHAPTER 1

Bianca

My whole life I've lived in a bittersweet symphony filled with moments that made me laugh and cry, where joy and sorrow intertwined unexpectedly.

Just like now as I stand in the airport, I am instantly hit by my most beautiful and saddening memories.

In movies and books, the bustling airport, with its cacophony of sounds and the constant movement of people, promises a fresh start and a step towards a new beginning. For me, it promises a return to the painful chapter of my life, where the healing wounds of my heart and mind will reopen—threatening raw emotions to flood.

Here goes to the beginning of the ending.

Never thought I'd be back at this airport. This place holds the

memories of the many painful wails and screams after I lost my everything.

If there is one thing I have learned in these five years, it is that nothing comes easy, but it can leave with the snap of fingers. One moment I have everything, the next … nothing. *Nothing* is permanent; once you taste it, there is no power that can make you feel fully complete.

It's a sudden hit of nostalgia as a gush of chilly air greets me through the opening of the automatic doors. My hair goes flying back with the impact, exactly how I left it. The same clouds, ready to pour down any minute, are hiding away the sun. It proves my memory right, because especially in the winter months, starting in June, finding the sun is harder than finding my favourite shade of blue among all the shades.

I can tell myself I'm back solely for the company project—the voices in my head will say otherwise.

Australia's well-known interior designing company, Florals & Bells, assigned five of its deserving candidates to go to the five different states in the country, explore them, and come back with a completed 'revolutionary' design set or at least something that could give new sense into the industry.

Luckily for me, it was the city I had grown up in. So, after the two-hour flight from the Australian capital, I find myself stranded in the waiting bay for my best friend to come and pick me up.

I had told the girls of my return a week ago on our weekly video call, and if they could have come out of the phone and kissed the hell out of me, they would've. After my hiatus of five years, I can't believe I would see and feel them in flesh and bone.

They had the entire itinerary planned for the days I am here, successfully ignoring my constant reminders that I would also need to do some work, but that piece of information fell on deaf ears. I'd gotten a rough run of the spa dates we would go on with Sage, the shopping sprees with Eva, and exploring clubs with Kiara.

My first stop is at the Archers' home—an hour's drive from the airport. Eva promised to pick me up, but when she comes, I'll have grey hair. There is no sign of the woman with dark hair and green eyes waving a welcome. I may love her, but Eva is going to get a piece of my mind.

The waiting area is a filtering station for people being dropped off and picked up, and I've been standing here long enough to know that I'm in neither of the categories. My patience and loyalty are being put to their test, and things are looking south—for Eva.

"Pick up, Eva … pickup." My phone presses against my cheek, and my feet tap an impatient beat as I wait. It rings again, rings, and dies. *Again.*

I huff in annoyance as the phone rings only to decline again. To top it off, the wind has my dress flying in all directions. I know I should've worn the navy suit, and not a dress that can give any bystanders a flash.

Well, that's a great welcome back.

From my peripheral vision, the couple next to me hide their daughter behind them, shooting me death glares as if I put pineapple on their pizza.

I hold Ma responsible for my dislike of pineapple on pizza. Being true to her Italian roots, she made pizza a comfort food—beside her baking—and putting pineapple on it is equivalent to grabbing a bucket of sand and eating it raw.

Feeling embarrassed, I move up the waiting area to keep my breakdown away from the public eye.

Reminder: Kill Eva.

At the thought, my phone vibrates with the name of the victim.

"Hey Bee! I—" The silky sound of her voice fills my ears. No matter the warmth, I am still giving a piece of my mind I've been saving.

"Don't *Bee* me. Where the hell are you, Evalyn Archer?" I grumble. With my hands on my hips, I try to take a deep breath.

"So, yeah, the thing is, rush hour has started, and I'm stuck in a snail race. It could take an hour, so I—"

"What? It's fine. I'll call a taxi or an Uber. It'll be here sooner."

"If you would just listen to me." If words could widen their eyes, hers just did. "I've already called him, and it's better if you come with someone you know and trust. He's in the area and will be there any minute." Eva's smooth voice comes through, and I can hear a distant honk in the background.

"Okay … wait. Who is *he?* For all I know, he could be a serial killer," I say.

A phone rings in the background, replacing the honking.

"Give your girl some credit for being responsible. Hey Bee, I'll call you in a bit. Helly's on the line," Eva explains. Helly is Eva's assistant. They first met at university when Eva was doing her degree in fashion design and Helly in business administration. Since then, they have opened Eva's boutique and have successfully launched each season's clothing.

"If I don't call or text you, please tell my brother I love him," I say light-heartedly. I can never be upset with Eva for long.

"Sure. Steven would be heartbroken." Her laughter fills the air with a sweet sound. My heart drains all its blood from hearing her, and if this is me right now from only her voice, I don't know how I would survive when I see all three of them in front of me.

Now that I'm back, I didn't want to remind myself of what I'd left behind. The late nights at Sage's, where we talked about boys, our brothers and cousins included. The beach rides and dips. The cries after teen breakups. I will always cherish those moments. From the late nights to the early mornings and everything in between is worth more than any block of gold. And somewhere deep down, I missed this place more than I like to admit, but I'll keep that buried deep inside me.

I'll thank Floral & Bells for giving me the push—the chance to hit two targets with one arrow. To get a promotion but also to be back.

The icy wind breezes past me, calmer this time, and I smile into it with my eyes closed. *Home.* At least it was.

Honk!

A honk from the parking lot beside me shakes me back to reality. The window of the pastel grey Porsche Cayenne rolls down so silently I'm surprised it's even there. I peek inside the SUV, adjusting to its dark interior. It's him.

Jason Archer.

Of course, she sent him. *Can this day get any better?*

Eva's big brother, and my former childhood crush. Told no one and have no intention of doing so either. It's safe to put the blame on the developing hormones for the many years I drooled at the nerdy glasses-wearing boy.

Hot bodies. Our bodies. In such rhythm, I can believe I finally have him—

I block the thought before it even fully opens the gate of the memory, which should be locked.

But the man I'm looking at now has taken on a whole new transformation. *Who are you, and where did those glasses go?* He is far gone from the boy I left. The glasses have come off and have been replaced by the perfect showcase of his emerald orbs. His stubble, covering the lower half of his face, is so elegantly sculpted that it makes me want to run my hand through it. It's the absolute balance between the dark brown to his milky skin.

My gaze bounces back to him as he stares at me with those hypnotizing green eyes. Ever the silent type.

"Jason." Bitterness spreads through my tongue as I remember the last time I said his name.

"Put your luggage in the back and hop in." Simple and to the point. Shivers of pleasure run down my spine from hearing his deep, dark voice once again. He doesn't even bother with any pleasantries. I feel a pang of hurt hit my chest when he turns away to look straight ahead, not wanting to give me another second of his attention.

Okay, I deserve that. I let out a defeated sigh and place my two suitcases in the open boot and my bag in the back seat.

The moment I'm in Jason's vicinity, I get swallowed by his fresh mint scent—nostalgia eating me alive. Without casting me a second glance, he firmly presses the pedal, and we swiftly exit the parking lot. Well, it's going to be a hell of an hour's drive. *And three months.*

He's a god wearing the skin of a six-foot two man with the power to be victorious in any war. From the evergreen shine in the forest of his eyes to the thickness of his forearms, he is a package made in heaven to bless us poor souls, so we have a piece of eye candy.

Hello. Hello. Brain to Bianca, getting off track. Come back. The voice of White Wings warns in my head.

She is my companion alongside Red Horns. Mostly, they've calmed my restless mind, but more time or not, they have been the reason why I am restless.

For the first ten minutes of the drive, the silence is thick and uncomfortable, not that I was expecting him to pour his heart out. I bounce my feet with the nervous beat in my chest.

I breathe in courage to have a conversation when I know he would rather be anywhere else than be with the woman who pushed him away.

"How are you?" My voice is soft as I ask, not wanting to shake the still water.

I look at his side to take in his profile, which has changed drastically for the better. If I run my finger along the edge of his chin, I sure will bleed. His nose joins the league to cut things with a touch. The sharp cheekbones sit high on his face, giving enough space for his eyes to rest. Running the course from his broad shoulders, his thick arms showcase the paths of those sexy green veins I've drooled enough times over. He effortlessly rests a hand on the wheel while the other holds the weight of his head by the window.

He finally speaks with a single, "Good." No more, no less.

Silence.

"It's good to be back." My stomach tightens once again when I attempt to break the enveloping silence.

"Hmm." His tone holds more judgment than I applied for.

Does he really hate me so much that he doesn't even want to talk to me?

I deserve it—but it just … hurts. He knows why I left and why I did what I did, saying no to what we could've had together with his trust. His rare trust—trust I had rejected.

Tears burn the back of my eyes, and I turn my face to the window, sucking in a sharp breath. I blink rapidly and pout my mouth, pushing back any leaking traitors from my eyes. It's too cold in here; not like the heat I used to feel in his presence. *Nothing like it.*

The clouds have taken on a darker shade of grey, heaving with impending tears of their own. At least one of us can cry openly. On instinct, I grab my bracelet as if the piece of jewellery can take me out of the night I've lived too many times in my head.

"Still afraid?"

My head snaps in his direction. He is looking straight out at the road.

Still a charmer, isn't he? There she is. Welcome the voice of the devil with red horns in my head. My nemesis and saviour in one.

There's no change in Jason's posture, no muscles move. His eyes are stuck to the road, observing the paused traffic. Judging from the people on the road, the quick hour's drive could take two.

Great.

"No," I answer, taking his approach to one-word responses. Releasing the bracelet from its demise, my hand carries itself to the volume switch and turns on anything to distract me. Anything right now would be nice, fuck, I would even listen to the dingoes barking— anything.

I thought the day couldn't get any worse. I was wrong. The radio flips me off with a double bird as it plays the most sensual tunes. Dingoes are still the better option.

And now, suddenly, the heart-chilling atmosphere has turned into a sauna. A sauna that has sweat trickling down into the valley of my breasts, making me remember why I had left and for whom.

The rumble in Jason's throat lingers between us. I don't dare to lift my hand again to switch to a different station as my body paralyses, reminiscing about the last few moments I had with this man five years ago.

The sound of his grumble is so deep and heat throbbing, it intoxicates the oxygen in my lungs. Blood rushes to every nook of my body, letting heat tease the memories I want to bury.

"Do you have any playlists?" I ask with another attempt to take out more than one word from Jason and ignore all the heat.

"No." Again.

"Did someone take away your dictionary?" I *try* not to snap.

His dark brows furrow as he narrows his eyes into slits, watching the road with eagle vision.

I turn back to the window, and just as I do, rain begins to pour— giving relief to the sky that held the heavy clouds. I trace a single drop running down and watch it getting faster as it joins the others. Then another starts the same journey in the water-spotted window.

I didn't get a second of shut eye on the flight as the anxiety of coming back and the constricting space in the plane did wonders to keep my brain alert. A slow snail slithers down my back at the reminder of sitting in the middle row far from the exits. Even now, the thought chokes air from my lungs. It has been a solid five years since that night, and I tell myself that with every year I will get myself out of the rat race playing in my head, but I end right back into it, in complete spirals.

As I track another drop, my lids become heavy, and I allow myself to close them. For now, I can have a break.

"Bianca … Bianca!" A shake on my shoulder takes me away from my mint and honey covered waffles with ice-loaded orange juice. *Wait, mint?*

"Bianca!"

I shriek when I find Jason towering over me, his green eyes digging holes into my probably drool-decorated face.

"We're here." He doesn't bother hiding the crease of his brow as boredom clings to his words. I slide up to sit straight and stretch to get every bit of laziness out of my system. As I do, a blazer falls and pools in my lap.

I eye it for a good second before the scent of mint invades my senses.

"You were shaking," he says in explanation when my eyes flick to meet his. I look deeper into anything else I could get—nothing.

Jason Archer is a book with blank pages—carrying a plethora of stories which no ink can write. *Or dares.*

As I lift the blazer from my legs, the faint smell of his cologne becomes more prominent on my clothes, legs, and hands.

Bianca, it has been five fucking years, for fuck's sake, get over him!

I chant the words in my head, but it does nothing to stop me from taking the biggest inhale to store the scent to keep as my dirty little secret.

"You're staying with us today, and then you can head to your place after the party," he states simply, rolling his sleeves further up, if they can go any higher on his thick forearms. They are surely cutting off the circulation, making his arms bulkier than they should be. My throat bobs at the sight. The flashes of those arms come into view with the steam from the night when he was pounding—

"Party?" I say, distracting myself from the roar in my pulse.

"The CEO transfer party. Did Eva not tell you?" he asks, still with no emotion on his face.

Of course, she didn't. The woman has been undercover since her winter collection finished up. Maybe she did mention it here and there in one of our group calls, but I don't remember.

"Oh, well then. Who's becoming CEO now?"

He returns to his blank and bored stare as if I should already know the answer to the question.

"What?" My eyes dilate in size when realisation hits. "No bloody way. Oh, my God, I'm so happy for you," I squeal. I don't know what spirit takes over me as I throw my arms around his neck. Jason had dreamed and talked non-stop about leading Archer Enterprises ever since I've known him. It was the life presented to him on a golden platter, and rightfully so. He has all the skills one would need to tackle the ups and downs of this career.

My arms snake around his neck, bringing him into me. I don't see the consequences of this when he doesn't return the hug with his arms by my sides, letting the cold air strike daggers in my back.

When we break apart—when I let go—heat surges up my neck to cheeks as I tuck a strand behind my ear.

I may as well have run a marathon and sat back inside this car, judging by the rapid beat of my heart.

"Thanks for the ride." I give a tight smile before stretching to the back seat for my bag. When I come back, Jason hasn't moved. I land exactly a breath away, not too far back or forward, enough for our noses to skim.

His stare is a killer. His eyes take me deeper into the forest of his making. The forest that once had me prisoner and deluded for what was beyond it. The delusion was pretty in imagination, but dark and dangerous in reality. Yet the twisted part of me is still searching for the truth in the delusion.

Suddenly, the spacious SUV seemed to close in on me and take away any breathing space. Our eyes shift between our lips and then back up. Hot air dances in the space between us, with silence ringing in our ears.

"I'll head out." I throw a thumb over my shoulder, washing an ice-cold bucket over the situation. I've always been the person who ruins and washes away other's happiness from their eyes—lives.

I turn to get to the boot, but Jason's voice stops me. "They'll get to your room. Head in." He needs to work on his conversation skills, ironic for a tele*communication* and electronics company owner.

"Great, thanks." I get out of the SUV, and he drives off without a second glance in my direction. Oh, how much I want to wrap my hands around his neck and mine.

CHAPTER 2
Bianca

The grand white brick house—mansion—that I had grown to love over the years welcomes me with warm familiarity. Soft lavender bushes still bordered the pebbled walkway. The large windows are their usual glossy clean, letting the sun peek through.

"Hi, Stewart," I chime to the Archers' long-serving butler.

"Miss Kennedy." He nods with the same old smile, melting my heart on the spot. He is wearing his morning coat and an earpiece in one ear. Stewart has been in my life for as long as I can remember. He has devoted himself to the Archers for countless years—his black hair turning grey.

"It's good to have you back. The house wasn't the same without you." He lifts his lips in a soft, genuine smile.

"Thank you."

It is good to be back.

"How are Chelsie and Rachel?" I ask.

"Rachel is Rachel. Chelsie has indeed turned out to be a wonderful woman and enjoys her time as a psychologist." He flashes me an even brighter smile. Stewart really loves his daughter.

Chelsie is Stewart and Rachel's daughter, whom they adopted from the Beating Hearts charity. A charity Kai's family has run for years. Despite being two years older, we hadn't seen her around much. So, we don't really know much about her other than that she is practicing at her clinic in regional Victoria and some clients from the metropolitan area.

"That's good to hear," I say, hurting my cheeks from the way I'm smiling. "Is everyone inside?" I ask, cocking my head to the entryway.

"Find out for yourself," Stewart answers. His posture is straight as he nods his head towards the expansive hall—the heart of the Archer residence.

I smile as I stroll inside with my bag slung over my shoulder. The spotless white marble stairs, edged with roses, lead me down to the main entrance room.

In its glory of crystals and gold, a chandelier hangs from the high domed ceiling, and smaller lights are scattered throughout. The black-rimmed, high-ceiling windows curve at the top, giving the room more air and light.

There must be over six stone pillars supporting the building. Flowers, vines, and birds adorn the stone carvings on each pillar. A sense of calm washes over me as I walk deeper into the silence and rustling of the indoor plants in each corner.

Where is everyone?

The seating area has a grand set of grey sofas on my right facing the back garden. The garden is two glass doors away, and it's beautiful enough to bring tears of joy to my eyes with its vast collection of flowers, trees, and fountains. To my left is the spacious white and grey marble kitchen—every chef's wet dream. In the centre of the room, there are opulent white, and gold tiered marble stairs that split in two as they reach the floors above.

I can stand here and admire the interior all day and still won't get enough. Every corner of the residence showcases the Archers' love for nature.

But that's not what has me raising my eyebrows. *Why is it so quiet?* Not a single soul is here when there are usually many helpers running around with their daily duties.

"Eva?" I take a careful step deeper inside. "Kiara? Sage?" My voice is calm as I call. "Is anyone here?" I say louder, my steps are tentative— not sure what will jump at my face.

Ping!

The sound, like a phone notification, comes from my right on the other side of the sofa.

"I told you to turn it off!" My ears perk up at the sharp whisper. *Kiara.*

"Shut up! I forgot, okay?" The song-like voice retorts back. *Sage.*

Oh, they are here, all right.

"You two both shut up!" Eva tries to keep quiet, but that's the last thing a woman with a loud and outgoing voice can do.

I cover my mouth, keeping my laugh in, and not wanting to blow their cover up for them. "I don't think anyone's here. Maybe I should try the garden." I think out loud to get my words to the ears of the three trying to be undercover.

A loud boom echoes as I reach the back of the three-seater sofa, and then strings of colourful confetti fly out, spreading like a rainbow.

"Welcome back!" my three sweethearts cheer, jumping out from the back of the large grey sofa. They are wearing the biggest grins that exceed their faces' limits. Even Sage.

"Fucking hell." My hand clenches the material of my dress over the thumping heart. Tears well in my eyes as I take in the sight in front of me.

All the memories of what's happened right here in this room and house come flooding back to me. It hits me now. I missed everything; I missed *them*. It's been too damn long.

A sob comes out, taking away my ability to plan any words. My hands cover my face to avoid putting on display the tears coming out.

Reminder: I'm home.

I meet them halfway, and we tumble down to the floor, our arms interlocked. Half-laughing, half-crying, our emotions run wild, making our embrace even tighter.

The well of my tears deepens and overflows with their touch. *They're here with me.*

"We missed you so fucking much," Kiara whispers when her voice breaks in an attempt not to cry.

With her deep mahogany waves and chocolate-dipped eyes, the free-spirited photographer knows all the ways to provoke emotions in anyone—especially me. I'm not surprised she wanted to opt in for a career *"full of adventure and bitches"*. She is the last person who would give a damn about anyone's opinion.

"We're not letting you leave now." Sage's sweet, melodious voice swells my heart even more.

Sage Joshi is the pacifier of the group when Evalyn Archer and Kiara Kozlova grow horns. It's in her instinct to shy away from the world, but not when she's on the stage and mesmerising the audience with her Indian classical moves connecting back to her heritage. On stage, her marrow fills with liquid, and her eyes take on a personality of their own. The moment allows her to free herself from her worries of the world beyond the auditorium. Namely, with her parents.

I wish I could stay, but I know it's not happening anytime soon.

"Sorry for not picking you up." Guilt plays in Eva's tone. The mastermind behind all my headaches. Yet she can treat them with a mere stretch of her lips in a smile. If I ever want any clothing opinion, Eva is my woman. Miss Archer is a feisty pack of emotions and care.

"Oh, don't get me started on that." I squint my eyes at her, and her smile widens.

We pull apart, but keep lying on the floor, with our heads moving towards each other in the centre—like a star.

"At least I got you a ride. It took me a life and a half to get him there," she says.

"Thanks for setting me up with Mr Grumpy. The guy needs to learn how to talk." I roll my eyes, thinking of the car ride. At least most of what I can remember pre-nap. It wasn't exactly a heart-warming welcome.

"Excuse me, my brother can converse just fine." The chuckle in her voice speaks quite the opposite.

"Yeah, sure, I only got around four one-word answers from him. That happened twice in two-hours." I raise four fingers, then lower two.

"You should be glad it wasn't a serial killer," Kiara says. "Although, I was tempted to do a skit out of that." She stretches her arms towards the ceiling. Her purple painted nails complement her glowing skin.

I close my eyes and sigh. "It's good to be back in all your chaos."

Coming back is one thing, but leaving is another beast. I don't need a wake-up call to realise I've lost another piece of myself and returned empty. The choice was never mine to leave in the first place. If I had one, I wouldn't look at any place other than here.

Steven and I faced a huge change, going from living with everything to nothing. Steven was always there with me, from my first period to the last day of university. But I still felt lonely. He got the best big brother award every year, yet something was missing all this time. Now that I'm here, it's clear what it was. My place, my people—my everything.

"You say that now. We'll see in another week. Wait, we won't, because you will run up the hills by then." Kiara smirks as she rests on her elbow, her hair cascading gracefully over her shoulder. She observes me as if I am the centrepiece at her exhibition.

"I'll love you in every way, even if it drives me mad," I murmur. My voice is weak as I try to push back my tears. Not today, not in front of them.

They pass me their soft smiles and give me a hug again. *God, if this is a dream, I don't want to wake up.* I'd rather sleep for all eternity frozen like this.

"Now, get ready. We have something planned for you." Eva jumps up on her feet, taking me with her.

"What?" I ask, confused.

"You'll see."

Oh, I don't like where this is going. The malicious grins on their faces make it clear they plan to kidnap me.

"Good luck on your first shopping frenzy," Sage whispers in my ear as Kiara and Eva gush over something they said to each other.

I chuckle and widen my eyes. "Great."

CHAPTER 3
Jason

"**I** don't trust you or anyone! I lost my everything tonight. You can't expect me to just stay behind when I have no one here!" she screams in my face. Her tears stain my own cheeks as I bring her close to me—

"Son!" Stewart's voice snaps me out of my spiral of thoughts. "Come on. Hand over the keys. Caleb will get it parked," he says and nods through the open window.

I get out and slam the door behind me and pass the keys to Stewart, who returns me with a smile—almost sympathetic.

I always imagined—against my better judgement—what it would be like when she returned and thought I would feel nothing, exactly what I'd felt for these past years. But I was wrong. The moment those

ocean-blue eyes saw me, the knot tightened in my chest, and all I could do was live the last moment we had together on repeat. Right before she took the flight.

It's ironic that we met again for the first time after five years in the same airport where we once swore never to see each other again.

It's been a long five years, six months, and two days. Not that I was counting.

The girl who had once left shows back up in the skin of an adult. From the outside, she looks like a bird of passage who joyfully smiles through everything. Yet the hint of sadness in those bright blue eyes gives her away. They always did.

The dreadful night when everything fell apart had transformed the course of our lives dramatically, and we were never the same again. The boy and the girl, who saw each other for the first time, never had the chance to live up to the promises they made.

Only because putting trust in me she couldn't afford.

I took a breath of relief once she flew on that plane, ignoring the crack in my chest. It felt like the last piece of my life's puzzle had vanished, leaving me with a painful, incomplete mess.

Bianca might have come with fresh energy, yet all I see is her as the girl with the toothy smile, covered with her rainbow-filled braces and glasses. Her glasses never stayed too long on her nose. They were a size too big and would just slide off, but she never got them changed.

When we would all have ice creams, she'd make a face, but keeping her lactose intolerance in check was the biggest hurdle for us all. One run to the hospital after being food poisoned from drinking milk was enough to keep our guard up.

When I saw her in that purple dress gleaming under the shadow of the clouds, pressure prohibited the flow of air to my lungs. Her collared dress hung effortlessly from her shoulders, hugging each curve, dropping high on her thighs. Brown boots came up to her knees, and a loose ribbon tied her brown hair.

Though she only arrived hours ago, she's already turned my world upside down. Her cries, shouts, and retaliations haunt my memories when the flashes of the night make an appearance. It was the most broken I'd seen her. The shine in those usually bright eyes had dulled, taking away their life. I had my arms wrapped around her to stop her from going into the house and becoming a burning tragedy herself.

"I love you." Bianca's familiar honey-smooth vocals grab my attention the moment I step into the living room.

"Hey, princess!" Eva screams, waving like she sold a million of her blue-flame jackets. They're in season for this year's winter collection she's launching at the end of the month.

"We're heading out to the boutique. Wanna come? I've booked the private rooms and displays at the boutique." Eva grins through her words. My sister is one proud woman. She followed her undying passion for fashion and clothing, leading her to be one of the most popular designers in the nation and going worldwide.

Eva notices my silence and urges, "Come on, Bee is only here for three months, and we don't know when she'll be back." Her watery eyes come on display that rival the colour of my own pupils.

Only three months.

"I have a meeting," I confidently state, then climb the stairs. Before I can enter my office, the blue eyes I've been dying to avoid collide with mine. From here I can see the outline of the girl-turned-woman, showing the depth of the orbs. A deep ocean with no end.

The scene from the car brushes my memory. Bianca's sweet, steady snores were the only sound I could hear as it took me back to the time she slept on my chest.

Fuck, why is it difficult to breathe?

The way she slightly shivered as she jumped in her sleep made me pull over and cover up her annoyingly irresistible body with my blazer. I, again, lost over the temptation to leave her be when I tucked her silky hair back into place.

All my thoughts collided into one when she stretched to get her bag, making me eye level with her breasts that I would have a perfect grasp over. The valley between them took a squeeze at the action, pressuring her sensitive skin and sending signals down to my—

Only three months.

Eva, Kiara and Sage push their long-lost friend towards the exit, but Bianca doesn't dare to leave my stare until she's entirely out of the room. She's searching for someone who isn't here.

I don't have a meeting. I know, guilty. Today was a reflection day on the yearly earnings for the end of the financial year while individual teams discuss the new components in our telecommunication services.

My phone vibrates in my pocket, and *fuck,* even I smell like her. Cherry-fucking-blossom.

It's a text from one of the few people I can't block even if I wanted to. Kai. Fortunately or unfortunately, someone I call a friend.

> *Kai: A little birdie told me you're free today.*
> *Come to Cornella's, we need to talk about*
> *your latest endeavour*

Typical Kai. If a fuckboy billionaire had a face, it would be Kai Jeffords'. The man works more and fucks even more. Being the owner of a multi-billion-dollar event organising company, Kai is the slackest of them all.

At least that's what he offers to the public, but no one has access to the pure heart he keeps deep inside. He has donations open for orphanages, cancer patients, the disabled, you name it, and it's under his league.

Having lost his mother to cancer provoked it out of him. But it also shattered him and left him in a place of no return.

Jason: *Coming.*

As if he were stuck to his phone, which he would be more figuratively than literally, the reply is instant.

Kai: *I'll be waiting at the usual spot*

The three floating dots appear, then disappear. Then appear.
Come on, get there faster.
Then it all goes blank. I guess in person it is then.

Entering Cornella's is like getting into a blanket and curling up in the deep of winter. I grew up drinking their hot chocolate, which quickly turned into their almond milk white chocolate latte for a reason I don't allow myself to think about.

The cafe started off small, with only one room for serving, and a two-person kitchen at the back. That was the best the Cornella's could've afforded when trying to recover from bankruptcy. Now, there are two stories of serving area with a large and modern open-concept kitchen. The lobby has a mix of two-and four-seater tables, while the upstairs floors accommodate larger groups, commonly used for pre-booked events.

The instant hit of the soothing baked goods takes me into a warm hug—something I haven't been getting much of. Since the transfer of the CEOs in our company, I've been so caught up in meeting the clients, investors, board members, and so on that finding space for anything else is just not possible.

Cornella's was our hideout. The girls and us boys had our weekly meetings here as if there was anything to discuss at all. But the memories made here are worth all the years of my life on this planet.

Despite Kiara's arguments with Steven and Eva and Kai's food fights, everyone ended up with a pleasant smile.

My phone rings.

> **Kai:** *Don't stare at the waffles too long, they might burn.*

> **Kai:** *Twelve o'clock*

I see him beside our usual spot by the glass wall with his phone in hand and an angel's ring over his head. Did I say angel? I meant the devil.

Approaching him, I notice his happy-go-lucky demeanour morph into a deep frown.

"What the fuck did you do?" The first thing I say while unbuttoning my blazer and sitting opposite him. Leg crossed and hands on lap.

He already has his short black waiting for him. His dark blue eyes glow with anticipation. Not the best news.

"I did nothing. You did." He points an accusatory finger in my direction.

I remain silent with a questioning eyebrow lifted on my forehead.

"Oh, giving me the silent treatment now, huh?" He lets out a huff and runs a frustrated hand through the nest of dirty blond on his head. Frustrated at what, I have no clue.

"Okay, let me get started. Why did no one fucking tell me that Bianca came back? And two, it was you, *you.*" He points again, leaning forward. "Who picked her up when your driver could have easily gone? Care to explain?"

"Eva asked, and I did it." I shrug with a bored expression. "There is nothing more to explain."

"Oh, sure. And did Evalyn ask you to run after the flying plane?

Or did Evalyn ask you to stalk Bianca's every move?" He throws the questions at me.

I can't decide what bothers me more: him calling her Evalyn or that he trapped me. I know he got me as his smug smirk appears, his deep dimples taunting.

"*Stalk* is rather strong. I would prefer being *informed*, not only for her, but for Steven as well."

"Oh, really?" *Kai, that bastard.* "Then please, if you'd care to explain all the files you have saved of her in the folder named, and I quote, *Bee*. And we all know that can't be a coincidence and has nothing to do with Steven, per se."

"Kai." I rub an exhausted hand over my face. "I thought we went over this. There is or will never, *never* be anything between us. If you need a reason for whatever happened, blame it on the raging hormones. I'm in more control now."

And a lot has changed since then. Taking public responsibility for Archer Enterprises and starting Phoenix to attract the wealthiest and most powerful people out of the reach of the ordinary. What started off as a simple group of four teenagers turned into a monster of an organisation that stayed under the links of the public world.

My partner in crime snickers while a reply lingers in his big mouth.

"Here's your order, Jay—the almond milk white chocolate latte with extra cinnamon." Sylvia interrupts us with a smile so wide it hurts my lips to look at her. Her recognisable autumn red and brown hair winks in the light as her lightly tanned skin glows. When she's about to leave, her eyes flick to Kai, and her face genuinely softens.

"Thank you." I take a sip of heaven and close my eyes to let the drink work its magic. The drink was there when I needed it, through the grey hair days, months, and years.

"Almond milk." Kai scoffs. "Look, I'm only saying this because I care about you. We don't know what's going on with Bianca, but you know another heartbreak you can't handle. Especially when we have so much on the line and becoming soft won't help."

And there goes the magic. Kai leans forward and places his hand on the table.

I don't have a weakness, and being soft only blinds you from the havoc that brews on the outskirts. One thing is clear: I cannot afford to be trapped by a woman who has nothing but heartbreak to offer.

"She's only here for three months—not a lifetime," I say, not sure who I'm reassuring.

"If it was a lifetime, then what?" Kai takes a more subtle yet confronting approach to the question.

I don't fucking know what I would do then.

"I bet on your Porsche you will get laid *very* soon by the one and only woman that could get the great Jason Archer out of his bearing. Although I don't want that for you." I'll never understand the dichotomy of this man. One moment he is telling me to stay away, the next he is placing bets on me getting laid by the *same woman.*

"Why my Porsche, huh? Don't you trust your instincts?"

"Oh, I *know* you will get laid, because it's only a matter of time. I need to think of what I can get out of all this as well, so the Porsche is the only thing I have my eyes on." Mischief takes over the earlier scowl.

"Fuck off."

Before our conversation progresses, the bell rings over the door. There is an instant hit of the unforgettable cherry blossom. *Great.*

The four girls I'm all too familiar with enter, their hands full of bags.

Kai follows my line of sight and sighs. "Oh, fucking hell. Think of the devil."

"Calling your sister and friend devils?" I point him with a look, and he knows he will have to take it back.

He fakes a smile and drops back into his seat with his steamy coffee. "There's only one devil there, and she looks a lot like you," he mutters over the rim of his glass.

I grab the nearest menu and slap it on his arm like a whip cutting through the air. He proudly smiles, not hiding his dislike for my sister.

To say Kai and Eva go well together will be the biggest lie. Since their paths collided, there was not a day that went by without them pulling out their hair.

"Someone massage my feet." Kiara slumps down on the couches, only a few tables down, and the others follow suit.

This day could not get any worse.

CHAPTER 4
Bianca

A groan leaves me when I slump in my seat. All my remaining energy screamed out of me, begging to be restored. The craze these girls have for shopping has multiplied in every way possible. I thought I was a shopping freak until I entered the boutique with their arms linked to mine. There was no comparison.

Regardless of the throbbing in my feet, I am content. Content that the girls I love most are here with me—physically. Content that I can share my space with the people I want to. Recently I hadn't wanted to see anyone or be with anyone, especially *him*. In the past years, I never felt it, but the rush of being *alone* was the strongest ever since my birthday this year. I guess that's the aftermath of the breaking of a two-year long relationship.

A year after we moved to Canberra, I left our family home and bought an apartment in the city. The move was supposed to reinforce a sense of freedom and take the burden off Steven's shoulder to provide care for another human, but I'd overestimated my abilities.

The first few months were at the speed of a rabbit with all the moving in, unpacking, and settling. That was when the turtle entered the race. I had never lived alone before that, and settling in with myself first was terrifying because I was stuck with nothing but my head. That is not a place I want to visit again, if I can help it. So, I went out with my work colleagues and only came back to sleep.

"We've got the dresses, shoes, and now there's only the jewellery left." Sage ticks off the items on her checklist.

"Guys, just so you know, I packed clothes," I say. "You guys have already pulled me in every direction in the eight hours I've been here, like Lucy." I bring up my wrist, holding my watch to show the time. Lucy was our once shared Victorian doll Ma found somewhere in a thrift shop.

"Be it eight hours or eight years—we will never get enough of you. And let me tell you, Lucy was adorable. Little creepy, but adorable. Plus, Kiara had her joined at her hip." Eva smiles as she rolls her eyes.

"Happily," Kiara chimes, flicking her eyes over the menu.

"I still have nightmares of it staring at my face at night." Sage shakes and straightens her back as if ants had crawled on her.

"Will you guys ever get over her?" With a shake of my head, I scan the menu. And would you look at that? Their top drink is a tropical orange punch.

"No."

"No."

"No."

All three of their distinct voices sing together.

We share a silent look before erupting into laughter that breaks the cafe's stillness. Our laughter radiates through the place to bring us back to the times when there were no worries or anything to deal with. We had everything a group of teenagers could ask for: happy families, friends, and a life where sorrow didn't exist in the closest distance.

"I could've had Lucy showcased if it weren't for the damn fir—" Kiara cuts herself as our laughs die a slow death. She doesn't need to finish saying for us to imply it.

Fire that brings light into the dark, and the fire that heats food for survival, had brought lifelong darkness and hunger for love for the rest of my life. The crackling of the wood under the flames, the smell of burnt ash from the smoking bodies of my—

No, I have given those events enough power to have them rule over me. *This year is better.*

But sometimes I let myself wonder how life would've been different. I would wake up every morning with Ma baking in the kitchen, and Dad discussing the next move in the company with Steven at the breakfast table.

"Sorry." Kiara shrinks with regret. A burn starts anew in my chest at the effect I have on my close friends. As if I am a fragile porcelain doll and will break at the wrong words or touch. It's not their fault—it's mine. I can't control my emotions and stop the voices in my head.

"It's okay." My eyes blink in understanding, a subtle smile playing on my lips. "That's why I can't stay here. I'd feel trapped in a time capsule, reliving the fire endlessly." Their faces melt into a series of sympathy and pity.

Can the earth open and swallow me?

Merely talking about it creates a golf ball-sized lump in my throat, impossible to swallow. I lie to myself again: *it will get better this year. Promise.*

You wish, the voice of red responds.

We used to come here to Cornella's all the time. Ma, Dad, me, and Steven. My first memory here with them was when I had the craziest blend of juice that shook my taste buds out of their place.

"I need to use the bathroom."

What if I had a last moment with Ma and Dad to get closure? To see them for one last time and prepare myself to live without the shelter of their security.

What if I had stayed behind that night and burned with them? Maybe that would have been better than burning every day.

What if—

"Take your time." Sage places a soft hand on mine and gives it a few squeezes. Dragging myself up with the last of my energy, I keep a poker face as I weave through the customers towards the restrooms, my feet racing. If I wait, the tightness in my chest will overwhelm me, and I won't be able to hold it in.

I let muscle memory guide me to the bathrooms. The lights blur past me, as does everything else, when I slam myself shut in the bathroom stall.

The buildup of emotions and what-ifs finally runs down and relieves me of the burn in my chest for the moment. It hurts more now that I'm standing in the place where the ghosts of my memories resurrect from their graves somewhere deep in my brain.

"Stop it." It kills me to say the words. I still struggle to handle myself when the conversation comes up, even after five years. "Stop it." *I give up.*

My fingers dig into my scalp. I sink to the floor, threatening to rip out my hair. The burn from the stretch is nothing compared to what is boiling inside me. I tried everything I could to come to terms with my new life. I screamed, ran, cried, hid, but nothing worked. Helpless now and helpless then.

Steven became my everything, but I couldn't be that for him because I was too deep in my grief. I forgot everything else. I never gave him the chance to pick himself. I was so stuck in myself that I forgot about him. He was hurting too—he was also just a boy at a loss.

I'm so … so sorry, Steven.

I sob, sob, and fucking sob. That is what I have been doing all this time—the only thing I could do. *Pathetic.* I doubt there's a single wall in Canberra that hasn't heard my poignant cries and seen how useless I am.

Although Uncle Gareth was with us, it did nothing to ease the pain of the reminder of who had left. He was the walking version of Dad, thanks to their identical twin genes.

"I'm sorry for your loss." Despite the many condolences offered at the funeral, the pain in our hearts and the guilt we felt remained.

Tears keep rolling down my cheeks, dripping from my chin to my dress. The stains on my dress are a reminder that I can never trust myself to be strong. No matter how I appear to the world, I'm not the same girl who dreamed of being like Ma. There's no one I can look up to who makes me feel that way now.

Come on Bianca. You can do this. White Wings comes in.

I take a shaky breath through my nose, and I pick up my weight from the ground. *There is nothing I can do to change the past, so why doesn't it leave me?*

No voice in my head has the answer to any of the questions I put in front of them. Maybe there are no answers.

The lock of the bathroom stall clicks open, and I get taken aback by what I see in the mirror. My mascara runs down my face, making my eyes look devoid and devastated. Cracks mar my makeup at the corners of my lips and eyes.

I am such a mess.

After two painful minutes, I reapplied my makeup. Then for another horrific minute, I take myself in through the wide-stretched mirror.

Do you really think you can survive coming back? The devilish voice in my head questions.

I don't know if I can survive or not, but by the end of the three months I will leave with a wrecked soul. My soul will hunger for the love and peace I get here, yet I will starve it. *Once again.*

After rehearsing for a perfect publicly accepted smile, I close the door behind me, smooth my dress, and turn—

Ouch!

Was I so far gone that I bumped into someone? *Pathetic Bianca, just pathetic.* I let out a harsh breath and rest my forehead there for the sake of disappearing for this second.

The person grabs me by my shoulders and pulls me back. What I see, or rather who I see, is a person who is both emotionally and physically unyielding, like a wall.

"Jason?" I ask, squinting my eyes at him to make sure he isn't a fragment of my imagination like he has been for countless years. No, these cheeks seem real, and these muscles flex under my touch.

"What are you doing?" He grits each word through his clenched teeth. His voice of darkness makes my heart climb flights of stairs, exhausting it more than it already is.

Yep, definitely here. He was never the touchy one. That gene went to Eva. I remove my hand from his cheek and drop it by my side.

"Nothing. What are *you* doing? Didn't you have a meeting?" I raise an eyebrow as my arms cross over my chest.

His eyes trail the movement and settle on the stain on the collar of my dress. Shit, forgot about that.

He looks back at my face, not pressing the issue.

Thanks.

"I have a *personal* meeting," he says, as if I am the biggest inconvenience to him. His responses need serious improvement, or else this winter won't be as easy as I hoped.

Personal meeting. With who? Not that it matters to me, but…

But what, Bianca? You must be curious. Maybe he is on a date and has moved on from us. One day soon I will take control of the voice with red horns in my head. She needs to shut it.

We stand there, me with my arms crossed and his hands in his pockets.

"So, are we going to stay here or…" I jerk my head towards the rest of Cornella's behind his muscular body.

He lightly shakes his head as he comes out of his daze. "You go." Moving out of my way, I take a step away from him.

"Hey, Bianca?" The sound of his deep decibels saying my name makes my gut clench. I pause as I look over my shoulder.

He hesitates for a moment, pondering his words. "You have people here who love you. Don't hide from them." His voice is steady as he holds my stare.

We linger there for another beat. Something in my chest grows. *Hope.*

I don't want to give myself hope that the people he is referring to include him, too. Even if he offers anything to me, I don't think I will return with a heart in my chest. I would rather hand it over to him. It would be easier to carry a space in my chest than an organ that is dead. He fed it life once and stayed there.

My heart beats so rapidly with life after being dormant for years from the way he watches me with careful consideration. He is begging me to say something, anything that could reverse time. I can't. I have no words that can change time. I wish I did.

I'm sorry, Jason. Sorry.

He takes a steadying breath, as if reading my eyes instead of my lips sealed with unsaid words. Jason takes the lead in breaking the tension by stepping into the bathroom.

I stare at the empty spot where he once stood.

I miss you, Jason. I wish there were a wand that could've stopped time at that beach. I wish…

With my racing thoughts, I take my seat back, my eyes staying glued to the bathrooms.

Jason comes out, his thick forearms on full display as he rolls them down, blinding my sight from the muscular flesh.

I wipe my face, scared I might have drooled. Highly unlikely, but for good measure.

"Here you are, girls." A sweet voice breaks my stare, bringing me back to the table. Eva and Kiara pause their discussion about the next hot cricketer they're in for, and Sage looks up from her phone.

"Here is your Strawberry Crush," a man in his late twenties says as he places the ruby red drink in front of Eva.

He looks familiar.

"There's the iced long black, Kiara," he says in a deep and hearty voice. He sets down the darkest and richest drink for Kiara.

While I only get the side of his face, I know I've seen him somewhere.

"Your lemonade, Sage." He has a brighter edge to his voice this time. The dancer in Sage doesn't allow for all the calories that we take in a day.

"And finally, for our guest of honour, your freshly smashed tropical orange juice with *extra* ice," he recites my order when he finally straightens to his full height and glances at me.

There's a bounce to his brown curls and a shine to the smile showing a broken tooth at the far side. Bells ring, but I can't say where I've seen him.

Maybe it's the expression I'm wearing because he looks at me with wide eyes and a hand placed on his chest in mock offense. "Don't tell me you forgot me?" He huffs in disbelief.

I know.

"Tickler Tony. No way." I spring up from my seat, taking him all in. My hands find my mouth as a smile appears on my face—another genuine one. I haven't seen him since he left to train in the defence force after enlisting. He returned last year for a year off to assist his parents with the expansion of Cornella's.

He takes me into a hug filled with the scent of freshness and sunset. "It's so good to see you."

I almost tear up again at the sudden recollection of Tony Cornella, a.k.a. our Tickler Tony. Stay away from those saucers of hands he carries because once they play their trick on you, there's no going back, but with teary eyes. Tears flowed from the uncontrolled laughter.

It's embarrassing to admit, but I was once a victim of his attack and accidentally gave him a broken tooth. What can I say? My body runs wild when I'm laughing.

Tony helped us get free goodies from the cafe when his parents, Adison and Tessa Cornella, opened it. Their story is tear-provoking, but it's for another time.

"How have you been?" he asks with soft eyes as I still hold on to him by the waist.

"Well enough," I say, which is true. I breathe in to avoid having round two of a bathroom run.

"That's what we need." He passes me a smile as we come apart.

"How was your service?" I ask, taking my glass from the table.

"Like sheep with a Shepard. Only that the sheep are trained with weapons." He stands casually with his hands in his pants pockets. His professional white ironed shirt and blue pants are trying their best to hide the muscular body—but fail.

"Every sheep should know how to fight," I say, "especially when the world is full of wolves."

Tony smiles and nods. "Let's not limit it to sheep only. There are even birds out there that need the training." He leans his elbow on my shoulder.

"Why would you want to cage a free bird?" I say, taking a sip of the orange juice. "Any bird would rather fly free than be tamed." Flavours of citrus with a tinge of sweetness burst in my mouth, giving me a renewed sense of satisfaction.

"Freedom comes at a high price, my bird. Would you pay that price?" He pumps his two eyebrows.

"If it means peace in here," I say, tapping his forehead. "Then yes."

"Accepting the fact makes you one step closer to your peace." He stands straight and darts his gaze behind me for a second before coming back to me.

"I'll see you around?" I ask with a questioning tilt of my head.

"You sure will. I'm heading out for the night. Only came in to see you and to see if there were any changes in the grump you left behind for us to deal with." He flicks his eyebrows behind me.

When I turn, I'm rooted to the spot, unable to move as Jason pins me down with his hard stare.

Jason is facing our table with one leg crossed over the other and his hands settled on his lap. He is nothing more than the epitome of power. A man who can equally make and ruin. His stare is unwavering, not missing a beat of our conversation.

"News flash…" Tony says, his voice hushed, "it'll take every single one of you and more to get the Grinch out of his soul."

Tony is not wrong about that. If the Grinch and Jason had a standoff, Jason would defeat the Grinch with flying colours. The scowl on his face is permanent, and the tightening around his mouth grows deeper.

"I'll leave you to it." Tony squeezes my shoulders and walks away.

Another figure, equally broad and dark, sits in front of Jason. After a moment passes, the said figure turns around and our eyes lock.

My heart cracks open yet again.

"Kai?" My voice silently breaks into a whisper as he stands up. The girls turn their heads towards Kai and visibly wince.

Kai's eyebrows shoot up to his hairline. "No fucking way. Queen Bee!" He takes two quick strides in my direction and engulfs me in his warmth, lifting me in the air.

I giggle and can't help the smile blossoming on my lips. Every girl deserves a friend like Kai, and we are truly lucky to have him. I don't remember a time he wasn't there when we needed him—or not. He would pick up any call, even if it's the middle of the night. The heart in his chest doesn't just beat blood, it beats the blood of gold.

"I missed you." He places a soft kiss on my temple. The light touch of his kiss makes me want to burst with happiness.

This man deserves all the love in the world after what he went through. It's hard to imagine how he's coping. Losing a parent to cancer, but also one who is living with addiction and laundering of all things materialistic isn't anything anyone should go through—much less Kai and Asher.

"Don't even get me started on how much I missed you." I swipe away a traitor of a tear with the back of my finger.

"For sure I missed you more." His dark blue eyes soften as he takes in my face. So many emotions glimmer through those protective eyes.

"You wanna bet?" We both laugh at our bad habit of betting on everything we do. From who eats the leftover lactose-free chocolate to who can jump the highest on the trampoline.

"Is Steven here?" Kai asks with a glimpse of hope of meeting his friend.

Shaking my head in disappointment, I share, "He mentioned the chance of coming. No promises, though." A small smile crosses my lips as I look at him.

"At least we have you. And you guys…" He tilts his head, eyeing the three women with their heads on their shoulders—not Sage. Their guilty expressions betray their confidence. "Exactly when were you going to tell me Bianca was back?"

Feigning disappointment, I gasp and cover my mouth. "You didn't tell him. How dare you not tell *him*." I stifle a giggle, barely getting the words out.

"Maybe check the device you pushed up where the sun doesn't shine. You *will* find the multiple texts and phone calls." Kiara's fake smile is sharp as she speaks.

"Probably busy putting his dick in someone," Eva grumbles, not even looking in his direction. "I'm surprised it hasn't fallen off already."

"Oh really. This baby here has rocked the world of many and will continue to. Sorry, some won't see Magic Mike's powers." He points under his belt with a smug smile.

We all shudder at the visual.

"Please don't tell me you call it *Magic Mike?*" Kiara asks, clearly unimpressed.

"One of the many names." He winks. I wish I could erase this moment with all my might because I am scarred.

"Cut it out already. We go through this every time." Sage sips her drink, her breath coming out in a puff. Most likely exhausted from being the broken record.

Clearly ignoring Sage, Eva suggests, "Or you can always leave and move to Mars. Wait…" Eva's excited voice bounces around as she straightens on her couch chair as if struck by a genius idea. "That's an excellent idea. You'd be great company for the Martians—you're clearly not made for humans."

"Eva." Sage's voice lowers in warning.

"No need to calm a kid, Sage. Evalyn is going through an inferiority phase in her life. Let her be," Kai says nonchalantly, although sparks zap between Eva and Kai.

My gaze shifts to Jason, still in the same position, eyes glued on me, as their playful conversation continues behind us. A sudden heat rushes up to my cheeks. *How can he still have such an effect on me?*

Don't hide from them.

"Guys, guess who's organising the grump's party?" Kai smiles mischievously, throwing a thumb over his shoulder.

"The poorest man in the city." Eva points at him.

"Rich enough to go to Mars," Kai fires back.

Their banter is in the background when Jason's deep green eyes hold me captive.

This bird is better left caged.

CHAPTER 5
Jason

I don't know if I can leave this night with a sane head. This celebration marks my acceptance of the Archer name and my position as the heir to the legacy. But my mind is elsewhere, far from this place.

"Is the new position stressing you out already?" A trembling hand lands on my shoulder when I take my whisky from the bar. It's Jacob Carter, the head of management. He has worked his years off well, and I truly respect that. But not when he sticks his nose in any hole he can find.

"You've downed four glasses, and we're only halfway through the night."

Not enough.

My eyes sharpen towards him like an eagle to its prey. "Maybe you should move to accounting after all that's where your skills seem to lie," my steady voice replies.

His lips thin.

"Hope you're enjoying yourself?" I gesture my drink around the venue. Here goes another round of conversation I could've lived another second without.

Carter ponders, his upper lip lifting as he strokes his moustache thoughtfully. "Very much. You got quite a celebration out there." He follows my movements, and we look out at the crowd filling the open space.

Lively chatter and slow dances fill the open-spaced dance floors on either side of the larger centre stage. I lean my elbows on the bar, taking in the deceptive smiles and even deceptive motives of the attendees.

Warm-scented lights wrap around the central large willow tree from the root to branches. By the entrance is a large arch surrounded by welcoming flowers of lilies and pink roses. Servers buzz around, carrying orders and drinks to tables of four and six placed throughout the venue.

"So, what's your plan for the future? And I don't mean for the company." I can feel his pupils stretching to the far corner, pinning me. I know the hint. Mr Carter has been the only persistent one—aside from my parents—interested in whomever I commit to outside the office. No one from Mum's blind dates ever made me want to see them again.

That person simply isn't here yet. *The only woman I had ever wanted has turned her back on me.*

"Nothing as of now," I reply, looking out to the crowd.

"I'm here." The same loud voice takes me away from the deep amber of the whisky kissing my lips, and search for its owner.

With unmatched elegance, Bianca finds her way through the crowd, her feet barely touching the ground.

It's been a day since I saw her at Cornella's, and I can't get rid of the fire in me after seeing the despair in those blue eyes. I would burn the entire world if anyone hurt her, no matter how much she pushes me away. But burning would do nothing to give her happiness because it only started the cascade of our downfall. Yet a part of me will do it again and again, if that means I can feel her in my arms one last time.

But here I stand, helpless—unable to take away her pain. Her pain, masked by her silence, has worn out those magnificent blue eyes, sealing the trauma she hides.

I don't know if I should follow the instincts of my heart again and fall back into the trap of those beautiful lies that come out of her mouth. The only thing I know is that the heart in my chest needs to quieten its beating for her. I'm getting drawn back to her, and I realise it's a path to heartbreak for both of us. I'm still recovering from the last time I had one. Back then, I longed for her—*craved* her. Now, though, those feelings seem to have dwarfed in comparison to the longing and craving that eat away at my sanity every time I see her and can't claim her.

A small part of me held onto the hope that she would be mine someday, but I'd neglected to realise that wanting her was a game I could never win.

Humiliated by Bianca's rejection after pouring my heart out, I learned a valuable lesson: feelings are flawed—hollow. Nothing could've prepared me for the rejection she slapped me with when I had asked her to put her trust in me and let me help her take care of her after the events of that night, which changed what we knew of the world and ourselves.

I tried so damn hard to move on, to find myself a space where she didn't exist, but I soon recognised no such place existed. She existed everywhere I could breathe and live. I'm incomplete without her, trapped in a puzzle I can never finish alone. Without her, I am a lost piece, finding my way to the right place.

In the sea of heads, Bianca smoothly guides herself and waves to Kiara, Eva, and Sage on the other side. As she does, her slender body comes into view, which makes it even more difficult to look away.

Her long, shimmering blue evening gown has a daringly high slit positioned on her hipbone, hugging every contour and shadow. From where I stand, I have the perfect view of her lightly tanned legs.

I don't need to see or acknowledge the spark in those blue eyes whenever she is near them. The four *are* inseparable. Even if bound to the farthest corners of the earth, their bond would draw them back together—they will make sure of it.

As Bianca settles at the four-seater table, Kiara hands her a glass of pale red liquid.

Even though she's in the farthest corner of the outdoor area, I can hear and smell her perfectly. The way her full lips move when she talks or the *clink* her bracelet makes when it hits the glass, holds me utterly spellbound.

Kiara says something, and Bianca falls back in her seat, covering her mouth as she laughs. A flutter stirs in my stomach, recalling how much I adored—*missed*—seeing her that way. The loose and carefree Bianca is the most attractive. When she's like that, the weight of her obligations and unhealed pain is freed from her shoulders.

"Is that Bianca?" Mr Carter comments, who I had forgotten is still here.

"Hmm." I nod, taking a swig of the strong whisky. But today it seems to be less strong than usual.

"She has grown to be quite the woman, I must say. Mr and Mrs Kennedy would've been proud. We do truly miss them." Mr Carter's condolences are futile to the ears even if he tries to sympathise.

The period of gloom and darkness creates a thick fog difficult for any sun to take away. I'd witnessed the way Steven had gathered the broken pieces of his sister at the funeral while forgetting to pick up his own. From that day onward, he had become the sword and shield who would protect the person he loves to hell and back. His sister.

Bianca was a couple of months off her twenties, but the violent trembles from her made her seem like a child left in the cold. Her screams, cries—

It had left a scarring mark not only on Bianca's life but also on mine. I learned fast that Bianca is the mirror of my devastation and salvation. The only way I can survive is seeing her reflection by my side. *With me.*

Fuck. I've tried so hard to let her go. It's as if I get pulled by an invisible string whenever she tries to step away from me. I'm cursed to see the one person I can't survive without but must live without.

"She would make a splendid wife, don't you think?" Carter speaks. His speech gets hushed as he takes the last gulp of his drink.

My silence, and the tightening of grip on my glass, speak volumes. His frail grey eyes notice every one of those. Men like him will always see women as their possessions, but their dense brains fail to comprehend the natural power of a woman. She could bring down worlds if she merely wished.

"I think Will would love to meet her one day. He believes it's time to find a beautiful woman and give her the life she deserves. Bianca fits just the role. Don't you think so?"

Fit? Fit. She does not need to *fit* with anyone, rather, others must find ways to even think about standing beside her.

When I let out a deep growl, Carter carefully steps back.

"Well, Mr Carter, I think we have better things to discuss than

Miss Kennedy and her love life. Should we perhaps discuss why the marketing team has been using up all the resources yet hasn't produced the results?" My voice is controlled, but the fire in my eyes doesn't get lost in translation.

He looks around to find the next best escape as he nods at me. "I'll have a look into it. Excuse me, I think someone is calling." With hurried steps, he excuses himself and makes his way to the other side of the venue.

I scoff at the sight and empty the remaining whisky, letting it burn the walls of my throat. It's a better burn than the one in my heart.

Her gaze, her smiles, even her sadness, each moment tightens the invisible lasso around my neck, bringing back memories of that night and the nights that followed.

Years have gone by, yet the pain and memories persist. How can one recover from losing everything? If I had any power to edit the dictionaries, *healed* wouldn't be a word because nothing—no one— truly heals. Recovery is an ongoing process that stays with you until you die, scarring every part of your life.

As my thoughts run wild, I see Mum and Dad making their way to me.

"How's our son doing?" Mum speaks first with her green eyes sparkling brighter than any light.

With a content heart, I soak up the view beyond me. Dad's hand sits on Mum's back as he guides them to me. "It's been well. How's your night?" I ask.

"Nothing we can't handle." Mum pats softly on Dad's arm with a wide grin. "I am so proud of you, Jason." She takes me in a tight hug.

I return the gesture and take in my mother's warmth. For the first time this evening, a genuine smile appears on my face.

"I knew you could do it. I mean, after all, whose son are you?" Dad smiles broadly.

Mum chuckles at his self-obsession. Brandon Archer oozes confidence in every way, while Catherine Archer walks with her confidence beside her.

"Brandon, at least leave this night for Jason, will you? We can hear all your self-praises tomorrow." Mum gently taps his chest while softly laughing. "Besides, have you seen your sister? The last I talked to her was this morning." Mum holds a questioning stare in my direction.

"Where else can she be other than with her troop?" I lift my fifth whisky of the night towards the opposite bar where the four women sit.

"They look good. It's been some time since we got them to be this happy." Dad points out, sticking himself next to Mum. It's true, the three of them hadn't been themselves in a long time.

Despite myself, I can't help but look at Bianca, who continues the facade to project an air of calm. Her smile speaks volumes, momentarily replacing the forced happiness with genuine joy.

My parents' conversation gets blurred as my stare lingers on the shimmering blue woman. As if finally sensing me, she lifts her lashes and our gazes collide.

She blushes instantly, and her chest moves with heavy breaths. A wave of heat washes over me, nothing to do with the alcohol.

Dad notices. "Bianca seems happy."

Once Bianca recognises Dad's eyes on her, she gives a nod, to which my parents lift their glasses.

The music softens, and the dancers move at a slower pace. The warm yellow lights fade to a romantic pink, the venue becoming a haven for couples to sway in each other's embrace.

"Oh, honey, will you have this dance with me?" Dad takes his hand out in front of Mum, and bows.

"Can I ever say no to you?" Mum says softly as she places her hand in his.

As they make their way to the dance floor, Dad stops and looks over his shoulder with a smile that means trouble. "Before I forget. There's something crucial we need to talk about tomorrow morning," he announces before heading to the dance floor.

I raise an eyebrow at him. The *crucial* conversation could go in countless directions—all unpredictable.

Brandon Archer may deceive others about his true self. But the one thing he shows openly is his affection towards Mum. They are always holding on to each other in happiness and grief, as they fight at every stake. They live on the strength of their love for one another.

Love is a tricky game when played with someone who doesn't want to play along, which is nowhere to be seen in the pair beyond me.

I do envy them—envy what they have—and somewhere deep in me, it's something I desire to have, too. With someone of bright blue eyes and a smile that could put the sun to shame.

But I can't let that happen, and I won't.

No trust, no heartbreaks. They don't call me the wall of emotions for no reason, because I have nothing left in me. All black and burned.

CHAPTER 6
Jason

I'm going to kill Kai.

He's begging to taste my fist on his damn face. The bastard knows exactly what he's doing when his hand lies dangerously lowers on Bianca's back.

That's why I didn't want her to come back, and fuck with my head, because right now the decision it's making will have the servers cleaning blood off the floor and not drinks.

The attendees have lessened, with only a few close correspondents left. The dim lights of the dance floor cast long shadows of those who are still swaying to the soft sounds. Including Bianca and Kai, who cling to each other as the music pulses in rhythm with the regulated pounding in my chest.

Slow, steady, and calculated.

Bianca is facing away from me, her hands resting on his shoulders. My ears ring with the rush of blood as Kai's playful glance over her shoulder holds a mischievous spark that makes my stomach clench. He should be grateful for our friendship, or I would've easily pinned him to the ground without hesitation.

I'm afraid I may have to suffer some glass cuts instead from the grip I have on my … I'd lost count by my seventh glass. But it's enough to make me drunk with irrationality. Kai knows he is playing with open fire when he bends again, too dangerously low to her ear, saying something while having his midnight blue eyes flick to me.

Bianca's back rumbles with laughter, but Kai's face is of a sly fox. *Fucker.*

Everything burns, especially the heat in my head that travels through my body, and rests in my clenched fists.

Fuck. My timid rage, curdling red in my eyes, overshadows all the good of his work for the event. The dance, his hands *off* her, and especially this fucking night are enough. He needs to get out, or I need to let go of this excessive energy. Somehow, somewhere, on *someone.*

Kai smirks and twirls Bianca around on the tip of his finger with the music, giving me full access to her wine-affected face.

Throughout the night I'd glanced and didn't *dare* to leave those blue eyes that made me adjust my pants more often than required. It's a surprise in itself—getting turned on was harder than battling my emotions in these years.

As Bianca focuses on something Kai says, her eyebrows pinch together in thought. Looking past his shoulder, she meets my gaze, a spark of recognition flickering in her eyes. The once vibrant light in her eyes, as bright and pure as a mockingbird, now held a hint of the darkness—another reason I needed to stay away from her. The darkness around me is enough to make hers shy away.

We keep staring, her sea on my forest, devouring each other until nothing else exists.

A surge of adrenaline courses through my veins as I spring from the sofa, my eyes shining with anticipation as I stalk towards them. My fingers buzz at the thought of feeling her touch, holding the warmth and cold all at once.

"A dance?" I ask, nudging Kai's shoulder to shoo him away, not even bothering to look at him. Kai's victorious grin fills the corner of my vision as I offer my hand to Bianca.

Bastard.

Bianca glances back and forth between my hand and my face, as if the thought of holding my hand is the most ridiculous thing imaginable. Ignoring the pinch in my chest, I slowly shake my hand and look through my lashes at the flushed-faced brunette.

"Sure," she replies in a singsong voice. She recovers from her minute-long coma and fills my oversized hand with her small one.

Life.

Fire.

Death.

Her.

I breathe through my nose, and I pull her towards me until her hands get splayed over my chest, and mine find grip around her waist. She fits perfectly in my hold. Bianca's breathing gets fanned over the brim of my neck, signalling to my heart to beat faster at the proximity.

"Breathe, or I might think you're still fan-girling over me," Bianca says, more relaxed. She bites her bottom lip and looks away.

"Hmm. That might be hard to do," I reply, spinning her in a circle. "Considering I might be fan *boying*."

Oh God, Jason. You did not just say that.

Bianca gasps when she faces me again, her eyes are wide. "Oh, so he jokes."

I nod, my insides heating—boiling—in every corner. "*He* is human."

"But don't try showing this skill to others. They might not survive this miracle."

I roll my lips, and for the first time, I want to laugh. "You've survived many of my *skills* and haven't complained."

The indication of which skills doesn't get lost as Bianca's eyes twinkle with renewed energy. Heat becomes palpable between us, an entity of its own, fulfilling yet empty.

I hold her tighter, hoping to grasp at something tangible, anything to quell the growing emptiness. The music pulses through the floor, our feet move in perfect rhythm, and after a minute, I finally speak, "You look beautiful. Blue suits you."

Instead of answering, she takes me by surprise as her head rests on my shoulder, letting the weight settle.

"It's been some time," she whispers, barely audible.

"It didn't need to be." I bite my tongue, stopping it from speaking. I know if I spill my heart and tell her how much her absence has affected me, we will be running in circles of confused emotions all night—three months.

The best I can do is wrap my arms tighter around her with the sense of possessiveness and protectiveness from years ago returning.

I'm four years older than Bianca. She is someone I had seen grow into the woman she is today. I craved her presence, her voice, a single sign of life, and yet, the distance between us mocked me, whispering every detail of her absence into my aching heart. Keeping an eye on her was the only thing that could quench the hunger I felt after she left. From the university she enrolled at for her interior designing degree, the local agency she did her internship with, her local grocery store, the bar she went to weekly and stayed longer than needed, to when she started at Florals & Bells.

I had always contemplated opening the files I received from Teal every month. My inner demon tormented me. He scratched at my sanity, leaving me frustrated to the core. The only solution was to click on the files.

"How are you?" she asks again, ignoring my words. Her voice vibrates on my shoulder as her head rests there.

"Fine with what I have."

"I can see that. But how are *you* doing?" She looks up, and the earlier smile has dropped an inch. When I remain quiet, she elaborates, "I mean … how we left things. I wasn't in my most mature shoes, but it's a conversation we still need to have." Her gaze flickers up, a tremor in her chin, and the glimmer of unshed tears glistens in her eyes.

"There is nothing we need to talk about. You made the best decision for you, and I did the same. *To let you go.*" My stomach clenches as I say the words.

The hurt flashing on Bianca's face comes forth, but there *is* nothing we can truly do about anything now. Her lips stretch into a weak, pleading smile, begging for understanding and a glimmer of hope in the face of despair.

She nods. Once. Twice. The sight of her eyes welling with tears sends a wave of sadness through me, squeezing my heart tight. She looks away, pouts, and takes a sharp inhale.

"It was nice to have the dance, *Jason.*" Her voice cracks at my name as her arms slide off my shoulders, giving way to the chilly emptiness in her place.

Fuck.

The world blurs as she hurries towards the bathroom. Her head is bent low, her breathing heavy and quick, as she disappears.

I return to where I was sitting—my heart in my mouth. As I sit, Kai shoots me daggers from his eyes.

"Happy?" he barks, sipping his bourbon.

I point to the bartender, and he gets right on my drink.

"You know you're a dick, right?" His hands fly in the air in pure disbelief and land with a smack on his lap.

"Weren't you the one who said to stay away?"

He huffs. "I did, but that didn't mean to make anyone cry. You really must be blind not to see what I can."

His words are no less than knives digging into my chest and twisting. "Oh, pray tell," I say mockingly.

"Listen to me carefully. I know you are hurting, and so is she. If you have nothing to do with her, then let her go. Don't hold on to the thin rope of hope that one day she will come back. Because I *know* you are. She will only come if you let her, and right now … you're just being a possessive jerk who wouldn't have her and won't let her have the choice, either." Kai takes deep, ragged breaths as he taps his index finger continuously on the arm of the sofa.

"Done? I didn't hire you as a relationship counsellor."

"I'm only telling the truth. I am done seeing you cage yourself within a wall that we can't come through. Either you free yourself, or her," Kai calmly requests.

If I could have, I would've done years ago.

I know he is right—there is no denying it—but I've lived as an open wound for the past five years, waiting to be treated by a cure that doesn't exist.

I was never the man who was so trapped by someone's presence that there was nothing else I could see or feel. For her I am.

"Kai, please listen," I croak, the knot of dread tightening in my chest as I turn to meet his stormy gaze. With a heavy sigh, I gesture towards the restrooms. "This is a disaster waiting to happen. Her life and mine are not coming together anymore." The words burn through my lips when the same pinching returns in my chest that I have felt since the brown waves invaded my vision at the airport.

Kai's silence is thick with the shade of disappointment. I know what I want and need. The bridge between them isn't easy to cross. *Not yet.*

"Gentlemen, I'll let you continue and brief me tomorrow," I say to the group of men around the table.

They give me a nod, and I stride towards the exit, letting the chatter die down behind me.

"So, how is our new CEO feeling?" The voice I avoid every waking minute pauses my steps. I hear his cunning smile before I see it, and I close my eyes as I take a deep breath.

Adrian leans against the wall by the entrance. I am on the verge of smashing his head against the very wall, imagining it splattered with his bright red blood. The sadist in me wouldn't mind it one bit. Maybe a little violence can help in cooling the uproar in my head.

"Not well, I assume from the crook of those growing creases." He squints to focus on my forehead.

"Don't you have better things to do than fuck with me?" I walk past him, my fists balled, fighting the urge to punch his perfectly pale face. He returned from the States a few months ago after he finished up some business.

"I do, but something caught my eye today. A *brunette* with pretty blue eyes." His sharp words have my feet halting at the first step down and looking up at him.

I want to keep him far away from me, even further away from

Bianca. Unless he is eager to have a taste of the dirt of his peace.

I'll give my shoulder to Aunt Stella to cry on once I label his death as an *accident* from the many ways I've learned to be discreet.

"It couldn't have been better timing. We came and left at around the same time. Maybe it's a sign." He finishes with a shrug of his shoulders, and the mischievous glint in his smug hazel eyes speaks volumes.

"I will suggest to you one thing, dear cousin." I smile, keeping my words calm to mask the green mist clouding my thoughts. "You go near her, I will make sure you can't go near anyone, and no one comes near you."

He stands there, amused by my reaction. His hands, which were once crossed, come undone, and he rests one on my shoulder, wiping off a piece of lint. "You might be more delusional than I put you for," Adrian says, his voice shielding the Satan dancing within him. "Let *me* tell you one thing, *dear cousin*." His stone-cold eyes hold me as he straightens my tie. "Nothing in this world can stop me from having what I want. Especially not you." I had thought I'd met a fair share of demonic men with crude ways, but I might have missed their lord.

Adrian Carson is not your typical man. He is a store of information with technical skills wrapped around his palm. By exposing your most private secrets, he can make you kneel and bark, all the while keeping you on a leash. Despite being my cousin, his personality remains an enigma, yet he possesses an uncanny ability to understand others deeply.

I take a slow, warning step up the stairs. "If that's so. I have no interest in you or whoever you have on your radar but be warned. You come after me or anyone that's mine. You'll see a man you haven't seen before." My warning sits heavily between us as Adrain matches my stare with his heated one, which he instantly melts into something less discernible.

"Woah, woah. Hold it there, Jason. I was only trying to get on your nerves. Guess I just hit a weak one." He chuckles darkly with a wink.

The blood in me boils and curses through every vein. The temptation to follow through on my previous thoughts of punching him is coming off strong, but I know better than to feed into his satisfaction. He was never one to fear any violence—he feeds off it.

"Fuck this!" Bianca comes rushing into a conversation she doesn't belong in, especially not the one with Adrian. Her hands pause in the air, with her phone in one and the other fisting her hair.

Great fucking timing.

There is another layer of makeup embedded on her face, especially under her eyes. Her deep, red-rimmed eyes lock with mine, conveying words that make my tongue taste bitter.

Kai was right. *I am a dick.*

Adrian steps back and examines Bianca with his head bobbing up and down. How much I want to take that off him.

"It's been ages since I saw you," Adrian says, putting on a face that doesn't belong to him.

Bianca silently—*carefully*—watches between Adrian and me. My nails dig into the heel of my palm, preventing me from doing anything that would be in the headlines tomorrow.

The heir of the Archer empire, now CEO, sentenced to a lifetime in prison for the murder of the CEO of Carson Technical.

The idea is tempting, like a siren song, to get rid of someone who the world is better off without.

"Adrian, it has been some time, hasn't it?" Bianca smiles, temporarily forgetting whatever had her hand in her hair.

Adrian's pale fingers wrap around Bianca's hand. She stands frozen in her spot, stunned by the sudden move.

Get rid of them now.

He kisses her knuckles, unexpectedly and intimately, causing her to stiffen and me to hear a deafening roar in my ears.

Fucker.

"Sure has, and what magic pill did you take?" His back into the socially acceptable Adrian Carson, who hides behind the fake smiles and softness of a caring man.

Bianca chuckles. "Same goes for you. The last I remember, you had light hair. But New York sure has drained their colour."

Adrian tenses, a muscle flutters in his jaw and his lips thin, but the smile doesn't drop. "Not just my hair. Though I'm back, I think I'll find my colour."

"Bianca, let's go. The car is ready." I take a step up and wrap my fingers around Bianca's wrist to pull her away. I suck in a sharp breath at the feel of her soft skin in my palm. Just like how I remember it, smooth to the touch, and a cure to my rough and used skin.

She is too stunned to speak and recovers only when we get to the car. My ears ring with controlled anger that has an urge to be released. The cool wind around us helps to calm my head from its heat as it weaves through my hair and lets me breathe.

"What do you think you're doing?" Her voice is raspier than before and more worn out.

"Getting out of here." I open the passenger door and gesture with my head for her to sit inside.

Bianca stares at me with narrowed eyes, her jaw set. "And why would I do that? I have my ride coming in…" Her voice fades when she lifts her phone, and her face brightens in the darkened carpark.

"In an hour," I complete for her, my gaze fixed on her screen, getting a glimpse of what she's looking at. The car on the screen is moving at a snail's pace, slowly eating away the black line to the flag that shows our location.

She lifts her chin. "I can wait."

Why is this woman so fucking dense? I drag a frustrated hand over my face, exhausted for multiple reasons.

"Look." I release an exasperated breath. "Your house is on my way, and waiting around at this hour isn't safe for anyone. So, Bianca, in the car *now*." I tightly string my words in demand, but Bianca stays rooted in her stubbornness, further sinking her heels in the ground.

"You don't need to worry about my safety. I have learned to take care of myself just fine." Her tone is sharp with defensiveness. Her ocean blue eyes become glossier than they already were.

"I don't care what you have learned *there*, but you're *here* now. Not everything will go according to what you want—whether you like it or not." I lower the decibel of my voice to a growl and lean down to her ear. "Bianca, in the car. *Now*."

She stares me down, even though she looks up at me. Her nostrils flare and her jaw tightens. "Nothing has ever gone the way I like. You, of all people, should know that."

Then she slips inside the car. Slapping me with her words.

CHAPTER 7
Bianca

My rage burns like wildfire, and I just want to tear the earth apart with my bare hands, to scream at the top of my lungs until my voice is raw. I'm more angry at myself than anyone else.

I want to take out every drop of these traitorous tears and dry the well of infinite emotions. I now understand the emptiness and sorrow that must have consumed the women of Troy after the war. They say the Trojan War lasted ten years. It's a mere blink of an eye compared to the eighteen years I've spent locked in battle with this man—my Trojan Horse—who somehow kept my peace to him. The weariness of this war has seeped into my bones, leaving me uncertain of when, or if, it will ever end.

Jason is right. I made the choice to leave, and *he* let me. End of story. Then it shouldn't hurt as much as it does.

The memory of that night hangs over me like a shroud, each echo of laughter and joy turns to ash in my mouth.

Is it too much to ask for a moment of attraction with someone who wanted me as much as I did him? Or was it too much to think I could have even a small amount of happiness? To feel loved and belong in his arms?

Maybe it's better this way, so I don't drag another soul into my world filled with a scarred fate—to live in the depths of pain and loneliness. *A life without love or the ability to give love.* I think I don't have it in me to love anyone anymore. I've lost too much in the delusion of love and that it exists. *Twice.*

I don't know what hell I lived in my past life that it followed me into this life. There must be a way to break this curse and find the clear horizon by the sea as the sun rises.

My grip around my bracelet tightens as I remember the things that could've happened, but fate ripped them away from me like a Band-Aid on a fresh wound.

Everything will be fine. Ma's gentle voice reminds me, the only voice that can break through the mist of my sorrowful brain. I don't hear her as much, and I know my brain does it to distract me, and I also know it's not normal to hear *any* voices in your head. But here I am, an anomaly.

The car comes to a halt, and my family house faces to haunt me. It's nothing but a building with shallowing walls that crush me the moment I enter.

The girls and I had come yesterday to unpack and make me feel at home. Nothing there is comfortable, instead, everything reminds of the little things that were left behind. Like Ma's baking utensils or Dad's fishing rods, and even Steven's posters of his favourite boxer, Timothy

Drago.

In a normal situation, I should smile when I'm thinking about all those things, but I don't. All I can think of is … nothing, because I have felt so much in the past few years that I've run myself into a phase of numbness.

Loneliness and I are the only company under that roof. We suffer together and suffocate together, leaving me with no option but to accept myself with a hug every time.

Jason has his stare trailed in the distance through the windshield. I didn't mean to snap at him earlier, but he deserved it. If he can't be nice, then he doesn't need to be so uptight either.

Throughout the drive, I had to make sure he was even breathing. The vein running down the side of his forehead ticked and pulsed as his knuckles lost colour holding the steering wheel. His demeanour is so controlled that a poke of a finger could've been enough to make him burst.

"Jason…" I whisper, looking out the windshield as well. I don't have it in me to speak to his face.

He presses a button on the steering wheel, and the opening of the locks sounds in the car. "Leave," he says.

"Seriously?" I scoff, turning to face him. "You know what? Fuck you. I can't deal with this right now." I open the car door as a hot liquid anger eats me and shut it with a slam. "Or ever," I say to the open window. The window rolls up, and so does any lingering hope for a beginning. Or even a small *'I missed you, Bianca.'*

Because you *did*. White fills in the blanks.

My feet are slow and tired as I walk up to the main door. I expect the engine to begin and take off, but it doesn't. Instead, everything goes as silent as the night, making my steps speed until I reach the front door.

I dig into my purse in search of the keys. Even though I could put the numbers into the keypad easily, I don't have it in me to lift my finger when I'm completely drained.

Nothing is going right. Hasn't been for a long time.

My forehead meets the coldness of the door. I smile when I know my life is colder than this piece of wood. But it's nothing compared to the coldness I'd felt after leaving Jason's arms. I couldn't stop myself from running away and hiding in the bathroom until Sage came and took me out. The sympathy on her face was enough to tell me how wrecked I may look. Only if she knew how wrecked I am from the inside.

Pathetic.

A silent, desperate sob rips from my throat, leaving a wet, trembling trail of a tear on my face. It's a plea for solace in the face of my mounting despair. I let out a hollow chuckle, which echoes around me, becoming a thin veil over the sorrow choking my throat.

Pathetic.

I am losing it. I am losing myself somewhere I will never find myself again.

This is it. This is where I give up and wish for luck to pick up the remains of my burned soul.

My hands keep at their work to find the key. I laugh for no good reason—I just laugh on the edge of hysteria.

I'm laughing at myself.

I'm laughing at the world.

I'm crying at who I've become.

I don't know when my laughs became loud sobs, but I know my emotions were never my strong suit. They had always betrayed me whenever I needed them the most.

Pathetic

If someone were watching me right now, they would seriously consider sending me off to a mental hospital. Not that I would mind. A heavy ache settles in my chest at disappearing from the world. The thought of pretending to be *normal* is too exhausting—too lonely. Perhaps among those labelled *mental* I'd find solace, a shared understanding of our inner turmoil no *normal* could ever explain.

Oh, there it is. My fingers graze over the cool metal of the keys. I insert the key into the keyhole, and the gears click. Before I can enter, the car door opens, then closes, and the sound of Jason's heavy steps becomes louder and louder, until they pause.

Just leave me alone.

"Bianca," he says, breathier than he should be from only a few steps.

"Go away, Jason. If you care even the slightest for me, please leave." I don't look behind me and enter the house, greeting me with its usual coldness. The tears on my cheeks dry instantly like permanent tattoos.

"We need to talk." He's louder and closer this time. The heat from his body meets my bare back, and all I want to do is curl in the comfort.

"No. We don't need to talk, *we* stay away." I can feel the muscles in my face relaxing after my sudden episode of unplanned laughter. My movements are unhurried when I enter and place my purse on the entrance table. With one hand on the wooden surface, I reach for the lace on my heel.

"I didn't mean to hurt you." His words, delivered with a finality that makes me stop in my tracks, hang in the air heavy with meaning.

I lift my head as I feel him breathing near me.

No, not today. I've had my fair share of emotions today, and I don't think I have any energy left to take more.

"You didn't. Now go," I reply nonchalantly.

"I know I did. I hate how things have turned out. But if I had the control, I would never have let you leave. You know that."

I turn around to have the crack in my heart deepen. He runs his thick fingers through his dark hair, his tie is loose, and the top buttons of his shirt are undone. The corners of his eyes have dropped, and creases coat his forehead.

My empty eyes find his emptier ones. They carry more hurt than I've ever felt in anyone.

Fuck, I did this to him. I do this to everyone.

"You might have left me physically, but it was your invisible pull that had me looking for you in every fucking atom. You were nowhere to be found, and that … killed me." His voice is thick with emotion. He takes one step towards me, leaving only the space of a finger between us.

"Stop…" I gulp. I am on the losing end when it comes to him.

"You asked if I was okay?" He takes a deep inhale, the muscle in his jaw flutters. "I don't even know the fucking answer to that. You know why?"

"Why?" I whisper, matching the intensity of his dark stare.

"You. I replayed all those fucking nights and days to the point the only person who could take me out was *you*." He takes another lethal step, mimicking those of a panther out to hunt at night with its green eyes shining under the moonlight.

I take a careful step behind, trying to leave enough space between us. "Jason—"

He pushes us further into the cloak of darkness.

"No, let me finish." His voice is deep and dangerous. It has goosebumps erupting on every corner of my skin.

"You wanted to know if I remembered? I do. I wish I didn't, because living with the memories was like living in hell."

Another step.

"Because living with the fucking memory urged me to find it *only with you.*" His green, dark eyes examine me in the darkness.

Another.

"You're a drug I would happily overdose on," he whispers, each word pulsing with each beat of my heart.

My swallow is loud in the bubble of our heating silence.

"And what's more terrifying is that I would die happily knowing you were the last I saw and tasted." Jason's eyes are battling with the mixed emotions of anger and sadness. I can't tell which one is winning among them. "Now I'm going to ask. Do you remember when you were learning to ride the bike and fell?"

Yes. You ripped your shirt as quick first aid for my knee. Then rushed me to the hospital, when you didn't need to.

"Or do you remember when you ate all the cookie dough Lina made?"

Yes. Everyone loved her baking. I also had a bad stomachache, which you soothed by rubbing the peppermint oil on my stomach.

"Or do you remember when the scoundrel of a boyfriend you had ended up in the hospital and jail for even touching you without your permission?"

Yes. I helped bandage your knuckles from the punches.

"Or whose shoulder you cried on when you needed it the most?"

Yes. Yours.

If this was his way of being nostalgic, it was fucked up.

"Or—"

"Shut up!" I let out a guttural scream as my hands claw at my ears, a desperate attempt to silence the relentless tide of agony as tears stream down my face—*fucking again.* Each is a fresh wave of sorrow. *"Shut up,"* I sob, weak.

Jason stands unaffected by the power his words hold, truly penetrating all the defence mechanisms I once thought I had but are shrivelling in his wake.

"You can't even hear them. Each day, this land whispered tales of what I'd lost. It was a constant reminder of the fact that escape was the best route for you to deal with grief alone, than to put trust and faith in those who care for you. It was a slap in my face for ever having feelings and emotions for someone who gave up at the first sign of adversity."

This is the most I had heard him talk, but I never thought the words would entail the most hurtful truth.

Yes, I had escaped.

I wanted to save you from myself. I didn't want to spread my misery to you when you had so many better things to do in your life than take care of a void person. Instead, I wanted to be an outlet for myself in a twisted sense of being independent.

I wanted to stay, I wanted to be in the arms of the man who stuck himself to me as I tried to run into the burning house. The same man who had his arms around my waist, letting me loose during the funeral.

I couldn't. I just couldn't linger around and let everyone get consumed in the black hole of my making. It was agonising to admit my fear of being less, but choosing cowardice felt like the safest option.

"If only you had listened, things would've been different. If only you had listened, Bianca." His voice loses its earlier rage and dominance.

If it weren't for the subtle shake in his voice, I would've thought none of this affected him. That he had indeed grown a heart of stone, being someone he isn't.

I was too far gone in my trance that I didn't notice how I became trapped between the entrance table and Jason. It was then that our proximity melted into reality. We're so close, too close. His hands land on either side of me, his ethereal outline standing out even in the pitch-black room, with the only source of light being the distant streetlamp outside.

"Was I not enough for you?" Jason asks, for the first time tonight he had softened, yet the fire in his tone still left burns in my ears.

You are more than enough.

"Jason, don't do this." I trail my gaze towards the ground, trying but failing to hold back the flow of tears. "We were nothing for me to stay behind." The words claw through the walls of my throat as the lie bleeds from my mouth.

"Really? Then how do you explain the tremendous night we had? The night when you let your emotions loose and milked my cock," he taunts in his voice of intoxicated rage.

What the fuck!

My anger boils hotter than anything I've ever felt before. He knew those feelings—those moments—we shared were sacred. How dare he weaponise them against me? My hands ball into fists, the tightness constricting my fingers until my nails bite into the skin, a sharp, painful reminder of my frustration.

"You do *not* get to do that. My feelings are not yours to meddle with. The world might see you as a king, but don't you dare use that language with me? *About* my feelings," I hiss as I heave from my built-up anger.

This is not me. I don't get angry this easily, but this man has proven to bring out the worst and the best in me.

He stays silent as the hardness in his eyes returns.

"I'm so naïve that I thought the Jason I knew—the Jason I *liked*—would be here somewhere in your heart, but I was so fucking wrong. He left the moment I did." I poke his chest as I grit my teeth, holding back from scratching the flesh of his exposed skin. I'm not a person who resorts to any sort of physical talk, but if he as much as speaks another word, it will be an impossible task to keep my hands at my side and not imprint my fingerprints on his cheek.

My heart aches with every passing second. His eyes, a cold, unyielding mirror, reflect the weight of my own mistakes. For ever thinking about us, and a potential relationship we could've had.

"Leave," I echo him from the car. Our chests brush as breathing becomes an effort too difficult when sparks of red ignite in my eyes.

The slight graze of my breasts against his hard chest sends a zip of electricity through my veins. My body betrays me, reacting in ways I can't control, sending the wrong signals at the worst times.

The only sound we could hear was the rhythmic rise and fall of our breaths. The smell of his mint, sharp and refreshing, overwhelms my senses.

"Jason, I said, leave." My voice falls to a near whisper. The command in it is so palpable that even the wind, howling through the open door, seems to stop and obey.

I don't want this man near—*not now.*

He holds my eyes for one lingering moment. Silently pleading me to say something, anything that would reverse everything.

I can't.

"Goodbye, Bianca."

CHAPTER 8
Jason

Why does it fucking hurt?

Each sip of this whisky is fuel to the fire consuming my very being. Even the shirt I removed didn't help cool me down.

I knew there was nothing between Bianca and me. The house burned fiercely, and in its wake, only the sombre echoes of the past remained, a canvas of blackened ash where our memories once danced. All gone with the wind.

Yet a stupid, pathetic part doesn't want to accept the fact. I know we've moved on in our lives, and the saw of time has severed any connection, leaving remnants of pure agony and mistrust.

The familiar burning sensation from the alcohol is almost gone,

replaced by a bland, watery taste. Instead, the strength of the sting lives in my eyes with the imprint of Bianca's tear-stricken face, paired with her bloodshot eyes.

It was a wake-up call to clear the distinction between the roads we have taken in our lives. They run parallel with no end of meeting. I feel her absence as a gaping hole in my life, and I know it will always hold me in its shadow.

Fuck.

Her tears streamed down her face, and I could only watch despite my hand's yearning to touch her—wipe away her sorrow.

For the first time in five years, I'd lost the key to the cage in which I'd rightfully restricted myself. The bars of the cage stopped any nuisance from coming until Bianca slipped right through—once again rendering me powerless in front of her allure.

Tonight, she was in my grip, only a touch away. Had I let my emotions guide me and become lost in their intensity, the night could have unfolded very differently. A direction I was a step away from taking, including the stripping of our clothes, much like our souls.

Everything fell apart that December night, slipping from our grasp like sand. Despite time's relentless march, our shared faith fortified us, making us believe we could overcome any obstacle as one. It was only that—a belief that is far from reality.

Every detail is so painfully clear. Living the night had come with the price of my sanity, keeping me on the edge of the cliff as I ready myself for a flight with the skeleton of my burned wings.

The brain is indeed a wondrous thing. It compels one to recall the memories they'd rather bury, yet it holds them captive in the darkest recesses of their mind. And they come to the surface at the most inopportune moments.

"Aren't your grandpa legs carrying you well?" Bianca yells, running

backwards near the shore. We had planned to take a dip before calling it a night, which explains why I'm carrying an entire house with me.

I drop our bags on the soft sand, feeling them sink in. With a burst of energy, I run towards the girl, her shriek ringing out as I scoop her up and throw her into the water.

"Jason!"

Her scream gets swallowed by the rushing current as she disappears beneath the surface.

"These legs can carry just fine." I chuckle.

She emerges from underneath the water, and I don't think I've seen anyone so otherworldly as the glimpses of moonlight awaken the beauty she keeps tamed. Water drips from the loose ends of her short hair, rolling down to the shirt clinging to her skin. Her curves give free access to stain my eyes with the thoughts I would rather hold back.

She is Eva's friend. I should see her as a sister, but the only thing on my mind—God forbid—has everything to do with me seeing her as a woman. My woman.

"I will get you back for this." She lunges at me, but I shift my weight to the left, sending her tumbling back into the water with a soft thud.

"Not today."

For the next minutes or hours, we stayed in the water, floated, and swam. The summer sea is warm and inviting, and nothing seemed out of the ordinary until our hands met beneath the surface. We stayed oblivious to the connection, allowing the thumps of our hearts to fill the air.

My feet sink into the sand as I push myself to stand and bring her close to me. When we face each other, our eyes sparkle with delight—mirroring the vibrant stars above—filling the sultry summer night with a sense of pure desire.

A silent understanding holds us captive, and electricity zaps between us. Her intense eyes sparkle as she steps closer. "We should go," she whispers—another step. Our wet bodies further heat with the slight collision of her breasts on my chest. My veins come alive with energy as her perky nipples skim my chest, sending a surge down to my cock.

I nod, swallowing. "We should."

As clear as the water we stand in, Bianca's blue eyes mirror her intentions when she parts her lips. Everything's muted, the gawking of seagulls, the crashing of the sea against the nearby rocky shore, and the calmness in the air. They are all too distant from the lust enveloping us.

"Jason," she says my name as a blessing and a curse.

The last thread of my control breaks, and I bend down as my lips capture hers. Their softness and pleasure intensify everything within me, creating an explosion of emotions. We move at a rhythm aiming to savour all her flavours, all the fucking cherry blossom.

With a moan, she opens her mouth and gives me access to taste the rest of her. Sucking, biting, nipping, and repeating. Everything fades away in the moment, leaving only a sense of unadulterated affection and desire.

"Jason." She holds my arms, digging into them for support as our feet sink in the sand and the warm water floats around us. "I want you."

I pause and watch her. She can't be serious. I know I want to do things unimaginable to her, but is she ready for it?

Am I?

She is my first.

"Are you sure?" My voice is a quiet whisper when I cup her cheek.

"Yes," she confirms, and kisses me again with more force this time. "Do you want me?" she asks when we pull out of the kiss.

"You have no fucking idea," I say.

She releases a needy whimper when I step away. Her hands curl around my forearms as she pants.

I chuckle. If time pauses here, I will happily be trapped. "I didn't know you were so desperate for me, Bee."

"Desperation is a two-way game, Jay." *Her arms come around my neck and pulls me close to her face.* "I will have you begging on your knees, being all desperate for me." *Her voice is seductive as she trails the tip of her finger along my jaw.*

I have no doubt. This girl can have me crawling to her for all I care.

"Forget knees, my whole body is at your mercy." *I raise her chin up with my thumb and claim her lips again. She moans when I suck her tongue, and the first of heaven greets me.*

I lift her up, letting her slender legs tightly wrap around me. We shiver when the breeze hits our wet bodies, but nothing can cool the heat between us.

Our kiss deepens as she pulls my hair to get me closer to her. The warmth of her body oozes out and sinks into my every pore, and my fingers instinctively squeeze her ass.

When I place Bianca on the blanket—looking so defenceless—I finally see why the red string between us pulled me towards her. Despite being Eva's friend, she somehow became mine, too. A friend I never want to lose.

"Now." Her voice is a quiet whisper when she finds the hem of my shirt. Together we raise it and toss it somewhere on the sand.

Her eyes greedily take me in, from the top of my chest to my abs, and then audibly gulps when she stops at my sharp-cutting V. Bianca's touch is cool and deliberate as her fingers glide around the ridges of my abs. Intimate and desired.

I hiss at her touch. The chill of her fingers doesn't bother me, but the very act of her touching me sends a frantic cascade of shivers.

"I'll get the condom from my bag." I lean down, saying the words on her lips.

"You carry condoms around with you?" she asks, getting on her elbows as I reach for my bag.

"Kept them with me all the time for my first." The foil feels foreign between my fingers as I take a step into new territory.

Nerves dance inside me, my eyes bouncing between the condom and Bianca. I am not a nervous man, but it's Bianca. My Bianca, and I'm finally having her.

"I thought they were for other girls," she says, a slight tremor in her voice.

I hover over her again, this time with fire sparking in my eyes. "There is or was no one before you. It has only been you and will always be." For a moment, I take in her soft smile. "I will give you my everything. My virginity is not even a part of it."

We look at each other for an extended time to let the words sink in. To let the truth *sink in.*

"I am yours, Jason Archer."

"So am I, Bianca Kennedy."

In seconds, we were both naked on a deserted corner of the most popular beach in the middle of the night. I might have found my heaven on earth, as I see Bianca ripping open the condom foil—never taking her blue eyes off mine.

"Put it on," I demand, my voice deep, full of the undying lust.

She kisses the tip of my straining cock and slides on the condom. I bring her face up and kiss her again until she is a writhing mess underneath me.

"Please, Jason."

"Oh, baby. No need to beg, I will fill your every hole as mine."

I lay her down and position myself at her entrance. We suck in a deep breath when I push the tip in, and she clenches. Bianca screws her face in pain, and I immediately stop.

"Keep going," she urges with a nod.

I slowly push in, and both our breaths get hitched with the foreign sensation of being so connected to someone that you feel one with them.

Bianca gasps. Her fingers find my arm as I move in and out. Her breasts move rhythmically with each thrust. I reach out to take her stiff nipple between my fingers.

"Jay..." she breathlessly moans, and I clench my ass, stopping myself from coming.

"You're fine. That's my girl." I pull out and then push in with a force that has us panting for air.

Our eyes drift to where we connect. My cock pulses with appreciation as it revels in Bianca's tight cunt, coated in blood. Home. *It has found where it belongs, right inside her. This is true ecstasy. A vice I never want to let go of because living without it is not an option.*

"You see that." Thrust. "You are bleeding for me. You are going to come for me on my cock, aren't you?" I growl in her ear, my voice deep and raw as I drill deeper.

The sound of our skin slapping echoes all around us on the empty beach. Bianca's breathing gets heavier with each thrust, and I don't think I can hold on much longer.

I take a perky brown nipple in my mouth and let the sensation of her filling me take me higher on her addiction. I have become the animal that has just woken from its lifelong hibernation and is ready to feed—to take.

"You are mine now, Bianca Kennedy. All fucking mine," I whisper against her skin, leaving paths of kisses between the valley of her breasts to her lips. "You hear me? Who are you?" My ears need to hear her lustful voice.

"Yours." She breathes on my lips, and pulls me down in a soft kiss.

Fuck. I never knew I needed to hear that one word from her mouth. But now I need to hear it every hour—second—of every day.

"Yours," I echo.

With one hard thrust, Bianca convulses with a scream, providing me with the only blessing my ears need. I follow soon after her as I empty inside the condom.

My eyes darken at her vaginal blood on me, flooding me with a euphoric sense of want. She is mine, and I'll be damned if I let her go.

Through the simple touch of our lips, I'd discovered a whole new high, something I hadn't felt in my short years on this planet. This petite girl has ruined everyone else for me.

After changing into dry clothes, we took the longer path to the farmhouses—hoping to make this night longer. Beyond this night of clouds and rain, there is something to look forward to. Reality.

Bianca clears her throat and breathes before speaking. "This is going to be stupid, but what we did, is it right?"

I look at her with a frown. "You tell me. How did you feel when my coc—" Bianca slaps her hand on my mouth, cutting out the rest.

"Shh! You know what I mean!" she whispers sharply, tugging tightly on my arm.

Smiling, I reply, "I don't know about you, but you're my most true person. Sometimes I wonder if I ever would be enough for you, because I know you deserve everything there is." The words sound so strange, yet I know they belong in this moment with our hands linked with each other.

A dark hue of red decorates her cheeks and neck, radiating even in the darkness. "Oh, I…" she murmurs and turns her face the other way.

My chest and shoulders feel impossibly lighter—a massive boulder pressing down on them has vanished.

A wisp of burnt wood, almost imperceptible, dances in the air, teasing my senses. It must be one of the tourists having a midnight barbecue.

We are only a corner away from the houses, our bodies finally dry from our emotions and water. The sky rumbles, and a heavy raindrop lands on my eyelid. It rolls down my cheek followed by another and another. Before we know it, it pelts down like it has never rained in the year.

"Shit." Bianca shields her face by making an impromptu umbrella of her

hands. It's unusual for it to rain in the middle of summer when it's the sun's season of glory.

I grab Bianca's hand and sprint down the road to our houses. Our feet hit a muddy puddle and splashes on our clean clothes. A laugh bubbles out of us as we keep running into puddles until we reach the gates.

"What the…" Bianca gasps. I don't hear rather see the sizzle.

The smell wasn't of a barbecue, but of the burning wood of a two-story building that had Oliver and Lina inside. What the fuck? Are we at the right house?

We stand frozen as lightning flashes behind the house, a horror movie incarnate. This can't be happening. A second later, a loud, ear-splitting sound echoes around us as if the sky tore in half.

Bianca flinches beside me, coming back from whatever trance had her still. "Ma…. Dad…" She begins to pant, her hold around my hand loosens. She takes a step forward, her feet sinking into the soft, muddy ground—more like quicksand.

Bianca stands there with her soul slowly and painfully detaching itself from her body.

Words ghosted from her lips in a breathy huff. "I have to go. I have to save them!" Bianca mumbles lost in her trance, while her eyes widen as reality settles. Deep, simmering waves of worry crash in my gut with the growing paleness of Bianca's face. This can't be happening, not to her.

"Bianca, listen." I try to tug her to face me. She's too far gone for me to reach.

"Ma! Dad! I'm coming! I won't let anything happen to you!" Bianca screams, her voice straining.

Our connected hands stretch out, daring to break apart. I pull her back, and she comes colliding into my chest. We face each other, and my heart breaks at her wet face and red eyes. Her tears become one with the showers pouring down on us. Using the palm of my hand, I wipe her cheeks, but they instantly *get replaced with tears or the rain I wouldn't know.*

"Listen to me. Stay here, and I'll have a look," I say calmly, forgetting the uproar of dread in my stomach.

"No! My Ma and Dad are in there. I can't just wait here. I can't lose them!" Bianca shakes her head frantically while her fingers claw my chest in frustration.

She pushes me with all her strength and stares at me with empty black eyes. There are no signs of life in them now, not like what was on the beach. My breath gets caught in my throat when our hands slide away—the last of her fingertips are the only memory that she was touching me once.

She's gone. And the growing black hole keeps getting darker and inkier.

I run after her, the wind and the rain hold alliance as they burn my eyes, obstructing my vision from whatever lies ahead. The lingering flames begin to sizzle at the foot of the smoking house. The skeleton of the house won't be able to hold on any longer.

"Argh!" I groan as I come crashing down to the muddy ground with my feet over a rock. A sharp sting awakens the nerves on my wrist as I see a long piece of wood penetrating into the side.

It's the wooden stake from the fence we put up together, Bianca and me, when they first brought the house.

And here I bleed infinitely for our loss.

"Bianca, stop!"

"Jason, there's a problem in the systems." The intercom in my room speaks and works as an ice-bucket to bring me back to the present.

The voice of the security head at Phoenix is the perfect distraction. Her unwavering loyalty, like one would have to the King, has proven her well. She wasn't born into this life of protecting others rather pushed into it.

"What's the source?" The sound of my hoarse voice surprises me.

"Currently, nothing. We're working to change that." The

conversation is monotonous, and it feels far removed from a normal human interaction. It's clear, concise, and objective—exactly what I need.

"Keep me updated, Teal."

"Sure, Jason."

"Do you think he's doing all right?" A piercing high-pitched voice disrupts my sleep.

A different voice, softer this time, replies, "We should just leave him. I'd like to live to see another day."

"You wouldn't want to pass up something like this. It's Jason we're talking about. He's an early bird, and look, it's past noon." That's Eva for sure.

"He probably got laid yesterday. Let the man live, sis." The squeaky voice barges in again, Kiara.

"Or hungover," Eva adds, and I can imagine her giving Kiara a side look. "And I don't know what's worse."

Did they say noon?

Fuck.

I jerk awake, nearly striking my head on Kiara, who hovers over me like she would when examining a broken camera. Not only her, but also Sage and Eva with their heads together in a triangle.

"You were awake!" Eva and Kiara react with a startled jump, clutching their chests. Sage remains calm—almost indifferent.

I'm still on the couch opposite my bed. After talking with Teal, I remember closing my eyes and then blank. The high ceiling curtains are pulled to the sides, allowing the sun to warm the room as it reaches its peak in the sky.

Kiara's eyes go wide, and a slow, suggestive smirk lifts her lips. Her emotions are as vibrant and bold as her neon clothing, a contrast to Sage's muted black-and-white attire and restrained demeanour.

"Cover it up, princess." Eva throws me a shirt. "No one needs a view of your mini army at any time of the day." Her pointed stare goes to my abdomen, then back up again.

I sit up with my bare chest exposed to their bored glances, at least two out of the three.

"And what the fuck are you doing?" Eva continues as she crosses her arms. Her denim jumpsuit sits easily on her shoulders with a peak from her white shirt underneath.

"I should ask you that. What the hell are you all doing here?" I say as I pull the shirt over my head.

"Us? It's you. The five-a.m.-er is waking way past his time. We're checking if you're still breathing." Kiara's high-pitched vocals are hard to avoid, but her concern is real.

I don't remember the last time I woke up so late. "It was a long night," I explain, getting off the couch. My body feels like a taut bowstring, the tension pulsing through my muscles, refusing to release.

I stride towards the bathroom to clean off the high from last night and finally come to my senses. God knows how much I need to. I look behind me, and they stay rooted. "If you don't mind. I need to get ready," I say, but they don't move a muscle. "That means leave." My finger points to the door as I walk to the bathroom.

"Have you heard from Bee? She hasn't answered my calls or texts," Eva casually asks.

I pause in my steps at *her* name.

Eva carries on, oblivious of the heartstrings she's pulling. "I had to leave the party early for international clients. After that, I heard nothing from her. Do you know anything?"

I meet her innocent stare and balance my breathing. "No idea."

Once I reach the bathroom door, I pin them with a stare. "And you should be gone before I come out. Otherwise, Stewart will let none of you in."

"Okay, okay." Kiara holds out her hands in front of her as if taming an animal. "Don't go King Kong on us. The world can't afford another grumpy monkey."

I huff and shake my head, not bothering with anything and anyone right now.

Sage also shakes her head but tries not to smile. "King Kong was an ape," she states plainly.

"What's the difference?" Kiara faces Sage. "They are practically the same thing, correction police."

"I will be both a monkey *and* an ape if you don't get out. *Now.*" I widen my eyes. I don't wait for them and lock myself inside the bathroom.

Three months. Three long and torturous months.

"Get this to McKenzie. Let me know what he says about the contract," I tell Oscar, my assistant. He confidently nods and takes the papers for the new office construction.

The day is drawing to a close, and the setting sun paints the sky with vibrant shades of orange and pink, creating a mesmerising symphony of colours. I got here after lunch, right after being woken by the three alarm clocks.

And luckily for them, they had disappeared when I came out. Saving them a King Kong scene.

I swivel in my chair, looking out the glass to the city sprawling out before me. People of all kinds continue with their lives, walking and running through the streets by the Yarra. All have their happiness and problems to deal with and are just moving. *Moving, moving and moving.*

Nothing like my sedentary life. A lot is changing and happening in my public and private lives, but … nothing is *truly* happening.

There's nothing that would make me jump from this chair and run home as soon as possible. Or look forward to anything because somewhere along the line, I think I've lost the connection to my emotions.

"May I come in, sir?" A familiar voice intrudes my thoughts.

"You know, this was your office," I state the obvious, turning around to face my father by the door, flying his cane as he struts inside with an overly appeasing smile. His cane is a more flamboyant display than a means of support. He only had to get it after his stroke last year.

"So?" I ask as he takes a seat across the desk.

"So what? Can't I visit my son?" He sounds offended, but I know he is far from it.

"Save us both the time. I'm sure the Chairman doesn't have a lot of time to spare," I say with the lift of an eyebrow.

"No, the Chairman does not, but your old man does." A wide, playful smile stretches across his face, crinkling the corners of his eyes. "Care for a drink?" he asks, heading over to the bar by the corner—his cane forgotten.

He doesn't wait for me to answer when he pours two glasses of whisky.

Whisky.

The last time we shared whisky was when I made my first investment. Five years ago.

Taking a swig, he says, "As you know, Bianca's back."

And here I was thinking I could've escaped a conversation without her in it.

He pauses, selecting his next words with care. "She's working on an interior design project with Florals & Bells. I was considering assigning her to the new office opening in mid-city. It would be like getting two flowers with one *bee*." My father smiles proudly to himself.

I lean against the counter and sip thoughtfully. "Assign it to Jelena or someone in the creative team to handle." I suggest ignoring the devil on his shoulder speaking everything it shouldn't. "What do I get to do with it?"

"She needs a friendly face in the workplace, and you two are already close-knit," Dad says as he takes a seat on the bar stool.

"*Close-knit* would be stretching it. It would be a relief if we could hold a civil conversation," I reply. My brain ticks back to her reduced form from last night. "I don't want to get involved with her."

Dad scoffs and reaches behind his back. He brings a few pieces of paper and gently glides them across the counter to me. "I knew you would say that, so I brought this."

"What are these?" I ask with raised eyebrows.

"Cancellation of McKenzie's construction for the new site."

"*Excuse me?*"

"You heard me right. I had Castillo rock up these to take out McKenzie and put in the Fosters. There shouldn't be much problem. Should there?"

The company's head lawyer needs to start discussing these sorts of things with me.

Mitchell McKenzie isn't a saint, but compared to Simon Foster, he may as well be. Not to forget, Foster has been pulled in on cases of fraud and money laundering, which he has successfully covered with the dirt of his money. It's no wonder my father is pulling this stunt on me. Not only will having the Fosters leave a questioning mark on our new offices, but it will also give him access to information of the internal build which he can use against us—not can, *will*. McKenzie has proven to be the *most* loyal in the years I've known him.

The answer to his proposition is clear, and Brandon Archer came into this room as a man on a mission.

The light-heartedness has vanished, replaced by a tense stillness, and I feel the weight of Dad's stern, unforgiving look. It's the same look he uses to assert his dominance, burning his opposition to their graves. Now, I stand as a target of his brutality.

"The terms are simple. You agree, and nothing changes. Disagree, and I will happily have Foster Construction replace McKenzie Corp." His lips curl into a sharp, predatory smile, a clear signal of his intention to manipulate the situation to his advantage. "The choice is yours."

"You're kidding me, right? Taking out McKenzie will largely cost us, and for what? A person who came temporarily." My disbelief radiates in wavelengths.

"*That person* is my daughter, and she has lived through circumstances no one should. She is trying to grow, and if I have the power to help her even in the smallest way, I will. Not only that, but her skills are also ones to look out for, and Florals & Bells agrees so." His expression softens in the slightest. "The last I remember, you two were joined at the hip. It's a shame small five years have changed so much."

Silence. The silence in the room hangs heavy, punctuated only by the rhythmic ticking of the clock.

This is a rare showcase of his authority. He may be an easy-going husband and father, but he is not like that when he handles his business.

My gaze drifts back to the glass wall, watching the clouds hover close by. "Nothing was small about these five years."

A hand, been through decent age, lands on my shoulder. His voice is considerate as he replies, "Then it's time to change it. You know Bianca, and coming back isn't easy for her or any of us. So, if she sees a familiar face along the way, it *will* help."

"I know."

He clears his throat and grips the papers. "I'll hold on to these. Mark my words, you will thank me. Stagnant things, *relationships*, just need a small push, and they roll." He stands and touches his glass to mine.

"Have you asked her?" I ask instead of lingering on his choice of words—*relationship.*

He pauses and looks up at me, telling me more than I need. "I wouldn't be here if it weren't for certainty," he says.

We drink in silence, and I let out a chuckle. "How do you do this? You walk in and just slip the ground beneath my feet."

"There are many lessons you will learn and let this lead you: there is no situation you can't control but just need to see it from a different perspective." He lets the words set in before continuing, "And after all is done and dusted, you will see why a bird always returns to its nest." Dad's voice is soft and slow, like when he did at the Gardens. Telling me and mesmerising me with his tales of the birds we watched.

"I return to your mum." He pats my shoulder as he pushes off and straightens his suit. He clears his voice, slipping on his professional mask. "Don't let me hold you back. You need to be there at seven sharp. Bianca will be waiting at the site."

"Way to ruin the life lessons," I say, taking the rest of the drink back.

"Anytime." Dad chuckles and walks out, saluting me behind his back.

I lift my wrist to see my watch ticking away the minutes I have to prepare, and it's not long enough.

The speaker on the intercom buzzes with Oscar's call. "McKenzie has declined to sign the contract."

The day just can't get any fucking worse.

"Why?" My voice is hard as I lean over my desk to speak to the intercom.

"He said the turnover period for the completion date is clashing with his already committed dates, which are intangible," Oscar relays.

Oh well, that's fucking great, isn't it?

"Okay," I reply to the receiver. The line goes silent.

McKenzie is no easy fish. He knows his abilities and sources are the best the construction world has seen. But scoring a deal with the Archers is no easy feat as well, so if that man wants an ego massage, he better be on his knees for it.

Now, though, is the time to give a site tour. A tour leading me to hell.

CHAPTER 9
Bianca

The moment Brandon proposed designing their new office, I jumped at the golden opportunity. My presumptuous thinking had me believing it would be a small cosy office with a couple of rooms, one main and a reception, but I should've known the Archers don't do cosy. How could I forget? They do extravagant, too much for one person to handle. Especially if that person is a small city interior designer.

Most of my colleagues took their leagues into big commercial settings and industries. Me though? The allure didn't attract me. All I wanted was to find my space while doing things I love—bringing life to empty spaces.

And I also know I need to step outside of my comfort zone to get

that promotion and build my league.

"Just stick to small things. You need to be in your zone when designing." His voice comes to me again. Like any other time, a fiery rage, hot and sharp, ignites within me. A bitter taste takes over my mouth when the years I've wasted by my timid adherence to the status quo. Not only was I grieving, but I had been a fool to let *him* judge my worth. I can't believe I'd hung on to his every word when he was only spitting lies at me. But it was only a matter of time before the effect of his magic had shattered, like we did.

Aaron. My ex. Once upon a time, I thought he would be my everything, someone I could rely on. After being crushed by the walls of my apartment, I found peace in Aaron's presence. He embodied everything I'd ever desired: intelligence, compassion, and attentiveness. Yet I failed to see a bigger than life hole that sucked all the good and left a man who was a hollow nothing.

The universe slapped me in the face when he did. I didn't waste another thought in his presence. I wasn't so far gone as to have ignored myself in him.

Shedding away the bitterness, I take the first tentative step towards the site. This is where it all starts, with me believing in myself, and a small push from the wind.

I put in the code Brandon gave on the keypad at the main entrance. The heavy security doors slide open, and I step into the cool, dimly lit building. Brandon said I would meet with their construction team member around seven, and I still have five minutes to spare. An early scouting of the location doesn't hurt.

A hard-cased helmet, other PPE and a torch wait by the entrance, and once I slip them on, I take another step inside.

The excited hum of the city life shuts with the door behind me. An oddly calming sense surrounds me within the empty room and plain walls.

The construction still seems underway, with some areas of the seemingly large space marked off. From the limited light I have of the floor, it expands over a vast area looking a lot like a reception and front lobby.

The sun has set, and the site overlooks the other buildings, so light is close to non-existent save for the one from my torch—

Crash!

I still.

My grip on the torch tightens, and my toes freeze, locking me in place. *What was that?*

I don't think when I slide my feet towards the sound of the glass breaking. If I were in a horror movie right now, someone somewhere would be screaming at their screen, calling me to stop. But the idea of waiting here for whoever—whatever—there is to find me is not my way to die.

I would rather see myself die than be caught by surprise.

"Anyone there?" I whisper. The cold air that clouds in front of me is the only tell that I'm still breathing.

Stupid, you don't ask them! Red screams.

What do you think they'll say? White joins. *Oh, I'm here, and kill me now!*

I can see them shaking their heads and twisting their lips, in laughter or disappointment I wouldn't know.

The sliding on my feet stops when I get close enough to the sound, and someone else whispers something like, *"Fuck this."* And. *"I will see you."*

The sound comes from the corner, sharp and deep. Slow and tempting. I swallow and slowly unzip my bag and take out my deodorant as an impromptu pepper spray. Both work in your favour when used right. With my heart racing and sweat beading, I ready myself.

Well, it was nice knowing you. White and Red hug each other.

Cowards, I snap.

I cut the corner and spray with all I have. The sound of the spray can and the floral scent rushing out are the only things I feel before a hand pushes on my mouth and slams me against the wall. The air gets knocked from my lungs, very much could be my last.

The deodorant drops lifelessly from my hand as I search to hold anything but meet with nothing but the shadowy darkness. The torch in my hand flickers, and I slowly bring it up.

Our eyes widen when my stark blue clashes with his comforting green.

Relief and dread battle within me when I mumble against his hand. Jason is as shocked as I am, but instead of backing away, he pushes further into me. His hard planes hug mine perfectly—like pieces of a puzzle sliding in—and the delicious feel of his thighs seep warmth into my cold ridden bones, making me forget where I am.

I growl, and no reaction. I even bite his palm, and no muscles move. He almost seems to be enjoying this too much. "Is this how you protect yourself?" Jason whispers.

My frozen hand finds the courage, and I wrap it around his wrist. As if touched by a live wire, Jason jerks back.

"What are you doing here?" I ask, straightening my orange jumpsuit. Today I woke up and chose the brightest shade of orange I could find. Especially after last night's events, I needed something to make me smile.

"Before you wanted to blind me, I was trying to get the emergency door to work," he responds after a moment, fixing himself. "But got this instead." He holds up a doorknob.

I shake my head. "Okay. But what *are* you doing here? Unless you picked up fixing doorknobs as a side business."

"For the site tour," Jason says.

"No, that's for the construction team, Brandon said."

"And you believed him." He looks at me as if I am a mouse in a trap. I'm sure I am when the locks click into place in my head.

I would never have said yes if I had known Jason would be involved in any way. Agreeing to the deal would've been way off my radar. In fact, it wouldn't even exist on my radar. Because if the past has any say, I cannot be me when I'm around Jason. He takes away my rationality the moment I see those hypnotizing green eyes.

"Great," I murmur, looking away. I suck in a deep, ragged breath, trying to calm the burning fire in my chest threatening to erupt. How do I get myself out of this?

"Trust me, I would be anywhere else but here," Jason says from behind me.

Oh, you have no idea. I scoff, rolling my eyes. "And you think I would want to spend my three months with a man who can't even communicate properly." *Especially when I can't stop thinking about the said man.*

I turn around as the words flow and see him standing unaffected, looking at me deadpan.

He inches closer to me, and I immediately get enveloped by his heavenly minty scent. His eyes search mine, but I can't for the life of me decode the emotion in him. *Annoyed? Intrigue?*

"Bianca." The rasp of his voice vibrates the lumbers on my spine, sending the already erupting goosebumps on a whole different level. *Focus, Bianca.* "Let's be adults and, most importantly, *professionals.* I am here as the CEO of Archer Enterprises. When it comes to business, I don't do rainbows and sunshine. I take it very seriously."

A sense of disappointment runs through me at the blank look on his face. He continues to lean forward, leaving a ghosting distance between our noses.

I don't back down and return the intensity of his stare.

"If you work with me, you follow my rules," he says with a hint of darkness, and my insides clench in appreciation. *Fuck me already*—not literally.

"If I don't?" I whisper in challenge, sharply.

The sides of his lips quirk up, and the heat circling us intensifies. "Then you get punished."

Oh, it's getting hot *in here!* Red and White sing all at once.

I'm trying not to see all the possible ways and on all the possible surfaces I could be *punished*. My sex clenches as fire runs through my insides at just the mere thought. That's right, it's just a thought. In my head. And it will *stay* there.

You hear me? It. Is. Not. Happening! I answer to the voices in my head.

Yeah. Yeah, Red taunts.

Shut. Up, I spit back.

His face darkens slightly, and he brings his hand close to my face. The heat from his hand radiates to my face without a single touch. "We'll start with the first floor and then make our way up." The next minute I know he is walking away and leaving me painfully trying to breathe normally.

A faint click of a switch sounds in the room, and soon enough a flash of electricity runs through before the lights stabilise in a cool white tone. I blink, recovering from the sudden brightness to take in my surroundings.

Woah.

This is amazing. What I thought was a normal-sized reception area turned out to be anything but. It spreads across the plain, appearing as a simple room with white walls to an outsider. But to me … each wall holds a whisper of potential and a lingering scent of inspiration for the future.

An ornate flowerpot, perhaps in a bronze finish, nestled in that corner, and a sleek, modern L-shaped sofa placed before the reception desk.

There a pair of perfect lips waiting to be taken. *Huh, hold on.*

Jason leans against the wall—the faint scent of paint still in the air—close to the future sofa's location, and studies me with a look of hunger.

His frame is tall and dark. It would have anyone on their knees for him, all genders alike. His forearms tighten when they flex across his chest. Not to mention the thighs that are begging to be relieved from the skin-tight pants, setting my stomach to flutter. How can someone be so devastatingly attractive and uptight?

For most of last night, I blame the stupid glasses of red wine for making me feel too much. In the last five years, I'd always imagined how our reunion would be like. It was nothing like the one in reality. Did I expect him to throw himself at me? No, but a simple conversation? Yes.

With a quiet push from the wall, Jason makes his way to me with sharp clarity.

"How many floors?" I ask, still awestruck by the sheer size and layout of this beast of a building.

"Twenty," he says casually.

"Twe-what?" My mouth hangs. Coming up with a design for this bad beauty is the work of half a year, if not more. Brandon surely doesn't expect me to do the entire building in three months.

Jason doesn't spare any attention to the look on my face. My mouth gaped open, so wide it felt like it could graze the floor, and my eyes bulged out in disbelief.

"I'm only doing a couple of the floors, right?" Please say yes. That would be enough to showcase some skills worthy of a promotion.

"No. Dad discussed this with you?" he asks. "You're lucky this is the smallest we have."

Of course, it is. Brandon! I am going to kill you!

"He did say to prepare for the entire building, but he missed out on some minor detail about how bloody huge this is." I stretch my arms to get the entirety of the mansion-like building and fail.

Insecurity and incompetence creep into my veins like a dirty little thing. *I can't do this much.*

Don't let Aaron dictate you, White fires. *He's not worth it.*

"But you can't expect m—" I try to argue.

"The creative team will work with you." He clears his throat, pocketing his hands. When he speaks again, there's a hint of comic. "Hopefully, your legs can carry you well."

I don't get to question why my legs are of any matter as Jason pushes open the emergency door he was near earlier. "You would not." My eyes dart from my heels to the stairs.

He looks over his shoulder, with a hint of a smile on his lips. "It's a construction building, after all. The elevators will be installed later. For now, wear these." He passes me a pair of shoes.

With little relief, I slip them on, abandoning my heels, and stand beside Jason.

"The first floor is for the technical team managing the basics. It has four major rooms and five smaller meeting rooms." Jason begins as we step on the first floor.

A long and interesting hour later, we finally reach the twentieth floor. The air feels lighter, but a little difficult to breathe, which also could be due to the workout we went through. The bright jumpsuit isn't doing much to keep the cold away, even for my mood.

"This one would be my office, and Oscar's there." Jason points to another smaller room beside his large and expansive office.

"Oscar?" I ask while looking at the small room.

"My assistant," he replies dryly.

"Hmm." I nod.

Quick and easy. Awkward.

Jason's office is a pristine glass cube offering a panoramic view of the floor and beyond. The room is set out in a well thought out futuristic style. I walk into his proposed office and examine it. A desk of his choice could dominate the centre, with plush, inviting couches balancing it on either side of the space.

Jason takes out his phone and opens an app. His thumb runs on the screen, and the glass walls surrounding us become opaque, leaving only the glass facing the city transparent. From the floor-to-ceiling glass, Melbourne's skyline glitters like a scattered constellation, a breathtaking sight that fills the room.

"Is this all on the floor? The two offices, nothing else?" I ask.

"There will be a files room to the left and more meeting and conference rooms. Like every office we've built."

I nod.

Everything around me pauses when I see the brightly lit city coated in the cool colours of the winter night.

"I missed this," I whisper, adoration filling me when I take in the city I spent years in. My hand feels the cold glass on its every pore, as if it's giving me the moments I've spent here.

My reflection stares back, but I can only see the little girl who used to laugh and smile all day with the people she cared for and loved.

I miss *her*.

My eyes burn and nose stiffens, carrying with it the bittersweet ache of memories from a life left behind. Instead, the universe has given birth to a woman who is still learning to live.

"It hasn't changed, has it?" This is the first time in this meeting Jason has spoken out of his professional tone.

"Not one bit. But other things have." I flick my eyes to his reflection towering behind me with his arms behind his back, a step away. My hint doesn't get lost in translation by him as he holds my stare with his heated one.

"It's for the better," he replies without missing a beat.

Is it though?

I want to ask what happened to the boy who kissed me like I was his world, only to find him in the shoes of a man that won't look at me?

But I don't. Maybe it is *better* this way, so I don't get caught up in my feelings and fall back to where things ended. It's *better* to keep a distance.

"Is this all?" My voice shakes from the unshed tears, and probably from the ridiculous temperature in the room.

"Yes." The mask comes back on his face, hiding away the slight glimpse I had of him.

"Great. Tomorrow, I'll meet with the creative team and get started with some proposed plans. Then we can discuss further."

"As it suits you," Jason says. He presses on his screen, and the glass becomes transparent again. I don't think I can ever get used to that.

After stopping every ten steps, we finally exit the building. No one says a word.

As the sliding doors open, a powerful gust of wind hits me, the force of it causing my carefully arranged hair in a bun to unravel down my back. Shivers wrack through me, and I try to mask it as much as I can, but with a piercing wind like this, it becomes an awful effort.

A soft material comes over my shoulders, warming me. I reach for it and feel the smooth dark velvet of the blazer melting in my fingers.

Then I look up at the man to whom it belongs to. For a quick second, he observes my blank expression and then walks past me.

"I will give you my everything..." His past words ring in my ear, meaning more than physical. He had truly given me his raw self, but *I* couldn't hold on to him.

"Why, Jason?" The words get caught in my throat like a whisper lost in the heavy air of his indifference. Looking up, I see his steps falter. He stops but doesn't turn like he did last night.

"I'll drop you off," he says over his shoulder in his *'don't mess with me'* tone.

Oh, we aren't doing this again.

"You can't order and expect me to follow you like a puppet." My voice is stern, not ready to take his bullshit two nights in a row.

"Fuck." He flips around and grazes a frustrated hand in his hair. "This is why I didn't want to do this. It'll never work."

"Because you won't let it. That's why. You are too stuck with yourself and think you can do whatever you like with anyone around you. I'm sorry to break your bubble, Mr Archer, but I'm not one of *those* people. I don't know what heavenly position you think you have, but you don't get to point fingers and expect me to waddle right where you want me." I heave and clench my fists at my side from the sudden outburst. "Come live in the *real* world."

"Bianca," Jason growls, taking a small step in front. "You think I don't. The fact is that *you're* just so blocked by your emotions that you see only yourself. You're not the only one who lost something that night."

No, I wasn't.

I stand stunned in my spot, barely breathing.

"I wasn't the one to escape," he finally says in his low and deep voice.

My eyes flick to him, and his figure blurs. "Sometimes we aren't given the choice," I whisper. My angry beating heart contradicts my weak tone.

I *did* escape. Not because I didn't care about him, I left *because* I cared about him. Being with a person who is lost in her own dark grief can only give darkness. Not happiness. Not love.

We stare at each other. His deep green, green eyes lock with mine and say every word he can't bring to his tongue. That's his problem: he can never talk about what he truly feels. He would burn himself from the inside than let others know about his inner turmoil.

"We are not in the right state of mind. It's better if I leave. *Alone.*" I walk past him, trying to hold back the tears.

I will not cry. Will not cry. Not cry. Cry.

"Where the fuck do you think you're going?" I hear his angry shout from behind as I exit the site. The city's Friday night traffic crashes into me with its extreme sounds—a wave of brake lights and rumbling engines spin in my vision. *This is just too much.*

Before I could consider another step, he grips my elbow, pulling me back. For a fleeting moment, the wind sweeps my hair across my face, a light, cool curtain briefly hiding me. At least there's somewhere I can hide.

"I asked you something. Where the *fuck* do you think you're going?" he demands.

"None. Of. Your. Business." I spell it out for him, clearing my vision.

"Everything about you is *my* business."

"No."

His neck cranes down to meet me in the eyes, and that's when I see the usual glowing emerald eyes are no longer glowing, or even green. They have taken to the shade of the forest at its darkest.

All dangerous and consuming.

"Jason, leave me." I look up at him with the intensity to burn him with my sight.

He doesn't as much as move a muscle. "Not until you tell me where you're going?"

"Why do you care? I can do whatever I want. I can go out there, get wasted, and disappear. Or I can go find myself a hot stripper, let him have his way with me to give me the best fuck of my life. Sounds nice. What do you think, *Mr Archer*?" His eyes twitch and his jaw ticks at the name.

"That's if you care for a human life. If you don't, go ahead and you'll see how a man cries for his life," he grits the slow whisper through his lips.

"I'll watch. At least that'll be more entertaining than us having the same conversation again and again," I say with certainty. "Now, leave me."

He releases my elbow, and I stumble back and look at him one last time before sprinting away. My heart pounds in my chest as I run. His presence is a magnetic pull, and I can't risk giving in to the temptation *again*.

If I know something for certain, it's that I can't handle a relationship—whichever it may be. A sister, friend, colleague, and—especially—girlfriend. In each one I've failed and burned a little of myself every time. I don't want anyone else to become collateral damage when I blow up.

That's exactly what happened to me on the night of the fire. It's ironic we were so close to the sea, yet our lives burned with a fire no water could've saved us from.

I keep running.

Run, cry, and run. Everything is a blur, with tears consistently blinding me. His blazer sticks to my shoulder with my hands resting on it, becoming my cape.

Reminder: Return blazer to Eva.

CHAPTER 10
Jason

Against my better judgement, I follow her.

The wind whips through her hair as she runs with my dark blazer on her citrus-coloured shoulders.

I don't give a flying fuck what she thinks about me, but I can't let her roam around on a Friday night of all nights. This city may be safe, but not safe enough for a brunette who can't think or see past her tears.

I may not know much about women, but I know when Bianca's shoulders carry the weight of the world. I should be running the other way, but here I am.

At the end of the street, she takes an abrupt left.

Is she going there? *Can't be.*

An icy dread washes over me as I see the vibrant, yet menacing,

shadows of the Botanic Gardens. Just as I enter through the gates, I become the twelve-year-old boy who saw the eight-year-old Bianca.

"Dad, I'll set up!" I tell him as I run to the entrance of the Gardens.

It's the sunniest day of the year today—the clear sky is blue, and the warmth of the sun is just right. So, Dad decided to do some birdwatching while the girls have their picnic.

The trees are full of leaves, and the sound of birds comes from somewhere up there. Sunlight peeks through the shelter from the layer of branches and leaves above me, pricking the gravel path with spots of light.

Sniff.

Sniff.

My ears perk up at the sound. That's not a bird.

Sniff.

I snap my head to the left, and the sniffles sound closer. Who is it? I take a slow step towards the bush and peek over it.

It's a girl.

She's holding a book to her chest and crying.

Why is she crying?

She is sitting under the large oak tree, where I always see a honeyeater. She doesn't look any younger than Eva, if not the same age. Her eyes are closed as another tear drops, then another. I don't like her crying. I don't know who she is, but she is beautiful.

"Jason!" I hear Dad calling my name from the entrance, going to our usual place. I take a step back, still looking at her closed eyes and her fingers holding the book tightly with a rainbow on it.

Please stop crying, *I say in my head.*

As if she heard me, her head springs up and our eyes collide.

Blue. Eyes. Two shards of gems.

We stare at each other. She's still on the ground looking up at me with those eyes, somehow making my camera and journal seem heavy—frozen in place.

"Jason! Where are you?" Dad yells louder this time.

An elastic band hits my forehead and snaps me out of my trance. I take a hurried step back and trip over a rock behind me. With the impact, everything in my hand slips and crashes to the ground.

Oh no. *My new camera.*

Dad calls one more time, and I hurry back on my feet. I look behind to find her eyes already trailing my way. Those majestic blue eyes are truly beautiful.

"I saw two more birds than you," I declare as we pack up after the most successful bird watching.

"I let you, that's all. Be careful next time, young man." He smiles, facing the sun.

"It's okay to accept defeat. Repeat after me: I can also lose." I pat Dad's shoulder.

He chuckles, shaking his head.

Today I saw the mesmerising Robin. Seeing a bird quite like that in the city gardens is rare.

"They give you a sense of freedom yet teach you lessons no human can." The phrase of a wise man, namely my father, repeats every time we come here. I can't fight that because our flying feathered friends are truly a living source of freedom even though they live their lives under the threat of other predators. Not too far from what humans live by.

The tents under Dad's arm make the only sound as we get to the girls. As we approach the trio, their excited chatter grows louder, like a rising tide of voices. My ears perk up at the sound of a booming voice, which is completely different from Kiara's squeak, Sage's melody, or Eva's aggressive tones.

"Come on, girls, let's go," Dad says when we get near their checkered *picnic blanket with food spread on it.*

"Okay, Dad." Eva shines a smile, revealing a deep dimple on her chubby cheek, and stands to reveal the same girl from earlier sitting behind her. Blue eyes.

We stare at each other with wide eyes, and I immediately look away.

"Who do we have here?" Dad squats to get eye level with her.

"I'm Bianca," she mutters, talking to the blanket while fiddling with her fingers and brushing an imaginary strand behind her ear.

Bianca—that's a beautiful name, just like what it means. Beauty.

"We met today. She was alone, so we asked her to come," Eva explains. "She's my friend now," she adds.

"Mine too," Sage cheers next to Bianca, one of the few moments I've seen Sage this happy with her smile daring to break the lines of her face.

"Mine three." Kiara includes herself from the other side and topples over Bianca for a hug.

A hint of blush stains Bianca's cheeks in a gentle arch. The colour is a vivid contrast against the deep, captivating blue of her eyes.

"Me four." Bianca's loud voice makes me jump, but the girls giggle, including my father.

"That's nice." Dad breathes dreamily, admiring the four as I stand behind him with my hat twisted back.

There's a part of me that wants to stay when everything was so simple and understandable. Not like adult life, when the bridge between the heart and brain—the emotions and logic—is so convoluted, I can't fathom the courage to cross it.

Right now, I should be in my car on my way to the office to deal with McKenzie and address the virus in the system in Phoenix. Instead, I'm here, standing behind a tree looking at Bianca while she weeps away her colours, sitting on a bench. This time I'm near the tree, and still in awe of how captive this woman has me.

I have been weeping as well. No one has ever glimpsed a tear, not even me, instead, the silent, salty tears had over time filled the cracks in the seemingly impenetrable wall of brick around my heart. The same wall everyone keeps talking about.

With each drop of her tears, I am losing control at an exponential rate. I should never have let her in to curl and twist everything.

"Why?" she sobs, her hands covering her face. Instead of the sun this time, it's the subtle tones of the moonlight making her noticeable in this dark corner of the garden.

"Ma … Dad … Where are you?" A wail echoes in the space, fracturing another part of my heart. "I miss you. So fucking much…"

My fists curl at my sides.

I don't know when I became so weak at another's pain. Never in my life have I experienced this raw need to get the antidote to cure her broken heart. Yet I know it doesn't exist.

"I'm so alone. I hate this fucking … loneliness … it fucking kills… Steven …" She hiccups and grips her hair from the scalp, letting the veins on her neck stretch.

Steven. I haven't heard anything from him. Though Bianca and Eva called, there were no mentions of Steven. Was he even with Bianca? Just imagining her navigating this world by herself, so vulnerable and exposed, sends a fresh wave of anger burning through me.

Her wails get louder, piercing my ears and bleeding my heart. *How did everything go so wrong?*

"Jason …" She breathes, my name barely audible, causing me to freeze. Her head hangs low, and her hair curtains over her face. I want to see all of it, her swollen eyes and tortured lips, everything. That's the only thing I can do—watch. I might be the most powerless man standing on this earth, watching someone who is the best and worst thing that happened to him.

"This is the place I first saw you. I don't want it to be the last." For a moment I thought she knew I was standing here, but her head hangs low as she focuses on the ground.

"I fought with Steven that day … and ran from home with my favourite book… Ha. Did you imagine it would get me to you?" She laughs sarcastically while hiccupping.

"I wish I never knew you. I wish I was the one instead of my parents. I wish…" Her cries get muffled with her hand covering her mouth.

The crack in my chest seems to break with each word of agony. Not in my wildest thoughts would I've imagined this day coming, when the brightest girl ever to exist in my life has surrounded herself with so much darkness.

Consume me. Leave her.

The darkness surrounds her like a prison of her own making, silencing my real Bianca's cries for freedom. I can almost feel her trembling, holding on to the bars to break free.

Pressure builds in my chest, and I can't breathe. I turn around and lean the back of my head against the barky tree, letting her cries traumatise my hearing. The sharp, bitter taste of salt fills my mouth when a stream of silent tears of my own runs down my face.

I can't stop them. Not when the brunette behind me is wailing, her cries a raw, guttural sound that chills me to the bone. She's not the Bianca who grew to be the rainbow of our stormy skies. She has become the storm no sun can quieten or clear.

My eyes pop open when the buzz of her phone pauses her cries, making it eerily silent, except for some sniffles.

After clearing her throat, she answers the call. "Hello, Kiara?" Her voice is hoarse, not hers at all. And Kiara recognises as well when Bianca replies, "Yeah. I'm fine. What's up?"

Bianca's voice clears, but she takes her time responding as if stopping herself from tearing up again. "Performance next week. Yeah, sure…I'm fine, seriously. Yeah. I'll call when I'm home. Bye, love you."

A slow exhale leaves her when she puts her phone back on her lap. "Everything will be okay," she chants.

I face the other way when she gets up and use my clothes to camouflage against the tree. She passes me with her head held high, shedding away another piece of her light, and becoming one with the night.

"You know, I have better things to do than watch a grumpy man put together cardboard pieces." As usual, Kai complains about the puzzle I'm using to distract myself. The warm lighting in the room calms a fragment of my mind while a glass of whisky sits in its amber tone.

Phoenix is my sanctuary, a place where I can let my guard down and embrace my authentic self without facing consequences. Every study globally is owned and run by the high-class members of society to create themselves a place exclusive to their needs.

After making sure Bianca was in her house and the lights were off, I came to the only place I could be tonight.

It's a hidden retreat, shrouded from the world's view, where the wealthy shed their public personas and relax among themselves. Far from the prying eyes of the press and public.

When I don't speak, Kai releases an exasperated sigh. "What's so interesting about this puzzle, anyway? You haven't been able to put it down since it came two weeks ago. They're messing with you, and you know it."

"I know when they're messing and when they are trying to be smartasses." I stare at him as he returns it.

"You're reading too much into it. The last time we played into their games, we needed to save Adrian." Kai widens his eyes. *"Adrian, the big bad wolf, Adrian.* Let them do whatever the fuck they want. We can't lose more than we already have."

I slowly raise my eyes to Kai and put the back of my hand on his forehead.

"What the fuck are you doing?" He slaps my hand away.

"Checking if your brain is still in your head and not in *your dick.* And since when did you worry about Pyrosilk and their tactics?" I ask, going back to the puzzle at hand.

Kai, out of the four of us, has been the least bothered with Pyrosilk. He has seen the collateral damage they leave behind and never once thought of retaliation.

Yet here we are.

He drops back onto the sofa and takes a swig of his drink. "All I'm saying is to be careful. We have more at stake now than we have ever before." The icy fire in his eyes comes to life.

Just like good and evil coexist, so do Phoenix and Pyrosilk. It's not a matter of Phoenix being good and them being evil. Rather, our ruthlessness has boundaries while theirs does not.

We've been on their radar since our society had taken its leap with the number of members coming our way and possibly leaving them. So, when the puzzle appeared in my hands, it somehow felt like they had opened a gateway to their death with their own hands.

The truth lies in the complete.

The six words on the note that came in the package with the stamp of a creature resembling a chicken at the tip and descending into a dragon. The puzzle enveloped a silent yet threatening warning—with no other choice but to complete it.

"I know," I finally reply on my lingering breath.

Kai shakes his head and leans his elbows on his knees. "Also, did you see Nathan's innings? That man is going to change history." Lightness returns to his features, or at least that's what he's showing.

I give him a side eye and keep focusing on the puzzle. "What did I say about cricket talk in Phoenix?"

His obsession with cricket is stronger than the pull of gravity. Not just for Kai, but for the cricketing world, which feeds off the players' life.

Kai shrugs. "The next games are going to be crucial," he continues, as if I didn't open my mouth.

Just as I am about to connect another border piece, a voice interrupts the quiet progress and Kai's rant.

"Don't forget about Wakeham. He's taking the lead."

Our heads follow the sound of the voice. Kai immediately tenses and evens his breathing. "Did we forget to give you your lollipop?" He glares at his brother, who sits on the sofa next to him and sips the bourbon in Kai's hand.

Asher Jeffords is the youngest heir to the Jeffords empire. As lively as Kai can be, Asher is the North Pole, both uninviting and freezing. He's only twenty-one but has the knowledge of those who have lived their lives through.

"No one pays for generosity these days," Asher simply says in his deep vocals, nearly rattling the pieces off the table. "Jay, do you mind if I have a word with my lovely brother?" He smiles, a deceiving and cunning one.

"With pleasure." I sip down the rest of the bitter amber liquid.

"Hey! We still have a conversation," Kai whispers as I get up.

"We can play the broken record later," I say over my shoulder, only getting a grumble from the man, and leave the siblings to themselves.

I walk through the familiar warm-scented halls to find myself in the dimly lit library. It has everything one would find inside of prestigious palaces with dark wood tones, displaying both history and legacy. Instead of hosting a royal family, it hosts people in society who are beyond the normalcy and the typical royal status.

A grand spiral staircase dominates the centre. Its elegant curves enclose around an old willow tree whose branches reach out from within the staircase's embrace. Each branch holds a softly glowing lantern, casting a warm, inviting light across the expansive space. The staircase spirals upward, its turns culminate to reach the stunning glass mosaic of a phoenix on the ceiling. The mosaic's warm and cool colours bathe the space in an ethereal light.

When I come face to face with the book with an italicised capital *J* and a proud standing Griffin in the back corner, I know I can at least breathe for a fleeting moment. My fingers pull on the edge of the spine, and the shelves break apart with a yawn of soft light.

It amazes me to this day as the forest comes into view with its leaves rustling, flowers blooming, rivers flowing, and animals living. The Phoenix Forest is one place that can lower the background noise in my head to a whisper.

The lush green trees stand tall, dancing along with the wind. The crunching of the leaves under my weight holds the perfect melody to erase the cries of a certain interior designer. Despite my attempts at distraction, I can't forget those blue eyes welling up like a heavy cloud.

The flow of the nearest river smooths over the rocks, and ducks quack as they float with the current and head over to their nests.

It's as if I have a different personality whenever I step foot here. I lose *The Jason Archer* and come in as a man who finds enjoyment in the simple things like the flapping of wings and the singing wind in my ears.

Singing my life to me of all the things I have and those I don't.

A pink petal falls on my nose from the tree above me, its scent so floral and familiar.

The shock on her face, and the silent dare when she bit me were all enough for me to forget the world and be lost in hers. I hadn't recognised her attempts to get free until her fingers circled around my wrist and took me away from my trance.

Some may find the heart the most sacred part of someone. For me, it's the hands. The way humans are shaped is no less than puzzle pieces that fit together. I haven't held anyone's hand because I don't want to feel anyone's pulse—life—under my palm.

Only hers. The same one I have lost.

CHAPTER 11
Bianca

Busy is good. Busy is distracting. Busy is numbing. Busy is all I need to keep my head in one place.

For the past week, I've been laser-focused on building a fortress against any green-eyed man daring to upset my resolve. Even the air felt thick with my determination.

I met with the Archer's creative and marketing teams to discuss the different moods and materials suitable for a business like theirs. The pressure of working for them is slowly creeping up on me, overwhelming me. But I know the immense possibilities this project unlocks and all the doors it could open. Maybe the lust for that is making work my hours—

Or you just want to be close to him, Red Horns indicates.

I doubt.

I already had a call from Mitchell McKenzie. *The* Mitchell McKenzie. His widespread construction work has earned him millions in just starter packages. When he called, I nearly collapsed. He mentioned that my portfolio on my website sparked his interest. *But what was he doing searching me up?*

Because your work is worth it, White Wings whispers from some corner.

"Bee, are you done? We're waiting downstairs," Eva's voice interrupts my uncontrolled thoughts.

Tonight is Sage's first performance of the season at Excelsior House. I've seen my girl grow throughout her primary and secondary schooling straight through tertiary, and her passion for Kathak only grew. What started as an interest blossomed into a career which she thrives in.

I may not be an expert on the dance form, but when she performs, she captivates all attention. Her stage presence—graceful and polished—mesmerises every eye in the audience. Undoubtedly, the moment she takes the stage she's in her element, and once off it her own eyes search for the two people who won't be there.

Her parents refused to believe their daughter was in a career with no stability. Sage grew up among conversations and confidence of old money, surrounded by doctors, lawyers, and engineers. Her career choices, however, directly challenged her parents' definition of a fulfilling life—more so of her mother's.

Regardless, we were all there for her whenever she needed and didn't need us. The glue that binds her mended heart leaves a tight smile on her face, a silent testament to the pain she's overcome and the pain she still lives through.

"Nearly done!" I shout.

I'm wearing a soft yellow, ankle- length, backless dress that flares out as it reaches my feet. A flower-shaped bow adorns the centre of my waist-hugging belt, and a similar long scarf is around my neck. My reflection in the full-length mirror is of a confident woman, looking more beautiful than I've seen her. Only if someone were to truly look inside me.

Or it could be for him, Red Horns taunts.

Fuck off.

The thought of Jason makes me flick my eyes to the blazer folded in my closet behind me.

"Hey, Eva?" My voice carries to her through the door, the sound slightly echoing.

"Yeah," she says as she opens the door with a puzzled look.

"I need to give you something." Reaching for the open closet, I pulled out the piece of velvet—soft and heavy in my hand—that had kept me warm on a bitterly cold night last week. She looks at the blazer and then back at me again, confused.

"It's Jason's," I simply say.

Her mouth opens to question, but I put my index finger up. "Don't ask. It used to be here, but now it's with you." I give her a smile and return to face the mirror.

Reminder: Return blazer to Eva—complete.

Eva stays quiet, the gears in her head working. The blazer was a constant reminder of missed opportunities and regrets. But also, how much I started to hate the man for everything he stands for—for everything I crave.

"Cool, okay." She shrugs, feigning indifference. "That explains why he has been in troll mode recently and hasn't worn a black blazer. And mind you, he wore the colour like ink on paper," she says, yet I'm sure her imagination is running riot with improbable scenarios. "I could ask why you have it…"

I shoot her a pointed look. "We all know about Jason's mood swings."

She nods, but her lips are mischievously thin. "Hmm. Yeah."

The stairs sound with quick and excited footsteps, and soon enough Kiara makes her entrance. "Chop chop, people. We needed to be out of here like…" She looks at the watch on her wrist. "Now. It's our Sage's night!"

"Am I missing a part of the conversation?" I ask, confused as to why Kiara is wearing a brooch of Sage's face.

"About that." Eva clears her throat and holds her fist like a mic. "Please meet the *Sage Joshi Fan Club's* president." Eva spreads her arms towards Kiara, who smiles as if she's ready to shoot out of the roof.

Her happiness is contagious as a face breaking smile spreads on my lips. "Well then. Let's get this night started, babe."

Linking our arms, we can't help smiling like we've won the world.

As soon as we enter the prestigious Excelsior House, everything around me blurs, except for the wonder ahead of us.

The perfect shade of red kisses the elongated carpet. The entrance hall is massive, with people claiming the space and a drink in their hands. Shadows consume the ceilings, while the air flows with the scent of polished wood and lavender. Thoughtfully placed pictures and ornaments of peacocks, their feathers, and flutes adorn the walls. A central crystal chandelier gives off a spectacle of sparkling facets, bathing the space in a warm and welcoming tone.

"Why the hell are there so many people?" Eva whispers between Kiara and me.

"I don't know what you're on about, but this—" Kiara swirls her extended arm around the hall "—is awesome. Imagine the people you can meet and connect with." Kiara tugs us along with our linked arms to swarm through the sea of people. She took the meaning of sticking together a bit too seriously.

A woman's loud voice fills the overhead speakers, making us jolt at the sudden sound. "The performances will begin momentarily. Please head towards the auditorium. Thank you and enjoy your evening."

Eva's shoulders drop from her ears, and she sounds relieved as she says, "The connections can wait."

The auditorium is as promising and mesmerising as the rest of the House. There are three tiers of seating: the ground, middle, and balconies. We go to our assigned seats in the middle of the second row, with Kiara between me and Eva. A glass of white wine, cheese, and crackers await us at our seats.

"She doesn't say it, but Sage was so worried about this," Eva says. "We all know she's a natural." She rubs her hands together, eyes glued to the stage.

As the lights dim, the once bright room becomes completely dark, focusing our attention on the stage's light. The spotlight follows a slender figure that commands the stage, microphone and clipboard in hand.

"Welcome to the first night of the year to celebrate all cultures alike!" the confident host announces.

A burst of cheers and applause erupts, nearly making me spring out of my seat from the wave of noise.

"Before commencing, on behalf of our organisation and everyone present, I'd like to acknowledge the Traditional Owners and Custodians of this land on which we meet today. I would also like to pay my respects to Elders past and present, and to emerging leaders."

There's a comforting pause in respect, and he begins again. "In credit for the smooth running of the program tonight, we would like to recognise Jeffords Events for organising the event once again."

"Kai organised this?" I nudge my elbow into Kiara's arm.

"Hmm." She sips the wine, tasting it. "Every year. He's probably here somewhere with Jason."

My ears perk up, and nerves shoot.

"It's nothing much. He gets paid for it. What's the big deal?" Eva scoffs from the other seat, I don't need to see her to tell her cringe.

"We would also like to give our appreciation to an anonymous contributor for their great support in the smooth running of the night." A wave of claps and cheers vibrates through the hall.

"Who's this? It's the first time they're making an announcement of a contributor." Kiara munches on the cracker after taking another sip. I am sure we adopted a kid. No doubt.

"With no further delays, let's get the night started!" The announcer spreads his arms and bows before he leaves.

The performances begin. Sage's is the third of the night. The first one is a ballet performance of *Black Swan*.

During the performance, the seat next to me sinks, and the smell of soot and smoke invades my vision and nose. My lungs burn with intensity and blur my vision, triggering something ugly in me. The smell has left a traumatising scar on my memories. Even being near it makes me itch my skin until it's nothing but a bloodied, nail-engraved mess.

The night of my confession should have been the most magical night of my life, filled with the sweet smell of anticipation and excitement, but the flames, instead, cast an ominous glow on everything.

My head turns to the man seated beside me, catching his gaze. His eyes are intense, dark and manipulative. *Why do they look so familiar?*

He sits with his legs spread wide, making his thighs brush against mine. The sudden, unwelcome contact has me timidly shrinking in my seat.

It's so hard to breathe. The walls are collapsing again. It's so dark. So many people. I need light. *Take me out.* My heart threatens to beat out of my chest and sweat coats my forehead. My breasts become tight as I try to breathe, but no air is doing any good.

Bianca, stop! You're fine. Everything is fine. You have Eva and Kiara. You're fine, White screams.

The performance's faint melodies wash over me as I shift uncomfortably, acutely aware of his proximity.

"Are you okay?" Kiara asks, giving me her full attention.

I nod, afraid that if I speak, it won't sound all that convincing.

The final note of the performance plays, and the audience erupts in applause. I breathe a relieved breath, thankful for the moment to centre myself.

"Now, for the second of the night. Please welcome Elise and Denver marching their way with Salsa!" the announcer says.

As darkness envelopes the surroundings, a hush falls over the audience. Suddenly, a dazzling burst of red light, a viscous shade of crimson, illuminates a slender figure in a vibrant red salsa dress with black accents, electrifying the stage with their presence. Then another dancer, sharply dressed in a pristine white suit, joins in, expertly coordinating the dance steps.

"Miss me, Ice?" the same chill of a voice sounds.

My heart drops below the earth as I cease to think or do anything. It can be *him.* No one else called me by that name, and it's been three months since. *Ice.*

He had given me the name after how coldly I treated him at Florals & Bells.

Breathe. You're fine. The only mantra White Wings and, surprisingly, Red Horns chant.

I try to stop the knee-jerk reaction to turn his way, but I do it anyway. Like a scene from a horror movie, a blood-red spotlight slashes across his face, the harshness of it shocking. His light-coloured eyes and dark locks shine out, giving a horrific edge to his already ruined features.

Aaron Blackburn.

My blood freezes at having my worst reminder in my face. The innocence he shredded from me—and I let him. The fear of a prey evokes in my senses, knowing I merely avoided the lurking creature in him.

The sting in my cheek rectifies as his fingerprints rise from their graves on my skin. An icy dread grips my heart, each breath a ragged gasp as I recall the torment I willingly endured.

"I'm offended. You didn't even call me," his same smooth, practiced tone says—the one from his 'good boy' act—that had me completely captivated and falling for him. "Let's have a chat. It's long overdue," he whispers amidst the Spanish tunes.

Is he for real?

Poisonous drips of anger melt the earlier ice in my veins.

"You know well why I didn't," I grit. "Use your energy on someone who cares."

"That isn't very nice. I know you still care for me—you never stopped." He tuts, playing the role of a masked Grim Reaper. His pale and chipped skin stands out in the dark, which are obvious results of his addiction.

A hint of sympathy blazes through me but dies as quickly as it arises. My repeated efforts failed to help him. He always relapsed, falling back into the same toxic pattern of brief sobriety for a week, and then his nose would be deep again. In the smallest fraction of the two years I was with him, I tried everything, and for a moment I thought I could help him—or at least that's what he had me believe.

And a stupid part of me is still soft for him, but no, he's not the Aaron that came to help me out with my design at Florals & Bells. Not the one who made me laugh when I needed it or when I was not myself.

"Fuck you," I seethe.

He shakes his head. "Don't jump bases, baby, I know you always wanted me, but we really need a chat."

Although we were in a relationship, we never had sex. Sounds odd, but yes, we never did because whenever he initiated something, I froze. Completely blanked out, and he would stop there.

Bile builds in the pit of my stomach, slowly making its way up so I can taste it. I thought it was the red from the lights, but no, I am seeing everything in a dark hue of crimson. I always knew I was reckless and naïve, but how was I so blinded by someone's charm that I failed to recognise the sinister intentions hidden beneath a deceptive façade?

What is he doing here? Shouldn't he be high in one of his custom-made rooms in hell?

"I heard some flying news, something about a fire and the Kennedys." He shrugs his shoulders. "Maybe I got the wrong Kennedy." His tone is suggestive as he breathes in my ear, still looking ahead.

Everything freezes in me, except the ringing in my ears. I never spoke about my family in detail, certainly not enough for him to know about the fire.

The rest of the performances were a whirlwind of sound and movement, a blur against the backdrop of my inner chaos. The only time I had a moment was when Kiara sprang out of her seat, screaming Sage's name in the silent room.

I feel and think nothing as I go to the after-party where people greet the performers. Aaron left during the performances, but his venomous presence is still here, hiding somewhere, getting ready for an ambush. I can just feel him.

"Sage!" Kiara and Eva exclaim as Sage comes into the crowd, changed into an emerald glittering dress reaching her ankles and heels that carry her elegance with ease. In her hands, she holds a glass of lemon sparkling water, unlike the wines in ours.

Sage's lips twitch as her eyes land on the brooch of her face on Kiara's chest. "So, how was it?" she asks, running a thumb at the base of her glass.

"Seriously, what was that?" Kiara replies with apparent disappointment.

Sage's thumb slows its movement on the glass. The muscles on her face loosen, dropping any emotion.

Our heads snap in Kiara's direction, but she remains silent.

"Dance," Sage replies without missing a beat.

"Wait, let me get…." Kiara reaches behind her, and when she comes back, she holds her hands out, her fingers making a shape. "A crown for the Queen of dance!" Kiara exclaims and puts her fingers on Sage's head.

Both come in for a monstrous hug and laugh like this happens all the time. The warmth of their embrace is palpable.

"Tell me something I don't know." Sage returns the hug and physically relaxes from the previous tense.

Eva beams from my side. "There's the Sage we know and love." She hugs Sage once Kiara lets go.

"Thank you," Sage whispers, her voice laced with longing.

After I hug Sage, she looks over my head, her eyes squinting as if marking her target. When I follow her gaze, it lands on an almost too amused Adrian, who looks our way.

"Hey, Eva, do me a favour and tell your *cousin* to stay away from me. I think he ate too many snails in New York. He's sticking to every corner I turn," Sage says, her eyebrows coming together in frustration.

Eva smiles, shrugging her shoulders. "I'm afraid that's one thing I can't promise. No one has ever tried to control Adrian, and frankly, we don't want to see what happens when someone does."

"Maybe that day is soon." Kiara flicks her eyes suggestively at Sage as she sips her drink.

"Speaking from experience?" This time Sage smirks—*smirks*.

"Maybe." Kiara shrugs her shoulders.

I need to rephrase our adoption clause. We have adopted two kids. One who's feral, the other not so much but matches the energy.

Heat radiates across my right cheek, a burning sensation of a silent alarm. It's comforting heat yet challenging. Hurts yet soothes.

I turn my head to the right, and the comforting green forest eyes locked in my direction. Of all the nights, he chose this one to reappear. A part of me wanted to apologise for my impulse, for being a nuisance last week. Then Red spoke and hushed White's voice.

Jason has his drink in one hand while his other digs in his pants pocket. He's wearing a grey three-piece suit that is clearly custom made for his physique. The amber liquid in his glass brings out the warm glow of his milky skin, especially his knuckles as they pale from his tight grip on the glass.

He stands on the other corner with a group of men busy discussing God knows what. He doesn't acknowledge the people surrounding him. Instead, his eyes search for mine over the heads between us.

My heart flutters, growing its own wings to escape from its cage. Not only does Jason know how to assert dominance, but he also holds the most beauty that should be beyond illegal for a male to carry. It can cause many women and men to commit crimes and happily confess to them.

Someone tells him something to which he only nods to with sealed lips. If he knew the power he holds over peopl—

A crashing force causes me to take shaky steps back.

"I am so sorry," the server mumbles.

He holds an empty tray loosely in one hand as the other awkwardly gestures to the crimson stain spreading across my light dress. The remnants of the shattered wine glasses scatter on the floor.

This is the universe's sign: don't enter a forest you can't escape.

CHAPTER 12
Bianca

"**I**'m really sorry. I didn't see you." He bends down to wipe off the draining liquid, but I step back. He seems young to be doing a job as a server. Maybe just out of his teens.

"It's okay. I'm fine," I say, flapping my drenched dress to stop it from staining further. The deep colour of the wine stains the pale yellow with its bright red and drips down the length of my gown.

"No, it's not fine. Is this what you call customer service?" Eva steps in front of me and blocks my vision.

Trembling, he says, "I wasn't paying attention. I'm sorry."

A low growl comes from behind me before Kiara pushes me aside and positions herself protectively in front. "I'll give you a tip. *Look* where you're going…" Kiara props her hands on her hips and bends forward.

"Vincent. I might need to have a chat with your manager," she sneers. This is the sharpest I'd heard her talk, juxtaposing her happy-go-lucky tone only minutes ago.

"Agreed." Sage joins, standing beside Kiara.

It's a simple mistake, and they're taking it too seriously. Yet, there's a part of me smiling at it—for someone to stand up for my sake. I can speak for myself and put the tigers back in their cages, but I would trade all my good days for this moment.

"Guys, it's fine. It's only a spill. Leave him alone." I try to level their anger.

"I'm sorry. At least allow me to show you the bathroom." His features soften, but there's an edge to them—he's almost too careful.

"Sure." I nod.

"You'll be all right?" Sage asks.

"I'll be back in a second." I smile, well knowing if I say anything more, they will jump on him.

"This way." He gestures towards the hallway.

Then, the blur of curious and expectant fills my sight. Everyone's attention has shifted from their gossip groups to watch the events roll out.

Jason is standing as still as a statue, with the lines on his face growing deeper. If it weren't for the occasional flicker of his eyelashes, I would've thought a sculptor had left a masterpiece on display.

Jason's eyes follow me as I leave with the server and undoubtedly map my way for me. His hands have lost the drink, and now instead, they curl by his sides with his chest, taking forced breaths.

"Are you new here?" the boy asks.

I snap out of my head and recognise that we have entered the corridor. It's painted in shades of deep blue with hints of gentle green when the light hits the walls. The wooden floorboards here are also a darker shade of brown.

"No," I say, keeping my tone clipped.

He looks over his young shoulder, his small ponytail moving with the movement. "I haven't seen you here. Everyone in today is a regular or I've seen them occasionally, but never you." The sides of his lips lift in epiphany before dropping.

"I'm not a regular," I tell him. After a moment I ask him, "How long have you been working here?"

He may be nothing more than a curious person, but it doesn't hurt to investigate.

"Four years at the end of the month," he replies proudly.

"You started young," I state.

"Life has its way with everyone. It makes us do things we never imagined."

And very smart, too.

He turns around and faces me. His eyes are a light shade of blue, but what gets my attention is the small scar by his left eye. I hadn't seen it in the main hall.

"Here we are. It was nice meeting you," he says, pointing to the door behind him.

"Thank you." I smile.

We stare at each other for a split second before he walks off. I follow his back as he goes back to the main hall.

Something just felt wrong. The way he looked at me, and the way he smiled just *felt wrong*.

Shaking my head, I enter the darkened bathroom. The pungent smell of a lemon-flavoured cleaner with a hint of burned paper greets me. The lock clicks behind me, raising the hair on the back of my neck, and the light blows on, blinding me for a second.

"Long time no see, Ice," a cold, chilly voice says.

No. No. No. *No.*

"I really love your ass, but I rather talk to your beautiful face," Aaron says.

Slowly, I turn, my heels tapping on the tiled floor, to see him leaning against the locked door. His face wears his usual mask of composure as he crosses his arms and ankles, leaning against the door.

Aaron has an evil type of beauty with a dark edge to his high cheekbones and sharp lift of his eyes. Those bloodshot eyes, red and inflamed, are like those of a scarred soldier's, burning with a calm wrath. His attire, however, deludes everyone into seeing him as an immaculate prince with dark and wavy hair.

"I said I didn't want to talk to you." Finally breaking out of shock, blood fires with new renewed energy.

"So you did." He lifts his head up in thought. "As you know, I don't really do as I'm told." He smiles almost genuinely when his eyes come to me. "How has my beautiful Bianca been? I know we have a lot to catch up on."

"Are you for fucking real right now?"

With a mocking laugh, Aaron rises from the door. The crisp fabric of his suit whispers against his skin as he straightens it. Perfect depiction of the devil wearing a suit—could be Prada.

"Let bygones be bygones, Ice. I knew you wouldn't come on your own free will, so I had to pull some strings," Aaron says, his voice as beautiful as I remember. He throws a dismissive thumb over his shoulder.

Now the gears click in. The server. The wine spill. It was all a trap, exactly what this man is capable of. Trapping and baiting people. Like he did with me.

His interest in working with Steven didn't immediately grab my attention. I thought it was an innocent move for him to grow and develop his startup after he quit Florals & Bells. It was a terrible mistake, because the only language Aaron speaks is the language of manipulation.

"You gave money to the server to trap me? That's pathetic even for you." I scoff. "Maybe you need to go back to school and learn that no means fucking *no*."

He has the audacity to chuckle as he keeps stepping towards me. "Oh no, babe, you got it wrong. Information is more valuable than money. It's surprising what lies beneath, just waiting to be uncovered," he says. "That boy out there is far from innocent." He winks.

No murder tonight. White Wings comes in.

But a kick to the balls won't kill him, Red Horns recommends.

Shut up, you two.

"What do you want, Aaron?" I ask, breathing through my nose.

"Why would you think I want something from you? I was missing you, Bianca." His voice is sharp with lies and deception.

I cross my arms over my chest and glare at him, unimpressed.

"Okay, okay. You got me." He holds his hands in front of him. "I *do* want something, just not from you. *Entirely*." A deceiving smile pulls on his face. It sends a cold sweat dripping down my spine. I may have thought I've lived through all the shades of Aaron Blackburn, but this is different.

He takes slow steps towards me, showing me the gates of hell through the hidden rage constricted in his dark pupils. "What I want is nothing too big. At least nothing you can't do." He's up close to my face, nose to nose as he bends down, drowning me with his burned intoxication.

"Why would you think I would do anything for *you?*" My voice is stern as I level him with an equally heated stare.

"I came to do you a favour and shine light on your truth," he prods with suggestiveness in his tone.

My arms instinctively cross on my chest. "What truth?"

"Something about a fire." He shrugs his shoulders. "Like I said. Information is the new bribe. It takes wonders out of people and lets you use them to your benefit." His bloodshot eyes make an appearance, giving him an even creepier edge to his already damaged personality.

Fire. *The* fire. "How do you know about it?" The question jumps out of my mouth.

His breath washes over my face. *Dirty smoke.* "You really think I allowed you in knowing nothing about you?"

I stare at him. Why am I not surprised he might have done a background check on me?

"The fire was an accidental gas leak. *Accidental*," I spell it out for him.

He taps my nose, and I try my best not to bite his finger. "That's what the police said. It was a plan put in place way before the years we were born, and only came to fruition that night," he explains.

"What do you know?" I catch the insecurity in my voice before it comes out. I don't want Aaron to know how nervous he still makes me.

It's a trap. Don't fall for it again, White Wings warns.

"That's the catch. I can't be throwing around the answers. Let's play a game." He straightens and rubs his hands together. "Pass the levels and get the reward."

"I'm not playing into any of your filthy games and definitely not doing anything for your sick ways." The saliva in my mouth swirls, daring to land on his face.

"I'm so sorry. Did that come as a request?" He grabs the back of my head, pulling me up to him.

His fingers dig into my scalp, but not enough to make me jump in pain.

"At least if you don't want your brother to meet his untimely death. You're smart, Bianca, and you know taking a life isn't much of a deal for me, but I know you thrive on the living. So, be my girl and do as I say."

He takes his phone out of his back pocket and flashes the screen at me. My fingers and toes go cold as the last breath freezes in my lungs at what I see. It's a live feed from Steven's office—him sitting on his desk, completely oblivious to the murderous eyes watching him.

"I have my sniper ready to shoot at my word. It's up to you if that word is fire or cease," Aaron explains.

"Stay the fuck away from Steven," I spit. My eyes shut as he tightens his grip on my hair.

Worry bleeds from my heart at the mention of Steven. When I learned that Aaron's plan to date me was to bankrupt our major company and fund his own finances after his father rejected his inheritance, I'd ended things with him in the next breath.

His eyes darken with the heat of malice. "It's simple. I want you to gather some intel on Jason Archer for me and get all the information you can."

My breath gets hitched in my throat. *What does Jason have to do with any of this?*

"I'm also aware he is your most recent crush, or should I say, old times coming back. It would be a walk in the park for you to get under his skin."

My world becomes a hazy mess. Forget Satan. Aaron is the ruler of multiple underworlds, where he has Satan on his knees licking his shoes clean.

"Jason has nothing to do with any of your bullshit."

"Now, now, not everyone is what they seem." He dips his head, and a few strands of his hair sweep across his brow. "Like yours truly."

His eyes don't leave mine as he tests the tightness of his grip on my hair. My breath gets caught in my lungs, but I don't give him the show—not feeding into his satisfaction.

"So, if I have all that in my hand, you can have anything you want from me. *Anything.*" Aaron pushes me, my back hits the wall, and his hard clothed dick presses into my thighs.

I swallow down a gag, the taste of bitter bile cursing me. "I would rather see death than have your filthy touch on me again." Each word spits out fireballs that I hope burns in all the right places.

His grip tightens, and white buzzes across my eyes. "Get me the intel, and you can have the truth. I must warn you, things will only get darker from here."

A thousand possible causes for the fire flash before my eyes, each scenario accompanied by the ghost of the acrid stench of burning wood. My heart speeds, rushing blood everywhere all at once.

"So, what do you say? In or out?" He levels a questioning look at me.

Out.

Red and White rival.

This is your ticket to finally feel free—to fill the gaps with the truth. We can work together and get justice. Red Horns smiles maniacally at the prospect of the thought.

In.

Sometimes ignorance is bliss, *and knowledge is stress. Nothing good will come from more ashes at our footsteps,* White Wing warns.

Don't listen to that prude. She knows nothing. We must bring peace to the lost souls; this is the only way. Red becomes more adamant.

What about Jason—

Out.

He will understand. Red shuts White's reason with her own. *Do you want Steven safe or not?*

Red had woken up in the past years to find out what really

happened, but considering the circumstances, I had to shut her and take on White's subtle opinion.

But not this time. I need my answers and to keep my brother safe.

The race of my heart comes to the finish line as it completely steadies. "In." My chest moves in slow rhythms, up and down, as time stills when the word rushes out.

"Like I thought." Aaron muses, his pungent scent invades my space as he leans down to come eye to eye. I push his chest to move his boulder-like body, but all my efforts are worthless.

He wraps his other warm hand around my throat. The touch is not aggressive, but somehow a little soothing to the coldness of my skin. "Remember, Ice." An indiscernible emotion flickers through his eyes. "Sometimes we do things in the present to have a better future. But not before we pay the price in sacrifices."

My arms drop lifelessly to my sides. The word *sacrifice* bounces in my head. Isn't living a form of sacrificing? Every breath I take reminds me of the moments life forced me to sacrifice without giving me a choice. The moments when I could've seen the girls grow up to be the women they are now or the slow dances and conversations I could've had with Jason. The raging hands of the flames consumed the life I had planned with all the hope for a brighter future.

I learned one thing in my own company these past few years: when a storm comes, it comes to stay.

It takes all my power not to slap him across the face and push him away. Instead, I breathe. *Now is not the time to pick a fight.* "What do I have to do?" My voice comes out solid and lacking any shake.

"Welcome to the real world."

Fuck. I just sold myself to the devil—sacrificed my peace. *And any hope with Jason.*

Jason

It's been twenty minutes since Bianca disappeared, and there's still no sign of her. It certainly wouldn't take that long to clean up.

The whole incident was not a random accident. The way he looked around and kept his path to her suggested something more calculated than chance.

The ballroom is emptying like bears getting ready for hibernation. I'd ordered the drivers to get the girls home so that I could head to Phoenix. Not before I'd convinced them to take Bianca home when she didn't return by the tenth minute.

Kai left early with a blond by his side after coming here for appearances sake. By that, I mean he's fucking her in his car as I speak. He never enjoyed attending his own organised events, and says, "*It brings too much attention.*" My CEO's party was the only exception.

Like the attention seeker doesn't live for it.

Greeting the last few of the lingering guests, I make my way towards the bathrooms. I shouldn't be here trying to find a woman who breaks me down like no other. Yet the fire in me will never cease if I don't see her.

The cool-coloured hallway blocks out sounds from the close-by rooms, only the tapping of my shoes on the cushioned carpets fills in the silence.

"Gentleman," an elderly man—most likely in his early seventies—greets me as he passes. The distinct pattern of his suit blazer is the first thing I see. The letter *M* written in pink flames stands out from the dark tones of his suit.

I nod in return and keep on my path. Once I get to the bathroom doors and reach for it, it flies open. I come face to face with my destruction clad in a yellow dress and swollen eyes.

"Jason?" Bianca's eyes widen, her mouth slightly parting. The dormant part of my body comes to life, beating frantically just by the rise and fall of her chest. "What are you doing here?"

"Looking for you."

CHAPTER 13
Jason

"M e?" Bianca gasps.

"The entire House has left," I say, carefully glazing my eyes over her body. Only the red stain on her dress stands at attention, but…

"You didn't," she states matter-of-factly.

I shake my head once. "No. I didn't."

Silence floats around us while our breaths play between us.

Bianca straightens and fixes her hair around her neck. "Are those…" I look closely at her quickly covering up her neck. "Finger marks?"

An audible gulp comes from her throat, and my chest ceases to move.

"No." Bianca waves a dismissive hand in front of her. Those blue

eyes I've grown to study dart to the side. "I think you drank more than you can hold."

I narrow my eyes at her. After last week's events, I should rightfully ignore her and let her be, but the thought of anyone touching her and *marking* her in any way—or purpose—has my fucking blood roaring. "Who?"

Only one word, and the temperature around us drops multiple degrees.

Bianca laughs, her cheeks growing shades darker. "Not who but *what*. My dress scarf got too tight," she explains, holding up a thin yellow scarf. Her eyes drift to my neck and pause on the deceptively calm pulse on my neck and lingers.

I give her and her scarf a skeptical look.

Another beat of silence passes through us, and Bianca clears her throat. "Hey, Jason."

Oh God. The sound of my name from her lips is so pure and sinful, so much so that it will make me break oaths I didn't even take and promises I didn't make.

"Yeah?"

"I wish that night never happened." She pauses, searching my face for any changes. When she finds none, she continues, "I hated all nights after that. But I don't want to hate tonight."

Traitor.

The only word surfacing in my head.

I'm stuck in a conundrum of choosing between the right and wrong when their shades have blended into nothing but black, muting the other colours.

That's how I feel. An outcast who came to ruin the worlds of many, knowingly or unknowingly.

Jason revs his Porsche to life, pushing my head back to the headrest as we exit the parking lot. I hiss when my swollen head rests on the back.

I would be lying that when I saw Jason looking for me, the creatures in my stomach didn't come to life or that I wasn't relieved he had just missed Aaron going out of the bathroom. I would never understand how he knows when I need him and how he can warm the cold parts of me.

Tonight, I'm going to ignore the fact that I will betray the only man who feels like my safe home. Tonight, I want to be lost.

That's how I found myself in a car with Jason.

My voice is hoarse when I speak. "Can I ask a question?" I keep my eyes trailed to the windshield, focusing on the night unfolding before us.

"Hmm." Jason nods.

I clear my tight throat. "Why did you ask for my trust when I was leaving?"

The question has bothered me more than it should've.

His fingers on the steering wheel whiten. "Bianca." He breathes, the softness of his voice taking me by surprise. "I've grown to know that trust is a tangible thing that no riches can buy. It takes years to build and only seconds to break. And to put it back together, it could take forever. But I think I lost the power to trust, because I only needed to take the hit once."

His words, cold and yearning, fall over me like an angry waterfall.

I only needed to take the hit once.

I close my eyes as the realisation hits. "I'm sorry," I whisper.

"Don't be. You're not at fault." He shakes his head, but something in his tone tells me he is still holding on to the hurt.

And neither are you.

Silence and darkness cover the next moments. He rests one of his arms on the wheel and the other messes up his hair, sitting like the exact definition of power and my every desire. He doesn't need to say anything to get my attention because the serpent-like veins he has on his arms are enough.

Who knew I had a fetish for forearms? Out of all of him, it's the arms that have him wanting more.

Can I let loose just for tonight? My demons can wait at home and haunt me later. Regardless of the *deal* with Aaron, being with Jason was always a given, whether he was physically with me driving his car or if he was capturing every corner of my brain. He is always with me

Yet you know everything shatters when you come together, White Wing comments.

Aaron is psychotic at best, and has controlling, murderous tendencies at worst. I had front row seats when we broke up. The hunger for control, the need to possess what he saw as his own, consumed every part of his being. Exactly how he had treated me, and I still remember each demand as a fresh wound. Initially, I enjoyed his care, needing someone when I had no one. My innocent perspective was gone when I stepped out of the club on my birthday as a changed person.

The cold, clear night fuels my rage, every detail a sharp brand on my soul. Each star was a witness to my torment—to the slap across my face.

We were celebrating my twenty-fifth birthday earlier this year in March with our friends and colleagues. Drinks, food, decoration, perfect lighting and colour tones of the beautiful blues. Exactly how I had it planned.

I'd strictly said it was a no drugs night. It was a big ask for a man who breathed more cocaine than air. Of course, that went in one ear and out the other. I'd held on to the false hope that one day Aaron would break out of his pattern, but he didn't. Just like a dog that won't stop chasing its tail, he didn't stop chasing his next high.

They're sitting at the corner table, taking their next jab for a moment to get lost. Claws of annoyance scratch the walls of my skull, itching me to take the poison away from him. I had my eyes glued to his every move, and he was fine until now, when he began barking out nonsense loud enough for the next state to hear.

I march towards them, but my feet slow when Aaron's friend speaks. "Come on, get a new girl already, or at least share her with us. There are so many more bitches out there ready to shag. This dull nun girlfriend you have isn't worth it." His tone is bored and oblivious to the blossoming rage in me.

No way in hell does any piece of shit talk about me like that. Not in front of me, and definitely not behind my back, and that too with my boyfriend.

Aaron's jaw clenches, and he breathes deeply. I wait to see his response. Nothing. *His eyes are bloodshot red, displacing him in his tailored suit and face.*

Then Aaron says, "You know I can't. She's a fucking jackpot. Once I get my hands on … Steven, I'll let go of the leash. I may have all the riches at my hand, but Lord Blackburn *wants to take it away from me for whatever … fucked reason he has. So, I need some sort of leverage and security. After I'm done, you're … free to take her." Despite slurring and hiccupping, Aaron's nauseating words hit their target.*

Poisoned darts of his words pierce my heart with a venom more potent than any physical affliction.

Forget rage, I'm going to behead him and hang his lifeless and headless body at the top of the Parliament House for the world to see.

"So that's what I am to you? A bitch on your leash?" My voice sounds in the group.

Their heads snap in my direction with their eyes wide.

"Ice?" Aaron breathes. He's not surprised, almost expecting me.

"Don't you dare call me that," I grit out, my nails digging into my palm as I swallow my anger. The nickname only freezes the butterflies in their cages and locks them in with no key to be found. To freeze and freeze until they're snapped in half.

"Oh, come on, baby, you know I didn't mean that. These fuckers get me high, and shit comes out."

Lies, lies and fucking lies.

He rises and moves towards me, his eyes fixed on mine, but abruptly stops as my hand shoots up.

"Shut up, Aaron! I fucking trusted you!" My scream makes all partygoers stop and listen.

"I guess it was your mistake then. Should've never trusted the miser," his impersonal voice replies.

Who are you? *I want to ask, but I think I already know.*

A murderous smile curves across his lips. "Now that the cat's out of the bag, I can finally breathe. You do not know how frustrating it was to be a loving boyfriend.

"Did you think I would fall for a prude like you? You were nothing but a bridge I had to cross so I could secure myself. You mean and meant nothing but a bank. I've had eyes on you since the first time I saw you, and you know what I saw?"

He stares me down with his light eyes growing dark. His stance is calm as he leans on the sofa and speaks with no remorse. "A walking bundle of everything I've ever wanted. The money, the beauty, and the distraction. Everything."

My chest tightens at how I let this snake slither right in. I take an inhale and exhale like a drowning woman in the depths of air.

I can't believe it. The man I fucking thought was everything was nothing but a facade of a beautiful dream turned into a haunting nightmare.

Murmurs erupt around us in slow and quiet whispers, mocking the display of my torment. They are becoming witnesses to the crumbling of the world I knew into nothing but insignificant smithereens.

"Why? What the fuck did I ever do to you?" My voice cracks as a lone tear finally escapes and rolls down my cheek. "Forget it. I don't want to fucking know or see you," I sneer. Looking away, all I feel is the useless thing in my chest cracking.

"I'll see you try." His words are strong and sang in an order. A challenge.

Aaron slithers close to me at a slow and steady pace with a spark in his eyes I always saw. Tonight, I'm seeing the truth behind them.

"You will see," I spit as our chests collide, letting our breaths mix in the middle. "Find yourself another bank. *My money won't be enough to fill your black heart's desire."*

His dark eyes enlarge, and a smile spreads—spreads just like the chills on my spine. "I will finish the race I started, even if it kills me." He grips my jaw. I hear a crack as he crushes it under his fingers.

He blinks twice. Usually that's when he is asking for help, but I know nothing is the same anymore with him. "Run all you want. I will find you," he mocks in a loving tone.

"Fuck. You," I curse. More profanity lingers on my tongue, and before it could come to life, another nightmare does—a tight hit on my right cheek that sends me back.

He slapped me.

He slapped *me.*

More warm tears trail down my now senseless body. I may as well be in a casket, ready to be shipped six feet under.

Not thinking much, I push him and make a run for it. Not looking to the right, left, up, or down. Only straight out of the damn club, leaving as a woman completely changed.

A piece of me was gone—the unguarded part that readily trusted even the slightest kind gesture, a vulnerability I no longer possess. That part is at fault. *That's what I did to Jason.*

"What did that boy say?" Jason's voice brings me back to the present.

"Nothing," I reply, looking straight ahead.

I rest my head back. The sting of the pain courses throughout my head—a reminder of who came back.

The silent hum of the car beckons me to relax in the moment, and I do. I shut my eyes, blocking the sharpness of the night lights and the traffic.

The massage of my seat turns on and gently works on my head and my back. Slowly, I peel open my eyes and see Jason driving like he didn't just understand me without having to hear anything from me.

Jason might not speak much, but his sharp gaze absorbs his surroundings, silently noting every nuance.

We've been stuck in traffic for over an hour, and I had forgotten how busy Melbourne had gotten over the years, or maybe it was always like that. Even though the navigator had initially promised a forty-minute drive from the venue to my house, we've been here and staring at the red brake lights of the car ahead of us.

"Bianca?" Jason's quietened hush sounds.

"Hmm?" I reply distractedly in the haze of my mind.

"Where do you want to go?" he asks, and this time I look at him. I should reply in a heartbeat. *My house.* But that's the last place I want to be, and alone.

"With you." I pause, breathing courage for what I'm about to do.

"I don't want to be alone tonight." My voice is weak, but enough to be heard.

A sharp turn of Jason's head brings his deep green eyes to mine, a silent emotion hanging heavy in their depths.

I should stay away from emotional turmoil after the colourful bursts of surprises tonight. But do I? No. Logic was never the forte when Jason was around.

Reminder: Be logical. Later

He's the man who you will eventually hurt. White speaks up, blaming me with guilt.

I won't hurt him, I say with finality.

You can keep saying that.

Jason once again takes me out of my cycle of pity and guilt. "You would want to hold on," he warns, not giving me enough time to puncture the words when he revs the engine.

"Where can we possibly go in this *traffic*?" The word elongates in my mouth with emphasis. My breath and everything I have to say get glued to the back of my throat as it goes dry from the U-turn. Jason winds the steering wheel in full rotation, swirling us as the movement blurs all the night lights and stars into one.

Instinctively, I clutch onto the seatbelt for dear life. "What the fuck!" A smile spread across my face, surprise flicking through my veins. Adrenaline beats in every vein, giving life to the dormant neurons to fire. "Woah." My grin widens.

"I warned you." Jason matches my level of excitement as the smallest fragment of a smile flashes on him before I could truly catch it.

"I think I'll wear a helmet and kneepads if you go at this rate."

"And some glasses." He turns to look at me for a moment. "Where did they go, anyway? The grandma look was good on you, too."

I chuckle. "The great Jason Archer blesses me with another joke. I must have seen a handful of four-leaf clovers in the morning."

"Flatter yourself, not everyone gets it."

I am lucky.

"So, where are we going?" I ask.

"You'll see."

"Come on, just tell me." I nearly whine.

"No."

A dizzying swirl of city lights smears across my vision as our car roars ahead. The slow turtle race of traffic becomes a distant memory as we leave it behind.

"I'm sorry." The words come out on their own.

"Why?" he questions, his tone curious—almost offended.

For what's coming. That's what I want to say and should say. But the coward in me won't allow it. "For freaking out on Friday," I amend.

"I should apologise as well. I didn't have any right to act that way," he says. "But that doesn't mean what you were doing was any better." He looks at me from the corner of his eyes with his features hardening. "Listen to me, Bianca." His body tenses, making him appear bulkier. "*We may be* nothing beyond our connections, but know one thing ..." His grip on the wheel tightens, the earlier lightness lost. "For however long you are here. I will *not* stand by if someone hurts you. Man or not, nothing will stop me from making them pay for the slightest scratch. I promise you. They will not see the light of the next day—at least not in their conscious mind." Jason's warning burns with deep meaning, a promise he will always keep.

His words make me pause, trapping me in a temporary abyss of security with his words and presence. But, I also know all these promises and words will fade the moment I leave.

Yet his words don't sound empty. They hold meaning—meaning

that he will not hesitate to pursue his words if someone hurts *me*. For *me*.

I should revolt and tell him to mind his own business, but that's not what the flutters in the wings of my heart tell me. The volume of blood within me grows, getting pumped to all corners. Especially arousing heat in every vein flowing in my bloodstream, leading to the pulse settled between my thighs.

My sex aches at the dark possessiveness of his tone. To be handled with his roughness and merciless touches. I want him, and that's nothing new.

Alarm bells ring in my head as I dig deep into the part that will satisfy us both.

CHAPTER 14
Jason

"St. Kilda beach!" Bianca gasps. "It's been an age since the last time I was here." Unshed tears glisten in her bright blue eyes, their surface shimmering brighter than the ocean anyone could own. Even Poseidon would have a jealous fit over it.

Bianca spreads her toes on the sand, letting them taste the coolness. "Still got grandpa legs?" she questions randomly.

I face her. "What's your obsession with my legs?"

Her brown hair glides over her shoulder as her head tilts to the side, her teeth nipping her lip. "Nah. Legs aren't my obsession."

"Then what is?" I ask, a smirk fighting my lips.

Bianca's face lights up, even shining out in the dark, something I've only seen once on her. As she passes me, her fingers brush against the

veins of my wrist and then slide them up my arm. And it takes all my effort not to shiver. "Guess," she murmurs against my ear before leaving my world hanging off the axis as she walks off to the shore.

Taking off my shoes, I slowly follow her. The moonlight outlines her silhouette, hair flowing with the wind and hips swaying in a movement no one should ever have. It's a curse to only see her and not feel her beneath my fingers.

As we edge towards the shore, the incoming tide lightly kisses our toes. And for the first time, I breathe.

"Thank you for this. I needed it," she says, letting the chilly breeze softly caress her skin.

"Anytime," I reply, unable to keep myself from staring at the way calmness shadows the heaviness of her lids. "Bianca?" This is the second time I've called her, and she returns me with the same lightness.

Bianca stays silent, anticipating my next words.

"You look good happy. Always have." I surprise myself with the words.

She just smiles and nods, her fingers grazing over her bracelet. We stare at each other in silence, the cool moonlight catching the shine in our eyes, with a silent understanding passing between us.

With a playful grin, she leans in close, and her breath is warm against my ear as she whispers, "Did *you* give me a compliment?"

I suck in a breath. Not for what she said, but for how her hand rests on my chest. She stays there for beats longer, most likely feeling the hard beating of the stone behind my chest.

"I will take it back," my stern voice replies with a subtle undertone of caution. My desire for her goes beyond mere compliments. I want to claim her completely where her soul and body don't even begin explaining my hunger for her. I want *her* as she is.

"Oh no. You can't. It's mine now." She chuckles and looks straight ahead at the sea. Her shoulders graze against mine, letting her cherry blossom scent circle around me.

Quick beats pass as we witness the night sea and it us. Bianca speaks, giving me more than I thought she would. "You know, I never really thought I would become an interior designer. At first, I loved designing empty spaces, breathing life into them, and imbuing them with meaning. Then, it became about the smiles on people's faces after they saw their place. Somehow it made me feel special."

Our feet sink into the soft night sand, just as the incredulity in her tone sets in. Bianca was always the person who never restricted herself to one thing. Even when we were growing up, she took classes and workshops to explore whatever there was. From helping at the local animal shelter to volunteering with the local council.

I wasn't at all surprised by her decision to go into interior design. It will give her opportunities to connect with different people, and no project is the same, which gives her the freedom to explore.

"Special doesn't come close to describing who you are," I correct her when a slight frown appears on her eyebrows. She looks up at me with softness in her eyes.

Bianca is the brightness one seeks after escaping the dark. She brings questions that not only mess with your head but gives you what you were lacking.

Just like when she left, I had no reason to be excited, happy, or even sad. I was feeling nothing.

"You don't need anyone to tell you how you melt the sun when you smile or create miracles just by existing," I say. I will hunt down anyone who has ever told her she wasn't enough. They don't deserve another second of such a worthless life.

Bianca scoffs and chuckles. "Doesn't feel like it, though."

The weight of our shoes hanging off our fingers seems lighter than the weight of our words—even those that remain unsaid.

"Can we walk?" she asks. It's an innocent request that has my heart beating frantically.

She takes a step backward, and my arm shoots out to hold hers. Her skin is cold, too cold. Her heartbeat, breathing, everything is slow as if her body will give up on her any minute.

"Give me those." Before she could object, I take her heels and join them with my shoes.

"It's fine. I can hold them."

"No. You want to walk, we walk."

"But—"

I walk past her and get another hit of the cherry blossom. My jaw will break if I keep clenching it this hard.

"You're impossible," Bianca mutters before joining my side.

As we walk, the soft roar of the waves washing ashore creates a soothing soundtrack to our unspoken conversation. It's not awkward, but just empty.

"I would never have thought I'll be here with you." Bianca kicks a shell, sending it a small distance.

"I'm pretty sure I'm better company now than I was before." I look at her with a blank expression.

She chuckles. "No. That's not what I meant. The last time we were at a beach..." Her toes dig into the sand, allowing me to complete the sentence.

That's when everything fell out of place, when it only felt in place. I was still in awe of how it felt to be in our world of feelings. Especially understanding how amazing it felt to come together as a man and woman, not only for physical pleasures, but for the connection. For feeling the spark in my blood for the first time she *saw* me and wanted me as much as I did her.

As they say, good things don't last long. They didn't. Two days after the funeral, Bianca, Steven, and their Uncle Gareth sat on that plane and flew away. Far from my reach.

"So, I was saying we could add some pastels for the creative teams' floor and darker colours for the technical team..." Her voice slowly zones back to me. She's not even taking a moment to breathe. "Then we could add some plants, and I was thinking about a small library and garden on the top floor. What do you think?"

Facing me, she walks backward, swinging her arms at her side. Finally, taking a breath.

Fuck. I was so deep in thought that I didn't even know when Bianca started going on a tangent about anything and everything.

"Do what you have to," I simply reply. Not taking my eyes off the way her blue eyes get bluer with each blink. She has blinked twelve times already, and as addictive as they are, I can't forget the first time I saw them.

Innocent. Alive.

"Really? I was kidding." She raises her eyebrow and crosses her arms over her chest. "I knew you weren't listening to me."

"Do as you wish," I say, and slow my pace. "It's your design. I will not stand in the way of your special."

"I think you *did* drink too much. I'll ask the same question tomorrow," she mutters.

We walk towards the stone bench and, in quiet unison, face the horizon as we sit.

Turning to look at her, I am captivated by the serene moonlight illuminating her face, its gentle glow hinting at a hidden, powerful intensity.

"I didn't want to come back," Bianca says, her lips lifting towards the sky. A snarky smirk replaces her serious face. "Because I was afraid of getting judged for my loud voice. To not forget the first words *someone* said to me were—" Bianca clears her throat and makes it deeper, "—*'Your voice is deep, just like mine will be when I grow up.'*"

In my defence, I got nervous the first time I spoke to her when I went to pick Eva up from school and Bianca was there.

"Oh, come on. Get over it already. It's been, what? Fifteen years since that. And you say you've moved on." I push a smile back when I see Bianca's shoulders shaking with a laugh.

"Not until you admit my voice is now much sexier and sweeter, and nothing like yours. I will not let it go otherwise," she says as she looks at me from the side. Her soft brown hair cascades down one shoulder, revealing the warm skin of her exposed neck. My hands can still trace the slender curves of her neck with great familiarity, remembering how her heartbeat throbbed beneath my hand as I delved deeper into her. *Owning her.*

Without speaking, I grab hold of her wrist, feeling the warmth of her skin, and pull her slightly closer to me. Time stops as our eyes lock, and the only thing I feel is the frantic rhythm of her pulse.

"I don't need to tell you how you sound or *taste.*" A low growl rumbles in my chest.

Her bright blue eyes search mine as her chest rises with a steady rhythm. I let go of her hand and place it gently on her lap as she watches the movement keenly.

I say nothing, and neither does she, when we turn to face the calm ocean waves underneath the gentle glow of the stars.

"The last time we were here, we were totally different people with very different outlooks on life," her voice is low as she speaks.

"In a way, we're reborn. Just like a phoenix. Rising from the ashes, living for a glimpse, only to begin the cycle again. It's funny we think there is this one magical moment when everything changes, but in reality, it is the many smaller moments that lead up to it," I add. "The Phoenix is one creature that explains so many things about the living."

The subtle shift in the air causes Bianca to flinch, or it could be from a sudden realisation.

Bianca lets out a sarcastic scoff. "Rising and healing are never easy. With it comes memories that would rather stay in ashes. And no one witnesses the effect of those memories except the person themselves, when they break and break until they are nothing," she croaks. The soul-crushing message lies heavy among us. Healing is a solitary journey that no one can aid. That's why there is only one Phoenix shown to burn.

My heart bruises its cage with its thuds as the wounds from half a decade ago open fresh, oozing with pain and fury instead of blood.

I didn't know Bianca had grown beyond her age. To understand the meaning of living so deeply. Only the truly wounded could decipher that.

Those who lose more than gain.

Those who burn more.

The cool sand muffles the frantic tapping of Bianca's feet as her fingers fidget with the beads on her bracelet. "Sorry, I didn't mean to go deep. Anyway, it really means nothing. Ignore what I said. It's another one of my mind blurts, meaning nothing. You know me, nothing—"

I place my hand on her thigh, trying to ease the pain as much as I can from the parts that I can. "That's a lot of *nothing* in one go."

She pauses her rant and focuses her attention on my eyes. Hers are wide and yearning for the lost affection and care.

The drilling of her feet freezes mid-movement. Our breaths mingle as my fingers tighten on her thigh, our eyes lock in a silent promise. The chilling breeze, a stark contrast to our body heat, gradually warms up as it dances across our skin.

The anticipation crackles between us, becoming a palpable tension thick with charged glances. My eyes bounce between her glistening lips and the intoxication of her eyes. She takes in her bottom lip, bites and breathes through her nose.

Bianca places a soft hand over mine on her thigh, and the space between us shrinks.

I cannot take her pain away, but I can make her forget for this moment.

Bianca parts her lips, sending a clear message to be taken, which I will happily comply with. The salty air of the beach further dries the saliva in my mouth and intensifies my thirst for her.

A wave of the cherry blossom scent washes over me as we lean in, the delicate scent a prelude to the nearness of our lips.

She leans in and kisses the corner of my lips.

She kissed me.

"I'm sorry," her soft and low voice says. "There's no more I can give."

I shake my head. "I don't need more." *I just need you.*

For the past five years, I have touched no one and have allowed no one else to touch me. Not because I didn't want to, but because I knew—my subconscious knew—there is only one person I could give my all to.

In this moment I know who Bianca Kennedy truly is to me. A force that has given me a surprise I always wished to have but dreaded.

I don't dare to pull her close to me or take her like every cell in my body is screaming to do. It will be her who will *tell* me what she wants because I'm done reading between the lines. I want her, and she knows it more than I can explain. She will have to decide whether she wants me or leaves me.

With a sigh, the tension recoils from her shoulders, and she sits close by. If we were at the Gardens, crickets would fill in for our silence rather than the breeze.

I don't know how long we sit, staring out into the dark horizon, until Bianca yawns and drops back on the bench.

"Past someone's bedtime?" I tease, jolting her awake.

"Maybe yours." She yawns again.

I smile. "Change of plans. Let's go—"

"Let me steal a moment for myself with you." Her voice is like a cloud in a clear sky floating between us as she wraps her fingers around my arm. "Without the world."

"I'd let you steal me, if I could," I say.

A gasp of sadness escapes her, letting her eyes flutter close in a helpless surrender. I pull her near me, and the tremor in her chest becomes apparent in my own.

"If *we* could," Bianca repeats.

I contemplate how our lives would've been different if the fire hadn't happened. How close we would've been. *Would I be a different person?*

I relax back on the bench and watch as the vast ocean separates two late birds as they fly through the night, their forms almost lost in the starry sky. Only their faint calls give them away.

Parallel. Cursed to see each other but never meet.

A soft weight settles on my shoulder, and soon quiet snores vibrate through me. Bianca's sweet floral scent fills the air as she mumbles something, clinging to my arm.

Looking down, I see Bianca's closed eyes, her body relaxed against me, and the gentle rise and fall of her chest slows to a calming rhythm I've never felt before. A thick, unruly brown strand falls across her face, obscuring her peaceful, sleeping expression. I tuck her hair back to see her cheeks puff out when she inhales deeply before releasing a soft, rumbling snore as she exhales.

All I could do, and all I have done, is glue my eyes to her flushed face, drinking in the sight of her beauty until the moment fades.

"Only with you," I murmur, feeling her presence as the only one worth carrying the weight of.

I close my eyes and rest my head on hers.

A minute.

CHAPTER 15
Bianca

Whated my bed become so hard?

Did I leave the window open?

Why are my feet wet?

Bianca, wake up!

I snap open my eyes to get blinded by the morning sun, greeted by the salty air, and disturbed by the people walking.

People walking in my bedroom?

I shake my head to come back to earth.

No, this isn't my bed. Heck, this isn't my house.

Shit. We're still at the beach!

When did I sleep? Oh, fuck! The last thing I remember is being with Jason and then … blank.

Jason. I don't need to put in much effort to locate the bulky man,

leaning back open- mouthed, breathing in all the air. Not even the loud beachgoers are going to wake him.

His facial lines are smooth, a stark contrast to his usual frowning. This is the most vulnerable I've seen him, like a last leaf on a skeleton tree fighting bone to nail with the wind to not fly away.

My heart jump starts my body from the way his arm holds me close, and our legs intertwine. It's so innocent, yet I can't help but see more in it.

I don't need more.

But you deserve more, baby.

Jason shifts in place, his arm tightens around my waist, squeezing me close, as if the wind would steal me away.

Did we really sleep on a stone bench in the middle of the fucking beach? Earth, swallow me, please.

It doesn't.

"Jason," I whisper and shake his arm.

Nothing but a small grunt comes from him. His closed eyelids tense and then relax. Everything about him is praiseworthy. His perfectly formed lips, the sharp angle of his cheekbones, and his forehead framed by loose strands of midnight-black hair that fall across it. Beauty— masculine beauty.

What's that?

I freeze when I feel a wet slide of something on my feet. With my breathing stalled, I lean forward, and the sight in front of me takes a moment to decipher. A dog drools as a tongue shoots out to lick my feet, leaving behind an unpleasant layer of saliva on my feet.

"Aah!" I shriek, pulling my knees to my chest, and accidentally hit Jason on his chin.

"What the fuck?" Jason wakes with a jolt, wide and alert. In a quick movement, he digs his hand inside his pocket. When he turns to look at me, the action is so fast that our heads bump together with a loud thud.

I suck in a deep breath, trying to rub away the sting in my head.

Beside me, Jason holds on to his temple, rubs his head and chin at the same time. That's one way to wake up.

"Bianca?" He rubs his eyes and mirrors what I'd done exactly two minutes ago. His morning voice is so raw, raspy and deep that it shifts something between my legs. This man effortlessly has such an effect on me that even in the bright hours of the morning, I'm aching.

"Oh shit, sorry." I apply a soothing hand under his chin and wince when it doesn't get rid of the scowl on his face.

"Where are we?" he asks, leaning back again on the bench.

"The beach," I reply, squaring my shoulders.

"Oh, the beach. What? The *beach!*" He holds the edge of the bench and looks around with wide eyes. "Didn't we leave yesterday?" Jason says, shielding his eyes with a hand from the bright sun.

"Well, obviously not," I drawl.

Before he could reply, a chirpy voice calls for the dog still at my feet.

"Oh God, Lily, that's where you are!" A lady, somewhere in her mid-fifties, her grey hair catching the light, bends down to wrap a collar of lilies around the Doberman's neck. There's no remorse in the Doberman's eyes as she calmly licks her lips, a satisfied gleam reflecting in her eyes after her first meal.

Yes, my feet are the meal.

The lady has smooth neck-length grey hair, and a dimpled smile reaching her cool blue eyes, like mine—Ma's. Ma would've looked like that with the same ease in her words and facial features.

I stop myself from rolling down the same tunnel of *would've.* Instead, my fingers trace the smooth surface of my bracelet, its familiar weight a small comfort amidst my overwhelming feelings.

"I'm sorry. I was looking around for this little menace. Hopefully she didn't bother you too much," she speaks, her voice is that of the sounds of feathers falling with a silent thud.

"No. *Not at all.*" I muster a fake smile and *try* to adore the dog beside her.

Lily pounces for a bite. I react quickly enough to avoid having my fingers and toes bitten.

Don't get me wrong, I love dogs. I do. But some just take some *adjusting* to get used to. Guess that's the case with *beautiful Lily* here. She carries the face of an innocent but is nothing of the sort from within.

"Lily," the lady scolds. She looks up at us and uses her blue eyes to assess Jason and me with a light smile.

"I must be honest. You make a beautiful couple."

Suddenly, I become hyper-aware of the lingering pressure of his hand at my waist, the heat of his skin searing through my dress, and the solid feel of my hand against his thigh. We both freeze and slowly turn our heads to each other.

His green eyes search my face as heat rushes to my cheeks. We slowly peel apart and leave a good amount of space between us.

"We're not a couple," I say, not looking her in the eye.

But the wonder in the woman's eyes doesn't lessen. "That's what they all say at first." She flaps a dismissive hand with a widening smile. "Anyway, it was nice to meet you."

She walks away from us, but then slaps a hand on her forehead. "How rude! I didn't introduce myself. I'm Angel, people say I carry my name to heart."

"I'm Bianca," I introduce with a soft smile.

"Bianca. I like that. It rolls nicely off the tongue. And you, Mr Gentleman?"

"Jason." As unattached as he can be.

"Hi, Jason. That perfect face of yours truly brightened my day!" She sheepishly smiles.

Oh, to have the courage to tell him that. I chuckle at the tint of red on his neck from embarrassment or anger. I'm not too sure.

"Nice to meet you, Angel," I say, saving Jason from exploding.

"You too, honey. I'll see you around. Bye for now," she chirps, whistling to Lily. The she-devil dog bounces ahead, its joyful barks echoing, as Angel waddles after it along the beach.

I follow them with my soft gaze until they merge into the horizon, and a dull ache settles in my chest.

My phone buzzes in the space between us and brings me back. It's probably another one of my reminders telling me to get my ass up and go to work. When I see the text, I can't help but furrow my brows.

> **Unknown:** *Bright and shine, Ice. Time for piece one in the puzzle.*

Piece one out of the four.

Data files.

With that, he gave me a key, which currently burns a hole in my pocket.

The answers lie in the living. Aaron had said as he curled my fingers on the key. Something dirty and messy churns in my stomach from our interaction last night. Had it not been for this text and the key in my pocket, I would've thought I'd made the entire encounter up.

It wouldn't be the first time.

My grip on my phone tightens, my knuckles white, as worst-case scenarios play out in my mind, making my phone tremble in my hand. Like a persistent fly, Aaron had buzzed around the edges of my thoughts, but now he demands centre stage in my mind.

What he wants, I'm not sure I can do after all the ambiguous emotional rendezvous my brain is going through. I'm not that naïve that I'm not aware of the people who matter most to me, yet life is testing me once again to the brink of my damnation.

And you signed a deal with the devil against them?

White Wings, not the fucking time.

Amidst the adversities, everyone must survive without their respective companions. Do they die? No, but sure live the life of a fractured soul with the constant nagging of the missing.

That would be me if I don't get the answers to the long-asked questions.

Is losing those with you worth the price? White Wings reasons.

My gut clenches at the prospect of that answer.

I won't lose anyone, I retort.

Yourself?

I. Don't. Fucking know. I'll lose myself regardless. Why not let it be for a good reason? If Aaron is the dark light to being born again, then so be it.

Phoenix. The vision of rebirth and growth.

"Bianca?" Jason's voice comes to me.

I see the man I want, but I physically can't breathe as my guilt and desire personified stares at me.

"Jason, I have … to … leave. I'll see you … at the office," I stutter.

Fuck, Bianca.

"But—"

"Sorry, I have to go." I rush before he could say anything. Barefoot.

CHAPTER 16
Jason

To say Bianca is acting off would be the biggest understatement of the year. Seriously, the woman is obviously avoiding me. Colliding in the hallway, she flips the other way. Bumping in the elevator, apparently, the ceiling is more interesting. Being in the same room, I cease to exist.

I thought the time at the beach changed something between us. As small as it could be. That was two days ago. Rather than taking one step forward, she took two back.

The minute I promised flawed into an entire night, and then, with the click of fingers, the spell broke and the moment changed. So did Bianca.

Everything was perfectly in my grasp, a sense of power I held on to

for five years, until those captivating brown waves of hair and intense blue eyes interfered. They shattered my control with the swiftness of sand escaping my hand.

The constant reminder of her yellow heels trapped in the bottom drawer of my desk isn't any help, either. I had the temptation to give it to Eva when she returned my blazer this morning.

I couldn't.

Even now, my thumb hovers over Bianca's number on my phone. My instincts are shouting to let her go, and if she wants to avoid me, good for her. But that doesn't mean I will let her.

One call wouldn't hurt. To just hear her. Five minutes, that's it.

"Fuck. Jason, get it together," my hush whispers back to me. I slap my phone screen first on the table and run a frustrated hand through my hair.

I can sense that something is amiss. It's like my finger is hovering over the answer but not landing on it.

"Mr Archer?" Oscar's voice comes through the speaker. Today, his deep stone sounds like nothing less than chalk scratching on a board.

"What?" I snap.

Breathe in through your nose, out through your mouth.

"What is it, Oscar?" I try again.

Oscar clears his throat before continuing with a shake in his voice. "Mr McKenzie is here. He wishes to meet you. There is no appointment scheduled for him. Do you want to meet him?"

"Allow him in," I say. At least the muddle with McKenzie can be a good distraction.

I smell his arrogance before I see him. "Jason. My man! Sorry I came in uninvited." McKenzie enters with his arms spread out for a hug.

I simply extend my hand out instead.

McKenzie chuckles and accepts my hand with a grip promising ulterior motives for his visit. There would be no other plausible reason he'd rock up in my office after rejecting the contract a week ago.

"What did I do to earn such a visit?" I say, as I take my seat with him opposite me.

Now, there appears a sharp smile. "*You* did nothing specifically. Someone else has caught my attention on your team," he replies. His smile is deceiving when his brown eyes shine with unwritten excitement.

"I thought you wanted nothing to do with me or my company." I try to control the growl in my voice—*try*.

"Jason, like you, I monitor everyone in my circle, and there's gold in *your* circle. So, I have an offer," McKenzie explains. His eyes shine with their brightest brown.

I lean back in my chair and let him have his offer on the table.

"I am ready to get on the construction. *If* Bianca Kennedy is the one designing this project and my other planned ones." He smiles.

Everything in me freezes at the name.

Fuck off.

Something unsettles and shifts in my chest—something heavy and burning.

He said her name.

"It would be difficult. You see, *Miss. Kennedy* is only here for a short period. Three months, to be exact. So, I'm afraid that won't be possible." I rub my thumb on my lower lip in thought.

The words feel like raw ash on my tongue. It is the truth, albeit. And in no way I'm letting this bastard near Bianca, or any men, because we come from the same root, wearing deception and manipulation to thicken our skins.

"Hmm." He remains quiet, staring at his reflection on the black glass of my table. "Can I have a word with her?" he finally says.

Over my fucking body.

"She doesn't meet directly with any of our clients," I growl. My trying thrown out of the window. Or preferably throw him out of the window.

"This could be a one-off. I'm sure she wouldn't mind after our call. She seemed keen to have a meeting. Why not it be today?" He shrugs.

I want to fucking rip that smug smile off his face.

He's been *calling* Bianca.

We supply McKenzie with his technical needs and connections, but I'm considering cutting that connection. Again, I would rather have them talk in front of me than anywhere else. I take one powerful breath and then reply, "Of course."

"Great," he exclaims, clasping his hands together.

I press the call button on my desk. Oscar's voice immediately answers, "How can I help?"

"Call *Miss. Kennedy*—" I flick my eyes to McKenzie, who seems too pleased with himself "—to my office."

"Sure."

Half of me is hoping she won't come and will avoid me like she has been doing. But the other half is breathing to snatch the slightest glimpse of those ocean blue eyes.

The latter wins when two soft knocks sound on the door.

"Come in," I instruct.

In comes the only person on this land that can turn my world upside down. Today it's blue, Spix's macaw blue. Her blouse takes on dark tones, making the swell of her breasts more prominent than ever. The blue pants are doing great things for me as they fit smoothly over her waist and thighs. The belt securely holds up the pants on her hips, concealing whatever secrets lie beneath. How easily I could leisurely unfold, unhook the belt, and hold those thighs on my face and beneath my palm as I pound into her. *Stop.*

Bianca's gaze meets mine after what feels like years, and the earlier unsettling eases.

"How can I help, Mr Archer?" she asks, her hands resting out front with her bracelet dangling from her wrist. That thing has to go, and soon. She might think it gives her a sense of reprieve, but it only shines her moment of weakness in front of a pack of wolves.

I know she isn't a lamb, but wolves exist wearing the skin of men. The normal eye would see him as a charmer, but McKenzie is a fucking wolf.

"Mr McKenzie here wants to have a chat." I point my hand towards the man sitting in front of me.

He swivels in his chair and makes a grand gesture of his presence.

Bastard. It's too early for murder. For the day—not in life.

"Mr McKen—Oh my God." Bianca all but shrieks. Her hands fly to her mouth in awe with her eyes widening in shock as she gasps.

What's so special about him?

Bianca remains motionless, a statue of ice, almost as if frozen in time. She finally recovers and shakes his outstretched hand. "It's such a great pleasure to meet you finally."

And like that, I cease to exist once again.

Their connected hands move up and down, up and down. Isn't once enough?

My fists clench, knuckles white, as I watch the interaction. A chilling smile plays on McKenzie's lips, a smile that will have blood on my hands. *His blood.*

"Enough." My raw voice sounds in the room, in a fucking warning. "Another shake and I will make sure our connections are severed."

Their blank faces snap in my direction, one more taken aback than the other. McKenzie's eyes light up with a darker spark. "A handshake worth losing tens of millions of dollars? Impulsive even for you, Archer."

"Good to know you can read between the lines." I fix my blazer and sit back down. My equally dark eyes meet his.

They finally step away from each other. A much-preferred distance.

"What was it you wanted to discuss?" Bianca interrupts all the ways I was slicing him in my head.

"I have an offer for us to work together. If Mr Archer allows." He gestures confidently towards me with a sweeping movement of his arm. I don't hide the scowl on my face.

It felt like forever, but finally, Bianca's comforting blue eyes found me again, and I feel a rush of oxygen returning to me. *Fuck.* I swear I would do anything and give her my everything just to have her look at me.

"What is it exactly?" she asks.

"I want you to be a part of my next projects. We'll be handling every aspect of the building, from the initial design to the final construction—bringing it to life," Mckenzie offers.

Bianca's once bright face drops. "I would love to, but I won't be here for long, and working remotely isn't something I can put on my plate right now," Bianca explains.

"So I'm aware. That's why I've come with a proposal for you to join our company and stay here. We will cover all costs," he offers, oblivious to the storm he's inviting. Bianca staying for longer than three months is a ticking time bomb ready to blast.

"Florals & Bells has me in a contract, and I'm here to complete a task for them." Her confidence radiates from her stiff stance.

"Well. It's a shame, but if you're still up for the offer, you know where to contact me." He smiles and plants a rough hand on Bianca's shoulder.

The thin rope of my restraint finally breaks, and I spring up from my chair. "Th at settles it. Give *Miss. Kennedy* some time, and she'll be right back to," I say. Th e possibility of that happening on my watch is having the sea working for the sun instead of the moon.

"You may leave." I point to the dark-toned door. A silent challenge.

He takes the clue with a smug grin. "Great meeting you, Jason," he chimes.

Just get out, fucker. Th e words are at the tip of my tongue. Instead, I answer with a nod.

As soon as he leaves, Bianca's feet pick up in the same direction.

"Bianca, a minute," I demand. Her hand drops by her side before she could reach for the door.

I've had enough of her games. It's time to put a stop to this cat-and-mouse chase and get her where she belongs.

Bianca

I could ignore him and walk off, but his piercing stare glues my feet to the marble floor.

"You always loved to play hide-and-seek. I didn't know you still did." He prowls over to me, calculating each step.

"I don't know what you're talking about." I shrug.
Bad move, Bianca. Don't provoke the devil, especially whose eyes hold the shadowed depths of a forest—a place that calls me. Especially when I can't erase the urge to challenge every towering tree that dares to obstruct my path with the scent of pine and damp earth filling my lungs with each breath.

"Th is isn't how it's supposed to go." He tuts, moving his index finger side-to-side. "You do not get to do this." He seethes a few more steps in my direction.

I take an equal amount back.
"You have no idea what you do to me, do you?" He corners me at the door, his massive arms pinned beside my head. "How much the

stupid thing beating in my chest calls your name and no matter how many times I silence it, it beats again and again. *For you.*

Now *my stupid thing* is betraying my every demand to stop racing and slow down. I stare up at him. His eyes have hints of red at the corner as if the dark seriousness in his tone has wrapped itself in a crimson blanket in the white.

"Either you leave me or…" He dips low to my ear, and I'm scared he can hear the rush of liquid in there. "Cure me."

Cure.

Cure?

And him?

He is the one who attracts me to him like the opposite ends of a magnet. I'm the one who should ask for a repellent, so I can save us both time and heartbreak.

Especially when the sword of piece one hangs on my neck.

Piece one: Data files.

All the information there is about the Archers.

And yet that isn't the most prominent thing in my head, but the words from the beach are eating me alive.

"Did you mean it…" I swallow harder this time, the lump scratching the walls of my throat.

Jason waits, following the movement of my neck. His expression is unreadable except for the pulse running on the side of his forehead.

"That you'll let me steal you?" I whisper, my eyes flicking to his.

His fists tighten against the door, and his emerald eyes grow two shades darker. "Does it matter when I can't have you?"

Pain. So much pain in one question.

A harsh breath leaves me, and I drop my head back on the door. Before I could meet with the cold surface, Jason's big and soft hand captures my head, making my landing soft.

Something cracks in my chest at the softness of his gesture, the sound so audible and haunting. The ears of my organs wince and cry in pain that they haven't felt before.

"If you could?" My voice is raw and almost gone as I question.

He smiles, the most beautiful thing I've seen on a human, and glides—ghosts—his fingers along my jaw. "When I said steal me, I didn't mean my body at all. It's my soul I would lay bare at your feet. To give it a final purpose and stall its mindless wandering in rooms and gardens which call it."

With you, he didn't need to add.

"I'm sorry," I whisper.

His eyes darken, and he continues as if I didn't speak. "I would let you use me all you like. There would be no place on me you wouldn't touch. That is if you haven't already." He presses against me, his hard body everything I feel and see.

Jason wraps his fingers around my wrist, masterfully avoiding touching my hand. Words escape me when he slides my hands onto his hard chest, letting my fingers skim over his abs to his nipples poking through his shirt.

We share the air as we suck in sharply, our eyes witnessing my thumb over his nipple and Jason's pressing it down.

Logic battles with desire. My rational mind urges me to escape through the door, yet a force glues my feet on the floor. Not because of the wave of physical arousal cursing me, but the silent plea for relief on his face.

"Jason," I whisper. It's barely audible. He keeps moving our hands up to his chest, lingering in the middle, letting me feel the thumping of his heart. "We shouldn't be here. I'm leaving soo—"

My breath hitches when he goes higher and wraps my fingers around his neck. I try to jerk my hand away, shaking my head, but he doesn't allow me. "What are you doing?" I ask as he covers my small hand with his larger one and presses my fingers into his skin.

"Giving you evidence of the power you have over me. I'm at your mercy. You could give me life or take it away in this moment, and I won't say otherwise."

Tears well in my eyes. "Why are you doing this? I'm not the woman who can make you happy."

"No, you're not." He shakes his head. "You are the *only* woman who can. You are the Pied Piper I will happily follow. Even if I know I will disappear in your hypnotising tunes. I have to—*want* to—just follow you. I am fucking trapped, Bianca."

A dangerous spark ignites in his eyes, daring to set ablaze any remaining embers of my resistance.

The more I push, the more he will pull. That's how he's built.

It's exactly what you need. Get under his skin, get what you want— deserve. Red Horns appears, offering advice that felt both contradictory and strangely believable, like a whisper from the dark corner of my brain.

You can't do that to Jason. He will never forgive you, and neither will anyone else. Stop this nonsense while you can, White Wings retorts.

I need to breathe. I need space.

"Jason, move," I say, more sternly. I have to leave, otherwise, I don't trust myself not to give in.

"Not before I finish," he growls, leaving me no choice but to feed off the fire flaring in his forest, making it all grey.

He punches the door, the wood and metal silently groaning, and I instantly straighten my back. He leans down, confiscating my space, only allowing me to breathe the oxygen he provides. Some strands of his dark hair fall on my forehead, transferring the heat from him to me.

"I thought I had no weaknesses. But you, Bianca Kennedy, are my biggest weakness," he says the words of his every breath on my face. "But more than that, you're also my strength."

Finally, a single tear, cool and salty, traces a path down my cheek. This beautiful man with a heart of gold knows nothing about the darkness I bring into people's lives.

"Jason, please." My stomach constricts at his words when I'm unable to stop another tear from escaping.

He wipes the wetness and clenches it in his fist, feeling the lingering dampness on his skin. I devour every inch of him, all of it begging me to let him in.

"Tell me what's wrong? I may not have seen you in a while, but you're just as predictable as you were," he demands, the muscle in his jaw ticking.

Forget butterflies, instead, a kaleidoscope of birds—cardinals, hummingbirds, and eagles—invade my body, their vibrant colours a stark contrast to the frantic fluttering of newly grown wings on my organs.

His brows crease and chest heaves, brushing against mine.

"Your silence is louder than you think."

I finally find my lost voice. "Nothing is wrong. Trust me."

Such a blunt liar.

"Nothing that I can't handle," I say, ignoring White.

Lying to yourself, huh?

"Okay, whatever you say. I will ask again, and then you will answer." His words aren't a request, but a forceful demand, doing nothing to quell my rising anxiety. "Only then, you won't be able to speak because you will be screaming my name ..." he promises with a darker edge "... with me deep inside you. It's only a matter of time."

My jaw clenches at the visual, and how much I want that, but no. I can't let it happen.

He leans in close, leveling himself to my ear, and speaks. "You're dripping on the floor." His deep voice gives each hair ending on my neck a life.

"What?" I burst out, shocked. My eyes widen, and I snap my head down to see nothing but the untouched marble.

"So, you are wet, aren't you?" he purrs.

Those repulsive words should disgust me, but a primal arousal surges through me, swift and brutal as a crocodile's strike on an unsuspecting deer. In my case, Jason is the crocodile eating away at the deer of my logic, who dared to enter his waters.

I would've pulled out anyone's tongue for saying that, but somehow, I can't find the courage to do so as a twinge of excitement ignites in my heart. It shouldn't.

"Fuck. Off." I stress each word with my eyes, connecting with him.

I push him, and he finally steps back. My hand that was still around his neck falls by my side, and I feel the loss of his warm skin immensely.

Jason stands with his hands tucked into his pockets as those plump lips lift into a knowing smile.

When I slam the door behind me, all I have is the naked onslaught of my emotions, like a diary left open in the wind. All the dirty secrets flying out shamelessly.

For now, I close the diary and let my world of secrets remain trapped inside me.

CHAPTER 17
Bianca

"**B**ianca!" a chirpy voice calls from behind me as steady myself.

Max, a creative team member, waves at me as he exits the elevators. Max's long carefully crafted dark blond hair flies with his mini jog to me.

In the short weeks I have been working here, Max has become a friend who comes out to save me when things go south, or I save him. More often than not, he's the one who needs most of the rescuing when he breaks the printer or sleeps with one of the men from our team. There is no in-between.

"Hey, what's up?" I smile, relaxing my thumping heart from earlier.

"Nothing's up, but everything is looking down." He twists his lips in annoyance.

"There's no problem we can't handle." I pull the sleeve of my blouse, giving me the smell of fresh mint I'm all so addicted to at this point. "Shoot."

"Maybe this one. The plan we decided on for the fifth floor isn't going so well, and Jelly's on it."

Jelena is the head of the team and someone who ranks me below negative on the lovable scale. For sure. No doubt.

I may know why: Jason. He has somehow become the bane of my existence, crowding my every thought and breath.

I've been pointedly ignoring him and using every bit of my strength to push him away. I didn't miss Jason's stare or his posture while he was talking to the members of the team, but he truly was focusing on me.

As his eyes were on me, Jelena's were on him.

Jelena is around the same age as me, if not older, but when I see attraction, I know it. Especially when she silences curious onlookers with a single glance that makes them quickly avert their eyes.

"Argh. Great." I wince just thinking about her.

"First stop is the files room." Max groans, dropping his neck far back, making his tattoo visible. It's a figure that has the half body of a fox with a large mane of tails. "It's a literal history jungle in there."

"There will be a files room to the left and more meeting and conference rooms. Like every office we've ever built." Jason's words from the site ring in my head amidst the traffic of other thoughts.

It's right there, just do it, Red Horns encourages. Why am I even considering it?

It's just some information, and what could go wrong? Right? It's for the greater good.

White Wings doesn't speak.

Just fucking do it! In and out, that's it. Nothing more, nothing less.

"Hey Max, I can get it for you. We need someone to keep Jelly's ass in her seat." I pass Max a forced smile through the fog in my head. "Which one was it?"

"Yeah, that's true. I'm the best man for the job. Not something I want to be proud of." He places a soft hand on my shoulder. "Get the file of the systems we put in the Bendigo area. We want to go off the gold rush vibes," he says.

I raise an eyebrow in thought. A gold rush theme? *When did we decide that?*

"I'd better get going before Jel comes after me like a witch on a hunt. You didn't hear that from me." He places a finger on his lips and shushes.

"*Witch* part? I have no idea." I shrug.

We both chuckle at our bad joke, but it isn't too far off from reality.

Max jogs away towards the elevator while I stand here having a staring competition with the door that could become the door to my closure.

I slowly turn the knob of the door with my clammy fingers. I hear the door's gears grinding and feel the resistance of the turn as if it's telling me what White is screaming at me.

As expected, the room is nothing but a villa of cabinets upon cabinets, which I assume hold stacks of paper. The room is a beast in its size, just like its importance in the core of Archer Enterprises. There are no colours besides white and grey. The room is as soulful as its purpose.

I take a step inside and run my hands over the cold metal of the cabinets. Each displays a year label, starting from the beginning of the previous century. The Archers had started off with selling and making simple telephone services and connecting the local people. Now, they focus on global and more intricate paths Eva tried to explain but went over my head.

The first cabinet in every row reads their company slogan. "*From arrow to target."*

The room smells sterile, and the cabinets are glossy clean. As I walk deeper into the room, large desktops line up the back wall, assuming it has more of the recent data.

"Right, where are you?" I murmur to myself, searching the aisles to find the file for Max first.

I go to open the cabinet, but it remains stuck in place. *Locked* in place.

"Great. Not you too."

I bend to look at it, and the only thing on it has is a keyhole. *The key.* Without thinking, I take out the key Aaron gave me and put it in the hole. Surely, it fits perfectly as if made for it.

The door of the cabinet opens, and two stacks of paper come into view. I flick through and find the grey-looking file carefully put together. It feels heavy with my guilt, yet that's the price for the truth.

Shaking my head, I close the cabinet and distract myself by sliding my fingers on the cool metal of the cabinets and looking for any sign of the safe.

"They will keep it in the open to avoid suspicious eyes. The passcode you can work out. Your lover set it." Aaron's voice comes through.

I trudge through the many aisles of history and legacy. There are seven aisles going in ascending order of years until they reach the monitors by the back wall.

Every second, I look over my shoulder, just expecting the doors to open and a pair of handcuffs to curl around my wrists.

You know what? Fuck it. It's been ten minutes. I'm not doing this. I can't do th—

As soon as I make a turn to go back, the tip of my index finger smoothly digs into the end of the last cabinet of the last row. A perfectly cut square goes inside with my finger.

Beep!

A sharp sound echoes in the room, and for a moment, I thought I was busted. But no, the cabinet opens, and my eyes widen at what I see.

There it is. A safe like any other I've seen, with just a simple handle to open it up. No other security?

It hides in the far corner, away from plain sight of any intruder. But not anywhere no one will spot it.

Yet you found it. The intruder itself. White Wings finally makes her appearance.

The burnt and scarred bodies flash across my vision, and everything comes back into its pieces—my purpose. Then comes Red Horn's voice. *Keep them in mind. They're who you're fighting for.*

Fuck it.

Aaron had put this on me, and I'm doing this not out of loyalty or trust, but for his word, for giving me the answers he knew, and I didn't. Now, Aaron can be anything, but he holds on to his word. At least there is some sunshine in his body filled with the darkest storms and hell for a heart.

I reach for the small handle. My fingers feel foreign as they curl around the piece of metal, opening it up. This is too easy, isn't it?

Me and my big mouth. It *was* too easy until I saw the keypad shining with blue numbers and letters.

There's a passcode. It could be anything.

Jason. Think Jason. Jason … Jason … What can he put as a passcode? Fuck. This is such a bad idea. I knew I couldn't do this.

You're not going now after coming this far, surprisingly White says.

Okay, let's try *Archer.*

I punch in the letters, but it makes a loud screeching noise. "Please try again," a female voice responds.

I jump on the spot and place a hand on my chest. "Fuck. Keep it down," I hiss from where the voice came from.

"One attempt remaining," she says in her singsong-like voice again.

"The answers lie in the living." Aaron's voice bounces in my head after he went into the depths of the first piece. Maybe it was a hint. He could've gone straight to it and not riddle with the nerves of my brain.

Answers for the living.

The living. Or the dead.

Rebirth.

"Phoenix is one creature that explains so many things about the living." Jason's response intrudes from the beach.

Phoenix!

It's worth a try.

I lift a shaky finger and apply more force than necessary to the screen.

P.

Thud.

H.

Thud.

O.

Thud.

E.

Thud.

N. I. X. Thud, thud, thud.

My heart is like a car engine revving up—a powerful vibration that takes over my chest, the rhythm of my heart a fast-paced tornado.

As I type in the last letter, everything goes eerily silent for one itching second when the thuds echo in my ear.

Ting!

It opens.

"Welcome, Mr Archer." The voice greets and a hit of guilt fills me.

I let out a breath, taking in oxygen and getting rid of the bitter taste at the back of my throat.

In there sits a small USB. *Oh,* that's not something I'd expected. What I did was another stack of paper with a golden glow shining from behind it.

Tremors run through my hand as I reach into the safe and get a hold of the item that would have me one-fourth of my way towards the end goal.

As slow as my hand reached for the USB, it was gone just as quickly I retrieved it and slipped it into my pocket. "Help me out, and I promise I'll get you back." I talk to the inanimate object while tapping on my pocket.

Now, I need to get out. I will suffocate within myself if I stay here longer than I need to be.

After finding my way through the labyrinth of aisles, I reach for the door and twist the knob.

I go still.

Jason's voice echoes from the other side of the door, and bottom lip flips inward as my teeth nip on it.

With a slow, deliberate pace, I click the door shut, so quiet it gets swallowed by the surrounding sounds. The weight of the robbed safe and files presses down on me. They've become the physical manifestation of my guilt come to life.

With a hard push of my back, I keep the door closed and force myself to breathe. Each ragged breath hitches in my chest, a desperate, painful gasp that makes me fear my ribs will crack.

Jason's muffled voice speaks from the other side. "Prepare all the materials and get the technical team on it." There's a pause as Jason listens to someone over the phone. "Also, Teal, make sure there is no hint of this going out," he says with utter seriousness.

After a heavy second, he replies, "Good." A hush falls, broken only by the subtle *tap-tap-tap* of retreating footsteps on the glossy, tiled floor—the sound gradually fading into silence.

Waiting another tick of a minute, I slowly crack open the door and peek out.

All clear.

CHAPTER 18
Bianca

After such a shitty and adventurous day, I need to vent out all I can. So, I accepted Kiara's request to *cool down* at the club they follow religiously.

As I stand in front of it, I feel like a kid looking at the Eureka Tower for the first time, craning my neck up. I haven't seen such an extravagant place, especially among all the hidden gems Melbourne has.

I changed to the colour of the day: blue. There are no hints of any other colour. I ditched the pants and put on the sexiest blue skirt I could find, and might I add, the shade of ocean-blue of this skirt unexpectedly matches perfectly with the dark blue of the blouse.

I need some sort of distraction for multiple reasons, including but

not limited to Jelena's intolerable demands and the USB blinding my consciousness as it sits in the top drawer next to my bed.

The blue and pink neon sign breaks into the darkness of the cool night, reading *'Nicko's'* with the D crossed and replaced by an N.

Hilarious.

When I reach the front of the snaking queue, a bouncer checks my ID and steps aside. The hungry and tainted look in his eyes matches closely to someone I wish to eradicate from the face of the earth. Only if I had the guts to just punch Aaron, and for the life of me I couldn't hurt a fly with muscles I'm gifted.

Stepping inside, I'm assaulted by a cacophony of loud, pulsating music and a potent, almost nauseating smell of alcohol mingling with a host of other strong scents. People crowd the place like bees buzzing in a beehive. Rather than working, every person in here reeks of sex, others snorting all the white powder as if their life depends on it—it most likely does—while the majority have their drinks and losing off on the dance floor.

It doesn't take long to spot the bright red of Eva's professional suit, coming straight from the boutique. If only she could wear overalls to work, she would. My girl lives for those. By her side, the disco lights above illuminate Kiara's bright yellow neon dress—the brightest I've ever seen. Sage is wearing her neutral white shirt and black pants.

"How's our girl doing?" Kiara slightly slurs as she slams down a glass of beer on the table the moment I come to them.

"Not bad. Just needed some distraction after the day from hell. And Sage," I turn to her and place my hand on hers. "Where are your colours? At least tonight you could've ditched the fifties." I try not to whine, because I know my friend knows colours but just restricts herself to black and white.

Sage playfully narrows her eyes, and I love it for us that only we get to see this side of her. She presents a closed-off demeanour to the world, intensely focused on her dance, and giving people cold shoulders, at least to those who deserve it.

"You know, the last time someone tried to tell me about colour, they ended up having their car vandalised. I may seem soft and subtle, but don't test me." She fights a smile and nods as if imagining all the things she could do.

"Lucky me, I don't own a car." I straighten my back, smiling widely.

"Wait, did you hear car? I said *clothes*—colour-coordinated clothes." Sage widens her eyes and quirks her lips up in confidence.

I feign a scoff. "You wouldn't."

"Accidents happen all the time." Her face drops all comic.

"What about a spa date? Would that save my clothes?" I muse, looking at my golden-brown skinned friend with pleading eyes.

After a silent sip of her lemonade, Sage holds up her fist. "Deal." I bump mine with hers with a wide smile.

We chuckle like schoolgirls and fist bump each other—twice. This feels good, to be out of my head and away from the shackles of Red and White.

"I already chugged two beers, Evs only had one and a half and she's about to explode. Then we have Sage, the non-alcoholic. Imagine her type exists." Kiara gives me a rundown and takes another swig of her drink and bangs the glass on the table for dramatics.

"I'm sorry, I *choose* not to drink. Autonomy and freedom of choice do exist," Sage defends, crossing her arms and eyeing the lemon soda in front of her.

"Could you speak human, please, preferably English," Kiara requests, folding her hands in front of her.

Here goes our chaotic duo again.

Eva meets my stare across the table, and we hide our smiles behind our glasses.

Sage opens her mouth to begin with whatever she had in her defence, but Kiara holds up a finger, silencing her. "On second thought. I don't want to know, and I'm happy living in the dark if that means I can escape a Sage Session. I got over and done with those long ago." Kiara contorts her features to what should be disgust but appears as if she's in pain.

"Suit yourself. Alcohol is a waste of energy and not to mention dangerous." Sage elegantly sips her drink, sitting in her element.

In my many years on this earth, Sage has not touched a single glass of alcohol for reasons she gatekeeps and only gives us *my choice and freedom* lecture every time we ask.

"Okay, who wants to rock tonight and fuck great!" Kiara, as enthusiastic as she is, screams and holds her glass in the air, letting the dim light of the club reflect the amber liquid.

"Let's go!" Eva and I clink our glasses together when Sage simply raises hers.

Tonight, I am determined to resist the allure of my emotions and the painful memories of my best friend's older brother. Especially the feeling of his hardness following me around like a cute, annoying child.

"I think you should slow down. You already had two beers and three shots in eight minutes." Eva tries to pacify, but isn't going anywhere as I take down my fourth shot.

The citrus burst on my tongue from the lemon is no less than flying on the softest cloud after the rush from the tequila.

I don't know the time or the day, and truly, I don't give a fuck. Wait? *What's my favourite colour again?*

Everything is heightened, from the sound of the booming music to the brightness of the lights, like broad daylight. There is no annoyingly handsome, green-eyed man to have me under his spell and wrapped around his finger. I've escaped countless circumstances where I could've leaned into him, but I don't know how long I can deflect the urge to just have him.

"Let the girl live. It doesn't hurt for one night," Kiara slurs, the scent of alcohol heavy in the air as she clinks her shot glass—her tenth—against mine.

Watch me puke on one of these billionaires. It would be a sight to see them screaming like they met with the ghost of their souls.

Woah, that's dark. Tone it down, Bee. *Haha! I'm fucking losing it.*

The beer I drank afterward works to cool down the effects of the warmth the shot brings until it amplifies it.

I have Kiara to thank for telling me this. I'm questioning my alcohol-drinking skills and how I'd survived without her to guide me. *Just to feel this alive.*

"That's why you're my favourite. I love you." Kiara hums.

She's the best. "I knew I was. How can I not be?"

We hug each other, our bodies swaying as if we're balancing on a tightrope, until the sturdy table thankfully steadies us.

"Would you like to have this dance?" Kiara bends and shakily takes out her hand.

I giggle.

We take each other's hands, and we move towards the dance floor. The bass vibrating through our bodies as we guide each other through the swaying crowd.

"We'll be here when you topple over someone and need a break!" Sage raises her glass and clinks it with Eva, who has also resorted to a lime soda.

"Before that, I'll take someone to the dark corner and have some fun." Kiara waves her hand behind her back as we stumble towards the crowd.

"Woo-hoo!" The fiery beats of the music ignite a bounce in my feet, shaking loose the mental chaos. *Wow.*

The pump of adrenaline from the mask of alcohol does wonders in muting everything and giving freedom for a moment. The nights out in Canberra were nothing compared to this monster. I often went out with Aaron, so he could show me off to his friends and label me as his most prized trophy in his cabinet. Pathetic me didn't see it as such until earlier this year.

At first, I liked someone breaking into the cage of my loneliness, giving me importance and attention. But soon enough, I saw how Aaron made his way into my life, twisting and slithering like a venomous snake. He took over my brain as he slowly injected spurts of venom, exploiting me one by one.

That's how I got addicted to keeping everything in place and having colour-coordinated outfits with stashes of makeup that would, in literal terms, last me a lifetime. It was a coping mechanism, a way to quiet the relentless noises in my head that I had to abandon.

"Bianca!" Kiara shouts, and I return to the dance floor. My limbs move with the music while my brain deals with my past decisions. "Be in the moment. Fuck the rest!" Her beautiful, silky hair also bounces with the rhythm.

The loud sounds coming from our mouths probably make us look like idiots. I'm proud to be one, because apparently the world lacks them. Everything is so serious and gooey outside these walls, where people can't help stressing about life and coming to terms with the stupidity of their decisions.

Kiara places her small hands on my hips and slowly sways with me, following the rhythm of the music.

Our feral child.

My intoxicated brain follows suit as I wrap my arms around her neck and get lost in the moment.

From the corner of my eye, I can see Eva raising her phone in our direction as if taking our video. She smiles and speaks to it while Sage stands behind her.

Kiara gets near my ear and shouts over the music, "Look, there's a guy literally eye-fucking you? He's *hot*. I would take the bait." She winks.

I examine her for a second and can feel the heat reaching my cheeks. Everything hits me at once—the thrill, the release—and I laugh, a sound both breathless and liberating. Maybe I am too drunk, but even if someone faints now, I will laugh.

Kiara gets ripped away from me, her face reflecting the same shock as mine, but it soon disappears when she sees the tall and broody man. He pushes Kiara into him and holds her from behind. His long dark hair is in a ponytail, and he has tattoos climbing one of his arms. If I didn't know better, I would've thought he belonged to some sort of mob.

Ha. See, truly drummed.

The devil's child looks over her shoulder, and winks with every intention of getting laid. *Go for you, babe.* At least one of us can get that without feeling guilty.

Wait. Why should I feel guilty about something I want?

Because of the man you can't get out of your system. I need to learn to mute the idiots in my head.

The music dissolves into a meaningless hum, and I throw my head back, shedding the day's worries with the last notes.

No, Jason tonight. No, Aaron and his stupid puzzle. None of it. Tomorrow—I'll deal with all that tomorrow.

Reminder: Deal with my shit. Tomorrow

I let my hands run through the roots of my hair and take in the throbbing music.

As I move to the muted sounds, a—man's—body hits me, and he wraps his hands around my waist. I don't bounce back like my sober self would've, instead, I lay my head on his chest. Solid and hard.

"You look lonely, sweetheart. What you say I get rid of it?" His voice is deep like the Pacific Ocean, but nothing compared to Jason's Great Canyon.

"Hmm, wouldn't mind it." I nod, totally swallowed by the mood.

The world spins as he twirls me around, and I see who it is. My eyes go wide when I see him.

Jason. My fingers lightly skim the sharp edges of his features. No, he can't be here.

I look up at the ceiling. *Can't I get* one *night without thinking about him?*

"Eyes on me, sweetheart," his deep voice says.

I look back at him, and what I see is nowhere close to the man capturing and living in my thoughts, heck, existence.

His dark brown eyes spark with mischief, and his boxy grin spreads across his face like a sunbeam. I shake my head, but the man's strange appearance remains unchanged, his eyes holding an unsettling depth.

Good. I'm not as delusional as I thought I was.

He tightens his hold around my waist and pushes me closer to him.

My hands spread on his chest. The sharp, stinging smell of scotch fills my nostrils, but I don't move—can't move.

Lost in the music's embrace, we sway, the melody a shield against the anticipation of the stranger's plan for the night.

"You are so beautiful." He hums in my ear.

I lazily nod.

He buries his head in my hair, sniffing like a dog. As his neck cranes down, I see a tattoo. It's so large that his entire shoulder can't hold it. From what I can see, there's a large beak poking out, then it narrows until it gets eaten away in the depths of his black shirt.

"What do you say we take this somewhere else?"

Heat swallows my body, but going beyond this dance floor doesn't fit in. It doesn't seem right. I just want to be lost for the moment and nothing more.

But what's wrong with taking some time off from being the boring Bianca?

Red, shut up!

His hand slowly—so slowly—glides up and into my skirt. A wave of nausea and revulsion washes over me at his touch. It's so far from the lust shining in his eyes.

I want to throw up. I want to stop this.

"Stop!" I scream over the loud music. I push him hard, but he doesn't budge. His arms lock around me, their grip like iron bands.

"Not when you hold so much importance. I will fuck everything out of you tonight," he growls near my ear as he lifts me up to feel his hard dick. "Before giving you away."

Before I could open my mouth to respond, a raspy, *rageful* voice answers for me. "I would stop right there if you wish to have your head on your shoulders and not in my hand."

Both our heads turn to the brutal, silent threat that shakes me to the core. He can't be Jason. My stupid head is deluding me again.

No, there's no delusion.

That's Jason Archer standing there—with death in his eyes.

CHAPTER 19
Jason

"The recent intrusion in our systems has been traced to Bendigo," Teal reports. She called in earlier for an urgent meeting after Bianca left.

"The bug seemed to be implemented through a high-security vault, which leaves a possibility that someone from our tech team is a mole." The sound of ice and malice feeds through as Adrian comes with his vodka in hand. No matter my dislike towards him, he is one of the four pillars of Phoenix.

"What were they after?" I ask Teal, sipping my whisky.

"Nothing," she replies with a nod.

Adrian scoffs. "Oh, it was something all right." He tsks

condescendingly. "Our locations, and all the resources we supply and use to run Phoenix. That's information enough." Adrian looks around the room, giving each of us his cold stare.

"*Adriana*, you better put some fuel up your ass to work with fire then," Kai simply answers.

Kai has two shades to himself. One he keeps for the world to see and one that lurks in the darkness of his heart. We know both.

"*Kia*, I have, and it seems like your gears aren't working on this one. I thought you were the brutal planner," Adrian says, letting Kai release a challenged huff, sinking his chest into his ribcage.

"How about we also discuss *Excelsior?* You have been *so* generous to them these days." Kai hides his smirk behind the rim of his glass.

Adrian stands ramrod straight, and levels Kai with a warning stare. "Kia…"

Pyrosilk is getting more layered as we dig into it. First, they got into our storage facilities in the regional areas, and now they're aiming for the main control.

A vibration comes from the side table, taking me out of my thoughts. Eva.

Kai groans as he shifts to look at the flashing name. "Seriously, I was already having a shitty day. It's getting shitter by the minute."

I ignore him and pick up the call.

Adrian stands unaffected by the mini bar, sipping his vodka like water and filling it for seconds.

I don't even get to see her when the loud bangs from the pulse-beating music come through. The camera focuses on a pale cheek and red-eyed Eva.

"Are you at Nicko's again?"

The multiple bright neon signs crawl on every corner of the club.

Kai clears his throat, clearly interested in the matter now. If he were a rabbit, his ears would stand and watch out for any competition whenever he senses a club or alike. Owning multiple for himself, he can never get enough of them or taking them down. He is the king of his own kingdom.

"Where else can I be?" she hiccups.

"How much did you drink?"

"Two. I am a big girl." She lifts her biceps. "Meet Elizabeth." She kisses her left bicep. "And Jacob," she says as she kisses her right one. It's not amiss who she named them after. Her favourite designers, Elizabeth DuPont and Jacob Kriemler.

"Crazy," Kai sings, twirling a finger by his head.

I throw the nearest file to me at him, which he catches with a white-toothed smile. He must have started selling these things, after all, that's what he gets from me.

Eva has come a long way from those judging comments about her weight when she was a child to now becoming the designer she always wanted. The nights I held her when the world became too much were something I never thought would bring us together. Feeling the warmth of her body as she confided in me and holding me to release the day's pent-up emotions. Listening to her soft whispers as she wished she could just be like everyone else. But she always ignored the fact that she is beautiful in her own way.

That's when Kiara, Sage and Bianca came in and became Eva's anchors, providing her the shot of love.

But now, she faces her demons on her own. I can only imagine what she goes through. I've tried to step in, but she's put up barriers stronger than those at Phoenix. We know she hurts, yet we don't know what we're fighting with anymore.

"Okay, big girl." The phone shuffles around, and Sage's face comes into view. "Hey, Jay." Sage gives me a subtle nod from behind Eva.

Adrian pauses mid-pour and clears his throat.

"Hi." I nod at her.

"I think things are going to get out of hand here. I can only handle one drunk girl at a time, not three." Her eyes go wide as she huffs out a breath.

Three. Bianca's there. And drunk.

"We'll come."

"No, *we* won't, *he* will," Kai says as he jumps on me to get into the camera's view.

Eva giggles. "Stupid. He thought we were talking about him. I would rather eat my own nails than have him pick me up. Bug! I know you're there. Be a good cousin and come."

"A day will come when you want me and I won't be there," Kai says. Kai must've picked her up drunk countless times in their teenage years, and they probably got drunk together more.

Eva sighs, her shoulders dropping. "Dreams."

From his corner, Adrian smirks and places his drink down. "On my way, little fly."

"Where are the other two?" I ask, wanting to see Bianca.

"It's better if you see." Eva snatches the phone from Sage and flips the camera's view to the dance floor.

It doesn't take me long to spot the women among the sweaty bodies and flashing lights.

Bianca holds Kiara close as her arms cross around Kiara's neck. They move with the loud beats of the music and nearly topple into another group of dancers. Definitely had more than just two beers.

Kiara leans to Bianca's ear and whispers something. Bianca's cheeks redden, then she tips back her head and explodes into a laugh, loud enough to be heard by the surrounding people.

I search the club for anything unusual, from habit. I immediately notice a man, his stare unwavering as it rests on Bianca, making the hairs on my arms stand on end.

My knuckles turn white as I clench the fabric of my pants, watching him linger near the oblivious woman. The sight makes my fucking blood boil.

I am not a violent man. It's never been my true nature, but I've also never deviated from giving a slice or two when people crossed their limits and certain fuckers who want to meddle with my business—public or private.

I can deny all I want that I have nothing to do with Bianca, but I know she makes my heart beat like it's the first time, and that she's the only one who can. From the moment I saw her sitting innocently under the tree, she had become both my business and my deepest pleasure. A source of my loathing and fascination coiled in one.

Kiara gets pulled from Bianca when a guy cradles her into his chest, which she happily welcomes. She smiles sheepishly and winks, well knowing where this might end up.

Bianca's mood doesn't falter. She slowly traces the length of her side and curves, especially on the swell of her breasts. It's done so sensually, so seductively, that it's calling for me to get lost in the roots of her waves.

I want to throw her over my shoulder and hide her away from the world that will devour her whole. Because I am the world that will devour her like the animal I would become when I have her to myself.

My blood curses each vein when that bastard keeps his eyes on her and sips his drink.

Sage turns the camera back, but all I'm thinking is how I can carve his eyes out.

I could feel my eyes darkening with anger, refusing to allow him to continue with whatever intentions his lustful eyes held. Not if he wants to wake up in the hospital the next morning and not in his bed.

"How much did they drink?" My tone goes shades deeper, and the two girls remain quiet in shock. "I said how much?"

"I'm the only sober witness to the method of their madness," Sage answers, her voice strong. "And can say for sure I had lost count of their drinks after the fifth shot."

"I'll be there. Keep them out of trouble," I growl.

"It's oka—" I cut the call before Sage could say otherwise.

"Jay, are you okay—where the fuck you're goi—" Kai doesn't finish as I dash out of the room. "Seriously, would you tell me why you look like you're going to massacre a whole town?" Kai huffs as he catches up to me with our jackets.

"Nicko's." I only see rivers of blood leaking out of every creak in the ceiling and windows. "Teal! Surround the club," I order with my voice reaching a new high.

"On it!" She marches off and taps her earpiece.

"Evalyn's nail feast can wait. I'm out for mine." Kai rubs his hands in anticipation.

"Then why should I starve?" Adrian folds his sleeves.

The devil dances hot on our heads.

I didn't count the number of red lights we skipped or the horns and curses that came our way. I'll shove them up the asses of anyone who does cares.

Kai's Aston Martin speeds behind me, while Adrian's bike roars in the distance ahead.

Nicko's is a fifteen-minute drive when there's no rush. Five when the water overflows its surface.

The entire ride I saw the night painted with deep red all because of a motherfucker who would spend the rest of his life crying in his mother's lap. Thinking of anyone pursuing Bianca like I had, hearing her laugh for me and at me—no.

The club's atmosphere changes drastically as I walk in and witness his hand inching up her thighs, under her skirt. I fight for each breath, my chest constricting with the effort, while my fingers, robbed of colour, curl into tight white fists.

Bianca's shoulders became stiff, screaming with discomfort. She pushes him on his chest. *That's it.*

"I would stop right there if you wish to have your head on your shoulders and not in my hand." The words come out like burned coal with the only purpose to blacken rather than power.

Their heads snap in my direction, too stunned to speak. He recovers first and holds Bianca closer to him, suffocating her.

"Hey!" She tries to push him off. Her alcohol ridden muscles do shit to stop it. "Stop! Let me go!" She attempts another push but fails miserably.

"Hey, sweetheart, that's not how this works. We have the night together, like you promised."

"I didn't promise you shit," Bianca grits.

Her eyes fill with wetness at his words, breaking the last straw holding me back. The fucker called for it, and I wouldn't mind spending my life in jail if some misfortune happens tonight. Only doing a favour for the sake of humanity.

Slowly walking over to them, I place a hand on Bianca's shoulder and push her back with ease. When I'm sure she's at a safe distance, I throw my fist at the bone of his cheek, sending him to the floor on his side. A sense of satisfaction makes me smile as the aftershock of his jaw's crunch ripples through my hand.

There is nothing after as I lunge at him, and land punches one after another. I don't hear any groans, but the first trickle of blood that comes from his lips lessens some of the crimson clouding my eyes.

The sound of my punches echoes in the now silent club, leaving everyone in shock.

Punch!

"*Jason.*"

Punch!

"Jason!"

Punch!

Losing count, I allow my fist to disorganise his face with a drop of remorse.

I land one more for good measure before I assess the ripped skin of his lips and the cuts on his eyebrows married with his bruised nose. Energy works through me, even if my hand drips with blood from my torn skin.

"*Jason!*"

I lean in close, the smell of his sweat and fear heavy in the air and pull him up by his collar. "You're lucky I'm in a good mood, fucker," I growl, my voice low and dangerous, "that you're still breathing."

With a heave, I throw him back. His lifeless form hits the floor with a harsh thud, the stillness amplifying the grim reality. A spotlight flashes above us, and the trail of the blood travels down the side of his face to his neck. What I see is no less than a trophy in my scarce act of violence.

A Pyrosilk.

My rage has lowered dramatically, replaced with a twinge of pride and interest.

"Jason!" Kai's voice booms in my ear once I get up, bringing me back to the club and not in my ring.

My gaze flicks around the club to find Bianca. Before I can do anything, she comes into my chest and wraps her shaking arms around my torso. With a trembling hand, she clutches my shirt while her other arm curls against my side.

I let out a much-awaited breath of relief and take her in.

Tremors vibrate through her, wave after wave, a cold, tingling sensation that starts at the base of her spine climbs up to where my hand rests in her hair.

"Jay! What the actual fuck is wrong with you?" Eva grumbles, running towards more sobered than she was on the phone. Kai is on her side, and Sage follows wide-eyed with Adrian close by. Kiara is nowhere to be seen.

"We'll talk later," I reply curtly, not answering. I turn to Kai. "Take them before there's more blood on my hands."

He nods and guides Eva to the exit. Sage straightens, almost unaffected, and holds on to Eva, who glares as if she's ready to wrap her hands around my neck.

Once they leave, I look down at Bianca. "Let's get you out," I say with my voice softer. I lift Bianca off me and see her redden eyes fill with a layer of wetness that shouldn't be there.

It urges me to have a second round with that fucker, and this time I will not stop.

"Take me away from this hell," she whispers.

I'll take you to our *hell.*

"You know, I really thought you didn't like me," Bianca slurs as she messes my hair. Despite my many warnings, Bianca got two bottles of beer as we were coming out of the bar. And now she is just trying to breathe properly.

I parked five minutes away from Bianca's house, not by choice. By the time I could get into her street, she had opened the window and tried to jump out because it was *"getting too hot."*

Then, with a small, determined grunt, she scrambled onto my back, and I tried to think of how I ended up here with her on my back, whispering words her alcohol-ridden tongue couldn't hold. Clearly, I'd underestimated her ability to hold her alcohol.

"But you were really the hero in there," she giggles, whispering in my ear.

I'm a beast, not a hero.

Mental note: never let her drink *without me.*

But this woman with windows of blue oceans unravels the beast inside of me I didn't know existed to this extent, like tonight. When everything is red, and the only colours are hers.

"Ever since the night at the beach, I wanted to kiss you so…" She sighs. "So fucking bad. But you know we can't." She levels her chin on my shoulder.

I know. Yet the chemicals in my brain and the pulse in my neck sing otherwise.

"I shouldn't, but God, I'm a sinner and I want to," she mumbles, snatching a chuckle out of me. Her cold fingers crawl into my hair, allowing me to relish the feel of the cold against the heat consuming me.

I smirk to myself as I push her up. "If you're a sinner, I've sinned right beside you."

Bianca chuckles and keeps her hands rooted in my hair. *Fuck.* If she doesn't take that out, I will fucking have her on the wall of her family house.

"Oh God," she moans. Fucking moans at the back of neck as her hot breath fans my hair.

I inhale sharply to cool down the building arousal. *Control, Jason.*

"Could we just forget for one night?" Her voice drops to a whisper. "That the fire never happened, and we never had that argument when I lost you."

For the first time, I'm at a loss for words. She doesn't know what she's calling for. My *supposed* hatred of her is the only grace that keeps me at bay. Once that's gone, nothing in anyone's power can stop me from having Bianca—not even her. I'll be powerless on her battlefield.

"Life's short. Too short. And now, Aaro—" The house comes into view and the heavy cloud over us fades away. "My house!" she cheers, forgetting the noose of unsaid words around our necks.

Now who?

In the background, Bianca mutters, but my head is in a haze. She deserves so much better than me, and her sober self will never truly put her trust in me. She made that abundantly clear.

"What's the code?" I bend down and reach for the keypad. One hand holding her, the other hovering on the keypad.

"0612," she happily sings, but my fingers freeze midway when the numbers rock a crucial piece of memory.

06/12. December 6th. The night when everything happened. The night I lost and gained in equal amounts. Ironic in the relationship of the numbers six and twelve, half and double of each other. Perfectly encapsulating the night.

I put in the numbers and wait for the beep to open the door.

"I wish I had died that night, not them."

CHAPTER 20
Jason

Lead settles in my feet, forcing me to stop by the entrance table. "I miss going fishing with Dad…" She swallows loudly. "And braiding my hair with Ma."

A tear, warm and heavy, falls on my shoulder. It's a burden I'll take. I will collect each and every tear she sheds and make our sea of peace out of them.

"If you had died that night, they wouldn't have survived, anyway. *I* wouldn't have survived." My grip on her legs tightens as I bring her closer to me. "If you had died, you would have had three souls follow your path." My voice is not mine as I speak with a softness I don't have.

A huff leaves her, and we stay silent until I get to the sofa. She

doesn't make a move to get off, and I don't force her.

"Do you understand me?" I speak to the silent air in front of me. "Your soul costs more than any universe out there, and my soul is nothing without yours."

"Jay," she whispers, unwinding her arms from neck and coming to stand in front of me. Her eyelids shut tight, robbing me of the view to read her. When she opens them again, a shield blocks those blue pearls, and the lead from my feet spreads to my chest. "Take me away from this hell my life has become. Make me believe heaven exists." She breathes.

I don't need to take her to heaven when she is heaven embodied. *My* heaven is right in front of me. The sound of her voice is nothing short of being celestial, like the harmonies of a thousand angels singing in perfect composition.

The truth is: Bianca had never truly left me, yet I was boiling in the pots of hell in her absence. Now that she is here, under my touch, I know my peace is also in my hands.

Just like heaven, Bianca is too good to be true. For me. For anyone.

I shake my hand as I cup her cheek. "Not tonight. Tonight, you will love yourself the way I do," I whisper and pause, thinking the words through and feeling the utter truth behind them.

Bianca looks up at me, and I know she won't remember anything come morning. It makes me a coward for not telling her sober self all this, but I *need* to tell her to get it off my chest and let her believe herself because I do.

"Don't forget you can love yourself without me because that's who you are. You are full of so much fucking love that it radiates off every corner of your being," I murmur on her forehead, and leave a lingering kiss. My five-year long celibacy is wavering at her mercy, and all I can see is her face in pure bliss.

"Jason." Her eyes blur behind a sheen of wetness. There's a moment of silence before she erupts into a waterfall of tears. "Too much … everything is too much. The voices in my head won't quiet. They keep talking and talking. It's too much." Getting out of my hold, she drops back onto the sofa, and before she does, I pull her and sit her on my lap as I sit on the sofa.

"Cry, baby," I murmur through my tight throat into her hair. "Cry all you want. Let me hear you—let me be near you." My grip around her gets tighter as she wails into my chest.

I sit through her wails, which turn into cries and then into hiccups. All I do is let her be while I smooth my hand over her hair. I don't know when, but my own salty tears stung, and every time they trailed down, they tried but failed to provide solace to the torment my ears and heart were going through. The short five minutes felt like a lifetime and more.

Once her breathing evens, she looks up at me with the innocence of the girl I once saw but got robbed by the hands of time. "Sorry," is all she says before she leans in and presses a kiss on my chest. "I'm sorry for everything I put you through."

Unbelievable. This woman is more than I could have ever asked for. In a swift movement, I lift her chin with my thumb and level her stare with mine. "Don't you ever apologise for anything. And never apologise to me out of all the people—you can never do wrong in my eyes. Even if you do, you will have your reasons."

Bianca shakes her head and rests on my chest again, over my now calm beating heart. "You really like me, don't you?"

"Why do you say it as a question?" I smile, thankful for the dark to become my veil. "I've only ever known myself with you and for liking you. You've always been the one answer I search for in every question."

In this moment, I would confess my every feeling and sin because I'm done holding back.

"Would you do something for me?" She finally speaks after long and calm moments of silence.

"Anything," I murmur against her as I look up at the dark ceiling.

Bianca's breath fans over me, and so does her intoxicating cherry blossom. "Touch me," she says on a lingering breath. "I haven't been touched in a long time."

My muscles go rigid at her request, and oxygen fails me, as do words. She can't be serious. I knew she had a boyfriend. No matter how much it killed me to know the fact, I faced it. But I never mustered the courage to dig deeper and find who it was, or anything closely related to her sex life. I lost the privilege to that part of her once she left.

I shake my head against all the nerves in me coming back to life. "No," I say, "not tonight." Bianca Kennedy will remember me when I have her, and she will scream my name. "You do not know who you're inviting. I've claimed you once, and I will do it again. This time, the right way. We will soothe the parts you keep hidden and find my own for you to kiss better. Not tonight, though, Rainbow."

I always wanted to call her Rainbow because that's who she is. The colour to the lifeless palette of my life.

Disappointment clouds her beautiful eyes, and I feel it in the crack of my heart.

I swallow and feel my arousal building, not listening to my plea to keep at bay. "But…" I slide my hand along her arm and hold her wrist.

Our breathing becomes one as I drag her hand down the slope of her stomach. Bianca locks her eyes on me, confused yet not telling me to stop.

"You can," I say so slowly, unafraid to break the soft bubble we have created around us. "Touch yourself. I'll be here for you."

Bianca doesn't say otherwise and follows my hand as I guide her to the hem of her skirt. Once there, I remove my hand and lift her chin so that she's watching me. Her eyes search mine with such softness and somehow make me believe everything we lived in the past was only in our imagination and the truth is we never really got off this couch with her in my arms.

"Tell me what to do," Bianca instructs with her voice soft and not daring to leave my face.

I smile. "You're going to slide your beautiful fingers in your skirt." She does.

"Inside your lacy panties," I whisper. My desire to touch is reaching heights I've never felt before.

"How do you know their lace?" she asks with a lift of her eyebrow and lips.

I scoff. "Tell me they're not," I challenge her.

She smiles and slides inside. "They are."

My grip on her chin tightens slightly. "I know you better than you know yourself, Bianca Kennedy."

My eyes darken at her little nod and the way she folds her lower lip inside.

"Are you wet?" I ask.

She doesn't need to answer because I found my answer as her nose flares with each breath and nipples peak through her blouse.

"Are you wet for me?" My voice is so low and dangerous that it's taking every part of me not to replace my hand with hers.

"Yes," she hisses so softly, leaning into my touch on her chin.

I swallow. "Put one finger inside your tight little cunt."

She does. Her breath instantly hitches, and her hand outside grabs my arm, digging her fingers into my arm.

"You know what to do now. Be my good girl and show me how you like to fuck yourself," I say as I tuck a loose strand behind her ear.

The dark pupil of her eye dilates, and by the movement of her arm, I can tell she's getting what she wants. Her pleasure is so clear on her face, and nothing is left to question when she moans.

"What are you thinking?" I finally mustered words through my lust-clouded brain.

"You." She swallows, and her arm goes deeper into her skirt. "Your hands on me. Your cock in me," she murmurs, "all of you."

If she keeps up with her dirty mouth, I will for sure burst into smithereens of my desire. My cock strains against my pants, and I'm sure Bianca can feel it.

She closes her eyes and swallows when her movements become frantic. "God, Jay…" Her breathless moan teases me once again, but this time I'm on the losing end because, holy hell, she said my name in that voice.

"I know, Rainbow. Press your thumb to your clit," I say.

As she does, her chest harshly moves up and down while her fingers on my arm squeeze with all their might.

She smiles when she opens her eyes again. "I'm coming…" She doesn't get to finish her sentence as I feel her arousal leaving her and coating me as well.

I drop my forehead to hers as she breathes through her orgasm.

"How are you feeling?" I ask with eyes closed, cherishing this fine moment of her being so close yet so far away.

She nods. "Better." She cuddles closer to me and holds me around my neck. "For now."

"Come on, let's get you to bed." I huff as I take her to her bedroom upstairs with her clinging to my front. Her tender legs wrap around me, and her nose grazes the pulse of my neck.

The room is just as I remember. Her bed is in the middle, with two small bedside tables on either side accompanied by a lamp in the shape of a flower. The bed dips with her weight, and she groans with her eyes closed.

I pull the blanket around and curl it around her shoulders. "Sleep, it's been a long night," I tell her as I run my hand over her hair.

She fights against sleep when she holds my wrist, and I stop myself from closing my eyes where her thumb strokes the memory of the night I cried in blood. "Please stay. At least until I sleep," she whispers, barely audible.

I'll stay forever if you say the word.

I smile, and even if I wanted to, I couldn't say no to this woman. "Okay."

She lets go of my arm and allows me only a minute to remove my watch and shirt, grabbing my wrist and dragging me down beside her. I don't dare slide underneath the covers and have her close to me. Instead, she holds on to my arm and smiles.

Sweet and tender minutes pass, and we sit in silence. As Bianca wanders in and out of sleep, she mumbles, "I don't want to lose you, Jason, but…"

Before she trails off into her slumber, the words she mutters sober me from any lust as a name that's not mine rolls out.

Aaron.

CHAPTER 21
Bianca

I feel I wrestled armies, and they defeated me shamelessly. All I hear is the war cry of my muscles and brain in pain but, surprisingly, pleasure as well.

I yawn and stretch, feeling like a totally new person. The smell of freshly peeled oranges surrounds the room, paired with the warmth of something sweet.

Slowly, my hazy world becomes clear. A headache blossoms at my temples, and I hiss when I rub them. I'm never drinking again.

Red, we need a chat.

I support my head as I get up, throwing off my blankets from my body. The soothing scent of mint floats around me, and I freeze. *Mint.*

My head snaps to the rest of my body, and rest assured I'm wearing

every piece of clothing I remember I was wearing at last. Flashes from last night come forward with the headache.

The club.

Fight.

Piggyback.

Jason.

Fuck!

You're a total idiot, Bianca.

Wait…

A burning blush creeps up my neck, staining my cheeks crimson as my heart pounds a frantic rhythm against my ribs. No, we didn't. We didn't have sex. I'm sure because Jason hates me. But more importantly, he is a gentleman from the inside, and I've seen him put up boundaries when they need to be.

When I get up, I turn the lamp off on my bedside table. I smile to myself. He remembers—remembers I don't like to sleep in the dark. My smile softens when I find his Rolex there on the table, solidifying the fact that it was him.

With my mind filled with possibilities, I take a shower and come out fully dressed. Far away from the mint.

The colour of today is green. Emerald green.

The dress hangs low all the way to my ankles, enough to distract me from the comfortable tightness in my chest. Even after the longest shower, his mint swallowed me and chased me around my room.

Listening to my stomach growl, I head to the kitchen and meet with another pleasant surprise. A sweet and caramel scent swims in the air from the waffles on the kitchen counter topped with blueberries and honey, and next to them is a glass of orange juice with extra ice.

I drop myself on the bar stool, and heaven falls over me as the first bite melts on my tongue, a delicious wave of flavour blinds me. My body hums with delight as I sip the freshly made orange juice.

When I get to my second waffle, my eyes catch a bright yellow note on the fridge. I peel it off with the ice crushing between my teeth.

Breakfast is made.

Orange juice and waffles your favourite.

I had an early meeting.

And you're never drinking again. Alone.

- Jason

I let out a small laugh. He was nervous. The great wall Jason Archer was nervous when he wrote the note. Jason only ever writes and speaks in simple sentences. We get either a single-word response from him or nothing.

Maybe the younger Jason is still in there.

We'll see about that when he finds out you're the parasite sucking his blood. White Wings begins her early moral call.

But I'm not too focused on it. The threat and playful tone of his note makes my heart pound like a drum, a mixture of fear and anticipation.

Fuck. I think I'm going to call in sick. Because I'm having a heart attack.

I didn't call in sick.

It's past twelve, and I haven't been in Jason's radius. Good—great even. I don't need to know what I did last night, and I know I scarred him somehow and in some way.

"Who did *you* fuck last night?" Max nudges my elbow as we sit in the conference room, discussing the next set of designs.

We've finished the first five floors and are completing the material unit list to send to Jason for authorisation.

The shipping of the materials isn't until the end of the month, and that's only for the fourth of the building. Completing the rest of the project will take considerably longer because of the countries the items are being shipped from.

Who gets potted plants from Italy?

I will never understand.

The plan is to complete my designs for the floors and get them to the creative team. Then I'll submit them to Florals & Bells.

"No one," I say from the corner of my mouth, trying to focus on the meeting.

Max shrugs his shoulders. "Liar," he scoffs. "I can smell—" He leans in close, his fresh scent near me as he sniffs me "—sexual energy."

I swallow.

All morning and now afternoon I've been hot and bothered. All I wanted to do was pour an ice-bucket over my head.

"Not everyone is a sexaholic like you," I reply, trying to take the conversation off me.

Out of the corner of my eye, I can see him smirk as he puts the end of his pen in his mouth. Our heads face the front as Chris, the second in charge, does the presentation.

"You aren't addicted to orgasms. *Yet.* Once you are, we'll have a very different conversation," Max whispers in my ear, still looking ahead.

"See you in the next lifetime, then," I mutter, a smile fighting my lips. Maybe the next lifetime is near, and so is my addiction.

"Hmm." He nods, not convinced.

The speakers above ring on with the company's familiar tune, and Oscar's voice filters through. "Bianca, please see Mr Archer in his office."

Everything was going so well.

All the heads in the room turn to face me, especially Jelena's squinted stare. Her eyes ink a tattoo of her stare on my cheek from the head of the table.

Max leans into me and whispers, "Welcome to your next lifetime." He excitedly pokes my thighs as I stand.

"Shut up," I hiss. I kick him under the table, and he just smiles. "Excuse me," I say to the rest of the room.

Jelena's intense gaze lingers on me as I leave the room, suffocating me until I reach the hallway. All day I've wanted to see him and ask questions, and in fact, I was buzzing with energy, but now all I want to do is throw up and run for the hills.

The elevator doors open, and two men I've briefly seen around are already inside, standing with their heads high. They both wear expensive suits and have perfectly made-up hair. The only distinguishing factor among them is the colour of their shirts. One is wearing a soft orange shirt while the other is wearing a pale green. I don't know anyone around here; this office is a country unto itself with the number of people coming in and out.

"Hello," they say as I step inside the wide elevator behind them.

"Hi," I reply with a smile.

"Which floor?" Green shirt asks.

"Twenty-second, thank you." He clicks the button, and I see it light up to the beautiful shade of light green. I could've sworn it was blue yesterday.

We ride up slowly, and I tap my feet with nervous energy. Fuck, I couldn't have planned this any better than it is.

On the twentieth floor, the doors slide open and reveal the man I've been dreading all day. *Jason Archer.* Heat rises, and my heartbeat bruises my chest. The forest-green eyes melt me in place the moment they spot me.

"Caelum." He nods to Green Shirt. "Dagon," he says to Orange Shirt.

"Afternoon, Mr Archer," Caelum greets.

Dagon nods.

"Take the next one. I need some *privacy.*" Jason's eyes flick to mine behind the two men with untamed fire in them.

"Sure." They step out and let Jason come in. I begin to go out, but Jason stands directly in front of me and presses a button.

Privacy. My stomach twists with what he might need privacy for in a fucking elevator. The doors close and silence fills the metal walls.

His thick, meaty finger opens a merged small flap and presses on a button inside it. The elevator stops its smooth rise with a slight jerk.

He locked us.

Jason turns and faces me with the expression of a hungry panther eyeing its prey.

"Do you know what they call a bird in a net?" he purrs.

Really? Now is the time he finds for riddles.

He strolls, calculating each step towards me. When he is close enough, I can see the hardened lines on his otherwise constructed face.

I shake my head, silenced by his calmness.

"*Trapped.*" His thick, rough hand cups my cheek, and his other hand gently tucks in my hair at the back of my head. "I am the bird trapped in your net, and that was the last thing I needed to be."

Oh no, he doesn't. He can't come and trap *me* when I should be the one asking the questions. Like what the fuck happened last night? Keeping my alcohol intake down was never my strong suit. And in moments like this, when I'm clueless as a sloth, I don't like it one bit.

I attempt to glare at him—an attempt—which morphs into wide eyes as Jason leans down and whispers in my ear, "Who gave you so much power over me?"

My heart beats like a hummingbird, and my breath pauses midway. "Right now, you're the one with power."

He shakes his head and closes his eyes, a small knowing smile on his lips. "No." I wait for him to continue—he doesn't.

No better time than now to approach the elephant in the room—the elevator. "What happened last night?"

The small smile on his lips stretches to a smirk. "It's better I show you." His breath fans my lips, and I try my best not to squirm and melt into a puddle of mess. He keeps lowering until his delicate lips kiss the corner of mine, teasing and alluding to the truth.

Warmth stronger than the sun caresses my skin, and I become a breathing furnace. This didn't happen last night—*this* sudden rush in heat and the pulsing in my core.

His green eyes find me again, but the earlier lightness is clouded. "We have a lot to talk about. Let's start with *Aaron*," Jason demands.

The floor underneath my feet slides right across, giving no time to take the loss.

Laughs and quiet conversation float around Cornella's as we sit in the corner by the window. The fresh smell of coffee and muffins dances through the air, with the staff serving each table in the wide area.

A cool winter vibe captures the cafe, with a large pit lit in the far corner, enough to warm up the entire bottom floor.

Jason's persona has shifted as he sits opposite me, palpable tension replacing his usual calm demeanour. I thought I would bounce my legs with the heat of embarrassment, but here I am dawning the feeling of dread.

I absolutely will not tell Jason about Aaron's manipulative games. Not when so many answers lie among them. Not when it could cost us our lives.

This girl won't listen, will she? Enter White Wings to wreak havoc.

Seriously, where the fuck is the button to their voices?

I don't see when the waitress places our drinks in front of us and leaves with her bright red hair pulled up in a tight bun. Like fire tamed by a single band of darkness.

As soon as she leaves, darkness dawns on his features once again. "Now, where was I? Right, Aaron." The fury in his tone takes me off guard.

Without answering, I pick up the cup and stop before taking a sip, looking closely at the hot drink.

"It's almond milk." He reads my thoughts.

I nod and take a sip. My eyes widen at the taste of the sweetness of white chocolate complementing the richness of cinnamon.

Jason keeps staring at me, branding me in his way. "I have my ways of getting what I want, Bianca. If you don't tell, I will find whatever you're trying to hide, and if it has anything remotely to do with your safety" —Jason levels me with a stare, so dark and hard, I don't believe it's him at all— "I will turn this world upside down to have you safe," he declares.

The ice in my glass rattles, not from my bouncing feet, but from the tremor in my hands. A sharp, metallic sound against the chill of the glass, matching my nervous energy.

"Jason, trust me on this one. Please." I sigh, deflated of all energy.

He smiles and lays back in his seat, his own hot cup in his hand. When he speaks, his voice is that of a businessman. "There's a scenario used in psychology. The *Heinz dilemma*. Let me give you my version of it." His green eyes lock me in place. "A poor boy who worked for a blacksmith needed a specific metal to make his sword, and he couldn't find it anywhere but with the rival blacksmith. The boy went to him and asked for it, but the blacksmith was selling it for double the price. They had an argument for a long time, and the boy left hot headed.

"The next night, the boy went inside the rival's store and stole the metal, and some other things he saw in the dark. Just to kick the blacksmith's ass. The blacksmith came in the morning to find some things missing. He quickly searched for the metal, and it was exactly where he had left it, but his gold and silver were missing. So, it turned out that the boy did everything for a metal that he still didn't get, yet he got something else equally valuable."

Jason sips his drink, his not leaving as they look over the rim of the cup. "Now tell me, who's more at a loss? The boy for still not getting what he needed or the blacksmith for being stubborn and losing his gold and silver."

I sit in thought, not sure where he is getting at. All possibilities run through my head as the drink warms my tongue. "The boy," I finally say. "He was a blacksmith himself. All he needed to do was show the other blacksmith some skills, and he could've made a deal to work for the blacksmith. Then the entire store would've been his at one point, and he could've made his sword with the metal, all the while getting paid," I reply.

Jason shakes his head with a condescending smile on his lips. "The blacksmith. He should never have allowed his rival onto his territory. Never should've spared him a second of his time. The boy played with words for enough time to assess the shop and see around."

I did not let *Aaron* in. He came on his own.

Aaron saw a metal that only you had. Jason. Red Horns informs.

I sit there, silenced. The realisation hits me like a powerful wave. "I am not the blacksmith, Jason," I whisper, dropping my head.

"I didn't say that." He sips his drink, satisfied with himself.

After a long-stretched minute, I heave and then speak. "Aaron's my ex," I say in one go.

Silence.

"It wouldn't be Aaron Blackburn by any chance?" His foot shakes as he sits one leg over the other.

I look at him with each breath releasing from me, silently answering him.

The movement of his foot pauses mid-movement just like everything else on him.

"The spoiled brat of the Blackburn Group. One who has been under the radar of the police for drug trafficking. Quiet the pick," Jason says.

I truly lived under a rock for years on end.

"Yes." I nodded, even though he didn't ask.

"I didn't take you to be into such types."

"How would you know *my type?* Please enlighten me," I say, mimicking his posture slightly annoyed.

"*Me.*" His dark eyes find me.

My eyes search his face for anything that would tell me he's mocking me. No, there's nothing.

"Arrogant much?" I cross my arms over my chest, shielding myself.

"Only with you," he says, sipping his drink.

"Get over yourself."

"Only with you."

"Will you stop saying that."

"What? Only *with you?*"

"Jason, shut up—"

The ringing of my phone saves Jason from being strangled if he said another word. Yet if I had the option, I would stop time right in this moment and listen to this man all day and night. I knew deep down in one of the dark corners that I can't truly be lonely, not when a man with the height of a tree and eyes encompassing them exists.

The vibrations continue. I lift my phone and see a video call from Kiara.

"Hey, Bee!" she screams over the phone, a bit too excited for a girl with a hangover.

"Hi."

"So, how's my girl doing?" Her grin is suspiciously large. The glint of mischief in her eyes and the knowing lift of her lips tell me she is planning something.

"I'm fine." I carefully choose my words.

"When did you wear a Rolex?" she asks, her face light with a curious stare. "I thought you never took off your watch."

"I don't. Are you still drunk?"

She giggles, and the camera drops.

That's my room.

"Kiara, what are you doing in my room?"

She laughs. Like a hysterical *hyena* laugh. God, she's fucking crying.

"I wanted to give you a surprise. But you were a step ahead. So ..." She pumps her eyebrows. "What happened last night?"

"Nothing," I lie through my teeth.

Ignoring me, she continues, "If not you, who does this magnificent Rolex belong to, then?" Kiara sings, swinging the gold piece of clockwork.

Jason's and my heads snap to each other, sharing a look of shock. "You left it?" I whisper-scream to Jason, tucking away the camera.

He passes me a bored look, screaming *obviously*.

How the fuck he is this calm now is beyond me. I am sweating, ready to leave and never come back.

"Well, whoever this belongs to seems like your type." She hums to herself as she closes her eyes and thinks of whomever she's giving approval to. The rosy flush and dark circles from last night are gone, replaced by a healthy, radiant glow on her fair skin.

"Kiara, seriously. How the hell did you get in?" I question when she finally settles and lies on my bed. Her mahogany spreads across my pillow, and she smiles up at the camera.

"Your keys, obviously. You guys left me, and when I came back, there were stunned faces and your bag on the table." She groans and digs her face into the pillow. "All I want to do today is … nothing."

I close my eyes, and I can't help but smile. She's still the same. "There should be painkillers in the first cabinet in the kitchen. Fruits and your favourite watermelon are in the fridge."

"Life saver. Also, get almond milk. They were out when I went. Love you," she chimes as she cuts the call.

I'll have to run to the supermarket to get some things before the evening rush starts.

"The groceries will get dropped off," Jason says, breaking our silence.

I look up at him, raising an eyebrow. "Where and why? I don't need you or your beehive buzzing for me. It's fine."

He doesn't reply.

"In the future, don't wear watches. If you do, then don't leave it on my nightstand next time."

An eyebrow lifts on his forehead. "Next time, huh?" he asks as smugness colours his face.

"That's all you got from that?" I throw my hands in the air, face in shock.

"This may sound direct, and it is." He leans forward, and I stiffen at his serious tone. "You've done enough for yourself. Give me these two months, and I'll show you how a woman is treated. I know you're independent but just share some of your thoughts with me. Lean on me, even if it's just a finger," Jason says, his eyes almost pleading.

I don't breathe. This man takes everything away from me, leaving me naked and vulnerable. As I try to process his existence, Jason stands to his full height, overshadowing me.

"Let's make a start now." He holds out his arm for me to take.

There's no way out of this. *Yes or no?*

It's a risk. The last time I left him, it almost broke me into pieces I could put back together. Knowing how much I felt for him, and ignoring what we had was the hardest thing I did in my life. The feeling was unbearable, a physical tearing sensation, as if my heart was being brutally ripped.

What if it's like my relationship with Aaron? Will I go back to being that Bianca again?

Jason is not Aaron, White Wing states.

He is the dream of every dreamer, Red Horns adds.

I look at his folded arm, open and ready for me.

Yes.

Reminder: Escape the trap of feelings.

CHAPTER 22
Bianca

"Where are you kidnapping me?"

"You'll see," Jason replies, satisfied with himself. The green veins on his arms, thick and pulsing like tiny snakes, coil across his skin with powerful confidence.

To quiet my restless desire to touch and feel the warmth of his skin, I tuck my hands under my thighs.

Jason takes another turn, and the surroundings look familiar. *The site.*

When we park and Jason opens the passenger door for me, I ask, "What are we doing here?"

"You *will* see," he stresses.

I get out of the car and breathe in the fresh air. It's getting colder as the sun sets, giving full permission for the wind to sneak through the thin material of my coat and dress. Should've never underestimated Melbourne's weather.

The rocks and leaves crunch underneath our feet with each step we take towards the main entrance.

When we arrive at the doors, a red light blinks as the scanner verifi es Jason's thumbprint. With a sigh, the doors swing open, and I'm carried inside surrounded by the sudden infl ux of his minty scent. I stop dead in my tracks, awestruck by the view before me.

"The materials are here already?" I gasp, cupping my face. *That is not possible.*

"Sure are," Jason says, nodding proudly.

"The se chairs and plants were coming from Europe. How?" I ask, my wide eyes sparkling with a smile.

"Nothing is impossible," he answers. I feel his intense gaze burning into me from across the room, an irresistible force pulling me towards him.

"We were still finalising the costs of the materials and the designs. Possibly bringing it down because we exceeded the hundred-thousand-dollar limit." A bright chirp escapes my lips, like a bird's song, as I bounce on my toes, impatiently awaiting the answers.

"Hundred thousand?" A frown comes over his forehead.

My eyes widen, reflecting my surprise, every time I think of how much a hundred thousand dollars is, especially for just the materials. "Yeah. You guys really need to turn it down a notch with your spending."

He shakes his head, his lips twisting in disappointment. "I'm sure I set it to a couple million after our budget analysis meeting early in the month." I don't know whether he is mocking me or whether he is truly genuine. Regardless, my mouth unhinges from the jaw and grazes the polished tiles.

"I—"

"There's more." He cuts me off and guides me towards the now-operating elevator. We ride to the top level, every atom in me simmering in excitement while Jason stands unaffected. If I thought downstairs was a wet dream, anything beyond this is orgasm territory.

"Come." Jason's mint envelopes me in a hug and tows me with him to his soon to be office. One thing is for sure, Jason is not a man, not human—no human has ever made me *this* awestruck of them. Not that he will ever find out.

The soft blue light of the winter evening sky streams through the expansive glass wall and bathes us as we enter the room. Immediately, my gaze hits the slice of the room marked off.

"This wasn't here before." I stroll towards the section in investigation.

Jason follows right behind me, the heat of his gaze imprinting on my every move.

"No way." I cup my mouth—*again*. "You. Did. Not."

"Yes, *we* did."

"I was only bluffing about a garden library," I burst out with excitement I've never felt. "I was only checking if you were listening to me. I didn't mean it."

Because, oh my God, am I in heaven?

One, I have never done an internal garden or library, simply because the corporate world doesn't like to mess around with the norms. Two, this is what I always wanted to do.

"Nothing's a bluff when it comes from you. If you think of it, I'll give it to you." Something shifts on his face. Gone is the professionalism as he steps towards me. "If you say the sun's too hot, I will fucking take it out of the sky and feed it to the sea. You say the word, and I can even serve myself. So, Bianca, there is no such thing as a bluff with you." His voice is deadly deep as he takes slow steps in my direction.

I'm unable to think, do or feel anything. My hands have dropped lifelessly by my sides, and my feet try to balance on a thin beam as his words hit me.

"What are you thinking?" Jason says when I don't, and I somehow get a sense of déjà vu from his words.

I look at this beautiful man, who shows the world nothing when he is everything.

"I'm thinking about how I should run away from you—to save you from me—and that I'm terrified." The words flow out of me, and I have no control over them. "But all I know is you, Jason Archer, are the man every girl dreams of," I say, my voice thick with emotions.

My stomach drops at the loss we have experienced. The moments we could've had but were stolen from us. The arms I could've had ripped away from me.

He clucks his tongue, stopping only a breath away. "Only *you*. You've run and hid enough, I know you have. And when you decide to stop hiding and running, a man who wants you is waiting for you. If you don't come to me, I'll smile knowing you are happy wherever you are…" He pauses as if saying the next words are extremely painful "…with whomever you are." An emotion I haven't seen in him flashes—longing, yet he masks it with great precision.

The string I've been holding on to for so long and so tightly snaps. Snaps like it was never there. I don't think when I take the last step between us and capture his lips in mine.

Everything bursts into a pop of colour.

Jason hums as our lips move in perfect rhythm, a silent dance of longing, waiting for the sweet reunion of a kiss. It's been five fucking years. Five long years.

The taste of this man is fucking torturing, yet soothing. Empty yet filling. It's all in one. I feel a harsh bite on my bottom lip, and soon a metallic taste spreads through our mouths, the sensation lingering for moments. Regardless, I open with a moan that echoes hauntingly within the refinements of the large office room.

I pull apart and scan the emotions on my beautiful man. "How dare you think I would be or ever was happy without you," I whisper. "I always wanted you."

Jason *smiles*. "Perfect," he growls, a sound so guttural and territorial. With swift movements of his tongue in my mouth, he claims the rest of me.

I don't have time to fight for dominance because there's nothing to fight for. Jason doesn't fight; he conquers.

That's exactly what he does to every inch of my mouth, leaving no area unmarked, like an animal to its mate. Mates who are bound to each other for the rest of their lifetime. *Timeless.*

The onslaught of emotions is nothing I've ever felt. It's softer with more need. More hunger. *More, more, more.*

Our tongues tangle, tasting each other and wanting to know each other better. Jason grabs my thighs and lifts me up. My legs wrap around his muscular waist, and my arms around his neck.

He rushes us to the wall and slams me against it as he keeps devouring my lips. I feel a rush of air escape me as his hard, rock-solid cock presses against me.

"Jason…" I moan, digging my hands into his hair. "Tell me we didn't do this last night." I breathe.

"No," he confirms, his hands kneading my thighs. Taking my lips again, his fingers breathtakingly slow skim over my inner thigh, inching closer to where I've been imagining him for so long. Heavy pants escape me as anticipation builds.

I haven't been touched in so long. My body hungers for his thick fingers on me, giving us both the pleasures that could remedy our need for each other.

We pull apart, our lips still lingering on each other as they refuse to breathe separately. His bright green eyes take me in as his thumb dusts my sex over my panties.

We inhale together as Jason's thumb feels my arousal. I am wet—and I want him.

You shouldn't want him. A shade of voice—I'm too damn gone to know—rebuts.

"Fucking hell," Jason curses under his breath as if he were dying for this moment. Then he puts me down. "Not here. Not like this. This time, I will take you the right way. Only if you are going to give it your all for *us.*" His gaze locks with mine for an answer.

I could jump on him and cry my heart out because there is no world I would say no to this man. Every fibre in me wants to have him, but I can't.

All my efforts will be in vain. I left to save Jason from who I am. He can't know what goes on in my head—especially when grief hasn't loosened its grip on me.

I just nod and step back. The cold glass wall hisses under my palm, also not agreeing with me. "Not yet. I'm sorry."

Hurt flashes on Jason's face, and he takes a step back. "I told you last night, and I'm telling you now. Never apologise when you have every right to choose for yourself."

A choice—his giving me a choice. Something that the universe never gave me. He understands me like no one else ever has, and even in this moment—when we want each other—he steps to the side, giving me a way to walk ahead. "I will always wait for you."

CHAPTER 23
Jason

"**I**s he here?" I demand. My voice bounces off the bland basement walls of Phoenix.

"Inside," Teal says with her posture straight and hands behind her. Her tight bun held back her dark hair, and the red leather of her uniform gave her a more lethal appearance.

In silence, I dropped Bianca at her house to deal with Kiara and the girls.

The sweetness of her lips still stains my own, and the euphoria I felt in that moment was nothing no one else could've given me.

I know I've fucked up a lot in my life, and there are many things I wish I should've done differently. And at the top of the list is our fight

at the airport five years ago. I should never have let her go. She was grieving, and so was I, only for two different things.

The stench of stale blood reaches my nostrils the moment I enter the basement. I usually let Kai or Adrian handle the bloody work, but when time calls for it, let's say, they hide away too.

The half-conscious man kneels, his wrists raw and bleeding from being hung by the barbed wire. His head drooped low, hiding his purple, bruised face.

My shoes click as they meet each step with the floor. The metallic walls amplify the sound, making the bastard flinch and jerk back.

"Van. Three years with Pyrosilk," Teal begins, her voice crisp.

I circle him, folding my sleeves, like a butcher with his knife would, measuring the meat before slicing it up.

"That's all the information we have so far. He has been chanting something to avoid his mouth spilling," Teal informs.

I turn to Teal. "I'll handle it now. You can leave," I direct.

Teal nods and, with practiced footwork, she leaves the room.

Last night, I recognised him as a Pyrosilk from his demented tattoo of the creature. The creature, a grotesque fusion of a chicken and dragon, with its small, sharp beak contrasting the immense dragon body, descended in a flurry of scales and feathers.

Slapping on gloves, I stride towards the man. "Van." I grasp his sweaty hair tightly, pulling his head back to expose his face to the bright spotlight. The evidence of my punches is bruising well.

"Fuck. Off." He grits through his bloodied teeth.

"Now, now. That's not very nice." My fingers tighten in his hair, the roots screaming in protest as I threaten to rip them from his scalp.

"Look, I want to have a friendly chat. Man to man," I calmly say.

"I wish for no sort," he sneers with a heavy Italian accent.

"Wishes are not my specialty, rather, ruining them is. You messed with the wrong people, Van. We're not gods but devils with the face of gods." I drop his head back against the wall, and it hits with a loud thud.

His cold brown pupils don't lose their fire. He bares his teeth and clenches his hung fists in retaliation. It takes everything in me not to murder the bastard on the spot.

"So, this is how it will go. I ask a question, and you answer. If you don't…"

I walk towards the table, feeling satisfied with the glint of steel from the knives, guns, and iron rods as they catch the light. My hand reaches for the Modern Bowie, the familiar wood of the handle feeling cold and strong against my skin.

Knives were always my pick. The feeling of it slicing mercilessly through skin had always been a sensation I preferred over guns. No emotion comes from guns, when the shot is gone, it's gone. Nothing. But knives are different—*lethal.*

"This here really likes the taste of the blood of overconfident fools." The small knife twirls in my hand, and it too winks with anticipation. "You seem to have plenty of it. Overconfidence and blood," I say, my eyes not missing a beat from him. With slow and controlled movements, I pull on my gloves and drag a chair in front of him. The legs of the chair let out a high-pitched shriek off the cold metal walls, a chilling sound to the bone.

My words, calm and collected, are a stark contrast to the furious fire within as I replay the image of his hand, calloused and rough, gripping Bianca's thighs.

The blade shines under the limited light, showcasing its sharp edges, holding no delicate promises.

"No answer, one finger. No rocket science." Sitting on the chair behind me, I grip his fleshless, bony hand, its coldness seeps into my own. The *same* hand that had been where it shouldn't have been.

Leveling the blade to the knuckle of his index finger, I stare into his eyes once again. "It's no coincidence you're a Pyrosilk and laid your filthy hands on her. What do you want?"

I get no response except the silent movement of his lips. The blade sinks into his flesh, meeting with slight resistance before touching bone; a thin layer of skin was all that separated the two.

Blood spatters from his fingers, and I can feel the warmth of the thick liquid coating my gloves. It's only the beginning.

"What do you fucking want?" I roar in his face.

This time, the blade tears through the bone with a sickening crunch, the metallic tang of blood filling my nostrils as patience leaves me.

The useless piece of bone and flesh drops to the ground with a sickening thud.

"I will not repeat." I silently rage, leveling the knife at the second finger.

He wheezes, grasping for anything he can. His hands shake violently, a tremor that mirrors the turmoil in his body grappled with the crushing weight of his loss. "I want nothing." He speaks, and I stop moving. "They assigned the task to me."

"What task?" I ask, applying more pressure on the finger.

"They … Argh …" He winces in pain. "They are coming. For you. *All of you.*" He smirks knowingly.

"Who assigned you?" I growl.

Silence again. The blade digs deeper and deeper, moving like a saw on a wooden plank, until the finger dangles from a thin string of flesh.

I twist the hanging finger, earning me another deafening wail. The volcano of my anger simmers for an eruption.

His other hand moulds into a fist, trying to soak in the pain. The knife works on the next finger, repeating the same slow procedure.

"Boss …" He pants with heavy breaths. "Boss wants her," he blurts. His face scrunches in agony when I rip the finger from its hinges, allowing the initial rush of blood to drip onto the floor.

"Name," I demand.

"We don't know." He struggles to breathe, his chest rapidly rising and falling, while drool trickles from his mouth and mingles with the thick blood beneath him.

I don't wait for another answer and snap out his middle finger. My patience is leaving me with every passing second.

"We don't know. We never see him!" Van screams, deafening my ears.

I let the dam of his blood stain my gloves. It's no less than a trophy.

This proves one thing. Pyrosilk exists, but more importantly, with clear attention for an attack after years of passive threats.

"Why Phoenix?" I stand up from the chair to my full height and see him from my nose.

He cranes his head up and observes with bewilderment. "You're first to shake their ground. Now they want to remove yours."

I get on my haunches and have his eyes watch my every move. "If they want power—they have enough."

Van smiles and drops his head. He laughs, with a violent shake of his shoulders. "Fools, all of you. They don't care about power anymore. They want all four of you and what you have taken. The loved ones will come first—ruin them and let you watch." He smirks.

My grip tightens on the blade, and with a sudden, brutal movement, I plunge it into his thigh, eliciting a painful wail for life. Puncturing the same thigh, he laid his filthy hand on.

"They will see their lives burn in the fire we will set," I say, my eyes daring to come out of their sockets as I widen them.

The blade seers through the thick flesh on his thigh, and I twist it, gathering everything inside in one mess.

"It was nice meeting you, Van." I smile hauntingly and leave the bastard in a bloody mess.

He yells and screams, shivering like a fish out of the water as he pulls on the barbed wire. His efforts are causing him more harm than any good as with each pull, the wire digs into his wrists enough to ooze blood but nothing fatal. *For now.*

"Oh, also Van." I look over my shoulder. "Think twice before coming near my woman again. Never become a target of an archer. Our aim never misses."

The door slams behind me, not giving another look to see the bloodied snarl on his lips.

"Clean it up," I instruct Teal, waiting by the door.

With a subtle nod, she turns towards the room.

"Teal." I stop her, fixing my blazer buttons, then my cufflinks.

She pauses and nods again while listening.

"Get me everything on Aaron Blackburn."

"Not the best day?" Kai asks as soon as I sit at the society's bar. The low hanging lights highlight the maroon-coloured walls and dark bar counters.

Bartenders and their workstations take up half of the space, accompanied by the sound of distant conversations and utensils mixing cocktails.

I point my finger up at Cheryl. "The usual," I order.

"Coming right up!" she chirps as she gives me a wink and moves to make my whisky.

"What gave it away?" I huff, staring at the dark-toned table.

"Your aging face, or maybe the murderous look on it." Kai points at my face. A low melody plays from Kai's phone, and he groans. "Fuck off, will you?" He drags his hand down his face.

"Let me guess, that's *your aging* relationships, or lack thereof," I say, pointing at his phone that keeps vibrating.

"The latter." He rolls his eyes. "I would rather have a relationship with a snake than a clingy woman. I make it super clear when we get into this. Sex and nothing more. But here I am shooing them away because they want me at their feet and tattooing their names on my heart." He drains his glass, and it immediately gets filled by Tim behind the counter.

"All I'll say is wear the shoe that fits."

"So, you mean two women at once?" he genuinely asks.

"No." I drop my head back, exhausted. "Stop running around the truth. You know who you are, and a playboy you're not."

Kai mocks a gasp and holds his phone. "Give me one second. I'm just going to call Williams Media about the news. My friend has gone all lovey- dovey, it's making me cry. I'm a proud mama bear." He wipes away an imaginary tear from his cheek.

"Fuck off."

Kai snickers and leans back on his bar stool. His deep laugh has some eyes straying to us. His dark blue eyes glisten with tears. Kai Jeffords or drama queen, I would never know.

I watch the bartenders work busily around the place as they serve the members with their drinks. *Are any of them part of Pyrosilk?*

I shake my head at the thought. They're screened thoroughly before being offered the job, not to mention an oath of secrecy.

"Do we know anything about the Pyrosilk leader?" I ask, crossing my legs and holding my hands in my lap.

Kai drops the comic, his expression serious as he turns back to me.

"Nothing at all. I thought they were a myth until the puzzle appeared. Is he a Pyro?" Kai points over his shoulders. Leaning on the table, he takes a sip of his bourbon.

Cheryl comes with my drink and slides it over. "Thank you," I say, holding my glass to her.

She nods, and her bright pink hair glows from all the bottles behind her. "Anytime, Jason."

With the first sip, the whisky sends a fiery sensation down my throat.

"Hmm." I nod, savouring the bitter and sweet taste in my mouth. "But he doesn't know their *Boss*."

Kai raises an eyebrow and considers the thought. "That's interesting. Pyrosilk has been operating for decades, and you're telling me that nobody knows who is in charge?"

"We have two things from them now. The puzzle and Van. But do they truly mean anything?"

"They could be treasures or distractions." Kai swirls the liquid in the glass.

We have been attempting to investigate their society since they landed their first hit on us when we started but came back with nothing.

"Guess we will find out when we have the last piece of the puzzle," I say.

"That we will." He nods thoughtfully.

Kai's phone rings again with a different ringtone. A little deeper and tenser than the other. He flinches and looks at me. He huffs and clicks the big red button. "Piss off."

We stay silent, drinking and thinking.

"So ..." Kai turns towards me, and continues, "Is he the same guy from last night?"

"Hmm." I nod, not facing him.

"The same guy who touched Bianca?" Kai asks.

"Kai." I caution him, sensing a mischievous glint in his dimpled smile.

"The same guy who made you lose your calm and choose punches?" He still opens his mouth.

"Shut up and quit it," I grit.

He shows me a smug smile, all-knowing. "So, you partly did all this for Bianca?"

"Stop playing matchmaker."

His eyebrows pump up. "We have a match to make?" he asks, poking my arm.

"I just took three fingers, don't make yours fourth," I say, gripping my glass.

He pokes me again.

I let out a sharp breath and angrily slam my glass on the table. I open my mouth to tell him to fuck off, but he lifts his finger, silencing me.

"Did you talk to her about your feelings?" Kai drops his smile and frowns in seriousness.

In more than one way.

"Why should I tell you?" My anger is now far gone, replaced by … dread.

"Oh great, I'm back in grade one again." He rolls his eyes as he throws his hands in the air. "Come on, Jason. I asked you at least to talk to Bianca. She needs to know what's going on inside of you, and so do you, about her," he convinces.

"We did. We talked and things are…" I trail off, not sure how to put it.

"Things are?" Kai encourages.

"Complicated."

"At least not untouched. Progress."

We share a moment of understanding as we sip our drinks, our minds racing.

When we're growing up, our parents say wait until you grow up to live in the world, but how can we truly live when deception and cunningness fill the world? Knowing that behind every smiling face could be another monster waiting to attack.

"I think we should tell the girls about Phoenix." Kai breaks the silence.

My glass hangs midway to my lips.

"Things are in a whirlwind, and it won't take long until they get caught up in it. You know it. Now they aimed at Bianca, anyone could be next," Kai elaborates.

"We should," I agree.

They don't need to know everything, but all things that would keep them safe.

Kai holds his glass up in a toast. "To saving our asses."

"To saving." I raise my glass.

Kai's phone rings again. The tone changed *again*. A chirpy sound with bells.

"Oh, will they leave me alone!" With a frustrated sigh, he closes his eyes and rakes his fingers through his messy, dirty blond hair.

Only wear the shoe that fits.

CHAPTER 24
Bianca

As soon as I entered through the front doors, I got tackled by Eva and Kiara, who then pushed me down onto the sofa. They hover over me, looking at me with squinted eyes.

"Is the flashlight really necessary?" I block the light coming from Eva's phone, blinding me. I glance over and see Sage sitting comfortably with legs crossed on the opposite sofa. She's in her training clothes, while Kiara is wearing her shooting suit. Eva has changed into her denim overalls with hair up in a messy bun.

"Who is he?" Eva asks, her brows furrowed.

"Huh?" I open my mouth in question.

"Don't play dumb with me, miss. You know who I'm talking about.

Rolex—who is he?" Eva points at my chest. "Didn't you leave with Jason last night?"

I hear my heart thundering in my chest and echoing in my ears. Fuck, Eva can't know—*yet*.

I look around for anything I could say. "I did but…" *Think. Think*— "He dropped me off, and I needed more, so I went down to the local bar down the road."

Fuck. Fuck. Fuck. This isn't going great.

Eva looks at me from the corner of her eyes, unconvinced.

"Oh, babe. Calm down, let me ask nicely." Kaira proudly places a hand on Eva's shoulder. "Who was he, honey?" Her eyes are wide and hungry for gossip.

"That's not nice. It's creepy," Sage says from her spot, her arms crossed over her chest.

"Agreed." I point at Sage.

"Answer the question," Eva snaps.

"Just a random hookup," I lie. *What?*

They look at me blankly. "You don't do random hookups," all three of them say together.

"Things have changed, and I needed to forget what happened. Don't you remember?" I stare at Eva, who is trying her best not to smile. "And you were nowhere to be seen." I look at Kiara. "Both too drunk and lost to pay attention."

Fuck. What the hell am I?

Oh! Oh! Let me guess… Red snickers. *A dirty, dirty liar. How close was I?*

"I was there." Sage smirks, her eyebrow raises in a challenge. "And definitely wasn't drunk."

"Nothing memorable to remember, anyway. *Right, Sage,*" I stress her name.

"Definitely." She slowly shakes her head.

"Back here," Kiara remarks, grabbing my chin, dark eyes pinning me. "So, just a hookup?"

"Correct." I nod sharply. "Just a hookup."

"Liar," Sage coughs into her hand.

I shoot her my best '*I will see you later*' look.

"Okay. Enough of the good cop, bad cop. I need water." I push them and make my way to the kitchen. My vision is a little spotty from the flashlight.

"I knew I should've played the bad cop properly. You're taking the role next time," Eva says to Kiara as they both drop onto the sofa, snapping her fingers.

"That's enough about me. How are you still awake? I thought I wasn't going to see you today. Guess he wasn't worth … *it*," I mock as I point down.

Kiara rolls her eyes and hugs a cushion. "He was fine, nothing out of the ordinary. Been there and done that. He had the dick, but in his head and not between his legs." She nonchalantly shrugs her shoulders. "I've wiped him off my list."

I can't imagine sleeping with someone I don't have a connection with. Despite being twisted, I couldn't help but feel drawn to Aaron even if we never crossed first base, and it fills me with so much resentment in hindsight.

Cliché as it sounds, sex is something you share with someone—a part of yourself. Every kiss, every touch, represents your emotions to the other person.

Maybe Jason and I share the emotions, even if they hide in the fog's thickness, and maybe I want it to be more. His presence in my life made me reevaluate my past relationship, making me wonder if I had ever genuinely connected with Aaron or if it was my loneliness speaking.

Kiara doesn't need to know that. She's a woman of her own type and happy with herself. I couldn't ask for more. Living comfortably in one's own skin is the greatest blessing of being human, and some live without knowing the fact. Someone like me, who took every word to heart, that put me in a mould *he* wanted to see me as.

"There is something more. Drumroll, ladies and ladies…" Eva stands and spreads her arms. She claps her hands and waits for us to find any surface for a drum roll. Me on the kitchen counter, Sage and Kiara on the coffee table. The drumming reverberates through the room as Eva carefully pulls out three cards.

"The show's invitations are out!" she sings opera style and flaps the cards overhead.

"No fucking way!"

"Oh, my God!"

With a burst of excitement, Kiara and Sage leap out of their seats and embrace Eva, one on each side of her neck.

Running towards them, I halt in my track to marvel at the unique sight of all three of my friends gathered in one place. My eyes had begged the universe to give me this. And it did. My heart trembles with emotion, on the brink of releasing tears of overwhelming joy and satisfaction.

"Come you. Are you going to stay apart from this as well? Hell no!" Kiara says, breaking apart from Sage, allowing room for me to fit in the middle, extending their arms in invitation.

I wipe away a single tear and feel the anvil lift off my chest. I run towards them and crash into their arms. "Congratulations." My voice breaks as they hug me back.

"Thank you," Eva sobs.

Breaking apart, we can't help but sniffle lightly. Except Sage, who just smiles.

"When is it?" Kiara asks, taking the invitation.

"The official purchasing will begin next month, but the collection will be on the ramp in two weeks!" Eva's face lights up with excitement as she proudly announces.

When we went to her boutique earlier, I tried to sneak a peek at the designs, but she insisted on keeping them as a *"surprise."*

"Finally, we can see them." Sage speaks up with a glint in her eyes.

"For sure you will, and I'll have tissues on the go." Eva beams through her tears.

"I'm so fucking happy for you!" Kiara yells as she jumps back onto Eva and nearly chokes the living daylights out of our friend.

"You know, this extra hugging won't get you a free ticket to an early," Eva says, pointing to the back of Kiara's head and giggles.

"I'm sure it will because you love me so much." Kiara chuckles and swings them in the hug.

"That I do. *Sadly*," Eva whispers the last part.

Kiara lightly punches her in the back.

"Who's up for a milkshake and the *Vampire's Bite* re-run?" I hold up the milk I brought and the TV remote.

"Who are we to say no?" Eva grins, snatching the TV remote from me.

"Matthew James is the man to chase." Kiara smiles with her hand under chin.

"Give me a break. Porter Lee is the one." Eva rolls her eyes as she sucks on her straw.

We are an hour into our re-run, and they're officially fired up with no water to cool them down.

Sage and I sit on the middle couch, while Kiara and Eva sit on single sofas on either side of us. The only light in the room comes from the TV, bright on our faces.

"He has the best eyes," Kiara argues.

"He has perfect hair," Eva fires back.

"How do we stop them?" I whisper in Sage's ear, her impassive eyes watching the scene of the handsome vampire drinking the blood of his love interest while they have sex, and the other vampire watches them.

She leans in, her fresh, velvety scent surrounds me. "We don't. Let them burn it off and stay away. Otherwise, you'll become collateral damage. Speaking from experience," Sage replies.

"But they will rip each other's heads off," I worry.

"Let them." Sage shrugs and digs into the popcorn bucket.

"How can you be so unaffected?" I ask, fascinated by her patience.

"Their arguments only last around a minute and then we're back to normal." Sage lifts her watch up and holds five fingers. "If you want a demo. Five…"

I look between the two fighting wildcats, still firing back arguments.

"Four…"

Still no change.

"Three…" Sage sips of her drink. "Two…"

Eva is ready to get off her sofa and attack. Kiara is holding on dearly to the armrests.

"I should stop th—"

"One." As soon as Sage says the number, Kiara and Eva relax on the sofa back to watching the TV.

Silence, except for the sounds of the episode.

"Matthew's eyes *are* gorgeous," Eva says with a shrug.

"Porter's hair seems soft." Kiara munches on her popcorn.

"The condition is called Feral Cat Syndrome," Sage explains as she turns towards me.

"It's when the client has a raging fit for approximately two minutes and then relaxes." Sage points between our two friends. "We have documented only two cases so far. One of Kiara Kozlova and Evalyn Archer. They're very rare," she says in a professional tone befitting a psychologist.

I laugh out loud, tipping my head to the ceiling. *This is unreal.*

"What's so funny? Becky just died!" Kiara cries, giving me a disgusted look.

I laugh harder. *How do I know these people?*

My phone vibrates with a text as I come down from my high, and any remaining laughter I had dies a slow death from the name on my screen.

Jason: *This is my number*

Jason: *If you didn't already know*

Electricity pulses through me from the two texts. Tingles, zaps, itches. I'm feeling all of it. He texted me, and he's *nervous.*

Bianca: *The ambulance is on its way*

The reply is almost immediate when the three dots appear and the text pops up.

Jason: *???*

Bianca: *Jason Archer is nervous and forgot I always had his number*

The last part is a slipup, but I let it happen.

Jason: *Like I did yours*

I sit stunned, looking at the message.
He replies again.

Jason: *What are you doing?*

Lost for words, I send him a picture of the four of us watching the TV.

Bianca: You?

He sends a picture of a signal tower he is standing under.

Jason: Approving another connection

*Bianca: Oh, so fun! *Star-eyed emoji**

I giggle to myself, and hold the phone close to me, stopping Sage from stealing a glance. Then she leans on me, whispering, "Tell Jay I said hi."

My head snaps to her with wide eyes. "It's not him."

"Sure isn't." Her smile tells something else. "I will remember your secret but will never speak of it." She zips her lips with her fingers. "Rest assured."

I smile at my childhood friend. "It's not him," I repeat weakly.

My phone vibrates in my hand.

Jason: I missed you.

Then he goes offline.

CHAPTER 25
Jason

"Jason?" Bianca's voice bounces in my sleeping mind.

I haven't seen her in three days.

Three days since I'd admitted something I hadn't dared to admit to myself.

Meetings and revisions of our company's policy to accommodate more connections and strengthen existing ones overwhelmed my schedule. It was a surprise I even had time to sleep.

"Jason!" The voice sounds more assertive and comes with a push on my shoulders.

"Jason, wake up. What's wrong with him?" Eva's voice murmurs.

"I don't know. Let's try the water on the side table—that'll wake up

any troll," Kiara's recognisable squeak answers.

"Let him live, seriously, he works more than any of us," Sage speaks.

It's one thing to hear Bianca and another to hear the others.

"No. Once is fine, but twice after noon. Something must be wrong," Kiara says.

Shit.

I snap my eyes open and take the covers off. Instead of seeing the white ceiling of my room, I see four surprised faces.

"What the fuck are you doing here again?" I mumble, shooing them away.

I lean against the headboard of my bed and close my eyes. *Fuck me.* Exhausted doesn't come close to describing the ache in my head. But all I was thinking about before falling asleep were two blue pearls watching me with the same curiosity as I was them.

"Again?" Bianca questions.

"Uh—huh. Jason has made it a bit of a routine to wake past his wakey wakey time," Kiara answers.

I open my eyes and see her moving her index finger from side to side, disappointed.

"Oh, I wonder why. What keeps you up at night, Jay?" Bianca says, with a light smirk on her lips.

What did she have for breakfast? Attack mode already.

For goodness' sake, I just woke up. Her saying my name shouldn't make me hard.

"I'm sure you know why," I reply, not trying to hide my hint. *Because you're the reason I sleep peacefully.* It's not a matter of sleeping late; it's a matter of sleeping. Full stop. Ever since she came back, I slept. I don't know what to make of it when I couldn't find even two hours of rest in the past five years.

Kiara scoffs and squints her eyes. "How would Bianca know what your ass is up to?" she fires.

The two oblivious girls and Sage look between Bianca and me.

"Do you?" Sage asks me with a raise of her eyebrows, all-knowing.

"You do, don't you?" I say with my eyes hard on Bianca.

"I do." She clears her throat. "I have *come* to know you very well and your workaholic tendencies. Yeah, *Jay?*" I don't miss the way her bottom lip rolls and she bites on it to hide her smile.

I lift my brows in challenge. *Don't play with fire you can't quieten, Rainbow.* "Yes, working for *someone* very important," I reply. "International client," I quickly add as the other three stare.

"Cover it up, princess," Eva says, and slaps me with a shirt on my bare chest.

"Good to hear the CEO works well with his people and doesn't *miss* anything. Like I *did*." Bianca nods as soft eyes hold mine, conveying words I want to hear.

I close my eyes and just pull the shirt over my head. Giving myself a minute to recover from what she truly means. I can read her like an open book, yet I've stopped on page one because I already know her, and no words can convey anything more.

"If you aren't aware, there's a phenomenon called privacy," I say, directing to the others.

All four of them clap hands over their mouths, a collective gasp silencing the room.

"Did you hear what I heard?" Sage says.

"I think I did. My ears are ringing for sure, or maybe I'm in a parallel universe where *he* can be sarcastic." Kiara points at me.

They come together in a circle like players before their game. "He has to be hungover," Eva mumbles quietly in the circle they've made.

"You guys know *he* is right here," I mutter, but they don't spare me a glance.

All four look up and give me a serious look, then they return to mumbling in their circle.

They can't be for real. "I'm still here." I squint my eyes.

"He did it once. Be sarcastic, I mean. I thought I didn't hear right, but no." Bianca widens her eyes as she cups the side of her face. "The myth was true after all."

"Wait, was this before or after the blazer?" Eva asks. I can feel the mock seriousness on her face, even though their backs are to me.

"What blazer?" Kiara's curious glance comes to me over their shoulders.

"Get out before I kick you out myself," I warn, getting up and making my way to the bathroom.

"Leave my sensitive princess alone," Eva coos.

Visible shivers run down their backs, and they retreat their steps. Compared to the others, Bianca is the least afraid, her eyes locking with mine as I look at her.

She's in a sunrise-coloured professional suit and skirt. A mix of orange and pink dance together on the material—not like her usual single-colour outfits.

"Oscar's downstairs," Bianca says. She gives me a small smile as she walks out with the rest following her. "To discuss some things."

But I want to talk to you.

The morning air is unusually still and quiet today, despite the bizarre sight of the sun glowing on a winter day. And even more unusual is the calm I feel deep inside me. It would have nothing to do with Bianca sitting in front of me as she concentrates on the plan, biting the end of her pencil in concentration.

Oscar arrived without the usual smile on his face to tell me the reception floor's construction was underway, and the first floor would start next week. While that's interesting, I just want to punch Oscar and send him on his way. For the last hour, my PA has been relentlessly discussing work, his words grating on my nerves, and his proximity to Bianca is making my blood boil.

Leaning closer, he points out a plant that could be moved to another corner of the office, where it will get direct sunlight. One more inch, and I'll move *him* to the most remote, godforsaken corner of the planet.

How hard can it be to survive without an assistant? Maybe it's time I knew.

"I think I would like to have a look," I blurt. My stern voice fills the air pockets in the wide living room.

They jump out of their seats, eyes wide, and their throats bob as they swallow nervously. As if the earth shook from underneath him, Oscar's hand lands on Bianca's thigh.

That's. It.

"Bianca, come here," I growl. Breathing becomes a bloody effort when all I see is red.

"Sure." Bianca raises an eyebrow, straightening her skirt and making her way to me.

Oscar fixes the glasses on his nose and digs into the tablet on his lap.

"Bianca! Oh my, what a surprise!" Mum's voice booms from the doorway.

Bianca stops and looks at Mum jogging towards us in her gardening clothes, with a little dirt smeared on her face. Whenever she has the time, she comes to tame my garden. Not because she must but wants, and if it makes her happy, then so be it.

"Cath, it's so good to see you," Bianca cries as she meets Mum halfway for a hug.

"Feels like I haven't seen you in five years." Mum chuckles, wiping away a stray tear.

"You haven't." Bianca laughs a little. She clears her throat as if coaxing it to give her the best voice for the conversation. "But let me assure you, you are aging like the finest wine." Bianca pulls away and looks at Mum from toe to head.

"Rosé if we're serving any. I hear it keeps the heart young, and frankly, that's all we need sometimes." Mum smiles, her green eyes shining with a renewed sense of brightness today.

They share a silent moment. To the outside eye, it looks like a platonic break in a conversation, but somehow, I feel the weight of the words they're exchanging without them being said.

"I think I'm going to steal you," Mum says after some time. "Maybe I can use a hand in garden design." My extra cheerful mother links their arms and makes their way out to the back garden.

Okay. Just leave and ignore I ever existed. Fuck, when did I become so fucking needy? But I am many things I'm not when it comes to this blue-eyed sorceress.

As if hearing my thoughts, Bianca turns around and just softly looks over her shoulder, saying *I missed her.*

If I learned anything from the other night, Bianca doesn't need everyone and everything around her. What she truly needs is the unwavering support of her people, a comforting presence that will follow her across any distance, a shield against the storms of life, no matter how far she travels.

I'll be part of the crowd to cheer her on and be there when she's taking on her demons while I keep mine at bay.

Bianca

"How's Canberra treating you?" Catherine asks as we enter the gardens, well more like a forest.

Bright red, yellow, and orange tulips line the edges of the stone pathway, a vibrant contrast to the carefully manicured bushes overflowing with a riot of colourful blooms. They seem to make a figure when put together, and if I have to guess, it will have to do something with Jason's love for birds.

Oh, and let's not forget the eucalyptus and palm trees. I don't know where and how he pulled those off and brought them into the city.

"Fine—a place where I live." I shrug, kicking a stone in my way.

"Doesn't feel like home?"

I look around and spread my arms. "This place here never truly left me—a part of me wasn't able to leave." I smile as I breathe through my nose when Cath takes my hand.

"I know," Cath whispers. She gives my hand a few squeezes before stopping us so we can face each other. "Bianca, can I tell you something?" she asks carefully.

I nod, looking at her, confused.

"You remind me a lot of your mother." Her earlier radiant smile flattens for a second and then bounces up.

I take a deep breath, dreading the conversation already. Cath continues, "She had the same brown hair, but her curls, oh God, her curls. They were a battlefield."

Our light chuckles fill the air.

"The same blue eyes and the same habit of holding on to something when in pain." Her gaze follows my pale knuckles, bone-white and lightly trembling, as they grip Ma's smooth beaded bracelet.

"Lina had this but never wore it." Cath runs her skinny fingers over the beads. "Always said the love of her life gave it to her, and never asked for anything in return," Cath tells me softly. "She kept it close to her, so she could give it to you on your sixteenth."

Love the truest. The engraved words were everything that forced me to get up every day and pursue a life she would've wanted for me. A life that proved I was worthy of being her daughter.

"I guess I am my mother's daughter," I quietly say as my chest cracks in half.

"You are," Cath agrees, and we keep walking ahead hand in hand.

We're enveloped by the calm chirps of the birds and the gentle breeze sighing through the branches. There is nothing I would change at this moment.

"Do you remember Lina's baking?" Cath interrupts in the stillness.

Ma's baking was legendary. The sight of her warm, freshly baked goods alone would make anyone who knew her dive headfirst. She was world-class famous in our small families. Her warm cookies were a handful, each one slightly crisp on the edges with a soft, chewy centre, and they were everything everyone wanted. Surprisingly, Sage sprouted a pair of horns and became incredibly feisty.

My favourite was the sun-kissed muffins with the plump blueberries nestled inside. As I think of them, I murmur, "I can practically taste the sweet blueberries."

"I loved the strawberry cake. Wish I had the magic in me." Cath chuckles. "Jason and Kai always dropped their controllers then and there, Brandon and Oliver abandoned their tools for God knows what they needed them for, and you girls away from Lucy. It was such a simple thing that we all came together for."

A strained smile stretches across our faces as we recall the memory, and our shoulders shake with a silent, but bitter laugh.

"If we came together in the good times, we were there for the bad. One call of distress and we're all yours." Cath turns to me with a softness I've always known her for. "We know what Steven and you have been and are going through isn't easy but let us in when you need it." She holds my hand and takes me to a bench underneath a large eucalyptus tree.

Each word, like a drop of rain in a still pond, creates ripples in the pool of emotions that swells inside me. I'm at the breaking point, another word from Cath, and I'll be baring my soul.

"Cath." I breathe. The smooth, carved wood feels warm and supportive beneath me. Yet all I can do is hold on to the edge and let a tear drop from my nose. "Sometimes calling out to others doesn't help. By this time, five years afterwards, I should be over everything, but I'm still holding on to old emotions—the grief. It's … hard."

"There's no time for grief. It's not too long or short. It just is." She simply offers me a smile. "It comes without invitation and makes a permanent house in you. Stella and I lost our mother when we were your age, and I still crave my mother's softness, and I bet Stella has her own wounds. But listen, you know we love you, and that's secret code for you're stuck with us."

She looks ahead at the gardeners doing their tasks. "Love grows the more you share, and pain lessens," Cath says, a small break in her voice giving her away. "It's a choice you need to make."

With the onslaught of emotions, I dive in for a hug, breathing in her comforting, homey scent. "I love you."

"I love you, my Bee," she says, running her hand over my hair.

We pull apart and stare ahead into the garden. There are workers maintaining the shrubs, and some are trimming the high trees while others are mowing the lawns.

They're all wearing the same uniform of dark blue polo shirts and white shorts with steel-capped shoes. A stitched golden bow and arrow logo complements the dark blue base of the shirt.

A worker near us is using tweezers to work on the lavender bush and prunes off a portion.

"Mind the hems, Gary!" Catharine commands, swiftly issuing further orders that Gary follows without question.

Cath wears a cream button shirt and long black pants, and she keeps her long grey hair well-groomed, reaching the length of her back. Her mastery of the garden and her work with the workers are admirable.

The sound of their work banter is light from where I sit. My mind's garden grows richer with each day's new perspective. Today, I just felt that I am not alone for the first time in a long time.

You always had them, Red reassures.

I didn't know you had a soft side, I think.

We all do. Some more, some less. Her words bounce in my head.

I stare at the sky and thank the universe for giving me everyone I know.

The connection between my parents and the Archers began with Eva and my friendship, but it quickly developed into something far more profound and inexpressible. Through thick and thin, they had each other's unwavering support, sharing in both happiness and hardship.

Unlike our extroverted selves, Sage and Kiara's family valued their privacy and the peace of their home above all else, rarely coming to anything we organised. They had their own busy lives, but always made time for Sage and Kiara, letting them come along. Although I met Sage's parents often in the city, I had encountered Kiara's mum and her younger sister once on her eighteenth birthday. Her father has always been an enigma. Kiara never really talked about him.

My phone vibrates against my thigh, a low hum that feels like a trapped bee, and I half expect a text from Jason telling me to come inside, but it's far worse.

> **Unknown:** *Piece 1 completed. Put the USB in your letterbox. It will be taken good care of*

My throat constricts as I swallow hard past the lump forming in my throat, with sweat prickling on my forehead. Dread washes all over me. I don't know why he asked for the USB specifically, but I know it won't be for anything good.

> **Bianca:** *Not until you do your part of the deal*

> **Unknown:** *That's my girl on the point*

> **Unknown:** *Check your letterbox after you give me what I need. Good things are waiting. Tick Tock*

CHAPTER 26
Bianca

"Bee, are you okay?" Cath pats my shoulder. I didn't see when she came back from her lecture about gardening to sit next to me on the bench.

"Yeah … yeah, I'm fine," I stutter. I plaster on my most convincing smile, hoping it will work as a cover for what I've done and will do.

There will be nothing protecting them after I give Aaron everything, and every fibre in my body is pulling me back from doing anything for Aaron. But this is my one chance to escape the memories that haunt me, to be truly free from the past's suffocating grip.

Yet deep inside, I feel the weight of their unconditional love and trust slipping away, a silent betrayal that echoes in my soul.

Then don't go ahead with it. White speaks up now, and I'm considering it.

No! We went through so much and can't let it slip out of our hands when we're so close. Remember your parents. Would they want you to give up? Red Horns battles.

"Cath?" I mumble.

"Yes, Bee," she cheerfully replies.

"If someone causes pain to those they care about, even unintentionally, or gains something for themselves, is it wrong?" I ask, bouncing my feet impatiently.

Cath's movements and swinging of her legs pause. She may not ask for the details, but I can trust her to answer truthfully.

After a minute of thinking and brow creases, she speaks. "All depends on their intention. One saying has guided my whole life: the consequences of your actions are a direct reflection of your intentions. Good intentions open heaven's door, and bad intentions are the devil's calling." She nods to herself.

We remain silent as we watch straight ahead at nothing specifically.

"But sometimes we find the middle ground, and that's when things get tricky," she says. "At times, we do things for ourselves, and there's nothing wrong with that, too. Only if it doesn't risk everything you've built with others, most importantly yourself."

I nod, digesting her words.

"I don't know why you're asking, but remember, no matter how challenging things seem, there's always a path to overcome them. Don't give up hope."

Cath places a soft hand over my fingers and interlaces them on the bench.

There's a stretched second of silence before Cath gets up, smoothing the non-existent wrinkles on her pants. "I'll get going now. It's not an easy duty to handle Brandon Archer." She places a sweet kiss on my cheek and rushes inside.

I look up at the sky, and it's the clearest I've seen, especially after the week of rain we had. The clouds have parted, revealing a brilliant blue sky sparkling with the morning sun, and the mental fog in my mind seems to have lifted as well.

My phone rings again, a shrill, jarring sound that sends a shiver of dread down my spine. But I can't believe my eyes when I see the text.

> **Steven:** *How's my favourite sister doing?*

I nearly tear up from the message and drop my phone. Weeks have passed since I last spoke with Steven, yet every call or text from him sends a flutter of excitement through me.

> **Bianca:** *I'm your only sister*

> **Steven:** *Favourite in all ways*

> **Bianca:** *Don't you have people to order around?*

> **Steven:** *I do. Thought of you, it's been a long time*

The fresh air fills my chest with a wave of contentment as I reply.

> **Bianca:** *I'm fine. It's good to see the others after so long. Nothing has changed, yet everything has. You should visit sometime*

He's always swamped with work and has so little free time that even a pleasure trip is out of the question.

> **Steven:** *Things are picking up at this time of the year. I'll try to make time. Maybe to pick you up*

> **Bianca:** *Where's my brother? How much money do you want? *Raised eyebrow emoji**

> **Steven:** *Ha. Ha. Hilarious. I can make time*
> *for you*

Hope blossoms in my chest. I stare at the screen, feeling nothing—or a lot at the same time.

> **Bianca:** *If that's the case, then I'm waiting.*
> *Love you, Stevy*

> **Steven:** *I thought you forgot about that*
> *name!*

> **Bianca:** *Always my Stevy *Kissing emoji**

> **Steven:** *Bianca!*

If one thing could put fire under his ass, it's that nickname. Our aunt gave Steven his name as her fingers tugged playfully, but a little painfully, at his chubby cheeks. When she left, her pinching made his cheeks double their size.

We only have memories to live off now, but hope is a thing that gives way to making fresh memories, even if it's in our head.

Steven would do anything to keep everyone safe around him, and I would too. It's my turn to take back what we all deserve.

Peace.

Jason

"There is something else you should know," Oscar says as he taps his pen on the tablet.

We're still in the living room, and Oscar has finished reading out my schedule for the day. Back-to-back meetings fill my schedule until late, not to mention anything with Phoenix.

The hairs on my neck stand at attention at his worried tone. I've never seen Oscar flustered, but the sweat beading on his straight brow is shocking. I nod, leaning back in my seat.

"There has been a breach of the safe." He lowers his eyes behind his glasses.

Silence.

"The safe in the files room?" I ask.

"Yes." He nods.

"Was the USB compromised?"

"Yes."

"When?"

"Around five days now. The security team went for their weekly check and found it empty, and ever since we've been working on it," Oscar informs. "You were busy with the business, so we thought we could locate it in time, but unfortunately we couldn't."

The USB has every detail on Phoenix and … fuck. If they get it, we're finished.

"Any camera footage?" Although a storm of thoughts rage within, my voice remains even in a mask of composure.

"No, that's where we're stumped. The security management tried to get the footage of your office for the last week, but there was nothing." Oscar straightens his back, his gaze unwavering as he looks me in the eye. "We did a security check of the rest of the building and other offices. It came out clean. It was only the main office," he explains.

First Phoenix and now my office—that cannot be a coincidence. "Keep me updated on all and everything you find," I order, my mind running a million kilometres a minute.

I get up and fix my cufflinks and face towards the door.

"Sir." Oscar's voice stops me from behind.

I turn around to see Oscar squaring his shoulders, his expression resolute, quiet strength replacing his earlier uncertainty. "This doesn't seem like a general hack. Someone may have planned it. I know I'm in no position to say this, but please be safe."

"I will." I give him a nod, assessing his soft brown eyes filled with sincerity. His words ring in my head as I leave with a cold and warm sensation battling within me. *Maybe* Oscar can stay.

If this is Pyrosilk's doing, then they have access to everything we've built and the means to get to our families and all the people involved in Phoenix. And *Bianca.*

I drag a hand down my face. My slowly growing stubble scratches against my skin as I force myself to breathe.

Adrian. If anyone can get access to the footage, Adrian can.

I pull out my phone and text him.

> **Jason:** *I have a job for you. You may have the chance to save lives than take them*

The reply comes immediately.

> **Techno:** *I'm all ears, hands, arms and yours*
> **kissing emoji**

Techno? I barely called or texted him that I hadn't recognised *someone* had changed Adrian's name on my phone. Kai!

I ignore most of his text and respond.

> **Jason:** *USB is missing. I have my doubts, and the footage was out*

> **Techno:** *Think it's Pyro?*

> **Jason:** *I'm sure. Check the footage near my office and anything around it*

> **Techno:** *What's there for me? And not a punch*

> **Jason:** *That sucks. Just get it done*

"What did I do now?" Bianca's voice jolts me awake. "That look on your face can sink the Titanic a second time."

She comes to stand beside me and has a smile on her face that makes the sun look dull. The adrenaline from earlier fades, replaced by a calming wave washing over me, the frantic pulse in my ears quieting, and my breathing slowing.

I put my phone away in my pocket. "The question isn't what you did." I lean close to her ear. "It's when did you grow horns? Getting me worked up in the morning."

"I always had them." The mischievous smile on her face makes her the same Bianca I knew.

"What's got your face smiling today?" I say as we walk to my car.

"Nothing. Just having a good day, I guess." She shrugs.

We reach my Porsche, and I open the passenger door for Bianca, but she stops and looks at me.

"Can I tell you a secret?" she whispers, cupping the side of her face.

"What?"

"Jason Archer doesn't have a driver," she whispers again.

Following suit, I whisper, "He does. Multiple. But he doesn't like sharing Bianca Kennedy's space with anyone else."

A blush coats her cheeks. "Possessive much?" She tilts her head and scans my face.

"Only with you." My voice feels foreign, a strange sound, as I stare into the eyes of the best person I've ever known. "Now, get in." I flick my head towards the seat.

A shy smile tugs at her lips as Bianca drops her head and gets in.

We're halfway to the office, idling at a red light. Bianca's humming a tune from Sloane Garcia's latest album as her fingers tap a rhythm on the window.

Without much thought, I press the play button on the steering wheel. And to no surprise, the familiar upbeat rhythm of the song Bianca is humming fills the air.

With a slow turn of her head, Bianca's wide eyes heat the side of my face, but I look straight ahead, feigning interest in the traffic light's shift from red to green. With a press of the accelerator, the car's engine roars to life, and I feel Bianca's scorching stare shift from my cheek to my exposed forearms.

"The last time I checked, this car was emotion-less, music-less, and most likely life-less." She counts on her fingers. "Music tick. Others are still work in progress."

It *may* have escaped Eva on the hottest trends in the music industry, and she *may* have told me about what the girls were into. Not that Bianca needs to know any of that. Surprisingly, Eva has picked up listening to some classic tunes—Sage to explain for that.

"It's called being minimalistic—something you wouldn't have heard of," I explain.

"Tomayto tomahto." She chuckles, rolling her eyes.

We reach the underground parking basement, and cold water washes over any warmth.

"Well." Bianca clears her throat. "I'll see you then." She opens her door to get out.

"Wait," I say before she could leave.

Her hand freezes midway, and she looks at me with her gorgeous bright blue eyes, like a cloudless sky.

I look at her, somehow feeling nervous as I ask, "Are you free at seven?"

Her lips thin in thought. "If I am?"

"Then you're mine." Our wide eyes meet, and I shake my head. "For the evening. I'm taking you out," I add.

"It's not a date," she reads between the lines and bites her lip.

"It feels wrong if it isn't," I answer directly.

Bianca closes her eyes and nods to herself. "On one condition." She points.

"Yes," I agree.

"Don't agree to conditions that could surprise you."

"I'm sure there's nothing in the world I wouldn't do for you." The words flow freely out of my mouth.

Bianca's wide eyes trace my face, searching for something that will tell anything else. She wouldn't find it.

She gets off her seat and places a soft kiss on my cheeks, taking away my breath. Her wordless response is more emotive than any words.

"You are so beautiful." I breathe, looking at her. Somehow, during these weeks, the small barrier between us has been broken with the hammer of time and patience.

"So are you." Her eyes, pools of warmth, lock with mine as her fingers gently glide over my cheek.

I caress the pulse on her neck with my thumb. "Only with you," I echo my words.

The day crawled by, each hour feeling heavier than the last as the sun sank lower in the sky. I was pulled from one call to another, every conversation was a monotonous drone about the breach in the files room. We had cleared one thing after Adrian came into the conversation. There was fake footage played on repeat for an hour before the recording resumed in real time.

Many employees go in and out of the room throughout the day. We employ them for their trustworthiness and ethics.

Something really isn't adding up because the safe can only come out when activated, and only Oscar, and a few other people, know where it is. There's no other way.

"So, what do you think about the Smiths?" Mr Carter's blurred voice comes through my hazy thoughts. I'm sitting in my last meeting for the day and had few postponed.

"They're good, and our history with them is strong," I reason.

As our most trusted partner, Luise Smith and her family have been with us since the start, their commitment is like no other. She and I have met a few times, but there was always something about her that bugged me. Maybe it was the fact that she only ever spoke when she needed to or that she had security guards lined up everywhere she went.

My eyes flick to the clock behind Carter as he informs me about their policies and whatnot. *Thirty minutes.*

Excitement climbs the lumbers of my spine as I impatiently bounce my feet. I feel the familiar flutter of anticipation, just like when I was a teenager, waiting for the school day to end to have hot chocolate on winter days. Only today, it's not a drink I'm looking forward to.

"Sure, I'll get it sorted. Have a good day, Jason," Carter greets. With a handful of papers and a playful moustache twirl, he waddles towards the door.

The file with the final security updates stares back at me. I feel the smoothness of the papers against my fingertips as I turn each page, and each one carries the weight of all the things that could have been compromised but weren't.

It outlines the execution of every security plan we put in place. The key priority now is to guard the entrances to our offices, including the AC ducts.

"Mr Archer, what a surprise," Carter says to a figure he is blocking by the door.

"Good to see you too, Carter," Dad responds.

With a soft click, Carter shuts the door carefully behind him as he leaves.

"Dad."

"Jason." Dad nods back as he takes the seat in front of me. "Have you heard from McKenzie? He contacted me and was over the moon to be working together. Should the credit go to you?" Dad teases with a smile.

"The company, maybe?" I say, returning to the file, the paper crinkling slightly under my fingers. "Who wouldn't be glad to be working with us?"

"I recognised something the other day." He pauses as he stares at me. A little creepy with his wide eyes.

I drop the files with a huff and give him my attention because he won't leave without it. "Enlighten me."

"Bianca won't be able to see the completed building. She's been working so hard on it, and deserves to see the outcome, doesn't she?" He sits back on the chair and rests his cane by the table. He looks up at me through his hooded eyes, a slight smile playing on his lips, and speaks with confidence. "The creative team checked in with me and said they would love to have Bianca when we open up the new office."

"The planned opening is not until the end of the year, and Bianca will leave in the next month or so. There's nothing we could possibly do," I explain.

He clicks his fingers and points at me, and the smile gets wider. "There's the loophole. *We* can't. But *you* can."

I shake my head, the scent of his impending recklessness heavy in the air, knowing exactly where he is going. "You want me to contact

Florals & Bells and put in a word for Bianca," I think out loud.

"My son is smarter than I put him for." He winks, settling back into his plush chair.

That is a loophole. And one I've been constantly thinking about, but I am powerless in stopping Bianca. She had made it clear that staying back isn't an option. Everything in me wants her to stay, but it's her choice.

The metallic click of the pen against the smooth glass table echoes in the quiet room as I sit, lost in thought.

"I'll leave you with that, which goes without saying that you want her to stay," he says, rising and holding his cane. "If you don't, then let things be as they are."

"I will," I say. The words linger as a sweet and uncertain promise, hanging heavy in the air.

Dad hums. "Bee, you are around. Oh, I mean, *see* you around." He laughs.

Who is this man?

He couldn't be funnier even if he tried. His words hit me like a bombshell, the weight of them pressing down, stealing the space in my head.

"What happens with McKenzie's termination contract?"

He pauses on his way to the door and turns around. "Not my decision." He shrugs, a glint of amusement in his bright eyes.

"Cancel them. McKenzie is staying, and so is Bianca. No need for them anymore," I promise.

"Very well, Castillo will be on it." He nods to himself, pleased.

"And Dad…" I rise from my seat, the squeak of the chair joining the click of my heels on the polished floor as I approach my father.

He looks up at me. As strong as Brandon Archer, but soft as my father.

I bring him into a hug, the warmth of his body comforting me, and my eyes close on their own. The scent of pine and damp earth fills my senses as if I'm in the garden again, watching birds with his gentle touch on my shoulder. It's been so long since I'd hugged him.

"Thank you," I whisper. "You were right, I did need to thank you."

"Your old man will always look out for his boy," he whispers as he rubs his hand on my back.

We pull out, and I feel Dad's firm hands on my shoulders as he gazes at me, his face coloured with calm. "I'm so proud of you. You earned all this for yourself. I would never have appointed you as the CEO if it weren't for your potential. You have exceeded all my expectations, and it makes me proud to call you my son," he says, his voice thick with emotion.

I swallow a lump in my throat, and it hurts. I never thought I needed to hear those words from this unserious man. But I did; the kid in me did. No matter how I appear to others, I will always become the boy I was with him.

I smell the cherry blossom before the door rushes open. "Jason, I'm off—" Bianca begins to declare. The scent of her life lingers in the air as she barrels through the doorway, her bag slung over her shoulder.

Our heads turn towards her, and Bianca's face pales, her eyes widening in shock as she finds us in the middle of the room.

"Brandon." She swallows. "I'll come back later," she says. Her eyes came to me for a split second before they went back to Dad.

"Ridiculous. Come here." With a warm smile, Dad opens his arms wide, beckoning Bianca forward with outstretched hands. "Don't make me wait," he whines.

Shaking her head, Bianca jogs and takes him in for a hug. Bianca fists his shirt at the back as she puts her head on his chest.

"How have you been? We haven't talked in a while," Dad says, pulling away.

"I'm great. It's been busy, you could say, or someone has been keeping me busy." Bianca's eyes shoot to me behind Dad.

Dad looks over his shoulder and smirks. "I'm sure he has."

"Anyway, I'll leave you kids to it. If he troubles you, you know who to come to," he says as he straightens his suit jacket and holds his cane in one hand. Dad bends and kisses Bianca's cheek. He then turns to me and squeezes my shoulder. "Remember what I said."

I nod, understanding everything he said and didn't. The quiet affirmation, though unspoken, fills me with a deep sense of self-assurance, like the warmth spreading through my chest. If I learned anything about my father, it's that every decision Brandon Archer makes, no matter how insignificant it seems, stems from deep-seated motivation.

I may not have a nest, but that doesn't mean I won't build one.

As the door shuts behind him, I feel my chest expanding with gratitude. *I have great parents.*

"We're lucky to have him," Bianca concludes, her beautiful blue eyes glance over me.

"Yeah." I nod, looking at the now closed door. "We are."

I shake my head and lean back on the cool black glass of the table. "You couldn't wait another thirty minutes without seeing me? Am I that special now?" I look over at Bianca in her bright outfit.

"Don't flatter yourself. I did myself a favour and escaped Jelena. I swear she's out for blood by the end of the day." Bianca widens her eyes, holding a pen like a knife. "It gets tiring really quickly."

"Hopefully, you saved some energy for tonight," I say, stalking towards her. "You won't be getting any rest." My arms circle her soft waist, bringing her closer to my chest.

"So, what are we doing?" she asks with a spark in her eyes.

Our heated eyes electrify the air between us, and the only thing I can think of right now is pinning her to the wall and drilling deep into her. My cock hardens as the image of her dropping her head to the wall as she comes in bliss. *Fuck.* We need to get out.

"Let's begin with that condition."

CHAPTER 27
Jason

"**I** can be patient," Bianca mutters, slumping back in her seat, "but you're really testing my limits right now." Frustration leaks from her silky voice.

"Let this be a surprise, and for once, stop worrying. I promise I won't chase you in the dark." I shake my head at the ridiculous thought.

"Not that I mind," she mumbles, a small smile playing on her lips as she looks straight ahead.

I smirk. "Did you say something?" I ask, eyes glued to the road, my ear inching to her mouth to hear her whisper above the thudding in my chest.

"Nope," she says with a pop. Her hands curl around her bag, and

she puts one leg over the other.

For years, I thought I needed nothing, but then she appeared. With her tiny bundle of bittersweet emotions, she filled the emptiness in my life.

The very thought is unsettling, not because I feel complete, but because of whom. A person who will never be permanent in my life. Bianca Kennedy is a ticking bomb waiting to explode, and we will all be collateral damage, yet I know I will happily stand next to her as she explodes.

But that doesn't mean I won't steal every moment I can with her. Even if it's a shared glance across a crowded room.

I take another turn into local traffic and enter the place where we first ate our first ice creams and sorbet. "Here we are," I announce.

Her eyes widen as we arrive at the lively market. Light music pulses through the air, and the warm glow of the string of lights illuminates rows of vibrant stalls, brimming with enticing aromas.

"Queen Victoria Market?" Bianca sits straighter in her seat, blinking her eyes.

"How do you feel about a market run?" I ask, the buckle of my belt clicking as I unfasten it and swing my legs out of the car. The rich floral smell of jasmine and lilies, thick and heady from the market stalls, fills the air as I jog to the passenger-side door.

"Unprepared. But you know what, I would love to win against your long legs." Bianca jumps down with springs in her feet and catches my arm.

Time slows—pauses—as she leans down, her lips brush my knuckles in a slow kiss, and those seductive eyes put a noose around my neck. I'm afraid if she asks me to get on my knees and bark, I will fucking bark. "Listen, I'm going to make it to that counter before you, and if I do—which I will—then you owe me an entire tub of sorbet.

Blueberry sorbet," she whispers seductively, the words loud and clear above the sounds of the near-empty market as she speeds past.

She looks over her shoulder and passes me a smile that warms every corner of my body. Her honey-brown hair, a curtain over her face, whips around her as she sprints towards *Rainbow Sweet Desserts'* counter. "Grandpa legs, again?" she screams.

Shaking my head with a lift of my lips, I take off my jacket, toss it in the car, and sprint towards her. A surge of energy, like a jolt of electricity, fills my bones. The icy wind whips against my face as my feet pound the ground.

Bianca makes it to the counter before me and slaps her hand down on the counter of the stall, heaving with her olive cheeks blasting red. The young man at the counter looks between our sweaty faces as we catch our breaths. This must be the most normal thing I've done in a long time, running like a normal man in a normal market after a beautiful girl.

"Guess who owes me two tubs of sorbet?" she sings as she dances on the spot, moving her hips from side to side.

"I thought it was one." A single eyebrow arches as my fingers impatiently snap open the top button of my shirt.

"You thought wrong. Better clean your elderly ears," Bianca chirps, her fingertips lightly tapping my ear. Her voice sounds in the quiet space as the boy behind the counter watches with curious eyes.

"Hi, I'm Edmund. What can I get for you tonight?" he introduces with a smile. His golden hair, pulled back in a neat bun, frames a face with light brown eyes.

"Hi! Can we have two blueberry sorbets and one chocolate ice cream on a cone, please? And keep the tubs on standby when we come back," Bianca orders, her fingers tracing patterns on the cool counter as she beams at the boy.

"Make those five sorbets on the cone and no ice-cream," I correct as I look around the market. The only other people here are the few attendants at each stall, who may not even be here as they quietly work.

"Right away, mate." He nods and gets to the order, and we turn around to the rest of the market.

Bianca shoots me a questioning stare, rubbing her hands together. She straightens, inhaling deeply, the now-dry sweat clinging to her skin in a thin film. "No ice cream?"

"I stopped having ice-creams long ago." *Because you couldn't.* I reach for her arm, my fingers brushing against her skin, and gently tuck it in my coat.

"And why five?"

"You'll see."

Bianca hums distractingly as she keeps melting further into me.

We stand still in silence, peace and calm singing as we dance with the free-flowing air. Yet I know better than anyone that this moment is a deception, with the storm waiting on the outskirts.

The looming weight of the missing USB is heavy, but the information taken from the intrusion in Phoenix is heavier. It will jeopardise the commitment and promise we made to protect the members' privacy and data if we don't get this under control.

"Here they are!" Edmund yells, jolting me awake.

"We'll take the three of them first," I say.

He passes them, and Bianca shrugs, taking her two from me.

She licks the sorbet with a quick dart of her tongue, enjoying its icy sweetness, but then stops before reaching the next. "Wait, you didn't pay for them."

"Already did," I say, licking my sorbet.

Bianca shrugs. "Oh, you *tele-paid*. Get what I did there? Telecommunication and *tele*-paid." She giggles, nudging my shoulder.

She's happy.

"When did you take the course in dad jokes?" I roll my eyes. My lips twist in an attempt not to laugh as we stay rooted, holding our cones.

Flash!

A flash blinds me, and I see spots dancing in my vision until they clear out. When I recover, Bianca's laugh sounds in the market, and I can't help but smile too. She's laughing like she's seen the funniest thing there is.

I'll take that as a compliment.

"You will delete that." I point at her, but she's too busy tapping on the screen, and the smile on her face isn't the most innocent. "What do you think you're doing? You will not send that to anyone."

"No, because it's now our group chat profile picture." She smiles, holding up her phone, and my face appears with my eyes looking up, filling the small circle of their group—*Mystic Maidens* with a cat emoji.

I hold back a laugh. "I don't know what traumatises me more, the name of the group or my face on it."

"Courtesy to Eva and Kiara and their love for the *Vampire's Bite*. Aside from that, since you thought I can't handle my sor—" Bianca's amusement is short-lived as she trips over her feet and clumsily drops her two sorbet cones. The sticky mess splatters on the ground, making her laughter abruptly end.

"Karma 101. I would say, 'I told you so,' but…" My hands go up in surrender as she lets out a frustrated sigh, her eyebrows pinch together. "I won't."

"Smartass," she mutters.

Clearing my throat, I turn around to Edmund. "We'll have the other two now."

We come out of the *Rainbow Records Store* with a mini speaker blasting tunes that has us nodding our heads in rhythm. Now because of that, we're listening to the speaker play "You and Me" by Sloane Garcia. The same song that was playing in the car.

Linking her arm with mine, she traces patterns on my sleeve as we stroll past each store. I haven't had the time to think about anything but to give Bianca all my attention and time.

Judging from the satisfied sighs and wide smiles, I think I've passed this one.

"Where is everyone else?" Bianca asks, her eyes looking around.

"I rented the place for the night." I shrug my shoulder, still walking ahead.

Bianca's hold on my arm tightens as she processes. "Oh, okay, you—what!" she gasps. "You rented a public place? How's that possible?"

"Like I said, there's nothing money can't do. There is no issue with legality when I got all the permissions."

"You would have nothing to do with all the store names starting with 'rainbow'?" She turns around, her eyes narrowed in suspicion, a slight frown furrowing her brow. "Now it makes so much sense."

"What can I say? I'm taking after my creative company." I take her waist and keep walking.

"What do I do with you?"

"Nothing, just be with me. *For now*," I whisper, not wanting to admit it too loud.

"Oh, I..." Bianca gulps, her eyes avoiding looking at me. I know it is too early for any promises, yet I also know I wouldn't want anyone by my side except her. That's a truth I learned from the many times we shared laughs and stolen gazes as we grew.

"Don't say anything—you don't have to. Come on, let's get you something warm," I say.

We walk towards *Rainbow Woolly Wonderland* in silence. Bianca scoffs, looking up at the sign. "I can't believe I didn't pick up on that. You couldn't be more original."

After looking around the vast collection of winter wear, we settled on a set of sweaters, scarves, and beanies. Bianca looks in the mirror with a soft, searching gaze as her fingers trace the intricate beadwork woven into the thick, colourful wool scarf. She sighs deeply when she looks up at the matching beanie.

"You know, I haven't worn a beanie since I left. They reminded me of—"

"Oliver," I complete for her. "If it weren't for Lina, he would've married the beanie instead. I never understood the fascination."

"You remember," she states. She smiles, looking at me from the mirror.

My hands climb her arm to set them on her shoulders, letting my fingers skim over the side of her neck. "I would need to remember something if I had forgotten it. Your memories sit in every corner of my brain, giving colour to the darkness."

And that's why you're a rainbow who quietens the beast in me. Who battles the grey.

"I like this." Bianca runs her hand over the woolly beanie. "Let's get it."

"We should." I smile, leaning down and pressing a kiss to the side of her neck. Our heated stares through the mirror hold a silent conversation of their own.

And in this moment, I feel the bricks around my heart slowly disintegrating for her. "Never think you're lost or alone. Because the beautiful eyes you have are the realm of a survivor who has been through things no one has. In there is a girl who is stronger than anyone." I speak softly and prepare myself for what I'm going to say next. "But now, you have us—all of us. Stay here and we'll be everything you'll need," I request.

I had Teal checking on her throughout the years, getting the weekly updates, and they were nothing out of the ordinary. But something tells me that's not the case because Bianca is a mastermind when it comes to becoming a people pleaser and doing everything to fit in.

Her eyes shine the brightest I have seen them. Not bright like the sun, but with a deep, luminous brightness like the ocean's depths.

"I…" She heaves and pauses. "I would stay if I could. Regardless of what reason I stay for, I will always live under the rock of my past. Those memories will never stop chasing me, and I will run to get away from them."

"Then let me run with you. Let my hand be the hand you hold." My fingers squeeze her shoulders reassuringly. "I can't promise to free you, but at least I can push you out of your open cage. However slow you want me to."

"I'm just … afraid." Her voice and eyes well with tears. "I'm afraid I will somehow fuck up and leave empty-handed. That thought alone drags me down a path I don't even want to look at." She looks up, and a sob chokes out of her. Her knuckles become white as she clutches her bracelet.

"Then don't. Only look at the path that leads you to us. *To me,*" I simply say.

A tear slides down the slope of her cheek, but she doesn't wipe it.

Bianca's a bundle of undying emotions, keeping everything buried deep inside her. I want to unfurl and pick every one of her emotions apart—one cry, one worry at a time, and replace those with smiles and laughs.

"Whether you come down that path or not, I will follow you on the path you find for yourself." I pull her close, my arms circling around her waist, and her back snug against my chest. My chin rests on her shoulder, and immediately her floral scent fills my senses.

"Jason." She shakes her head, and the drops of her precious tears fly away. "Don't say things like that. It only makes me fall for you, and that fall would get us hurt."

I didn't know I wanted to hear those words.

A fall for you wouldn't be a fall of hurt. The landing would be like finally finding the directing light from the lighthouse to guide the lost ship of my mind to your shore.

"Don't fall. *Fly* to me while you reach all the heights and glide to all your successes. Be your own kind of bird. I'll wait at the end of the rainbow as you colour the world." I smile, measuring each drop of her tears.

With a light, breathy laugh, Bianca inhales slowly through her nose. "You would give me a bird analogy, wouldn't you?"

"What can I say? They're my first love before you," I tease.

The words flowed so easily that I didn't get to feel their true weight.

Bianca's stare through the mirror hardens, and she closes her eyes, then looks away. She pulls away from my grip with the scarf and beanie.

"Let's get these." Then she walks off.

Bianca

"Why are you covering my eyes?" I let out a frustrated sigh as I follow the way Jason sets.

"It would be a lot easier if you just kept quiet and let me do my job," he grumbles lightly.

I don't know, but the earlier conversation has shifted something between us. I can't point at it, but I just feel it, and for the first time in a long time, I'm conflicted—it's getting too real— about us. It's just too real.

"And what's that?" I ask, tilting my head to the side.

"Making you happy."

"Yeah, yeah. You do nothing without calculating each move, Mr Archer. I know your games."

"Maybe not this time." His minty breath warms my ear as he whispers, "This is only *for* you." And then he softly kisses my cheek.

As the words escape his mouth, he removes his hands from my eyes. My vision clears, allowing comfortable light through from the view beyond us. *A stunning view.*

My mouth opens in a gasp, in awe—fascination. "You … This … Wow." I point between the setup and Jason as I think of the right words to say.

"This is the first-ever prototype of the garden and library for the top floor," Jason announces.

Our favourite song plays on the mini speaker as the music softly pulses in my hand. Each note matches every beat of my heart.

He spreads his arms to the display, standing as another one of my many dreams.

Rich, dark wooden bookshelves curve in a semi-circle, each shelf flowing with books, while small, round tables and chairs scatter in inviting groups, hosting a simple vase of flowers. Delicate and pleasing.

In the heart of the expansive lawn, a vast collection of classic and contemporary books lay as a rich tapestry of literature, and stringed lights shine under the open sky.

Lush Japanese blue wisteria cascades from each bookshelf and enhances the setting. Tiny bushes with pops of colourful tulips and dahlias scattered with vibrant hues in a pattern around the miniature library. Their leaves rustle gently when the subtle breeze weaves through them.

The light scent of lavender hangs in the air as it edges a small, winding gravel path leading to the library. A soft purple light emanates from each lavender bush, the vibrant colour of the flowers guiding the way along the path. It's a beautiful depiction of the vibrant purple blooms contrasting against the grey stone.

"Bianca?" A light touch on my shoulder brings me back to earth from my dreamland.

I sigh and lean into Jason, placing my head on his shoulder. Emotions taking the better of me twice in a night. "This…" I swallow before continuing, "Is beautiful."

"It's all you. I don't have a creative bone in me to save my life. Do all you want with it," he says and leaves a kiss on my temple.

The song finishes, but Jason puts it back on repeat.

"There's also one more thing." He points to a shelf as he stares at me.

"Wait? Is that…" I smile and laugh as I jog to my yellow heels hanging off a hook on the edge of the historical fiction novels. "I thought I would never see you." I take them off and hug them to my chest.

"You're welcome," Jason's soft whisky voice teases from behind me.

"Oh yeah. Thank you, too, Jason." I smile, afraid I'll break my face in half. I go back to hugging my heels, deliberately ignoring him.

"This is not how I imagined being thanked."

My cheeks burn red, but I straighten and hide my thumping heart from the visual. "Then what did you have in mind?"

The air crackles with unspoken emotions as we face each other, our eyes searching for the unsaid words.

"I think you already know."

I step forward, dropping the heels, and circle my arms around his neck. Instinctively, his hands find my hips. "In all seriousness, this really means a lot. No one has ever done anything like this for me."

"I'm not just anyone," he replies point-blank.

You're mine. Jason Archer is mine, and I am his. We can't escape the truth, yet it never escapes our lips.

"What was that condition again?" he asks, already knowing it.

"Catch me when I land," I say and press my lips to his. They perfectly mould together and unlock a burst of emotion within me.

The chorus of the song plays soulfully around us—the music swells, a wave of calm as the lyrics resonate deeply with our painful reminder. *We are perfect.* But sometimes perfection isn't enough.

He gives me his everything. Each touch and kiss is his way of losing a small part of the weight on his shoulders. He doesn't speak of it, but I don't need his words to feel it.

We pull apart and simmer in the warmth of each other's company. Finally, I understand the importance of having someone beside me who wants me to grow as much as I do for myself. Especially with him.

"I think I've already caught you," Jason says softly, running his knuckles on my cheek.

I'm walking on a path coated with burned soaring coal that will only lead me to the shallow and calm waters amidst taller than life trees and chirping of birds. Because that is where I will find my peace. *My Jason.*

"I have faith in you…" I sing as the song fades, and I fade too. Into the perfection of this man.

CHAPTER 28
Bianca

"Thank you for tonight." My voice is soft as Jason pushes my door open. We step into the dark in silence, energy buzzing in me like fireflies in the night.

Tonight reminded me of the boy I met who always replaced my broken glasses and the one who always knew what I wanted without me telling him. Like now, as he turns the light on and bends to remove my heels from my throbbing feet.

Chuckling, I say, "Stop, I can do it."

He doesn't stop, just shakes his head. "Let me." He looks up with an edge of softness in his eyes. "Please."

Something shatters in my chest at the loosening of his usual creases in his forehead and the familiar softness of his green eyes.

Jason finishes working on my other heel, and once finished, he places them neatly in their spot by the front table. Still silent, he places the bag from *Rainbow Woolly Wonderland* on the centre table and another bag I didn't see before.

Now the distance between us feels so close, yet so far away. It's as if we're beside each other but in a world that isn't ours.

"So…" I linger on the word.

His intense eyes stay on me, not wavering, even in the darkness he hugs me with his presence.

He's so close, White says.

"So that's it. I'll see you tomorrow," he finally says, picking his pace to the front door.

Even now, he's giving me the option. The feeling, the freedom to feel and choose, are just so foreign, I don't deserve it—at least not from the one person I'm using. In all the years I've lived, the universe decided for me—my mental state, my emotions, my situations, everything—but now the ball is in my court, and I don't know if I should throw it out or try to shoot the goals. I'm a true lost cause.

No, not tonight—not with him.

"Hey, Jason," I say as soon as he opens the front door and the cold air whistles through.

He pauses, his feet stilling behind me, awaiting my next words.

With our backs to each other, I continue, "We may not be perfect, and our past wasn't for us to decide. And I may not be ready for us, truly, but …" I pause, feeding myself courage. "… For you I am."

In a swift movement, we face each other, and any confusion fades when I see those lightly glazed forest eyes.

"I want you." My voice is clear, yet soft. "You know that better than I do."

Silence.

His stance is confident, and his words are strong when he speaks, but rolls them in empathy he always had. "This is a one-way road. Once you enter, we keep going forward," he says almost as a warning.

I smile and take a step forward. "Then that's what we'll do for as long as we can."

With one wide step, he grabs the back of my neck and pulls my focus to him. Not that I can focus on anyone else when he's concerned. "I never hated you. Never." He breathes, his mint scent overloads me as he continues, "I hated that I couldn't make you mine when, in fact, you always were."

The air gets knocked out of my lungs as the words escape him and float around me like the truth they are. There is nothing I won't give to have this man because whoever created him spent a lifetime and more to make him.

"Some things take time, but they all come to fruition if they are meant to be," I whisper.

"Not if. We *are* meant to be." His fingers wrap tighter around the back of my neck. "It has never been a question to me. You have been mine…" he says, stopping to look at me. The rare shine in his eyes comes through, and I feel him building a home in my heart that I can't break even if I wanted to. "And will always be, Bianca Kennedy."

He lowers himself and, for the first time, kisses me like he hasn't before. Kisses me like this is his only way to live, his only way to breathe. My hands instantly find his hair and tug him closer because in this moment he is my only way to survive. He is the one piece of thread I can hold on to and trust my life with.

He unleashes his well-kept hunger, showing me how famished he is. With the hold on my neck, Jason expertly guides my lips into the position we want.

One moment I'm a writhing mess on my two feet, the next I'm

being carried by powerful hands deep inside the house. I try to tighten my hold around his waist with my legs, but the only thing I have in mind is the way he's consuming me alive with the kiss.

When we get close to the sofa, Jason lays me on it and braces himself on his elbows, savouring the moment as I try to find the right words in my bewildered mind. Gone is the softness, replaced by comforting darkness I'll let consume me.

"No one gets to claim you like this," he murmurs, his forest-green eyes staring at me while he gently tucks away a stray strand of hair behind my ear. "No one."

His dark voice has my body alive again and boiling with arousal.

Warm and thick fingers go under my blouse and give my waist reassuring squeezes—squeezes for him to feel me—as if to make sure I'm here. The move is innocent, yet wetness pools in my sex, and I clench, thinking of him inside me.

I shake my head, wisely staying quiet.

Emotions of all kinds make my heart flutter. But one stands tall, the emotions of *him*.

"I burn those who get close to me," I blurt out the words before I could stop them.

Jason smiles—*smiles*. "Lucky for you I'm fuel. Together, we're a forbidden, yet necessary pair to give light to the world. *Our* world."

I lean up and press my lips to his. Because who the fuck is this man and how do I have him on me? My lips work his, but he stays still, allowing me to give my all to him—understanding the roar of unexpected emotions in me.

I cup the side of his face and bite his lip. It triggers something in him.

Jason takes my arms and pins them above my head, breathing near my ear when he growls, "Let's burn the world together."

Animal.

His hand travels between us and slowly lifts my skirt, teasing me with the light skim of his fingers on my heating skin. Our breaths mingle between us, growing heavier with every inch of my skin he covers, and gets closer to my wet panties.

We both steal each other's air when Jason drags one thick finger along the length of my sex. "*Fuck me*," he swears in his voice of darkness. The sound of his voice sends a cascade of shivers down my spine, settling deep within me.

I chuckle. "Am I wet?"

His eyes find mine again, and for a moment they widen but soon morph into something sinister. "Yes."

I smile and tug him closer with the collar of his shirt. "For who?" My words land as a whisper on his lips, letting him feel them more than hear.

"Me." He reaches for my neck and hungrily kisses from the base, memorising every contour as I tilt my head back to offer him better access. "Do you remember that night?"

I shake my head. "Not much." I don't know what night he is talking about, but I know I don't want to remember anything but this moment right now.

His fingers dance on the hem of my skirt as he looks up at me. "Eyes on me," he murmurs.

He slips in quietly, his touch light and teasing as he traces my folds to my clit once again. Only this time, the ghost of his touch is on fire, aiming to burn off any other touch except his own.

As he instructed, my eyes stay glued to him. Honestly, I wouldn't want to look anywhere else than in the dangerous calm of his forest. Jason rests his rough hand around my pussy as his singular finger presses my clit. *Fuck.* I dig my teeth into my lips to seal the sound of pleasure, allowing through only a small whine.

Jason shakes his head as he removes his finger. "No. Don't you dare rob me of your sounds. Be as loud as you can. Let me hear all of you. I want all of you."

He inserts a finger into me, and this time I let loose. Letting go of all that was holding me back, I take it out in a moan I've never heard from me. He adds a finger, and the shots of pleasure running through me have my chest heaving and blood cursing hot.

"You feel that. Only I can give you that," he hisses. His touch is everything and nothing at all. Possessiveness floats on every inch of my skin.

With a firm squeeze, he wrings out all the arousal from my core, letting me feel every time it drips out of me and onto his hand. The sheer sensuality of the scene is so captivating that it lures me to the brink of climax.

"Don't come—not yet," he warns. At his voice, my head dips into the cushions when he inserts another finger, dragging his digits in and out of my heat.

"Jay," I moan. Chills of pleasure and impatience keep me wanting more. He picks up his pace, and I curl my nails into my palm, looking for a release. Trying anything to stop the impending pleasure from taking over.

"Keep that up and I'll be coming before you." I feel a tug on my hair, gently lifting my head to meet his gaze.

Another finger and I'm done. Too much, too full. He slides them effortlessly in and out, as if a different entity from me, the wetness coating my entrance obeys to his very command.

The only sound in the room is my pussy swallowing his fingers and feeding off his addicting touch. Everything is heightened, truly sending me into another world with the amount of heat zipping through me.

My insides are waiting to be relieved, and my ears are hungry to hear the growl come out of this man's vocals.

He removes his fingers, leaving me empty, scarred from his touch. I whimper at the loss.

"Remember, we're doing this the right way," Jason murmurs, lifting my burning body in his arms and looks down at me as if I'm his important treasure.

"Are you going to fuck me?" I say, admiring my view. An odd sense of confidence fills me by just how his hungry gaze marks me.

"Not before you scream my name. *Then* I will fuck you like you own me," Jason says with certainty.

My sex weeps in appreciation at his words. *Maybe you already own me.*

My room is lit only by a dim lamp on the bedside table. Although I don't need a bright room to see this man with the beauty of the sun.

Jason gently places me on the bed, letting my hair spread on the pillows.

"I've seen you every night in my dreams," he says as he unbuttons his shirt. "Seen how you would cry my name when you come." His shirt drops on the floor.

My heart flutters at the sight of his broad chest with a light scattering of dark hair. Chiselled abs and rippled stomach muscles make him utterly irresistible.

"Tell me you felt the same, that I wasn't the only one boiling in the pots of hell to find my heaven." His eyes darken at the thought, and my chest constricts with overwhelming emotion.

A single tear forces its way out the corner of my eye and betrays my intention to keep my emotions at bay. "There was no time I didn't think of you. I was simmering in myself waiting for you," I whisper, removing my blouse. I shiver not because of the cold, but from the heated stare

Jason glides over me.

"I will devour you like a famished man. You're mine tonight. Mine to claim. Mine to fuck."

As I go to unhook my bra, he shakes his head and murmurs, "The right way."

The unzipping of his pants shoots thrills of adrenaline through me, and when they drop on the floor with his boxers … Oh *God*. My eyes hungrily take in the engorged veins and angry pulse of his cock as it stands heavily between his legs. *Man*. That's who he has become, and in all the best ways.

"Skirt." He flicks his eyebrows at my shirt that has ridden up my thighs.

Purposely, I hook my fingers on the waistband of the skirt and slide it down inch by inch. "Right way, remember?" I raise my eyebrow at his clenched fists and rapidly moving chest.

As soon as the piece of clothing joins his clothes by the bed, Jason, without so much as a warning, rips away my panties. I close my eyes and hiss at the burn, only to smile when I feel his warm breath on my pulsing sex.

"Eyes on me," he demands as he slides his arm above my stomach to chin, tilting my head down. I can feel the weight of his thick, veiny arm nestled between the valley of my breasts, drawing me closer to him.

"I need to see the bliss on your face when you come for me." Jason breathes on my heat, sending it into overdrive.

He drags his tongue from the bottom to my clit and flicks. Breathing doesn't exist anymore in my world as I only breathe in his touch—a touch I always wanted. He does it again and again, teasing me until I'm nothing but a writhing mess at his mercy.

"Make me come," I say, my eyes locking with his.

With just the simple ask, he bites my clit, and I can't help but clench my teeth as the sharp sensation mixes with pleasure. He drags his fingers over my clothed nipples and pinches the erect buds between his fingers.

His teeth graze my swollen pussy, and I stand at the cliff of my climax. Heat becomes my skin. Jason squeezes my breasts as his tongue licks me deep. My mind goes hazy from the overstimulation of my senses. With smooth movements, Jason's fingers dance over my skin, go to my back and unhook my bra, letting my breasts sigh in relief. All the while with his head between my legs.

Never have I felt like this before. Pleasured and calm. From top to bottom, he has taken over.

Jason bites my clit, and he squeezes my breasts with a touch that sends me out of this world. I convulse with a scream, letting it all out. My body deflates as my chest heaves to get in all the air I can.

He puts a finger on my lips, lingering on my bottom lip. "I want you to remember who belongs in your screams. *Me.* I belong in your every breath—in every memory. Just like how all of you belong to me." His eyes darken as he speaks.

"Prove it," I say with finality.

He doesn't need to. I already *know* I belong to him. I've been blocking the thought for the past five years, but the truth always comes to the surface. Jason Archer has become an inseparable part of me, woven into the very fabric of my being when he shouldn't be.

With a guttural growl, he stands to his full height and grabs my hips with a burning hold. My ass is in the air, and his hard erection is just a teasing distance off my entrance. His cock throbs as precum glistens at the tip, desperate for release.

"Hips up for me, Rainbow. Drop them and you will forget that you had your pretty little pussy," he orders.

My legs tremble as if I'm standing naked on thin ice. With my feet flat on the bed, I raise my body, keeping it there. *Breathe.*

Stepping back, he takes in the scene in front of him. I can only imagine how I look as my bare pussy glistens with the evidence of my arousal and his need.

I unconsciously clench as his gaze becomes fixed on my entrance, longing to be filled. A subtle smile plays on his lips, making him appear both heavenly and maddening in the dim lamplight.

His hard length reaches up to his abs, circled with blue and green veins. If I thought the forearms were delicious, *that* right there is *my feast.*

He reaches to touch his cock, using his thumb to spread the leaking wetness along his shaft. My mouth waters at the mere sight. I've never seen such a scene. This man is out of this fucking world.

He preps himself, groaning and moaning. My steady breaths come to a staggering halt when his dick teases me as he rubs on the entrance of my folds. We groan together, the sound so raw and desperate.

Before we could go further, Jason pulls back and gets a foil packet from his pant pockets and rips it open with his teeth. His famished eyes meet mine as he sheaths himself, and I instantly swallow through my dry throat.

"Please…" I whine when the burn inside me intensifies.

"Please what?" His tone is everything I need him to feel at this moment.

"Please take me," I shamelessly beg.

"I can only fuck you."

"Then fuck me, you animal." Frustration takes over my tone as I can only think of him buried deep inside me.

In one quick movement, he thrusts into me, taking my breath away, and my back arches off the bed from the sudden movement. Our sounds muffle in unison as we cherish the moment. That's all it took for him to rip me from my soul and to consume me completely.

He raises my leg and places it on his shoulder and drills his cock deep into me. Slow at first, teasing until I thought I would combust, then picks up speed, making us steal air from each other.

Stars bounce in my vision as the bed hits the wall, but it doesn't stop Jason from taking what he needs. In a moment of pure bliss, he throws his head back, closes his eyes, and becomes completely captivated.

As he thrusts into me eagerly, his mouth kisses my toes, and my hands clench the bedsheets tightly. Jason's mouth engulfs everything from my feet and along my leg as he nibbles, bites, and sucks.

"Say my name," he growls in my ear. "Fucking say it."

"Jas—son," I stutter.

"More."

"Jason. I'm comi—"

Before I can finish speaking, my arousal takes over. I feel my soul leaving my body and seeing myself from above. Jason Archer consumes you so much no place brings justice to the heaven he shows.

"So tight, Rainbow."

Rainbow. That's exactly what I feel now. Light and unearthly. Colourful and *special.*

"You're the colour in this plain world, the life to a grey sky after a storm," Jason murmurs in my ear.

I feel a telling twitch of his cock, and he soon too finds his release. He collapses onto me, his breath coming in ragged gasps.

My core aches for more, but after the two mind-fucking orgasms he has granted me, I don't think I'll survive another one.

"You were worth the five years of wait," Jason mutters on my neck.

I freeze. "You … waited? *For me?*"

For the first time his green gaze lightens, and he says, "My virginity was in your name, and so was my celibacy. Even if you rejected my trust, there was a part of me—alive and human—that always wanted to wait for you. For this moment." He takes a stilling breath. "And you don't need to feel bad if you didn't."

Tears well in my eyes, and I look up to the most beautiful man in existence. "In what world do you think I could find peace with someone else? For me, it's always been you."

His wide eyes meet my smiling ones. "I am yours." His fingers run over my eyelids, gaze lost in searching my face. "I always thought when you'd look at me again, and I would read your eyes—so blue—telling me you want me even for a moment in pleasure. I waited for a moment of *us*." He leans down and kisses me tenderly. "Because you are worth it."

I was wrong. Jason has the stamina of a beast who will satisfy his hunger at all costs. Once, I was mercilessly fucked on my hands and knees and then on my front.

The clock had shown eleven several minutes ago, nearing midnight. He should leave, but just a little bit longer…

I am destroyed by this man lying beneath me. His hair is soft under my fingers as I play with it and let my brain relax for just this moment. I don't know if I'll even be able to walk tomorrow, but I will cherish this sweet soreness.

"Jason?" I murmur in the silent room.

He hums lazily as he buries in the crook of my neck. The sheets provide little protection against the cold, but the warmth of our entwined bodies keeps us cosy.

"What are we?" I whisper before I could stop myself.

He tilts his head, studies my face, and tries to decipher the emptiness within me.

"We are whatever you want us to be," he answers without hesitation.

Jason gently hooks his pinkie finger into the small hoops in my ears, whispering, "Life is a circle. Sometimes we meet the same people again to complete a part of our story with them or start anew. Yet life has brought us into each other's paths more than we can count and tested us even more."

I stare at him blankly. "Life has also separated us," I argue.

"And look where we are. In your bed, naked and fucked," he teases and twists my nipple.

I chuckle, slapping his hand away. "You know what? You're right," I say with realisation. "Life is testing us. To see if we last, but I've seen so much, it will take a lot to break me down."

"So, you're a bad bitch." Jason leans on his elbows and smirks.

I laugh, getting used to his random bursts of jokes. Touching his chest, I say, "Yeah, I'm a real bad bitch."

"Everything can fuck off, but this is mine." He presses his swollen lips to my chest, just above my racing heart, causing me to inhale deeply. "Mine." He trails feather-light kisses up my neck, sending shivers down my spine. "Mine." A tender peck on my nose. "Mine." A soft kiss on my forehead. "And fucking mine." Jason's lips find mine in a deep, passionate kiss. "You put whatever label on us, I don't give a fuck, but one thing is for sure. We're the opposite ends of the magnet that will always attract each other." With a confident smile, he cups my burning cheek, his thumb stroking my skin with a tender touch.

Deep down I knew all this, but bringing it to the surface was like flying through the clear clouds and finding a full arching rainbow. A lone tear finally escapes, spilling over the well of emotions that had been building inside me.

What he said was far beyond my belief, giving me an element as pure as hope.

I hope one day to see Steven truly smile.

I hope my friends love their lives and live them to the fullest.

I hope Jason finds his happiness.

Jason's eyes hold the same hope as a ray of sunshine breaking through the dark forest canopy, hoping it would grow and spread. Becoming a vision as vibrant and clear as the morning dew on the leaves.

And it's you who's going to cast the darkest cloud over that, White sadly reveals.

The idea of hurting the person whose happiness means everything to me sends a wave of sickening dread through me. But...

"I'm sorry," I say, barely audible. I lift and press my lips onto his and try to take away the guilt. Jason pauses for a moment. We remain still, our bodies lightly touching, a physical connection lingering between us. I take the lead this time and have his taste in me. All the mint.

Jason parts his lips in invitation. They're the softest I've had, taking their time to hold me down in place and stay where they belong. *With him.* I want to believe this will last as long as we desire, but I know—he knows—there is a capped date to this.

I don't remind him of that as we taste the saltiness of my tears in the mesh of our lips. A true forever is a fantasy, not a reality.

We pull apart, and I smile through my tears. "I didn't take you to believe in fate and life bringing people together." I laugh.

"You do," he simply says.

"Don't." I swallow, drifting my gaze to his neck—to his pulse. "You don't want to." *I ruin people who believe in me.*

I try not to shrink under the unusual softness of his gaze. "What happened?" His question teases the air. "To the girl who always laughed and smiled," he clarifies.

My body stiffens under the scrutiny of the question that the answer to isn't easy. I swallow, averting my gaze. "She's lost."

"Let's find her." He brings me back to face him with my chin. Something shifts on his face—the hardness of his jaw tenses and the muscles around his eyes constrict.

"What about you? What happened to the boy who *made me* smile?"

He shakes his head. "I was only like that with you. Ask any of the girls, I bet you their answers will be very different."

My heart shatters—the pieces crumbling in his hand. Before I could stop, I say, "Ever since Ma and Dad died, everyone and thing changed. Steven wasn't the boy we grew up with.He became T*he Steven Kennedy,* living to keep the name running. He was working day and night to provide for us and lost himself. Whenever I approached him, he would turn me down each time. Uncle Gareth was never in the picture, he didn't stay long enough. The moment we landed, he left us to fend for ourselves."

I take a shaky breath at Jason's blank listening face.

"I didn't want to be a burden anymore because it made me feel helpless, so I took solace in isolation. That's when I met Aaron."

Jason flinches, heat flares from him, eating away at the earlier lightness in his eyes.

"We worked together at Florals & Bells. He was my trainee when he came in. After some months, we dated and were together for two years." We stare intensely at each other. "I never loved him," I answer his unasked question.

Jason visibly deflates.

"I thought I did. I mistook a companion to my loneliness for more." My eyes close, thinking through the time. "Like another story of my life, his part also burnt me. I found out he was using me to get to Steven so that he could earn a part of our businesses. It was all to feed his addiction. We broke up on my birthday when he got high and sla— assaulted my intelligence," I amend.

Jason fists the sheets as his nostrils flare. "Did he hurt you?" He speaks in a tight voice.

I shake my head, words abandoning me.

Luckily, Jason doesn't push the topic, but he quietly studies me. "You didn't deserve to see all that. I wish we had stayed behind that night," Jason whispers. It reminds me of the boy I fell for—the vulnerable version of him.

No. He's treading into dangerous territory. We—he—did nothing wrong. I've cursed myself for years thinking the same—not tonight. "There was nothing we could've done to stop the fire. Now or then. The truth is, it happened, and we can't do a thing to change it," I say with the certainty I don't have. "But we can do one thing now."

Distraction—now. I run my fingers along his cock as it rests hard in my grip. "How are you still hard?" I ask.

He chuckles darkly. "Always ready for you."

"Condom," I whisper on his lips.

Jason reaches for the bedside table, and rips open the foil and readies himself.

I slide his pulsing cock into my already wet pussy, and we both suck in a shared breath as I ripple around him. A moan escapes me as he rubs a slow and patient thumb on my clit.

"I will always come to you." I kiss him with the words.

"Or *come for* me," he says. Without warning, he lifts me and lies back down. "Ride me, baby."

I put my hands on his chest and slide onto him. I pull out, then push down. As I come down, Jason pushes up, and I see the stars, the moon, and the whole damn universe.

We find a rhythm, fast and slow, edging each other to the brink of climax only to be pushed back.

My insides tense with impending pressure as I get ready to come undone once again. We both groan with pleasure as we slow. He tenses and his dick violently jerks as he comes.

I'm not very far off. Just one more pu—

The sound of loud bangs from the front door makes me freeze instantly.

"Bee, open up! It's me, Eva!"

Our wide eyes collide as we mirror the shock of a deer in the headlights.

CHAPTER 29

Bianca

"**W**hat is your sister doing here?" I whisper sharply, gripping my hair.

Eva can't see us like *this*. Her brother is deep inside me while I'm so close.

Fuck.

"I would like to know the same," he grits, annoyed.

A vibration echoes in the room, and our heads snap towards my dancing phone with Eva's name. This girl is as impatient as a ticking bomb.

I slide my hands down my face and hold my breath as I sense his cock being removed from me. Jason holds my hips and lifts me up. I

whimper at the emptiness and soreness.

"Bee! Open the door!" Eva screams.

I leap out of bed, and as I do, the sheet gets caught around my feet. Before I could meet with the floor, Jason pulls the other end of the blanket, making me come back on the bed and straight to him. "My shirt … My shorts … Where the fuck are my clothes!" I shriek in a whisper. A horrifying rush of adrenaline floods me. The continuous ringing of the bell is doing nothing to calm my nerves.

"Bianca—"

"Fuck … What are we going to do? Fuck. Fuck…"

"Bianca—"

"Eva can't know—"

"Bianca!" In my chaotic thoughts, Jason's hands on my shoulders halt me, and he pins me with a stare. "Calm. Down. It's just Eva. It's okay."

I close my eyes and do as he says.

"Now get dressed. I'll stay in here until she leaves. Okay?"

I nod. Closing my eyes and squaring my shoulders, I find a shirt and pants, and I creep out of my room like a burglar in my house. The ringing of the bell doesn't stop for even a second. *Where's your sense of time?*

The persistent ringing of the bell fuels my rising frustration as I trudge to the door. Glancing back, I see Jason with his pants hanging low on his hips, showcasing his defined muscles. My heart takes another leap at the sight because I never would've thought of my childhood crush standing at my bedroom door—half naked—encouraging me to talk to his sister.

When I get to the front door, I smile and open it.

"What took so long?" Eva rushes past me. *These Archer siblings.*

I roll my eyes. "Maybe sleep." I'm going to rot in hell with all this lying.

Eva stands in her denim jumpsuit with her black fleece jacket. Red rims her eyes and nose, giving her a ghostly look against her pale skin.

"Where is it? Where is it?" she chants to herself as she turns my living room into a dumpster.

"You okay, Eva—"

The remote comes flying in my direction, and I catch it in time before it meets the floor. Then comes a cushion, a shirt, my bag, and lipstick? Oh, that's where it went. I spent all day yesterday finding it or thinking about finding it. I try to balance all these things, lost and forgotten, in my arms.

"I'm fine. I'm looking for … Oh, here it is!" she exclaims as she drops onto the carpet and pulls out a small file from underneath the table. "Yeah, forgot this." Eva holds a file of papers, smiling while avoiding my eyes. The lost colour slowly returns, looking less gothic.

I put the items in my arms down on the coffee table, and when I look up at my friend, I know something's off. "Were you crying?" I ask carefully, taking steps towards her, like approaching a wounded animal.

"What? No, why would I?" She flaps a dismissive hand.

My ears stand on end. *The answer came too quickly.*

"Eva, stop. I know you. What's wrong?"

She stands unmoving, still avoiding contact with my eyes.

"Seriously, it's nothing. I think I left them here the other night. Just some important files from work—nothing much."

"You came running for them here at midnight?"

"I need them for tomorrow," she blurts, her hands running through her hair. Eva is never nervous with us, but the way she looks anywhere but at me and fiddles, it's easy to pick her nerves.

"Okay. I won't press it, but you will tell me if something is wrong, right?" I ask.

"I will." She nods and closes the distance and gives me a hug.

I hear a sniffle as she nestles in my neck, but when we come apart, there is no sign of it. Her hair, darker than the night, is tied up in a messy bun with loose strands peeking out.

"You're wearing the shirt inside out," she says after a while, pointing to my shirt.

"Huh?"

"Your shirt." She flicks her eyebrows.

I quickly look where she points. Fuck, true. My cheeks flush unexpectedly with a wave of heat. Given the situation, I did the best I could.

"You were up to something, weren't you?" she reduces, squinting her eyes at me.

"If you mean sleeping, then yes." I tilt my head with my eyes wide. I can't seem to convince myself, much less Eva, the detective.

"I'll believe you." She flattens her lips, unimpressed.

Eva's eyes stray behind me and focus. "What's in the bags?"

Bags? What bags?

Turning, I see her pointing at the bags her brother had conveniently left on the coffee table.

Jason!

Eva leaps for them, and before I could do anything, she's already halfway through opening the ribbon-tied package.

"Ooh. Not what I was expecting, but cute," Eva coos, holding the package close to her face.

She takes out a package wrapped in blue foil with a note on top.

I go to get it, but Eva moves it just out of my reach. No. No. No.

"*All the colours for my rainbow*," Eva sings as she reads the note. "Who is this from?" She unwraps the package and holds out a pair of blue woollen gloves with a beanie to match it.

That's where he was when I was trying out the other clothes in the winter wear shop. But this…

My heart wells with warmth at just the mere thought. Did he know what he was doing buying me something that's so personal to me—to *us?*

"Could it be Rolex?" Eva's voice slowly comes into my head, so crowded with her brother. She pulls out the rest of the foiled packages, each one more colourful than the one before. Starting with purple, pink, red, orange, yellow and green. There's also grey.

My lack of response widens Eva's eyes in realisation. "Shut up, it is!" she shrieks. "He wasn't lying when he said all the colours of the rainbow, though."

Don't cry. This is Jason. He knows you like no one else.

"There's another note." Eva bends and picks up the note on the grey set. She clears her throat and deepens her voice. "*'A grey to balance your colourful world'* and a secret poet as well, someone save my poor heart." She fans her face.

I'm not crying.

"So thoughtful. The winter ahead is going to hit hard, and my fingers are ready to fall off already. Sometimes I can't even hold my own hand." Eva beams, holding a set of red gloves in her hand.

Reminder: Check blood pressure

Coming out of my daze, I shake my head and say, "It's getting late. Get home before it gets any colder." Guilt rides me, but I need a moment to myself after this.

"I'll need an update on you and Rolex's status after this." She winks as we make our way to the door.

I drop my head, trying to shield my small smile from Eva.

As I open the door, my shoulders deflate in defeat. Heavy showers of midnight rain give life to the sky. It's so ridiculous that we can't even see the nearest tree or the streetlamp.

Fuck me.

"Shit," Eva curses, speaking my thoughts.

"You know what? Stay the night," I offer with my hand on her arm.

"Really?" She turns around and looks at me with calm eyes.

"I can't let you out in this weather." I stretch out my hands to the rain. My breathing comes short as my hand tightens around her arm.

Each raindrop could be extinguishing a blazing fire of a crashed car or … house.

Smoke.

Ashes.

Rain.

I don't register when my chest heaves just to breathe and my mouth tastes the saltiness streaking from my eyes.

"It's fine. I'll stay tonight. Everything's fine," Eva reassures, picking up my worry.

Holding on to my hand, she drags us back into the room, taking off all her excess clothing and dropping them on the couch, leaving her in only her t-shirt and pale red leggings.

My heart beats with a rhythm I've only felt once in my life, and the mere memory transports me back into the inky blackness that night always brings.

Eva runs into the kitchen and fiddles around before bringing a glass of water and a bag of lolly snakes. Our favourite. Guess the Archers do have healing properties.

"I will not say forget everything and leave it in the past, but …" She holds my arm in a comforting grip. "Remember, there are three beautiful girls and …" She tilts her head side to side in contemplation. "Good enough guys waiting for you here. Always," Eva says. The soft smile on her face clears the blur in my eyes. "Now. Let's continue our tradition, shall we?" She passes me a raspberry-flavoured snake and a strawberry for herself. Ever since I've known her, she's been addicted to these snake lollies.

"I'm sorry … I know I was a coward to move away and escape," I murmur, everything in me going silent. "I don't and didn't know how to handle the situation," I confess.

Eva smiles, her hand giving me a squeeze in silent understanding. "No one does. In fact, we guess half our way through life and never feel the difference. Only that you do, and that makes you unique."

I stare at her. Watching this beautiful girl, who somehow became an integral part of my life ever since she hugged me when I was crying in the gardens, to become an even more beautiful woman who can fill me with warmth I can't find anywhere except in her calm heart.

"Thank you," are the only words I can manage.

Eva grabs an orange snake and puts it in my hand. "Let's go to your room." She jumps and walks towards the stairs. "I'm exhausted." She stifles a yawn with the back of her hand.

Oh. Fuck.

Jason is still inside, half naked on *my* bed, inside *my* house.

Everything happens in a flash as I run past Eva with the orange snake hanging from my lips, up the stairs, and block the door with my arms and legs spread like a starfish to each corner. The horror and sweat on my face are almost too much to imagine.

Fuck, can this night go down any further?

"What?" Eva looks at me through her squinted eyes, lips thinned.

"Y—you can't go in. I mean, we—we can't go in." I mentally slap my forehead as I stutter.

Her single eyebrow raises. "And why not?" She crosses her arms on her chest.

Yeah, why not, Bianca? Think, think …

"Because … I puked," I lie.

Is that the best you could come up with?

"You what?" Eva twists her lips in disbelief.

"I had something off today and then ran it down the bathroom. It stinks worse than Kiara's feet." Shaking my head, I flap my hand in front of my nose.

"Fuck." Her face dawns in horror as she sighs. "You okay?" Eva melts as she holds my shoulders.

"I'm made of steel. Nothing I can't take." I rub my stomach for extra effect.

Bianca, seal that mouth, please! White screams.

"Let's take the couch tonight," Eva suggests.

"Or we can take other bedrooms."

"Nah. Maybe some open space can help." She smiles.

"Okay." I nod.

You saved yourself from one ditch …

… To only land in another. White finishes off for Red.

Jason needs to leave this way.

As Eva opens the sofa bed, my fingers fire on my phone to text Jason.

> **Bianca:** *Eva's staying. What are we going to do?*
>
> **Jason:** *I heard. It's fine, you sleep. I'll be out before she wakes up*
>
> **Bianca:** *She came back for a piece of paper. Seriously? I might believe you guys eat your files for breakfast*
>
> **Jason:** *Very. Funny.*

I'm debating whether I should say what the tips of my fingers are itching to type as my thumb hovers over the letters.

Bianca: *Thank you*

I can't use the phrase enough tonight.

Jason: *For?*

Bianca: *For being the grey in my colours. A colour I never knew I wanted*

I wish I could say it to him, but I just need to get the words off my chest. I didn't know that was the missing part. The part where I had made my life so colourful, it hid my demons—the greys.

Jason reads the message but doesn't reply. My heart pounds. Maybe I should've kept quiet.

Then finally his reply, and everything stills.

Jason: *A rainbow needs a grey sky to shine. I am happy to be that only with you*

After making the impromptu bed and cushioning it, we hear nothing but our shallow breaths as we stare into the nothingness of the dimly lit living room.

"Do you remember the time when we went to our last camp together? Even Adrian was there, too. All seven of us slept under the night sky." Eva speaks softly, blending into the calm of the night with the echoes of the light showers outside.

"How could I? That was after we found out about your first boyfriend and—"

"Kai went all bizarre all night. I still don't know what possessed him that night. It was as if he was angry with me for having a boyfriend." I can feel Eva rolling her eyes, probably seeing Kai putting the extra chillies in Eva's bowl, so she would have to sleep in the tent near the bathrooms—which, conveniently enough, was close to Jason and Kai's tent.

Slowly Eva mutters, "And he says he is an adult, really doubt that one."

I chuckle. "Agreed. Then why don't you become the adult and not bicker like kids. He's a nice guy, and you know it."

"Easy for you to say. You didn't have to deal with his *phases,* and all the girls he brought to our place. Insufferable."

"Kids." I mockingly shake my head.

Her breath catches, but her voice comes out smooth when she continues. "I asked something that night."

"I remember. Where do the stars go during the day?" The time comes drifting back in waves, and a warm hit of sentiment follows soon after.

"I finally found the answer." She looks up at me with a dull ache in her eyes that reflects from the small lamp lit on the table. "They are always around us, but they give the day the chance to light up because only the stars can light the dark." She breathes, finding her next words. "In these five years, our stars were stuck in the day and nearly forgotten without you—and *maybe* without Adrian too," Eva says as her eyes glaze. "The darkness is equally important to bring out the light. We are light and dark together, the seven of us. Without each other, we are lost stars."

A silent stream travels the path of my cheek. My hand strokes her hair as she snuggles close to me. "I have a feeling everything will be fine," I murmur and feel the quiet truth in the words.

Eva nods and buries her face in my chest.

No matter the quarrels or the hair pulling fights we would've got into, at least I would've seen them be the adults they are now. Maybe, just maybe, things between Jason and me would've been easier—smoother. We would've been living on the high from the night at the beach. Walking everywhere hand in hand, he would've been smiling more—a smile that makes the gods proud of their human creation.

"I love you guys so much," I whisper.

"We love you too, Bee."

Another stream of tears rolls down. Not for our loss, but for everything we have despite it.

Jason

It's well past one now, and it's dead silent. The rain has calmed enough for me to leave unnoticed.

With my shoes in hand, I cautiously crack open the door. The high-pitched creak from the hinges breaks the still night, and I freeze on the spot when a whine comes from the dozing women. They shift in their places, and Eva makes a noise before she goes back to sleep. The world could crack apart, swallowing her whole, and she'd still sleep soundly.

I tiptoe towards the main door, but halt when one of them stirs in their sleep. Never would I have imagined spending a night with Bianca ending with me escaping from my sister.

Kai's face flashes in my mind as his usual smugness decorates his face. *"I told you, didn't I? You can't fucking resist her, not in this lifetime. I'm still waiting for the keys."* That's word for word what he would say if he saw me right now.

As I close in on the two women cuddled on the sofa bed, my heart does something weird. I don't know how to describe it. It's as if I'm feeling the rush of blood for the first time, feeling alive after being dead for years.

Eva sleeps nestled in the curve of Bianca's neck, her dark hair partially concealing Bianca's chest. Their chests rise and fall in perfect unison, as though connected by invisible hands.

Despite the dried tears on Bianca's cheeks, she seems more at peace than I've ever seen her.

I got snippets of their heart-to-heart, and I can only think of what toll it took on her. She's a person who hides behind all the colours she shows the world, scared to take on the greys which also shape her and make her more beautiful than anyone I know.

Earlier on the bed, it killed me to see and hear all the words hanging on her tongue that she wanted to say but never came out. On top of all the grieving, she had to deal with the poison Aaron Blackburn fed her, shifting her trust in relationships. She doesn't know it, but a spark of distrust flashes through her eyes at the thought of wanting more. I can still read her like an open book—one she tries to close.

I should walk off and leave, but do I? Fuck no. Fighting against my brain has become my pastime, because not even I can stop myself from wanting Bianca now. That's why I lean down on her forehead and place a soft kiss. She hums in her sleep and slowly peels her eyes open.

"I'm leaving now," I whisper.

"See you tomorrow?" she quietly asks.

I nod. "Every day."

As she relaxes and her hold tightens around Eva, my heart leaps again from the overwhelming rush of blood. I step back, but then Bianca reaches for my wrist, halting me as she lets me feel the warmth of her soul on my skin.

Only two months now. The fact screams the scarce time the world has given us, but I'll hold on to anything I can. Anything *we* can. The slightest of straw is enough to save us from drowning.

I lower myself to her ear. "You deserve the world and beyond, Rainbow."

Her soft smile feeds me with another rush of oxygen and drops my hand. But there it is again, that spark of fear in those blue eyes.

I feel the same. But I would be damned not to give this a go, because even if we don't work out, I would die knowing love exists somewhere—just *not for me.*

We stare at each other for a lost moment before I step back. "Good night, Bianca." I place another unplanned kiss on her forehead, and she melts right into it.

She yawns and her eyes softly shut. I pull the fallen blanket up to her chest and linger there longer than needed.

Walking backwards to the door, I see the only woman I will ever desire, and with the thought I shut the door behind me.

Although the rain has stopped, the stiff wind is still in its glory. With the clouds gone, the night sky's beauty shines brightly. Stars scatter like mini bursts of light across the sky in the moonless night, and after a long time, everything feels in the right place.

It's completely complete in the incomplete. Much like the webs of our lives.

CHAPTER 30
Bianca

A week later.

The crisp white envelope feels fragile in my trembling hands, nothing compared to the quivering quake in my head. Will the truth set me free or send me spiralling into a new abyss? I don't know, and truthfully. I'm not ready for this, but there's no other option. I have to open it. The air I'm breathing is also betraying my every will to stay awake as it feels heavy with my curdling fear.

As promised, I gave out the USB and the other pieces he needed. Yet I can't scratch the itch—an itch of guilt. Stealing from Jason marked the line of all limits, and there is nothing I can do to ignore my wrong.

The knots in my stomach tighten into a tangled mess as I breathe through my nose and out my mouth. Maybe I'll read it later.

No! Do it now. At least get something for all the guilt you're putting yourself through. Red Horns butts in.

The market trip feels like a lifetime ago. The week since has been a blur of sensory overload from sights, sounds, and feelings. These seven days were the most magical of my life. There was no moment Jason didn't pursue me like he said he would—by every flat surface we could find and emotion we could unfurl.

But the magic died down, and now I can't even look at my reflection in the mirror. The only person who looks back at me isn't me at all. She's an impostor, a coward, who has taken over, making me feel alienated in my skin.

I've also given the other two pieces, aside from the USB. Aaron had texted me through different unknown numbers every time, and if I wanted to find him, I couldn't. The last I saw him was at the House, and ever since his last text, the silence has been unsettling. I've known him for his patience and greed, and this time just feels like I'm a waiting deer unprepared for an ambush. Because there will be one.

Unknown: Piece 2. Internal people

That was it. *Internal people.* Those who worked closely with Archer Enterprises, especially those involved in internal affairs. Included but not limited to Jacob Carter, the head of management; Savio Castillo, the lawyer who is at the heart of the company's legal ins and outs; and Jelena, leading organisational responsibilities. There were others I had never heard of and most likely never needed to know. Aaron wanted to have the full details of their role and how they maintain the flow of income within and outside of the company's realms.

Unknown: Piece 3. External people

People who are powerful in their domains but have had significant connections with the Archers. Mitchell McKenzie and Simon Foster ranked at the top as powerful bodies of businesses known globally. Recently, Smiths' Security received approval to take over the safety of the main building.

I tried to connect the dots.

USB, internal members and external correspondents. How do they belong to the same cake? Given that I knew nothing of the USB. Admittedly, I tried to open it, but I couldn't. I was giving myself enough guilt trips to avoid another one.

From the high-class security and being locked in a safe, it's safe to deduce that the USB must hold the power to make or break the chain.

Yet you gave it away, White calls out.

All the pieces went out in the same way, through the letterbox. I had enveloped the information and stalked out in the darkest hour of the night. Every time I did, I battled to find the middle ground between the nagging of Red Horns and the rebuttals of White Wings. Both held their ground strongly, unable to be uprooted in the garden of my head.

The only piece left was the asymmetrical puzzle piece. I still don't know what I could do with it. In this game of deception and betrayals, where does a puzzle piece lie to view the wider picture? Maybe this is another cruel game Aaron's playing, designed to further my despair, and give him some twisted satisfaction.

The pain behind my eyes feels like needles, each prick a warning as my heart hammers against my ribs in a chaotic rhythm, making the air thick with dread.

"I'm okay. I'll be fine," I chant, sniffing with my nose tilted up.

If there is darkness, light will also exist.

"How were you always so positive, Ma?" I ask, looking up at the roof. "I wish I was half as strong as you," I mumble through my fogged head.

The four walls of the living room hold me captive in a toxic cage that I could enter of my own will but not leave. It's sad how a place where we laughed, sang, cried, and talked has been reduced to a place of deathly silence. The vast emptiness of the room echoes with a haunting lullaby, a chilling melody that beckons me towards an unending sleep.

A harsh sigh shudders from deep within my chest. "It's now or never."

My surprisingly steady fingers break the envelope's seal and reveal three smaller folded papers inside. A fresh wave of dread and hope crashes over me as I eye the three typed sentences.

The first one.

The giver can be the taker.

Second.

Never trust everyone around you, never.

Third.

Replay history, you will find answers.

Six words, three ambiguous sentences. And no straight answer.

What else did I expect from Aaron's fucked up head? He proves me wrong every time I start to think that he may have even the smallest parts of good in him.

I fell right into his promising words again, and now retracing my steps isn't an option when I've circled back to the same dead end again and again.

Does he think I have time for his fucking riddles! I don't have enough patience to crack an egg, let alone deal with this.

"Fuck! You!" I curse each word with all the strength I have. My lungs burn as I scream and scream. No tears escape. I'm left with only sucking air through my dry throat.

"Tell me!" With a desperate tremor in my hands, I shake the paper and envelope, the scent of fresh paper filling my nose, wishing the answers would fall out.

Ting! A sharp sound comes when something drops to the marble floor.

Everything in me freezes when I lay my eyes on the piece of jewellery I haven't seen in five years. No blood pumping, no decision-making, and definitely no breathing.

This can't be real.

The similar glint of the bright gold winks at me.

Dad's wedding ring. He always wore his ring.

In a rush, I pick up the customised gold jewellery. It's cold—so cold—lacking the life it once had, and the love that once shone in his soft eyes for Ma.

I can't be mistaken. *No.* I will recognise the *L* engraved with various diamonds from any corner of the universe. Ma had the same feminine one with an *O*.

"I don't want my love to get rusty," he always said when Steven and I commented on his peculiar habit of cleaning it every day.

"My love for your Ma will always live." He would step back and admire his handiwork before speaking with a proud smile.

I breathe—the one thing that grants me access when everything else in me is frozen. The cool metal of the ring feels more foreign than I've ever felt. Aaron's messing with me. He cannot get hold of such a precious and significant part of Dad. Unless he went to heaven and got it himself. No, that's not possible. Guards of heaven *and* hell will never let such a hideous soul onto their land. Satan wouldn't want to risk his position.

"Argh!" I scream again, out of frustration. Out of agony. Of anger—toward me. It's always me!

Blinded with anger, I snatch the remote next to me and launch it across the room. It lands hard on the kitchen counter, making the glasses rattle and jump with a sharp, high-pitched noise.

The sweat on my skin makes my pyjamas stick uncomfortably, making each of my movements a heavy drag.

"No. No. No," I chant. "This can't be happening. No. No."

The force of air is hard—ice shards piercing the back of my throat. I'm broken, only physically now. Ever since I was growing up, I have been emotionally and mentally damaged. We never knew what was wrong with me when I woke in the middle of the night, hearing voices no one could hear, and having dreams that terrified me beyond explanation because I couldn't remember them. My parents had me see psychologists and psychiatrists of all kinds but couldn't diagnose me with anything because I was too young.

Again, I was the odd one out.

But the voices had stopped when I met the girls. Their craziness and care were all I needed to be normal. For the first time I didn't feel like a rat under a microscope. I felt like a normal girl with a normal group of friends.

After I left for Canberra, the voices returned, and my world got divided between red and white. I've just made my peace with them. I can't get rid of them because if I exist, so do they.

My most profound lesson I've learned in my years is that no one or thing can destroy you like you can yourself. You can drive yourself crazy with all the secrets and thoughts you bury deep inside you. Fortunately for me, I have many of those.

It's happening again. The walls are growing their own set of feet. They're going to press me flat underneath their weight from the top, bottom, right and left. My throat swells, constricting the path of oxygen, suffocating me in fresh air. My trembling hands are pale and frigid, mirroring the glacial temperature of all the ice I've had.

"Ma! Dad!" I screech, holding my hair from the roots. The familiar ripping pain is enough to make me feel, yet all I want to do is turn the switch off to my emotions. To my thoughts. To me.

My limbs give away, and I collapse onto the cold, hard floor, the lack of support leaving me breathless and defeated.

My body feels like it's on fire, consuming me like the sun eating away at the moon's glory.

Did my parents feel like this when the flames were engulfing them? While knowing their life was slipping out of their hands with every breath?

Helpless. Hopeless. Accepting the universe's ultimate testament and giving in to it.

I haven't felt like this since the time I broke up with Aaron. He was the only one who had gotten close enough that detaching from him felt like an agonising rip. Now the wound has slowly reopened for reasons that stem only from the rot building in me.

Things didn't need to be this hard. White Wings speaks up, and this would be the first time I truly agree with her. I must face the consequences of my own doings. For betraying the only man I thought I could live without but can't.

It's like I was never away from this place at all. From the moment I set foot at the airport until now, things have changed drastically in the most memorable and beautiful way. Jason has grown into a man with so much buried in him, yet from every aspect he is a gentleman. He is learning to trust me, after I left saying I don't. Every word and feeling I expressed in the moment was nothing but my damaged brain speaking. I had no control over it, and that's not an excuse. Jason deserves the world, and I feel terrible I can't give him even a fraction of what he deserves.

Aside from the cold exterior he pulls out for the world, he breaks that apart for me. Allowing me to be a viewer of the nourishing forest he breeds within him. To see how he has kept himself closed within a wall but still be the man of my dreams. *To be the love of my life.*

What? My body hums with its every cell and nerve singing in agreement.

No, Bianca, pull back. You can't afford to go in too deep when you know you can't have a future with him.

It's only a matter of time until he finds out that the deceiver laid so close to him and his heart, White Wings comments.

The three words are on the tip of my tongue, vibrating in my whole being, but I can't muster the courage to bring them out. I have to keep the feelings buried inside me for however long, possibly take them to wherever I end up.

"I need to breathe. Breathe … breathe!"

Crash! Crash! Crash!

The nearest vase joins in the fate of the remote, creating more havoc. The cups, plate and whatever else was on the counter crashed down on the floor, splintering into a million pieces.

My heart is beating in my ears and throat rather than in my chest. I hear nothing but the screams and tormented calls of my parents.

"Help!"

"Someone help!"

"Bianca!"

"Steven!"

A symphony of Ma's smooth voice and Dad's hoarse deep calls out, and I can hardly see through my clouded vision.

"Stop…" I whisper. "Make them stop!" I grit through my tears, slapping my hands on my head.

"Bianca, you're such a failure."

I don't want to hear them, not like this. They won't fucking stop!

"We wasted our time on a sick child."

"Stop! Fucking stop!" I screech, punching the side of my head as I try to get them out of my head. They're so real, the words feel so real, the meaning behind them—the truth. They probably felt that way when I was growing up as a broken kid who they had to care for.

"Stop! Stop! Stop! *Please, stop!*" Tears leak from my eyes like an open faucet as my hands put deadly pressure on my temples. The tears don't stop—they keep coming and fucking coming.

Dropping my hands, I uncurl my clenched fist and feel the stretch in my muscles as they open. My fingers, pale yellow as a dying dandelion petal, open to a palm marked with the circular, blood-red engraving of the ring. The grotesque remains of blood and metal are the only things warm against my skin.

My flesh opens in a small, fresh wound. The slim flow of blood is another gate to breathe—to have the lost air come. Maybe more of it can help. More red—to finally see inside me and take out the infected bug that keeps buzzing inside me.

Bianca, snap out! The synchronised cries of Red and White echo, yet the sight of the dark red liquid, pulsing and glistening, is far more compelling.

The shards of glass are right there in the kitchen. One scratch of the wrist will end it all. Peace—peace, the one that will truly free me.

No! You will not. There's always a solution to every problem, and taking your life isn't one. We are stronger than that.

Don't waste your breath on me, White.

With a deep breath, I push myself up, stretching my stiff limbs before striding towards the jagged shards of broken glass. The citrus scent of the lemon diffuser is dull when I walk past it and it releases a puff of scented smoke.

One slit, that's it.

I bend down and pick up a shard of glass with shaking hands. It feels comforting and welcoming, warm against my stone-cold skin. I've lost all the heat to be human. It's better if I end it.

The shard precariously hangs a millimetre from the nerve on my wrist, its jagged edge gleaming a silent promise of imminent pain and blood.

Just think about everyone who loves you. Think about Jason. *How would he see you after this? You can ignore it, but he loves you. He hasn't said it—he doesn't need to. It's a fact that even the universe can't change. You have to work for it,* Red and White persuade.

A sob wrenches out of me as reality hits. I knew I was a coward and that part of me will live on as long as I do, but how can I forget the people who are here with me now?

They can never see me like this. The mess of a person who can't think away from her own hatred and suffocation in the air she breathes.

I need to scratch the undying itch of self-destruction. If it stays any longer, there will be no going back for me.

Milk.

Jason and the girls had brought in some extra supplies for the times they came over. It can't be fatal, but it can give a taste of what lies after life.

I stumble towards the pantry, bypassing the cabinet of my pills. They scream to be used, to silence the suicidal beating of my head, and to stop me from taking another step forward into the pantry. A place that will lead me to no less pain than piercing my skin with the glass pieces shattered underneath me that surround me like my fallen kingdom.

"Where are you? Where the fuck…" I mutter, throwing everything that isn't milk behind my back. "There you are." The carton of milk eyes me with competition, a challenge of who would stand glorious after the immense battle between the dairy product and my lactose intolerance.

Good for it, I'm not playing for a win.

My clammy fingers fumble with the lid, the smell of milk instantly assaulting my nostrils and churning my stomach. It takes all of me not to gag.

Without a second thought, I tilt the carton and the liquid cascades over my tongue, a rush of bittersweet flavour filling my mouth down my throat.

My stomach violently churns a cocktail of digestive chemicals, the doctors always detailed, letting nausea overwhelm me with surprising speed. The longest, loudest bang imaginable rings in my ears, splitting my consciousness and shaking my vision until I can barely stand. The world around me becomes a dizzying chaos.

Tears swell my eyes as they make their grand appearance, flowing at an uncontrollable rate. I keep drinking, regardless. I need to feel all of it.

For all the times I was alone.

All the times I was not enough.

All the times I was weak in my own shoes.

All the times I ruined everyone's lives.

All the times I was myself.

I tip the rest of the milk down my throat, and that broke my hump. I marathon to the bathroom, cupping my mouth.

As soon as I enter the bathroom, I dive for the toilet and everything comes spilling out, emptying my already empty stomach. It's early evening, the time when lunch is long gone, but dinner is still on its way.

The acidic burn in my stomach makes me smile, and the stench of my insides outside keeps pushing me towards the edge of the cliff again and again.

The yellow, unpleasant liquid quickly fills the circular toilet bowl. I feel like I'm pouring out everything inside me, but I worry that I'll be a heap of lifeless skin and bones when everything is done.

Dry heaving, my grip tightens on the edges and only strings of drool escape my lips. My insides ignite with their own loss and dare to detach themselves from me. The burn and helplessness, is this what death feels like?

"Bianca!" His gruff voice, a rasping echo in my ears, beckons me to him, drying the tears on my burning cheeks.

He's here.

He's always here.

He shouldn't be.

Bianca

The blurry silhouette of Jason's broad shoulders stands under the door frame. He looks perfect, even in my dizzy vision. He is everything a woman could ask for.

A man of his word, a man who is everything to me when he shouldn't be. The man of my life. A surge of delight and joy should fill me at his sight, instead, guilt and shame stand prominent. For what I am and for what I will be once he finds I used his trust.

A man that can't be mine, unless I take him down the path of ruin with me.

Another round of puke rips out for another reason, and some spills over onto the tiles. My cheeks flush with unbearable heat, sweat beads

on my skin, both second nature to my stifling body heat.

"Bianca! Fuck!" I think he screams, but all I hear is a jumble of roaring sounds. After a moment, I hear him scream again. "Do you fucking think I care! Get me the doctor. Fly them, get them fucking now!" he commands to someone as I go another round.

He falls beside me, and his cool, minty scent fills the air. A comforting wave crashes over me, and I instantly sigh in relief.

Jason's strong fingers gather my hair while he gently pats my back. "Calm down. It's okay. Breathe."

Exhausted and aching, with the taste of bile still bitter in my mouth, I sink against the wall, desperate for a moment's rest. My lungs burn as each gasp of air becomes a plea for my ravaged organs, which scream in a symphony of pain.

"Are you okay?" Jason's familiar deep voice comes through the haze in my head. He sits beside me and clears my forehead of any hair.

"I don't know," I say, closing my eyes with a weak shrug.

Maybe I should tell him about Aaron and all the shit he got me into. No! No. NO! I can't. What will he think of me? He will leave me—he will have no choice.

You know he won't, Red says.

"Fuck." His thick fingers slide into his dark hair as he looks at me with a storm of unspoken questions in his eyes. "Tell me who I have to murder?" His head thuds against the wall, a dull sound swallowed by the silence as we stare up at the white ceiling.

I chuckle, looking the other way. "I'm okay," I whisper, tears streaming down my face.

He carefully wraps the smooth velvet of his blazer around my chest and shoulders. It was then that I realised my limbs were stiff and numb from the cold, violently shaking with no end on their own will.

"You don't look okay," he says as he wipes off the remaining tears.

"Let's get you to bed."

His hands envelop my calves and back as he carefully carries my limp body from the bathroom to the bedroom. With every step, his biceps bulge, a sharp tick feathers in his clenched jaw, and his green eyes flash with fierce determination.

He is in his all-blue work suit. The inner vest, to the tie, to even the shoes are blue. Guess I am coming off well. I shouldn't want that regardless, it blossoms warm, appreciating heat in my chest.

His lips are in a flat line, all red and kissable. The taste of his touch and lips still lingers on me from last week. As long as I have him, I want to make him feel the wonders of the world that he deserves. He might not say what he desires out loud, but I don't need to hear it to feel it.

When our lips touched at the site, I knew his every breath had been a silent testament to his undying affection for me. He remembered every moment we spent together before the shitshow our lives turned into. He wants me as much as I want him.

A big ask from a person who is ruining his life just by existing.

Fuck off, Red Horns. I'd had enough of your shenanigans. If it weren't for you, I wouldn't be here, consumed by self-loathing, and weighed down by the actions and emotions I can't escape.

The walk from the bathroom to the bed is ten steps, but I may have lived all of the twenty-five years of my life.

"Rest. Doctors are on their way," Jason says gently, lying me on my soft bed. With a groan, I lift my head from the cold sheets stinging as they touch me.

"Please stay." *As long as you can.* My fingers curl around his wrist, feeling the cool, smooth metal of his Rolex against my skin.

"What happened?" he finally asks. He fills my glass with water from the side table. His mint and warmth wrap me in their hold as my breathing comes at regular intervals, ditching the pants.

I was trying to torture myself for betraying your trust to get to the only truth about my life.

I am trapped in Aaron's web, who haunts my every waking step to look over my shoulder. But please don't leave me.

I bite my tongue as I taste the words. They're so close to being spoken, a dreadful tremor of anticipation runs through me teasing me to no end.

"I…" I clear my throat. The metallic taste of ash and lies coats my tongue as I gulp down the water. "I thought it was my almond milk. It wasn't."

Lies.

Jason's touch is tender as he cups my face, but a sudden, vibrant green fire ignites in his eyes, a captivating contrast to their usual gentleness. "I was serious when I said who I need to murder."

Kill me then. "I'm serious as well, Jason. Just a slight mistake." I sigh.

"The last time this happened, we barely survived. It could be much worse—"

"Dr Jason, I'm fine. I won't be dying anytime soon," I scoff. "Much less from a small sip of milk."

My forced chuckle dies in the air, a pathetic attempt to lighten the mood. Darkness gathers in his eyes, mirroring the growing tension.

"Is there anything you want to tell me?" His voice drops several degrees until it rivals the darkest of caves.

I shake my head, not opening my mouth, scared that I would spill the truth.

"If it has anything to do with Aaron, he will be sorry for ever having known you." He holds my wrist in his hand, the same wrist that I was ready to slit. "I promise you, there will be rivers of blood to pay for anyone even if they said your name wrong." His deep, dark voice sounds dangerous in the quiet.

I've never seen him like this. He's walking on a path of thin ice. Each step hardens the surface beneath his feet because the ice that consumes him in this moment can freeze everything in its path.

His eyes lock onto mine as they promise annihilation. I know promises are often broken, a whisper fading into the wind, and this one will be no different. Someday, it will too fade.

"Wait, how did you get in?" I ask, changing the topic.

"I knocked, but you didn't answer. I knew you took a day off today. So, it was the keypad," Jason explains. His thumb gently strokes my hand—but never holding it.

"You know the passcode?" I furrow my eyebrows. "I don't remember telling you."

"Yeah, wonders can come from a drunk person." He looks at me deadpan. "0612." His words are soft as he says the numbers.

He knows what it means. A blush creeps up my neck, my heart hammering like a drum solo against my ribs.

06/12.

If the balance of yin and yang could be a single day, it would be the sixth of December. Yin's shadow casted a pall of darkness and destruction. The flames of the burning house painted the scene in a hellish light and then bled into our memories.

Yang is this man. His six-foot-two frame emanated warmth, a comforting calmness, and he was my only source of light in that desolate place. In his hands, I found solace—a balm for the gaping wound in my chest inflicted by that night's cruel losses.

He was my sweet oblivion. Yin and Yang don't occur without each other, and neither does my need for this man and the love he deserves. Two very distinguished concepts that belong in one, yet always pulled apart.

I don't deserve him.

"I'm sorry," I apologise as streams of tears fall from my tired eyes. My pale fingers cover my face, hiding from my shame and guilt.

"Hey. Hey." The scent of his cologne fills my nostrils as his arms wrap around my neck, pulling me into his embrace.

A mixture of drool and tears runs down my face, making it impossible to tell one from the other. I push myself into him, fingers digging into the fabric of his shirt as I lose myself in the feel of his hard chest against mine. The only sound is our hearts beating as one. To find my ultimate peace in the arms of the only person I would want to see in my final moments, before the infinite void of darkness swallows me—offering a single moment of serenity.

"Shh. Shh. It's fine," he whispers, his fingers gently tracing the back of my head with a feather-light touch. "It's okay, I'm here. Always."

My hiccups come in irregular bursts, each one a sudden, convulsive gasp that leaves me breathless and gasping for air.

"I'm sor … ry. I'm so … so sorry." The apology echoes in my ears like a mournful lullaby, a haunting melody I'd sing for a lifetime if it cleansed the dirt of my mind and heart.

"Bianca, look at me," he says as he pulls me up to see my face. "Breathe with me. Breathe. In and out." He slowly and deeply breathes in and out, his actions mimicking the gentle rhythm of a toddler's breath.

I do that, but the burning in my stomach and the clenching in my chest remain—no matter how deeply I breathe.

My chest heaves for air, but nothing comes, and before I know it, his lips seal mine. All else dissolves into a hazy nothingness, leaving only the intoxicating pressure of his lips against my own.

He holds me close, his arms a warm embrace around my waist, occasionally squeezing gently.

My arms instinctively find their way to his neck. His muscular frame is an anchor against my surging emotions, a reassuring weight as I draw closer and let him own my soul.

The movement of our lips is a slow, deliberate caress, a stark contrast to the fierce hunger we usually have. His tongue dances with mine as we find an escape in each other's arms.

The sensation of his teeth on my lower lip ignites a surge of energy, transforming my earlier thoughts into raw, primal lust for this man.

The sound of my gasp fills the room when Jason lifts me and smoothly changes our positions, with him now sitting against the bedhead and me on his lap. His hard erection is more prominent in this position. His suit pants stretch tight as he grunts deeply, gutturally, while my throbbing heat presses against him.

He unzips himself and takes out his hard and angry cock that stands between us. "Use me," he whispers against my mouth as he swipes my shorts and panties to the side in one smooth movement.

His tongue shoots in, declaring its dominance while it marks every corner of my mouth. The only audible sounds are the smooching of skin against skin, intermingled with my muffled moans and his grunts. I move back and forth as I begin to grind him. The veins and grooves of his cock and the leaking precum feel so alive to my sensitive heat. All I can do is obey and move back and forth. Fuck, what must I look like? Hair all over the face, smelling of vomit and now him.

"Jason…" I tap on his chest. He parted just enough for me to whisper each word on his lips. "I puked."

"Yet you taste the sweetest."

"Jas—" His tongue collides with mine, cutting off the rest of my words.

A slow, deliberate slide of Jason's hand under my shirt evokes a ripple of goosebumps across my stomach. His touch is warm and calming, everything that his lips, teeth, and tongue are not. They inflict a lethal caress that belies the gentleness of his movements.

As I grind on his cock, I feel his chest rise and fall with heavy breaths, his grip around me growing tighter. Zaps of pleasure course through me with each of his grunts and the way he digs his fingers into me.

Our lips are pasted on each other, moving frantically in a rhythm to find the purchase we're chasing.

"Fuck, what are you doing to me?"

"Jay … I'm coming," I moan on his lips. My fingers curl on his shoulder as I keep moving myself onto him.

"Come for me, baby." He rests his forehead against mine. "Take me the way you like it."

My strongest yet orgasm hits me, and with a soft and muffled sound, I hide in his neck, feeling every wave leaving me.

This didn't feel sexual at all. It felt a calm reprieve with my insides coming back to me and my brain finally resting.

I reach down for his cock and stroke him to give him his release as well, but he holds my hand, stopping me.

He shakes his head. "Not today. I wanted to give it to you."

We stare, breathing each other in. "Jason." I swallow, gathering the courage to speak. "Please…" I keep stroking him. "Let me."

He doesn't stop me. And my heart cracks for our—for the pain I'll give him.

"Jason …" I swallow, my hand not stopping as he breathes heavily, carrying each breath with the promise of everything he believes in. "I'm broken … and I don't know how long it would take for me to piece every broken part back together again." My eyes drift to the uneven skin on the side of his wrist. "You deserve a person so much better than me. Someone who can keep you happy."

My hand keeps at its work, going from the base until the tip and pressing my thumb to smear the precum.

"Mine." Jason finds a moment to speak through his heavy breathing. "You're my broken. My woman to love the way I have her. Broken or fixed. I don't give a fuck. All that matters is that you're mine. *Only mine*," he punctuates each word on my lips. "You're right, you don't deserve me because *I am* not worthy of you. If I wanted to find happiness, I would've five years ago when you left, but I didn't." His finger traces the outline of my hooped earrings. "You were and are the only girl I have ever kissed, the only girl who I have ever made love to and will always be. I never settled for anyone because no one gave me the peace I was searching for—you took it with you."

His forest-green eyes soften, *truly* letting me in for the first time. He shifts as cock pulses in my hand and heat builds between us.

"A lot has changed in these years, but one thing hasn't. My *need* to live for you and die for you," he speaks with a desperate need to explain. "You became my friend, only to become one for life."

His hand covers my own, the touch sending shivers down my spine. Each word, imbued with profound meaning, makes my heart flutter like a trapped bird, its wings beating against the cage of my ribs.

Regardless of what he says, I keep stroking him, my speed increasing. I lean down and skim his cock with kisses. I can't speak physically—I can't get the clogged words out of my throat, so I express my emotions through every kiss and stroke of my hand along his cock. I squeeze his balls, and it doesn't take him long to find his release. His groan echoes deeply in the room, followed by a sweet and soft *rainbow*.

He lifts my chin, pulling me back to face him. His eyes level mine in a stare. "You're not broken, but tortured. Life isn't fair to us, but it took a lot from you. I can't promise to return anything you lost—I can't—but let me be the gold that runs through your cracks, to hold your pieces together like you do mine." He nods when my brows furrow.

"I'm broken too, in ways that I don't even know yet. But the purity of the gold that runs in your heart is enough to fill my cracks and make me forget about them—however large or small. I want to be the same to you, even when I'm nothing compared to you."

I blink. A single tear falls, hot and heavy, landing on our intertwined hands. "I—"

"Rest," he murmurs. Jason lays me back on the bed. "The doctor will be here soon." He leans down, his hand smoothing my hair with a comforting pressure, his kiss a warm, silent promise on my forehead.

I close my eyes, feeling safe after years.

Reminder: I have him. For now.

CHAPTER 32
Jason

Blood roars in my ears, my skin crawls with a nauseating scratch, and a deep loathing consumes me as Bianca's tear-streaked face, full of helplessness and a desperate plea for an end, flashes before my eyes.

By the third knock on the door, deadly worry shot through me. I didn't need to think twice to nearly murdering the keypad, and the moment the door swung open, my stomach lurched with a sickening feeling.

The living room had been through hell and back. Cushions laid strewn across the floor, shards of glass crunched underfoot in the kitchen, and pieces of paper were forgotten on the couch, revealing shadowy, upside down script.

Then, the noises from the bathroom came, and I ran—ran like my life depended on it. Ran as if being chased by a bear. It wasn't my life I was concerned about. It was the life of the woman I went out to find.

It's all a blur after that. Bianca fell asleep after the doctor came. She advised rest and extreme care of her diet.

I close the bedroom door, letting Bianca sleep while I see the overturned place in front of me. My steps are slow as I walk around the kitchen counter. A harsh, ragged breath escapes me as I spot two crimson drops of blood next to an empty milk carton on the ground, the metallic scent faint but sharp.

My fingers crunch into a fist. The sight of Bianca curled around the toilet, her knuckles white from gripping not only on the white ceramic, but for the strings of life. Harsh breaths rattled in her chest, and drool leaked from her lips and fuck do I want to ignite this entire fucking world on fire.

After she responded to my kiss with her eager passion, I knew she was still in there holding on. In that moment with her lips on mine, the intensity pacified my inner demon, restraining its power.

She may not grasp the intensity of my possessiveness and protectiveness when she's concerned. Those who lay a wrong hand on her will face an agonizing, fiery death—a fate they'll desperately wish to escape.

Red blurs at the corners of my eyes as I crouch and run my fingertip on the slick drop of blood on the kitchen floor.

"You will fucking pay," I murmur darkly, savouring the slick feel of the metallic liquid between my forefinger and thumb. "I swear to you, Rainbow."

I get up, and the sight of shattered ceramic—plates and bowls in jagged pieces—screams in its own agony, the pantry an equal chaotic mess behind it. Stepping into the living area, my feet meet a thick plush cushion, muffling the sound of my steps. It has a soft, delicate texture, yet marred by the ragged holes for fingers.

I notice three sheets of stark white paper lying still and untouched against the sofa's dark fabric. Upside down letters peek out from under the papers, their meaning obscured, and I strain to decipher them. Reaching out with a steady hand, I pick up the first sheet and turn it over.

Buzz … Buzz…

My phone rings with Kai's calls.

"We have news," Kai says to the point as soon as I pick the call. His voice is cold and detached, something we rarely get.

"Hold it. I'll be there later tonight," I answer, putting the paper back and head up to the balcony.

Kai hums over the phone. The sound of a door shutting comes through the speaker. "Are you at Bianca's?" he asks seriously but carefully.

"Yeah."

"Is she okay?"

My eyebrows shoot to my hairline at the question. "For now. She had a reaction to milk but is sleeping. How do you know?"

"It's better if you see it for yourself. The bastard we caught is something, and he has some interesting things up his sleeves," Kai relays, but I can feel the dread in his voice.

"It's time they fucking burn off the face of this planet," I say, feeling the cold wind burn against my face.

"They will, and Jay?" he asks cautiously.

When I remain silent, he continues, "I've always wanted the best for you and Bianca, but when you see this … just know not everything the eye sees is true." His voice holds a light warning.

Goosebumps stand on my arms and the back of my neck. "I know, but be there to remind me," I whisper. "And Kai?"

He hums again.

"Thank you for all the years you've been there for me. But you were wrong about one thing."

He chuckles, knowing what I'm about to say. "What?"

"I can go through another heartbreak if she gives it to me," I answer the very question he asked me every time I thought about Bianca.

He scoffs over the phone. "Have the Porsche ready."

We laugh lightly, a brittle sound against the approaching tempest, ignoring all the things that are buried and well knowing a storm is coming fast and strong at us.

"Adrian is coming, and I'm off to see what he has," Kai says. "I'll see you."

I come off the call and stare at the evening, feeling nothing.

Not a chirp of a bird.

Not even a single movement.

For long minutes, everything was still and so was I, until the door behind me opens and out came the most beautiful human to be born.

"Bianca?" I rush to her as she leans weakly against the door frame. Her dry hair clings to her neck, and her swollen lips hint at our passionate episode.

"Jason." Desperation etches her face as she digs her fingers into my bare forearms, her nails engraving in.

A strange dimness falls over her eyes, their usual brightness gone, replaced by emptiness. "I'm here now. You're still weak. You need some sleep."

"No, I don't want to sleep," she says. "I'm hungry."

I nod and silently guide her down to the living room, and Bianca flinches when she takes in the room.

"Stay here. I'll see what I can make." I lay her on the couch while cupping her cheek. She leans into my touch and closes her eyelids.

Tears still cling to her cheeks like stubborn jewels, revealing the rawness of her emotional scars that time hadn't yet softened.

With a deep ache in my chest, I clear up the kitchen. The glass swept, and the pantry put back to normal and not a battlefield. Once I'm done, I open the fridge and check what I can make. Soup would be a pleasant reprieve as a light meal.

"Please tell me you learned how to cook?" I ask once I put the water to boil, then add the vegetables and chicken in the pot. "I haven't touched any thing pasta after the wonder you made."

"I can cook perfectly fine." I hear her huff before she shoots a sharp glance over her shoulder.

"Sure." I don't sound so convincing.

"Don't cry when you wake up with no dick tomorrow. I hear they're in demand in the black market," she warns, as she tries to keep her smile at bay.

The carrot cuts with a satisfying slice, and with it I look at her through my hooded eyes. "I'm not the one riding it, and screaming curses because of it," I calmly answer.

Her face burns crimson, but she remains silent.

"Unless I put it in your mouth to shut you up."

She bites her bottom lip as if imagining exactly that. She clears her throat, her eyes training on me. "Maybe I don't just want to drink chicken soup tonight." She comes around and leans against the sofa, the colour to her legs and arms returning to their usual light tan—to Lina's Italian roots. "I'm in the mood for something more ... *you.*"

"Oh, fuck," I mutter under my breath, my cock tightening in my pants. The knife lies on the chopping board with a slow thud as I will myself to keep it in my pants. "Shut up and sit your ass on the sofa, woman." It was supposed to come out as a request, but as my breathing becomes deep, I growl out the words instead.

Add the salt. I think to distract myself.

She comes closer with one foot in front of the other, her smile becomes a little sharper. As she sits at the counter, she swipes a piece of carrot and props it in her mouth. "So, how was work?"

Great fucking way to deflate the mood along with the beast in my pants. I give her a pointed look, and she chuckles, well knowing what she's playing at.

"Jelena had a meeting to mention some issues with the ventilation systems, and Carter came with the solution to the connections we made with the Smiths. Jelena requested a private meeting to discuss other matters." A conversation like this feels so normal with Bianca. So natural because I don't need to calculate what I need to say next, I just say it.

"So, what did you say? About the *private* meeting?" Bianca asks, her tone more clipped than earlier.

"I said whatever is necessary," I mutter, adding black pepper and watching the ingredients simmer.

"Did you now? That's great." She lets out a sarcastic laugh as I turn around to return the salt and pepper to their cupboard.

"Jelena is the best we've got in terms of her skills, and if having extra meetings could give the design a boost, then why not."

When I see Bianca again, her face is red, deeply creased with anger? Frustration?

"That's great," she repeats, rolling her eyes, the sarcasm dripping from her tone. "I thought your schedule was jam-packed with meetings, day and night, leaving no room for anything else. Wait, you can make time *for her*, can't you? 'Because she's *'the best we've got'*. Anything for the best." She holds up her fingers for air quotes to solidify the point.

I come around the counter as the pot whispers with its cooking, and Bianca boils in her turmoil. "Calm down, *jealous*."

Bianca scoffs and runs her fingers over my forehead, sliding my hair to the side. "I'm not."

"Don't be. There's only one woman who turns the axis of my world every time she breathes."

Bianca's chest rises and falls at a steady beat, her eyes glowing with new energy. "Who?"

I don't answer, instead, my lips seal hers, and we melt into the kiss. Nothing in this world is more important than this moment right here.

"Here. Careful, it's hot," I warn, carrying the steaming soup bowl to her, a rich aroma filling the air with the blend of spices and chicken. That half hour was well spent, although I burned my hands more times than I could count, but it was all worth it.

"All the emergency numbers are on the fridge. Just in case I don't make it through this." Bianca laughs, so lightly and heartily I can't imagine anything sounding better. "But right now you need to feed me, because I'm about to pass out." She fucking pouts.

This girl will be the end of me.

"Just drink the damn soup." I gather a spoonful of tender chicken and vegetables, blow on it and bring it to her lips.

Her eyes go wide as she sips, slowly chewing the chicken pieces.

I tilt my head towards her to hear the verdict and, oddly enough, I am nervous about this.

"Woah." She gulps, taking down the liquid. Her eyes widen when they come to my face. She

smiles and closes her eyes as she savours the taste. "Yep, I'm never touching the kitchen again when you're here. It's a four-star," she says, chewing.

I take a deep breath of the much-needed fresh air filling my lungs.

"Four? How about we wrap it up with five?" I suggest. My lips tilt as ideas come into my head. This is the most relaxed I've been in a long time, not thinking about what could happen next or where the next hit would come from. In this moment, I am … me.

"It's missing a touch. I don't know what it is." She taps her lips.

"There is one way I could get the five stars."

I take a spoonful of the soup, letting it cool in my mouth. Dragging her onto my lap, with my hand on her thighs, I softly take her lips, and slip the fragrant soup into her mouth. The warm liquid creates a comforting sound as she swallows.

She would taste every shred of chicken, every cut of the carrots and other vegetables, but most importantly, taste us. She cups my face as she drinks down the soup.

"Does that get me the star?" I ask after lingering close to her for a moment too long.

"It was missing the golden touch." A tint of red blossoms into a darker shade on her cheeks as she fiddles with her fingers. Her gaze softens. "The Jason touch."

It's eleven now, and Bianca is back to her soft snoring. Her koala-like grip tightens around my neck as she nestles deeper into my chest, and the scent of her hair fills my senses while she sleeps peacefully. Despite her rhythmic breathing and the damp spot of drool on my shirt, it doesn't diminish the affection and peace I feel.

But I need to get to Phoenix. Kai's text arrived after the call to have security placed in Bianca's place and the girls. The guards will be here, surrounding the house and out of sight.

Yet I can't ignore the heaviness each word carried, and the chilling emptiness flowing out of Kai at whatever they had discovered, a darkness that lingered in the silence.

I only hope that the door we're approaching tonight isn't one I'll regret opening.

CHAPTER 33
Jason

Nothing has changed since the last time I was walking past these same walls, littered with crests for the different members of the society.

Above them all is the perfect depiction of the mythical creature that holds ownership of the society. The Phoenix, sculpted in gold and silver, sits at the top with its wings spread in pride as the flames captured in the art of stone become its crown. The true symbol of living, the ongoing cycle of healing, dying and rebirth. No other miracle of a being could encapsulate such meaning in itself.

The first of the multiple crests is a Griffin. It holds the solitude of all creatures in one, carrying the head of an eagle and the body of a lion.

A powerful animal combining the two most heard of creatures that master in their own worlds—the lion, king of the land, and the eagle, ruler of the sky. They soar and rule their realms fearlessly, without the burden of the outside world.

It is carved effortlessly onto the stone board, capturing it as it stands facing the sun, straight and proud. The wisdom and power dripping from its every pore carry the good and evil within it. A dangerous combination of motifs that can bring the world to its knees if one ought to use it with righteous will.

For me. It will only have one face of light tan with soft features, carrying eyes deeper than any ocean, a nose with a sharp edge, and lips softer than any feather.

Anything I define within myself will always and only reside within her entity. I find the fact dooming. No one has ever claimed me in such a way as to have unconditional ownership of me.

The Griffin in me will always bow its head in the wake of her rainbow.

I am doomed.

"We're ready. This way." Teal comes in, interrupting my thoughts.

Back to business.

After taking the elevator to the basement, I find Kai and Adrian sitting opposite each other at the long table in the meeting room. They both stare at the dark wood of the table, lost in their thoughts, which is a concerning fact on its own. There is nothing on the table but a laptop and a plastic bag with a shadow of things in it.

"What's happening?" I ask, unbuttoning my blazer, and sit at the head of the table between them.

"It's better if you watch it," Kai says as he slides the laptop in front of me. He presses the space key and the video on the screen plays.

It's CCTV footage of Bianca's front yard. From early this evening, maybe an hour before I got there. Nothing seems misplaced until Bianca comes out to put a package away in the letterbox and looks to the left, then right, and heads back inside. The hair at the back of my neck sticks as I perspire. Not a minute later, a shadowy figure, muscles rippling beneath his black clothing, emerges from the corner, snatches the package, and leaves behind a white envelope.

"It doesn't end there," Adrian says as he presses the forward key and skips ten minutes. Bianca comes out, hard on her toes as she checks on her left, then her right, and dips her hand into the letterbox. Her hands tremble, her knuckles white as she clutches the envelope. As she does, her gaze fixates on the envelope as if drawn into a vortex.

What are you doing, Bianca?

The footage stops there, and a moment of silence stuns the room.

"Had it been anyone else, I would've ignored it, but we're dealing with Bianca here. She is an easy target for Pyrosilk to use against us. But what would they hold against her for her to help them—"

"She. Is. Not," I growl, cutting Kai off. I slam my fist on the table, rattling the laptop and Adrian's hand down. "How fucking dare they put her in the middle of this!"

"There's good news as well. We found it," Adrian says. His long fingers curl around the square package before launching it to me across the table with a flick of his wrist. "And some other things in her letterbox."

I examine the package, and my heart sinks another inch when a USB—*our USB*—and two sheets of names slip out.

"They took nothing, but..." Kai gets the USB from my hand and plugs in the laptop. "This."

Adrian skims through all the files and evidence of Phoenix's existence, but he opens the last folder, which wasn't there before. Pictures of the early Australian gold rush come through, which quickly became pictures from sixty years ago, but there is a red exclamation mark on that folder labelled *'Bendigo'*.

"What's this?" I ask, tapping an impatient finger on my thigh.

"This is why they wanted to get the USB. Not because they wanted to steal, but to give, and frankly speaking, it doesn't feel like a Pyrosilk doing." Adrain clicks on the file, and images of miners and publicans get displayed. My attention gets stolen when a picture of the Kennedy brothers appears.

"That's Grandpa Kennedy, Oliver, and Gareth." Kai points at the screen, clarifying my thoughts.

The two brothers look no older than one or two, their tiny hands gripping their father's legs as they stand beside him, who is wearing hardware clothing. I couldn't find a single difference between the two brothers. Their hair, eyes, and even the way they carried themselves were exactly alike.

"How can we be sure they are the Kennedys?" I question. My finger keeps tapping on my thigh.

"Because of this." Adrian clicks on the next image—twenty years later. It's them, older and more recognisable, holding hands of a beautiful young girl. She looks exactly like Bianca—no doubt that's Lina. "We scanned the images, and they're true. It's funny they're wearing miners' clothes when mining was low in the Bendigo area. That's where they lived, right?"

I nod.

"This photograph was taken around forty years ago," Adrian continues. "It's when Oliver and Lina got engaged, them being twenty and twenty-one." My cousin's light eyes come to me with surprising calm. "And ... that's also when the biggest gold nugget was found."

"But they never officiated it." Kai clicks the next button, and the picture of a large golden nugget fills the screen.

How do we know about it if there is no record of it?

Because we know where it is, and now, so do they.

"You're saying someone is trying to find it and they've located it?" I ask.

"Not only that. Nick called earlier after a virus spread in the New York study of Phoenix. Interestingly, the virus only affected the library's records, and you know what that means," Adrian explains, and his expression turns grim.

"They're coming for it," I complete his thought.

"So, what're we doing now?" Adrian says.

Kai's eyes drift to me, and even with the dark clouds surrounding us, I know exactly what he's thinking.

I get up and push my chair out. "What any sane man will do. *Research.*"

The dim light barely illuminates the otherwise spotless space, highlighting only the crimson blood dripping from the shackled boy slumped against the wall.

He is only in his pants and bare from the chest, giving way to the star tattoo inked in the centre of his chest to be displayed. His pale body stands strong with his hands tied above.

"Vincent Warren, twenty. Addicted to everything and anything he can ingest, smoke or inject. He fell into a trap that he can't escape and is being swallowed whole," Kai calmly roars beside me.

Vincent lifts his head and smiles hauntingly at us. He is enjoying this too much, not for long. The cold steel of the cuffs, chained to the ground, bite into his wrists, leaving barely enough room to move, let alone when pressed against the wall of needles.

I know who he is.

The server.

"Interesting," I hum as I stroll towards him and glare at his smile. "Why does a boy want to get involved in a pack of bloodthirsty wolves?" My voice is deceptively smooth.

I peel him off the wall like a Band-Aid from a wound—slowly and painfully. His chest spasms as he keeps his breathing even and does not heave from the pain.

My fingers curl around his shoulder and dig into the grooves there. He hisses and stomps his feet to escape, but there is no escaping now.

Vincent smirks, forgetting his pain for a fleeting moment. His head hangs to the side, and his golden blond hair drips with sweat. "Don't bother yourself. I'll tell you what you want." His voice is thick with the sound of local boys.

"Oh, that's not fun. What do you think, guys?" I spread my hand and say over my shoulder to Kai and Adrian.

"Nah, I like to see some red and maybe some purple around the eye," Adrian suggests as he draws a circle on his eye.

"Agreed. Mistakes come with lessons and punishments." Kai nods to himself as he cracks his knuckles.

I take off my blazer and place it on the heavy wood table, propped against the wall, holding a valuable collection of tools, guns, and knives.

I grab the branding iron carved with a phoenix. "This specialises in slow burns, making its mark for the long term," I say, twisting the thin metal piece from the wooden handle.

"It's been some time since I got inked. Thanks, mate, I owe you." Vincent laughs, dropping his head.

With the flame gun, I heat the end of the iron until it glows deep red.

"You do. But first, who are you working for? I'm not interested in vague answers. Tell me the purpose and intention."

"I work for myself." He speaks, looking straight into my eyes. His slumped body straightens as he grazes against the prickled wall, sucking at the pain.

I bring the iron closer to his chest, aiming it at his shoulder blade.

"You think you're so smart. In fact, too smart." My eyes widen with a mix of anger and frustration. "Now let's drop the act and tell me *who* you work for?"

His bloodshot eyes, filled with a chilling certainty, fix on me.

The head of the iron slowly pushes into his flesh, and a slight sizzling sound echoes in the room.

"Ah!" he howls, tilting his head back, and drool drops from the corner of his mouth.

My hand pushes the iron more, feeling the intense heat and pressure.

"Aaron Blackburn," he rasps, each word a strained whisper as his body trembles violently, barely holding onto consciousness.

I take a step back and examine his swollen skin, going from a deep red to a duller colour.

"He gave me jobs to do, and I got paid with what I needed. It was a simple deal," Vincent explains, breathing like it's his last.

"What kind of jobs?" Kai steps beside me, his dark blue eyes darker.

"The kind that keeps us alive. He's working under Pyrosilk but wants to play by his rules."

"Where is he now?" Adrian comes to my other side. He clenches his hands tightly.

"He's already here," Vincent says with confidence.

With my teeth grinding and my pulse roaring, I step towards him and grab him by his sweaty hair and meet him eye to eye. "You're very young, boy. Get out of this maze while you can. It's only for your own good."

"Guys, there's a call on the burner." Teal bursts through the door. "It's Aaron."

Our bodies still, and Vincent's shoulder shakes with unsaid laughter.

Before we all exit the room, I face Vincent. "Stay."

"I don't really have much of an option, smartass." He jingles his arm, making the chains rattle.

Shaking my head, I go to the door but stop when I hear him laugh. "*You're* a very experienced man. So, pack your big guns. It's only for *your* good."

I try my best to block the truth in his voice as I enter the meeting room again.

"We finally meet, Jason Archer."

"You wish you didn't, Aaron Blackburn."

CHAPTER 34
Bianca

"I am always here with you, gioia mia." She leaves a soft and lingering kiss on my forehead. The tender touch of her lips makes me smile as I close my eyes to cherish the moment. I just love it when she calls me her jewel.

"I love you, Ma." My soft confession turns into a scream as her face melts in my hand, the skin crawling away, revealing dark, grainy flesh. The horrifying sight and smell of decay filling my senses. "Ma!"

With a sharp snap of a finger, I'm in front of our farmhouse covered by the inky blackness of the night. It's raining and windy, just like that night. The storm outside is a perfect reflection of the tempest in my heart. The night is heavy with a scent thicker than death.

The house is getting bigger and higher—no, I'm getting lower. I'm sinking into the mud—blood. The metallic stench assaults my nose as the mix of green waste and blood *devours my feet slowly.*

But that doesn't take my breath away. Th e two burning bodies do. One of them turns its head with a sound of nails scratching a board so horrifying I will remember for the rest of my breathing life. Not in control of my body, I instantly convulse, dropping on my knees, deep in the blood-bleached mud, which creates a thick layer on my hands. My breathing comes in great successions, and my vision blinds with red, white and black as the body now opens its mouth.

No sound comes, but a black inky mist, which slithers to circle around my throat, choking any remaining air out of me.

My ears ring and limbs give up as the bodies reduce to ash from their feet.

"The end is coming … save yourself…" It's a sharp and haunting whisper which tightens the noose of the black mist around my neck, and my heart stops. A hiss like a snake sounds with the next words. "Leave."

"Bianca, wake up!"

"Ahh!" A fiery pain shoots through my throat like my raw nerves getting tangled and roughly stitched together.

"You're okay. I'm right here." Slowly, the voice pushes through the fog of my sleep-heavy senses.

I wake with a start, my eyes snapping open to meet the oppressive darkness of my room except for the lamp that always stays on. With a gasp, my back lifts from the bed as I suck in air like a vacuum. Sweat drains from my face and back, plastering my clothes to my skin. My aching fingers hold on to my bracelet, each pulse of fear echoing through my body.

Was it a dream?

"Bianca." Jason's blurry voice now becomes clearer when he hovers over me, my legs captured between his thick thighs. "Breathe," he reminds.

"Jason," I sob with no tears. My voice is weak and strained as I try to get it through my mouth.

"I'm here. You're fine," he murmurs in the quiet, his breath kisses my skin as a silent prayer for my wellbeing.

"Where are we?" I ask in a strained voice.

"We're in your room—your house." I could hear him, but his image is blurry as my eyes and mind recover from wherever I was captured in.

Jason stretches over to the bedside table and turns the room's light on. "Bad dream?" He wipes away the hair stuck to my forehead and the side of my face.

I avoid his gaze and will the trembling of my hands to cease. "What's the time?"

He flicks his eyes at the clock on the wall and, as he does, I spot a hint of red on his collar. That wasn't there before. *Is it blood?*

Bianca, come back to the real world.

"Seven. You want to go back to sleep?" His eyes fill with worry as he laps a comforting hand on my thighs, kneading my skin reassuringly.

"Can we stay? I don't want to get up yet," I mumble softly as I bring him down by the neck, resting his head against my chest. "Promise me something."

"I promise," he says without missing a beat.

I force out a strained laugh. My hands run through his hair as his breath warms me. "At least listen first. You never know if I'll ask you to kill someone for me."

"That would be child's play in front of anything you could ask. I will have nothing, but you and I would die a lucky man."

I ignore the quiet, menacing flutters in my chest from his words.

Instead, I continue, "Promise me, if *anything* happens to me and I'm not here—with you—you'll put flowers on the stone bench at the beach. That way I will truly rest," I whisper under my breath.

Jason picks up his head and glances deeply into my eyes. "I don't know why you're saying that, but what makes you think I can live without you? There will be no future where a Jason exists, and a Bianca doesn't." He's warm breath caresses my neck as he leaves soft kisses there. "I could say we're two sides of the same coin, but even they can go rusty. The golden glint of our coin makes us inseparable, forever bound by an unseen force, each defining the other."

When he looks at me again, I see a determination that could pull universes together. "That's who you are to me and have always been. My definition—you define more than I do myself."

I smile and brush the back of my fingers over his light stubble. "I see no good future for myself but … with you, I see everything."

"Only with you." He kisses me softly. "I want you to know, you came as Bianca, but you will stay as my Rainbow." He smoothly switches our positions and places my head on his chest.

After some quiet beats, slowly and softly, he whispers, "You shine so brightly that the world needs to stop and just admire you. Not because of anyone, but of who you are from within."

My arm curls around his neck, and we tangle our legs. A deceptive calm forms a bubble around us, and it's a matter of time when it'll burst.

"The end is coming … save yourself."

I ignore the insidious voice in my head and press further into him.

CHAPTER 35
Bianca

"That's the best you got?" Kiara pulls up her sleeves as she digs into yet another donut.

I don't know how I got dragged into umpiring a brutal round of '*Who eats the most Donuts?*' featuring Kiara and Sage.

Yes, Sage, the diet freak. In fact, she was the one who called us to Cornella's. Sage can do a lot of things, but one thing she can't do is avoid a good challenge. Being born into such a big family, with so many cousins around her age, fostered the competitiveness in her. Not forgetting she grew up with Kiara and Eva, who know the right buttons to press.

This is a welcome distraction after yesterday's episode. I've

never been this bad—never this eager to end myself in a moment of uncontrollable sorrow. Not something I'm proud of.

"We still have a minute on the clock. The results will be revealed soon," Eva announces, using a rolled-up piece of paper as a mock microphone. Her voice, a powerful resonant boom that dwarfs my own, draws the attention of every eye in Cornella's, both familiar and new.

From my periphery, I see Tony leaning over the counter, his lips moving silently as he mouths, *"Sage, Sage."* But when Kiara shoots her fiery gaze at him, he chants, louder, "Kiara, Kiara."

Poor Tony.

Today of all days, my hand hasn't left the bracelet on my wrist. A sense of calm circles me whenever my hand touches it.

"Ten seconds…." Eva counts on her fingers high in the air.

I join in with her at the fifth second. "Five … four … three … two … one … Stop!" We jump out of our seats when the last second counts and the alarm goes off.

"All hail Queen Kozlova, bitches." With a burst of energy, Kiara shoots up, arms outstretched, her skin glowing with an inner light, completely oblivious to the world around her.

I sometimes envy how easily she seems to let things roll off her back, though I suspect there's more to it than meets the eye.

Kiara dusts her mouth of any crumbs and smiles.

"You don't even know the results yet," Sage mumbles as drains her glass of water.

Eva stands between the two and shakes her head. "Ladies, settle down, please. We agreed to a safe and sound round," Eva says, spreading her arms between Kiara and Sage as they sit on opposite sofas.

"*You* set the rules, but that doesn't mean *I* will follow them." Kiara points to herself as she smirks.

"Don't be a sore loser and watch me get my trophy." Sage looks

Kiara up and down with her lips thinned.

"But you already have a trophy, don't you? From *Mr Secret Admirer*," Kiara sings, crossing one leg over the other. The neon orange dress brings out the best of her pale skin, and it's no surprise she owns everything she wears with pride.

"Watch it," Sage warns.

Kiara puts a finger on her lips and kisses it. "I will happily." She forces a smile.

"Guys, break it. Where were we? Right, the results. Kiara ate … drum roll …" Eva taps on her lap, and so do I. "Six!"

"Let's go, baby!" Kiara screams and throws a punch into the air. I know we should be in the adulting phases of our lives, but it doesn't seem like it.

"Hold your camera. You still don't know mine," Sage says in a relaxed tone as her eyes narrow.

"Sage had … six! It's a tie," Eva declares. She bows, and her dark ponytail, thick and glossy, sways with the motion, a pendulum of midnight.

A wave of disappointment washes over Kiara and Sage, their bodies visibly deflating as their excitement evaporates into the air.

"At least it's a tie. You won't be at each other's necks for not winning or losing. More pros than cons." I shrug. My attempt to cheer the mood doesn't do well when Kiara and Sage's eyes spark with renewed energy.

"I want a rematch," Kiara declares, her voice ringing with determination after the tense silence.

"Agreed." Sage nods.

"Girls, girls, put the claws away, will you?" A smooth and velvety voice comes through.

"May I have a word with our beautiful dancer?"

Our heads snap at the formal tone of a very familiar man. Adrian steps from behind Sage's sofa, dressed to the nines with his brown suit jacket and pants, a crisp white shirt and a brown tie completing the look. His eyes are the lightest shade of hazel, but the look on his face is the farthest away from being light.

"Cousin dearest, I haven't seen you around in a while. What's the pleasure?" Eva plasters on the fakest of fake smiles that would make a princess's trainer proud.

"Discussing some *business* with Joshi." He simply puts as he adjusts the middle button of his suit.

"I don't wish to have any chat, *Carson*. Not today at least." Sage doesn't as much as give him a look and talks to her second glass of water instead. "You can leave now."

What's the deal with them and saying last names?

"I insist. Otherwise, *Spencer* Street will get busier with every delay to this conversation." Adrian's voice is suggestive, and the suggestion doesn't get lost. Although I have no idea what just escaped his mouth.

Sage turns around to face him. I can't see her expression, but from Adrian's look, it's everything he was expecting. A palpable tension crackles between them, so thick I could almost taste it.

"Five minutes." Sage abruptly stands, shaking the coffee table in the attempt. She walks to the door and leaves a trail of pure lava with every step.

"Good to see you, girls," Adrian says with a small nod of his head. He takes a step away but stops and looks at Eva and me with a sharp look in his eyes, almost a warning. "Be careful," is all he says before turning to Kiara. "And Kiara." He pauses and intently stares at her. "I'll see you tonight?"

"8 o'clock at the usual," Kiara says and taps on her watch.

He smiles knowingly and winks. "Awesome. Now, let me deal with the *wicked witch* of the group.”

“Hey!” All three of us throw a doughnut at him, which he catches with ease and pops one in his mouth.

Brushing off his blazer and chuckling, Adrian leaves, his silver hair shining effortlessly, while we all stare at his muscular retreating back.

“Please tell me you are only seeing him for professional reasons tonight,” Eva says with her eyes closed and fingers crossed.

“Okay, if that’s what you want to hear.” Kiara shrugs. “But that’s not the truth.”

“You’re dating Adrian? Like *our* Adrian, the ‘I’m the big bad wolf Adrian’ and ‘Eva’s cousin Adrian’?” I ask. My eyes widen with every word, and every nod Kiara does at them.

“Well ... not dating *dating*. But yep, that’s him.”

“When did this happen?” I scoff as I try to run a timeline with Kiara.

“After Jason’s party. He was waiting for someone, and I was drunk off the world, so he offered to drop me, and one thing led to another,” Kiara drawls, playing with the straw in her glass.

“Let me warn you,” Eva begins as she leans forward. “He appears harmless, but so does every coral in the sea until you touch it.”

Kiara waves her off and leans back in her seat. “Talk about being dramatic. Plus, it’s nothing serious. A night here and there.”

Eva leans back and sips her ruby drink. “When we were growing up, Mum and Aunt Stella met every second Sunday for brunch. Adrian used to come along, but getting to talk to him was the hardest thing we did as kids.” Eva sighs, a sound so unfamiliar and sad coming from her. “He had high social anxiety, which quickly turned into antisocial tendencies—ruled by his psychiatrist.

“We first picked up his signs when he attempted to hunt down their dog, Jasper. Luckily for him, he knows how to be a sheep in the herd and fit right in. Lately, he's been under the radar and not making grand appearances at the occasional family gatherings."

"Wow. I didn't … know," I say as I take in the information. I direct my attention to Kiara. "Are you sure about him?"

"If we're getting all the orgasms we want, that's all I need. I'm not out for a relationship." Kiara smiles, showing her teeth.

Eva lets out another sigh, her shoulders slumping, a disgusted grimace twisting her features. "If you're going ahead with this. We *do not* discuss the sex life of my cousin. I have enough gruesome details in my life."

"Nothing that includes Kai?" I ask with a playful rise of my lips.

"Everything that includes him." Eva rolls her eyes, pursing her lips.

My phone vibrates in my hand, and my once-settled world stands on the edge of a cliff, ready to collapse beneath my feet.

> **Unknown:** *Time for piece four. Always keep it with you. Your answers are waiting.*

After being politely escorted by a driver who wouldn't answer my questions or even look at me, I arrived here.

Standing before an enormous modern house with a bag of shirts—a peace offering from last night's disastrous showcase—slung over my shoulder. The heavenly smell of the almond cinnamon white chocolate warms my hand, and it's taking all of me not to drink it. No wonder Jason loves these.

My eyes admire the building's grandeur, which surpasses any structure I've encountered, its scale and design defying all my imagination. The deep green of the towering pine trees hugs the border of the mansion, their scent mingling with the sweet fragrance of a vibrant ring of colourful wildflowers.

LED lights dotting the modern house create a brilliant, futuristic glow, highlighting the building's sharp lines and angles. The house is mostly glass, with only a few brick accents. A strong gust of wind could easily topple it, but its four sturdy stories provide ample structure to withstand the impact. Before I get a view of the door, a garden with a stone path leads to the entrance.

Typical Archer style.

Jason texted me the address of this place and sent a car to pick me up. First, I thought it was weird of him sending a driver but soon found out why because I knew if I saw him, I wouldn't have admired this house—if it could be called one—the way I do now. All I see when he is near me is him.

Yet you still haven't told him, Red Horns says. I hear her voice more than I hear mine.

I thought I was delirious when I read the words on the main gate, but the plaque on the opaque glass door read the same. *Senza Tempo*. It's Italian for … timeless.

I smile as I read it and press the button on the intercom.

My heart thunders in my chest as if I'm meeting him for the first time.

The door flings open, the sound echoing in the sudden silence, and those melting, comforting green eyes hold me captive once again.

Peace.

"Hi," Jason greets as he stands tall in a white shirt that stretches tightly over his broad shoulders, making my heart race. He is wearing grey pants that hang low on his waist, giving a peek of his milky skin. My throat goes dry, and I gulp.

"Hi." I smile at him and look into his forest eyes. I could get lost in them and never want to come out.

"Come in." He moves to the side, letting me step in.

As soon as I enter, my eyes go wide and my mouth hangs when I take in the design made in heaven. "This place is incredible."

I set the bags on the front table and then slide my fingers across the cool, smooth surface of the crystal ball ornament. Looking up at the high, transparent ceilings, with their celestial designs, creates the illusion of being under a starlit night sky. Enhancing the dreamlike quality, subtle sounds of distant music swim through the air. The only clue to the room's height was the massive, glittering crystal chandelier that hung from the ceiling, its light dancing in the air with vibrations of the sound.

"It doesn't come close to incredible if you aren't looking at it," Jason says as his muscular arms come around my waist, my back to his chest. "And if you keep smiling like that, I don't think I'll let you go."

My breath hitches and my insides twist. "Stop it. I can take the grumpy Jason. Even the unbearable Jason. The sweet and caring one is the one I'm getting used to." My hand rubs his arm as we rock side to side. "But seriously, this is a fucking dream. With its build and design, it's my personal heaven."

"You mean me." Jason kisses the top of my head.

You are.

Three plush velvet sofas dominate a third of the large space, their rich colours a contrast to the gleaming white marble of the spiral staircase, which elegantly splits in two as it ascends.

"That's why I thought I'd bring you here before it's too late. At least since things are well between us." Jason's voice has an edge he tries to mask.

"What do you mean?" I turn my head to look at him with a furrow in my brows.

"What I mean is that before we make things official. I need you and all your time. Then we have to deal with my parents, and let's not forget

Eva, the little devil."

"Are you sure about this? *Us?*" A cold sweat prickles my anxiety on my skin, and the relentless ticking of an unseen clock in my mind races through every failure. Our history of being together never brought smiles, instead painful cries.

Shut up, Bianca, White scolds.

"More than anything." He turns me around so that I face him. My arms go around his neck as I look up at this beautiful man. "Whenever I kiss you, I know I will go to hell with all the sinful thoughts I have about you. But at least I can go to hell knowing I've lived my part of heaven on Earth."

My heart hammers against my ribs, a frantic drumbeat as my breath hitches, and I struggle to comprehend his words. I smile and dust my thumb on his cheek, my gaze bouncing between his two eyes. "Maybe I'll join you. I am no angel when it comes to you," I whisper.

I squeal when he picks me up in his arms like he did last night. His arms tighten under my legs and on my back as he walks us up the stairs, but all I see is my handsome man. When we reach the top, Jason turns, and I can't help but thank my good luck—all and the little I have.

"Thank you." I breathe, my fingers trace his jaw, my other hand rests lightly on his chest.

He looks at me with a raise of his eyebrow.

"For everything. For being there for me, I wish I could be there with you when you need me the most. Because I missed you in all the years I didn't see you."

With a soft sigh, Jason leans in, closing his eyes. Our foreheads meet in a shared moment of intimacy, with a silent promise passing between us. "You're already there." When his eyes open, they hold the power to melt glaciers. "Make me forget we ever spent so long without each other. Make me remember you're here with me and will never leave," he growls. "Kiss me."

Tightening my fingers on his jaw, I bring him down to meet my lips, and I moan—moan for the taste of his desperation and longing. For every emotion he can offer me, I will take them all and bundle them up in a colour no one has seen or ever heard of.

Everything gets escalated as I get pushed into the wall with my legs around Jason's waist.

"I need more. Let me claim you again and again until I lose myself in you. For as long as we can." His desperation climbs higher with every time he kisses me.

My soft eyes speak for me, but somehow, I can't get rid of the voice whispering something is wrong. That Jason is hiding something. "You and me," is all I say.

I trail kisses along his jaw, down to his neck, his skin warm beneath my lips, until I reach his wildly beating pulse. My tongue leisurely licks from the base of his neck to his chin, and I suck on his beating pulse. Without thinking, I bite down, the skin yielding easily, leaving a small, tender mark.

"No matter what happens, you are *mine*, Rainbow." His voice is sexily dark as he grabs my hair and places my head in a position where I see nothing but his green, green eyes.

I smile at him and lick my lips.

"Get your fucking lips on me again," he growls.

"Yes, Mr Archer."

CHAPTER 36
Bianca

I bring down his head and crash my lips against his, a brutal force that pins me against the wall, moulding my body to the rough surface. The taste of him prominent with sharpness and urgency.

As my purple dress rides up, I feel Jason's hard erection press against my exposed pussy. My moan echoes in the empty halls for the ears of the walls and hidden creatures to be the witnesses of my ruination by the man I couldn't think another day without.

"No panties?" Jason raises his eyebrow.

"Thought I'd save you the hassle." I moan as his finger ghosts my swollen lips.

Jason's tongue marks everywhere he can in my mouth. Each wipe

and lick from him are enough for me to come on the spot.

This force and strength are new, nothing compared to before. It's more anger than anything. My hands instinctively reach for the roots of his dark hair, giving me something to hold on to as he passionately claims my lips.

His fingers dust my weeping pussy, making him hum. "Look at you dripping for me."

I am. My arousal slides down my bare legs, and a drop settles on the floor. "Are you going to do something about it?" I prompt, nothing subtle in my tone.

An animalistic sound escapes his deep vocals, and I'm pushed further into the wall with his fingers plunging into me. His two digits take me away from my soul. All I see are stars, and we haven't even begun.

The rhythm he moves at degrades me to nothing in his hold—at his utter mercy.

"Whatever happens to us. There is no power in this world that can make me forget you, and all the times I've thought of you when I shouldn't have," he whispers against my lips, his fingers curling, hitting a spot that makes me scream.

Something cracks in me at his words—my restraint, my emotions, *my soul.* "Jay…" When I think I will come undone, Jason pulls his fingers away, baring me from his addictive touch. My whimper barely comes out of my lips in protest when his cock drills into me. "Oh God," I moan.

I got on the pill soon after we had sex. Turns out there are not enough boxes of condoms in this world for Jason Archer.

"You will think of me." *Thrust.* "Every time you come." *Thrust.* "Because." *Thrust.* "It will be me who makes you come." *Thrust.* "No one else."

"Only with you," I whisper. My insides burn with the onslaught of his touch and his cock. *Him.* I am burning with him.

"Be my girl and come for me," he commands.

My body works at his mercy, and I come in waves crashing into me again, again and *again.* Everything stills, and my head drops to his shoulder.

"Good girl," he purrs. His fingers lightly bring my head up to meet his heated stare. "On your knees now," he growls with unsettling lust and affection.

He unwinds my legs around his waist, and I drop on my knees. I can't help but gasp at his straining erection—coated with me. My insides tremble with desire and need once again. I brush my fingers against his cock and collect my arousal off him, letting it shine on my fingers. Making a show of it, I bring my finger to my mouth, my swollen lips circling it while my tongue shoots out and licks the length of my finger like I would his cock.

"Tease." Jason drops his head back to the wall.

His sharp inhale empowers me, making me feel like I have complete control over this man, and may as well have him at my mercy now.

Heat consumes my body, flowing through me and causing me to feel the warmth from my pussy trickling down my legs.

I bite hard on my lower lip, feeling the pressure and the slight sting as I fight back the tide of drool. Desperation takes me captive every time I'm around him.

"Eyes on me, Rainbow," he directs.

My eyes flick to his dark ones with renewed energy.

"I love my woman in control," he murmurs darkly. Lust drips like honey from his mouth as he claims me with his green eyes. "Take control of me."

Slowly, I let my mouth take the straining head and map his shaft with my tongue, from the tip to the base. All he needs to know is that he belongs to me as much as I do to him. I release him with an audible pop and kiss the crown of his cock.

Jason yanks my hair, his fingers digging into my scalp, angling me in front of him. "Fuck me with your mouth." His deep vocals, on the edge of desperation, make me groan and rub my thighs.

With my hands on his cock, I take him in and swirl my tongue around him. He picks up his pace, going in and out, not only losing himself but making me crazy for him.

When he slides out and pistons into the back of my throat, I gag, drool escaping the corners of my lips. I raise my hands to his balls and squeeze them, taking out all my desire for him.

Jason's hand tightens on the root of my hair and groans, tipping his head back. "Fuck … so perfect."

I drop my hands to his thick thighs as I try to keep balance. He continues with the movement, and his swollen balls slap against my chin as they flow with the rhythm of his cock coming in and out.

"Mine … mine…mine," he mutters distractedly in the haze of his lust. He leaves more stings of praises, which escape me as he releases me and smooths my hair with a soft hand. "My girl, my good girl," he fucking purrs.

I liquefy on the spot.

For one last time, he pushes in my mouth, and a gag escapes my lips, echoing like our strange melody with his heavy breathing. He jerks in my mouth, enlarging with each throb of his pulse. It doesn't take much effort from here as he rushes the rip of his cum down my throat. He pulls out, spilling it on my mouth, dripping down my chin to the floor to mingle with my own arousal. *Drip, drip, drip.*

Marking me. Claiming me.

An animal in every sense.

"Remember this moment when you think no one wants you." His thumb collects the dripping cum and pushes it into my mouth. "I will want you for all my breathing life and beyond."

My tongue shoots and in a slow devouring stroke, licking his seeds off my lips, tasting every bit of him. A surge of electricity runs through me as the redness of the bite mark on his neck screams from his milky skin.

Mine, and I have everything to prove it.

He pulls me up by my chin and levels me with his more relaxed features. I balance my hands on his shoulder, my weak knees faltering.

"You're going to be the death of me," he whispers on my forehead as he kisses me there.

"Not more than you are going to be mine." My heart thumps dangerously, trying to come out of its housing valves and make an appearance to showcase its vulnerability.

"My Rainbow until the end of time."

"My Grey now and forever." Rising on my toes, I place a soft kiss on his lips.

Bianca, that's pushing you further over the edge of the cliff. White Wings worries.

I know the fall will not hurt as much as staying away from him will.

After the connection and a promise of our lips, we walk down the hall.

"This is the master bedroom," Jason says when we get to the door. It is the biggest and simplest. The colour scheme is subtle, with tones of white, blue and grey.

A beautifully crafted bed is centred against the back wall of dark grey stone with accents of white. I stand admiring the intricate carvings on its headboard and the soft texture of the blankets. It invites me to curl and wrap myself in the grey comforter and all the pillows on it.

There are two doors opposite the bed, one for the bathroom—which is nothing short of luxury—and a walk-in wardrobe. A large arched mirror, outlined in a soft golden light, separates the two doors, its surface reflecting the room.

"Why white?" I ask. "Dark themes are usually your thing."

"Peace. I want this room to be our peaceful sanctuary when everything goes south and lift us every night for a new day," he replies as his chest expands with a breath.

Our peaceful sanctuary.

Lift us.

Before I could question his choice of words, he walked ahead. "Come on, there's more." There are passages upon passages as we walk down the hall, and Jason points in all directions as he shows me the gym, two offices, a second kitchen, and a theatre room.

I stay quiet throughout the tour and melt as he smiles when he likes something. I haven't seen this man smiling so openly so often that I had tonight.

We get to the final room, and Jason stops, takes a breath, and opens the door. This room, far from typical, boasts a massive space and a glass wall offering a panoramic forest view, a striking element within the house's overall monstrous design. Muffled sounds of the forest filter through the glass.

But it's empty. Nothing at all.

It's as if the body is here, but the soul and heart are nowhere to be seen.

"And this is all yours," Jason states, opening the door wide and letting me walk in first.

"Mine?" I turn to face him and put a soft hand on my chest in question.

"I thought you could design and redesign this room as you practice for different projects here," he says matter-of-factly.

My shoulders drop in a defeated sigh. "I only have a month and a half left, Jason. Don't dream of things that can't come true." I hate myself for saying this, but it's better to rip off the Band-Aid in one go.

Reminder: Nearly time

"Not unless you stay." He turns to face me, leaving a space between us and my hand drops. "You can't keep running away from your demons, Bianca. Inside you is a strong woman who has fought with herself and won. Don't weaken *her* by going back," he says as his eyes soften.

"Jason…" I step forward and put a hand on his beating heart. The big and thoughtful heart I will eventually break. "You know I can't. Even if I get better at living here, it still won't change the fact that I have a life there now, too."

"A life you lie to yourself about," he deadpans.

We both stare at each other, and I search for the wrong in his right words.

"I called Florals & Bells the other day for a termination of your employment." The earlier smiles and softness fade. "They will accept it if you put it forward."

"You what!" I ask, dumbfounded. I shake my head and look back at him. "Okay, so I terminate, and then what?" Red, hot anger simmers in my head. *How could he?*

"We're thinking of expanding our creative team into a company, and I want you to lead it," he offers, hope reflecting in his eyes.

I shake my head until my vision blurs and hair slaps my face. "I can't do that. I don't want things given to me, especially if that means I need to carry a name like Archer Enterprises," I croak as my throat constricts.

"It's not part of the Archers. It's a separate entity under your name. We will be your investors, and you will run it as you wish," he explains and clears my hair from my face.

Frustration leaks from my every pore. I scoff. "You seem to have planned everything out for me. Could you tell me what I should wear tomorrow? Maybe a harness so you could drag me around."

Calm down, Bianca, White Wings reminds me. *He cares about you.*

I close my eyes for a moment, and I speak. "I mean, you can't come in and barge into my personal life, Jason." I shake my head in disbelief.

His eyes widen as if I insulted him but soften. "Your personal life became *our* personal life as soon as we kissed on the beach. That goes for me as well. I'll let you know everything I do and know this: I will always do things that have our good in it whether or not we can see it now." His voice is soft as his thumb dusts over cheeks.

"But that doesn't mean you make decisions for me. I know what's right and wrong," I counter.

"I'm not making any decisions for you—you are more than capable yourself." He swallows, stepping slowly forwards. "And you know what's wrong and right for you. But I'm asking you to trust me this time around. Listen…" He grabs my wrists and puts my palms on either side of his neck. His calm pulse beats under my touch. "This will only keep beating if you're around me, and the moment you step foot the other way, it will cease."

"I … I just … I don't know. This is just too much to consider," I say, looking away as I imagine myself living here. *What would Ma and Dad have wanted? Would they have liked me to stay here and live with their memories? Or would they've preferred me to stay away?*

"Hey." He turns my head to face him. "Stop thinking. Take your time." He nods.

I look back at his beautiful face and heave a breath. "I will."

"What's on the menu tonight?" I ask, sitting down on the sofa.

Jason goes into the open, large, black and wood-themed kitchen suited to be in a Michelin star restaurant. There are three strings of disc lights on top of the black marble counter, like the rest of the kitchen. Everything is clean and fits right where it is.

"Besides you?" I hear Jason's voice from the pantry.

I stop myself from giggling. "Yes, besides me." I roll my eyes.

"Pizza." He walks out and carries three boxes of pizza. Their heavenly smell circles around us.

"Without pineapple, I hope. It's a disgrace to the cuisine. Any Italian will agree."

"I can't promise anything. Everyone has their own taste," Jason says as he places the boxes on the table in front of me. "Let me get the drinks."

He runs off and comes back with two bottles of wine. "Hmm, someone's being fancy tonight."

"Only with you," he murmurs on my lips, leaving a quick peck.

A bashful smile touches my lips as I roll my eyes, the warmth spreading across my cheeks. The silence between us is heavy from our earlier conversation, and I'm at a loss for what to do next. I had my mind made up that after the three months, I would not look back and would just leave. That would be the end. Now, I don't think anything will end there.

"There was just one more thing ..." Jason's voice trails off as he reaches underneath the table. The room sounds with a soft click, followed by a low mechanical whirring, and then the curtains slowly draw back, revealing a dimly lit space.

Not just any space. The forest.

"Wow." I breathe in awe as my hands fly to my mouth.

I am captivated by the sight of the pine trees. The rough bark and sturdy branches frame a perfect silhouette of a bird with its wings spread wide. In its beak is a ring woven from pink, white, and blue flowers. The detail is so exquisite that I half-expect the bird to take flight, carrying the flower ring, chirping away.

"You're spoiling me a lot tonight." I smile, standing up and moving towards the glass window. I feel like a kid seeing her favourite toy for the first time.

Jason comes from behind and places his chin on my shoulder. "Dad and I got it done last year. It's like the one in my home garden, except that one lacks the garland of flowers."

"What does it mean? The garland?" I ask, keeping my wide eyes on the wonder beyond me.

"The circle of life. That a bird representing new comings and beginnings carries us through every spike of life. Hence, the pine trees. And it shows us all the colours that life offers, from the loudest cheers to the silent sacrifices." His voice brushes my cheek as I feel his gaze on me.

We stand in silence, my eyes on the view and feel Jason's on me.

He turns my head and kisses me slow. Nothing in the world matters in this moment. Not who I am or what I will become.

"Okay, let's feed you." He rubs my stomach and pushes me towards the sofas, which face the scenery.

I smile to myself as I sit on the sofa. In my world of misery and sorrow, Jason has become the beacon that calls to the little remaining light in me.

Even if I'm bearing witness to Jason eating pineapple on pizza. In this moment, all I want is him.

Timeless.

Him and I for however long. Because this is too good to be true.

CHAPTER 37
Jason

It's been two days of thinking, thinking and fucking thinking. I feel lightheaded, as if my brain might leave my skull, and my heart hammers in my chest, protesting to burst. That would be preferable to getting rid of the torturous ache.

I don't know who to believe and who to trust.

I am standing amidst the war between my emotions and logic. This time it's worse, way worse than anything I'd felt before. A tempest of chaotic thoughts and feelings rage within, incinerating anyone caught in the brain's crossfire and the heart's conflict.

Every second I spend with Bianca is every breath I am lying to myself about being truthful to her. I could ask her straight out what she

wants and why she did what she did. But I can't. I can face death, but not what the truth holds.

I gave myself a grace period at the house two days ago. That was all I had until this moment. In the same house I bought five years ago, thinking that one day I will share it with the one woman I see myself with. And if things didn't work out, I would live there alone because the walls would only call for her. Their loyalty would always serve her as much as I would.

"What's this place?" Bianca asks from the passenger seat.

"Phoenix. A place where I find my answers," I say with a heavy sigh. "Maybe you'll find yours, too."

"Maybe." Bianca shrugs, her eyes shining like bright stars in the night sky, as she looks through the windshield at the building ahead. We arrived at Phoenix a few minutes ago and are just staring at the phenomenon we've created. Yet all I have today are nerves dancing to a frantic beat of doom as I wait for the worst to happen. *And it will.*

She turns to face me and puts a soft hand on my arm. "I'm concerned now. How much do you really earn?"

"Oh baby, there is no time when I don't. They don't call the Archers monsters for no reason." I smile as I raise an eyebrow.

Bianca shakes her head with a lip-biting smile. "Very humbling."

"That we are." I exit the car with unnecessary guilt. No matter how the evening ends, one thing is for sure: I can never get enough of Bianca Kennedy. She has wriggled herself into my soul in a way that makes her irreplaceable.

"Now, if you'll allow me to escort you." I open the passenger door and hold out my arm for her to take.

"It would be my pleasure," she replies as she hooks her arm in mine.

"Pleasure is the one thing I can always guarantee. For me or you, that's the question," I whisper, and visible shivers ring down her exposed back.

"For us." She looks innocently at me.

Tonight, she's wearing a deep-ocean gown. Its glimmering fabric shimmers under the moonlight, tiny jewels twinkling like distant stars, and equally blue stilettos that click softly with every step. They give her some added height, getting her to my shoulders. Her small clutch bag completes the look—a subtle hint of organised elegance.

My fucking Rainbow.

My fists clench and unclench, a silent battle between my desire to hold her hand and my fear of rejection. Things have changed, and so have we, but the memory of her hand slipping from mine—so easily— as she ran towards the burning house still leaves me with a hollow ache. The crackling flames, the screams, the heat—it all comes back.

Bianca halts in tracks, as if sensing my inner turmoil. "I thought I was the lost one in this relationship. Maybe we both are," Bianca says over her shoulder. She carefully turns around and sighs. "You can claim me every way you want, but can't hold my hand? I know we have a long way ahead of us, and it's misty. That doesn't mean we can't enjoy what we can see. The present—the now."

Her ocean-blue eyes, like the deep sea, map my face as she steps closer. Her fingers trace my chin, sending shivers down my spine.

"Don't look at me like that," I tell her and close my eyes for the moment, relishing her touch.

"Like what?" she asks, already knowing my answer.

Like you love me. "Like you want to kiss me," I amend my thought.

"Then kiss me like the first time, Grey," she whispers near my ears, each word grazing my lobe.

I sure do. My arms wrap around her waist and meet her in a longing kiss. I found a girl when I was a boy in a garden full of birds and trees that defined me, and now I have a woman when I'm becoming the man who she defines.

Everything is so soft. So perfect. *So ours.*

As we pull away, Bianca gently takes my hand, her small fingers curling around mine. I can feel the warmth of her skin against my rougher one, and in this moment, nothing else matters but her and her hand in mine.

Bianca stares up at the building in front of her, that seemingly whispers tales of Medieval London. The multiple-story building, a testament to modern architectural prowess, boasts intricate details that could challenge the finest royal palace constructions, the sounds of the city a distant hum against its imposing presence.

Four sturdy towers, their stone surfaces gleaming, project an undeniable sense of authority, hinting at the power held within. A meticulously carved forest, redolent with the scent of trees and live creatures, surrounds the prestigious estate, effectively isolating it from the outside world. It offers a glimpse of luxurious living that demands a significant life commitment to attain.

"Do you own this as well?" Bianca questions her eyes scanning the expansive property, noting the quiet grandeur of the place.

"Part of it," I answer. "It's split between its founders. Me, Kai, Adrian, and Nick."

"Nick? Do I know him?" Bianca asks, deep in thought.

"In passing, maybe. He mostly stays in the States, preferring a quiet existence," I reply.

Bianca nods but pauses abruptly as her mouth opens in awe. "Is that a phoenix?" Her eyes focus on the golden Phoenix by the front.

The handmade creation of the firebird hangs in the air, capturing a moment as it flies in mid-air. This sculpture stills time when the Phoenix lives before burning, different from the one inside with the crests.

"Yes." I nod, pressing my lips together not to smile.

"So, this is your inspiration for all the motivational speeches I get." A thoughtful hum vibrates in her chest, and she pouts her lips.

"I wouldn't give it all the credit." I shake my head, leading us inside. "It's better when you get deeper." Gently tugging her, I pull her close to my side, the reassuring pressure of her fingers bringing me comfort.

On the way, we encountered Mr Anglos from Norway, Mr and Mrs Smith, the former owners of the Smith Security. Teal also came about as we passed the control room with Allie—the head of the technical team assisting Adrian—dressed in everything red, including hair.

"Hello, Jason," Alexa says from her desk. Her eyes move to Bianca and smiles. "Welcome to Phoenix, Miss. Kennedy. I'm Alexa."

"I'm glad to be here, Alexa."

She is the manager of the central bar, and at times takes overall management of the society. Her brown eyes search for everything and anything. It's been some time since we've heard about a mishap in the bar, and it's Alexa we thank.

I nod in greeting.

As we get deeper, Bianca stays quiet throughout the wandering conversation, reacting with a smile and smooth responses when introduced.

Finally, we arrive at the library. The rich, dark wood of the shelves and the matte finish of the floating floor evoke the feeling of returning home after a long time out. Each grain is a familiar comfort. I should feel apprehensive about having someone with me here for the first time, but I don't because it's Bianca.

She's always been my first.

"Whenever I need a break from reality, I come here and breathe," I explain as we walk to the back. I reach out for the same book spine labelled with a Griffin and the letter *J*.

"The library is a calming place. I wouldn't mind coming either," Bianca says from beside me. Her wide eyes scan the entire area as her mouth drops wide open. "I definitely won't mind coming *here*."

"Not the library. This…" I pull the book, and the shelves part with a soft yawn, opening to unveil my hidden sanctuary. I came here weeks ago with the burden of many things in my control and a lot out of control, and now I stand watching the soft dancing leaves and the returning birds with no heaviness on my chest. But dread … for what's coming.

"Woah." Bianca breathes, her shoulders dropping with a soft exhale. "I … Who did you blackmail to get this many cherry blossom trees?" she asks, turning her head to face me and tightening her grip on my hand.

Rows of cherry blossom trees frame the path, showering us with pink petals every time a gentle breeze combs through the branches. As we walk deeper into the forest, the musty scent of damp earth gives way to the delicate fragrance of cherry blossoms. Their sweet perfume soothing my racing heart.

"They remind me of you," I whisper in the air. "I didn't want to lose even the slightest thread of yours—I wanted to keep them buried in me as long as I could."

"I am not going anywhere, and even if we have to try long distance, we will. It's going to be a hard time getting rid of me." Bianca chuckles as she finishes.

A loud, melodic chirping snaps my attention, and I jerk my head upward. "Look, those are yellow-faced honeyeaters." I point up to the nearest tree, where a pair of honeyeaters perch among the branches. "They are the closest to hummingbirds we can get here. Dad always said one thing about them. '*Even the smallest of wings can carry the biggest load*'."

"You're lucky to have a father like Brandon. He is a clown as much as he is wise." Bianca pats my arm.

"Did you call my dad a clown?" I ask, deliberately ignoring the rest.

Bianca looks at me as she battles not to smile. "I also said wise. Talk about selective listening." She rolls her eyes.

We walk for several silent beats before Bianca speaks. "I was thinking if we could go on a beach date with everyone. Like we used to. Have a picnic, a swim, and just relax. What do you think?"

"It won't be a date if *everyone* is there, now, will it?"

"Okay, let me rephrase. We could go out for a *day* with everyone. How's that sound?" Bianca asks. Her brown waves curtain the sides of her face.

"Less romantic." I tilt my head as I think.

"Like you have a romantic bone in you, don't you?" Bianca sarcastically comments.

"In fact, I do."

We arrive at the corner of the forest, where a fragrant, deep green wall of ivy shades a secluded entrance. I swipe it away and reveal the circular table in the middle of the clearing, just off the lake, under the oldest, biggest oak tree. Time and weather wore its wood smooth. The crackle of the large campfire beside the table sends sparks from the wood flying in the air like fireflies.

Every imaginable cuisine, from the spicy aromas of Indian curries to the delicate perfume of French pastries, graces the table.

"Jason…" Her steps freeze as she turns to face me, holding my two hands. "You're spoiling me so badly."

"I just like *feeding* you," I say, pulling the chair out for her.

"By the time I leave, I'll be walking like a balloon." She chuckles, taking the seat.

I walk over to the opposite chair and find it hard not to smile.

"You're forgetting if you're eating then so am I. So that makes us the balloon couple."

The spoon in Bianca's hand drops on the plate, and the high-pitched sound flows in waves around us—from a faraway tree, birds fly, and the water in the stream beside us rushes the other way. I look up at her with wide eyes and mouth.

"I've seen and heard all. Please don't *ever* make a joke again." She drops back onto the chair and laughs.

"I can list a lot of things I hate about you." I raise a challenging eyebrow.

She chuckles. "Don't put words in my mouth. I didn't say anything about hating anything. Joke all you want."

I hold up my index finger and say, ignoring her, "One, you're so beautiful that it hurts to look at you every time you're around me."

Bianca's shoulders drop, and she fights not to smile. "Keep going."

"Two, your blue eyes make me drown in thin air every time I see you," I continue.

Bianca twists her lips and widens her eyes. *Blue. Two shards.*

"Three, the fucking cherry blossom you wear curses me with life every time you leave me," I say, not looking away from her.

"And…" She pushes her chair back and stands. The sapphire blue dress shimmers like the jewel as she moves with the alluring grace of a seductress.

"Four, I hunger more of your delicate touch whenever you touch me," I whisper as she nears me.

"And…" Her voice is a slow murmur in the air. She comes, stands in front of me, and puts her hand on either side of my neck. She swings her leg over me, settling onto my lap with a soft sigh.

I stretch out all my five fingers. "Five, I hate that I'm an addict to your sweet drug," I whisper.

Bianca leans in and presses a soft kiss on my lips. It's enough pressure to engrave her on me, but not enough to have all of her. *Yet.* She reaches up and intertwines her fingers with my lifted hand and brings it down.

"Do you know what I hate most about you?" Bianca asks, her voice getting heavier.

"No," I reply.

"That you're the grey people are afraid of, but I always needed and never had." Her voice is full of silent vulnerability as she slides our hands down her neck.

"And you have become the colours my dark world never had. If you leave, I will lose myself once more in that endless abyss of no return. A place that shows no mercy." She guides my hand to her breast and presses my thumb onto her peaking nipple.

I drop my forehead onto hers and chuckle, shaking my head. It was only some time ago I did the same for her, but that time I wanted her to know I was always at her mercy, and now *I know* she's the only reprieve I need.

Slowly, she guides our linked hands down the slope of her stomach. "This. Us. I want it." She swallows. "I want *you.*"

She leaves my fingers when we reach her inner thighs. The closer my fingers move towards her folds, the clearer her arousal becomes.

Bianca Kennedy is dripping for me. The thought still bewilders me to this day. I hook fingers around the hem of her panties, and a rip echoes in the air, filled with our breathing.

Bianca sucks in a breath of surprise as she holds my shoulders, mirroring the hunger boiling in me.

My fingertips brush against her swollen clit, gathering her wetness. Her fingers curl on my shoulders, digging into them for a release.

Slowly, I bring up my fingers and lick them, relishing the sensation of cleaning off her wetness. "Delicious," I murmur. "Take out what you need," I demand through the thick fog of my newfound emotions.

Using assured movements, she unzips and unbuttons my pants, exposing my stiff, pulsating cock. My dark eyes follow Bianca's movements as she wipes away the precum beads with her thumb while I rub her clit in lazy circles.

"I need to be in your pretty little cunt," I lean into her ear and whisper.

Bianca's gaze traces the line of my neck, stopping at the mark she'd given me. Her tongue darts out and does a slow lick of her lips, letting a renewed surge of desire course through me.

My dick gets hard and waits to feel her tightness around me. "Let me take you away from this hell and give you heaven. *Our* heaven," I murmur.

With each slow movement, she lifts herself up and ever so fucking slowly slides down on my cock, making us feel my every inch entering her.

She groans, and clarity shines on her face. "I lo—"

Before she could get the words out, I lift her with a strong hold around her hips. She slams back down, her breath getting caught in her throat as the impact makes us moan. Her movements quicken on their own, rising and falling, and I am once again serenaded by the sound of her moans mingling with mine.

The quiet of the rustling leaves and flow of the river with the occasional quacking of ducks, holds its position to witness our connection when flesh collides against flesh. When moans come after moans.

I slam into her from underneath, her muscles relaxing and shivering all at the same time. Bianca leans in, touching our foreheads when I can feel her clenching around me.

"Jason…" She barely makes it out as she lets loose and her release comes like a waterfall, warming me with its embrace.

It doesn't take me long to feel the warmth of her body as I claim her with my every touch.

Sex with Bianca isn't sex at all. It's another way we speak to each other when words fail us. To trust each other when our heads get trapped in pleasure so immense the world fades. To hold each other—to *love* each other.

"Rainbow," I heave as I bring her down and kiss her like this is the last time. *It is.*

"Grey." She breathes on my lips.

Six, I hate that I love you in our darkest time.

CHAPTER 38
Jason

"But seriously, how did you score this wonder?" Bianca says, surveying the rich polished mahogany walls and gleaming floors of the hall.

"It's Nick's ancestral landmark. His grandmother passed it down to me as an heirloom." I carefully select my words. We know more than Nick lets on about his family and heritage, but that isn't my story to tell.

"Did he grow up here?" Bianca asks.

"Yes. In fact, he went to the same school and university as we did. We wouldn't have found him if we hadn't had the excursion to the zoo in primary school," I say, walking ahead to the Commons. "He was by the snakes, and wasn't moving a muscle. Turns out, the snakes

fascinated him so much that he forgot to breathe." I nod to myself, remembering the bright-eyed kid, so lost in wonder he didn't realise he was sprawled on the floor, his hands pressed against the cool glass enclosure.

"Funny you never mentioned him or brought him to our group," Bianca says, her gaze lingering on the portrait of Stanley Coburg, the oil paint's thick texture almost tangible beneath her curious stare. He was the artist who sculpted the magnificent phoenix and kept his methods a closely guarded secret—a mystery that went with him wherever he did.

"He never wanted to."

I count my shared breaths with Bianca as we enter the Commons.

"Remember one thing, Jason. We do some things that will hurt us, but they will let our solutions unfold. And I will do anything to get what I want." Aaron's words from the other night ring in my head.

All I wanted to do at that moment was to grab him out of the screen and give him a taste of his words. Raw and unapologetic. But deep down I knew he was right, and his motivations were also there for his and our benefit. Bianca's benefit. She deserves to live far away from our world of darkness. She has enough of her own.

We walk in, hand in hand, to the largest hall room of the society. Our reflections stare back at us on the polished floor as light from the many medium-sized crystal chandeliers glitters across the ceiling. The arched windows stretch from floor to ceiling on all walls, filling the space with soft lighting. The night sky and stars shake in my vision as they, too, worry about the night's ending.

But what takes away the breathing space in the room is the nearly complete puzzle.

"Can this place get any more unreal? *Tonight* seems unreal," Bianca chimes as she twirls in a circle in the centre of the room. Seeing her so happy, and knowing it's because of me, swells my heart with pride.

"Bianca," I say quietly, holding her waist to get her attention. "Do you trust me?"

She halts, her silent eyes searching my face with a slight tilt of her head in confusion. "Yes," she finally whispers. "There was no time I didn't."

The jarred space in my heart fills with her words. I knew she trusted me, yet everything fell on us like an avalanche that I took her word for it then. "Just keep that in mind. Sometimes what we see isn't the whole truth," I say, cupping her face.

"Jason, what's wrong?" She instantly picks up on my wrong tone.

"Nothing we can't tackle." I smile.

Sometimes temporary pain is all we need to suffer to have a happy future—regardless of how much I die in that time. Avoiding the thought, I lean down and capture her lips. She doesn't resist and moves her lips as I move mine.

I love you.

"I'll be back, need to use the bathroom. Make yourself comfortable." I lift her chin and have a full view of her breathtaking face.

After leaving another lingering kiss, our hands untangle, and I leave her in the middle of the large and modern space. I feel nothing when I enter the surveillance room, except the regular beating of my heart and my slow, controlled breathing.

Seven, I hate that I have to let you go.

Something's wrong, White Wings echoes my thoughts.

The vast hall stretches before me, and with each step, a heavier weight of lead settles in my stomach.

It's everything one would imagine at a regency ball, except more modernised. I can almost hear the slow music as elegant gowns float around, and people mingle. A large, ornate table dominates the centre of the room, its polished wood gleaming under the dim light, intensifying my suspicions.

The puzzle. The table size puzzle sits almost complete except for the missing piece in the middle. It's the biggest of them all, nearly the size of my hand.

The puzzle shows a beach battered by a storm, with ominous dark clouds, powerful waves, and an unexpected covering of white frost adding to the scene's surreal quality. There's an incomplete sentence partially buried in the sand.

Could this be it? The puzzle that Aaron was talking about.

Do it. There's no harm in trying, Red Horns encourages.

A frigid chill shoots through me, my hands and fingers shaking uncontrollably. As I unclip my clutch, the single puzzle piece stares up at me, seemingly holding both my destruction and my salvation.

The plastic coated with four outstretched nubs hangs between the pad of my thumb and index finger when I bring it to the empty place. It melts in place, like ice on my tongue.

There's a complete image of the beach and the words sprawled on the sand in a haunting font.

The secrets shall come forth in the dark of dawn near the shore of the place where the burns can't be bygones.

Can this fucker not speak in plain English?

Shore. Burns. Dark of dawn.

The words' strings dangle loosely, unattached, as my mind searches for connections to make

sense of the sentence.

Shore. Burns. Dark of dawn.

Burns.

Shore.

Then everything knots into place, forming a coherent thought and the only possible answer to all the twisting of words.

Dread and realisation climb up my back, sending goosebumps in the wake of facing the place that burned my everything with it. If I go again, I will have to face everything—rewinding the nightmare, but in reality.

No. No, no, no. Please, no.

Breathing becomes an effort with everything running around in my head. Maybe the dream was real. The warning echoes in my ears, a chilling reminder to save myself. After this, I don't know from whom I'm saving myself. Fear or death.

I should tell Jason about this. It would be better to have him in on this than for me to serve my head on a golden platter.

With a deep breath, I step back, determined to extricate myself from the web of my own mistakes. A web I spun with my foolish innocence of letting Aaron manipulate me—*again*.

My weak and slow step gets halted when my back flattens against a hard chest. A relieved breath leaves from deep within me when the fresh scent of mint envelopes me, but it's not like the usual comforting, rather, challenging.

"Jason?" I mutter and turn around with my hand on his chest, but what I'm met with was never something I would've expected from him, especially directed at me. "Are you okay?" I ask when his green eyes take the shade of the darkest night and rim red out of anger or sadness or a mix of both.

His forehead creases with deep engravings, and his tie is loose around his neck with the top two buttons of his shirt open. Eerily mirroring the same look I had only met a month ago when the dread of losing him took over.

"Am I okay?" he says as he curls his hand around mine. He slowly stalks towards me with his tone matching that of a roaring lion out to feed itself.

He knows—he knows what you did to him. Betraying his trust, Red spills my dread to me.

"Jason," I whisper, staggering back a step, overwhelmed by the manic gleam in his eyes.

"Answer my question, Bianca. Am *I* okay?"

Another step.

"How could I, when the biggest truth I'd found was masked by sweet, deceptive kisses?"

Another.

"How could I when the person I trusted the most—something I wasn't able to do over the fucking years—used it like a tissue and threw it away without looking back?"

Another.

"How could I when the woman I love the most is the woman bringing me closer to my grave?"

Everything in me stills at his words. I wanted a confession—a confession that would tell me what I'm feeling isn't only one way. And I got it. But not like this, when his face is out of colour, pale as the ghost haunting my every step. Not when he looks as if he would rather not look at all. Not when my heart is beating erratically for a reason rooted in fear of losing the only person I wanted the most.

"Jason. Listen—" I gasp when the edge of the table digs into my lower back, giving Jason the best opportunity to tower over me.

"No, Bianca! Listen to me." His voice is deep and ravaged with unspoken anger. "When that motherfucker said you would have the last piece to this fucking puzzle, I refused to believe. You know why?" He pauses. "Because I knew my Rainbow would never do that to me. She would never be in the devil's den trying to lure me. Or so I thought." He heaves as more profane filled words hang low on his tongue with his index finger shaking as he points at the puzzle. "Then I realised the woman who was with me the whole time wasn't my Rainbow at all. My Bianca is a lost angel that guides my soul. But you took mine right out of me."

Tears come pouring down like a fountain. *Jason talked to Aaron.* Aaron could've said anything. I know his insidious and labyrinthine ways of influencing others' minds. Aaron Blackburn is a master manipulator with every trick at his command.

"Jason…" I stammer. My insides violently shake as I try to keep myself up and not collapse into a crying mess. "I would never let anything happen to you or anyone. I don't know what Aaron told you, but it's not true. Know one thing: I will do everything in my power to protect everyone I love."

His green eyes darkened before me, fading into an inky blackness. *I did that to him.* He thinks I used him for Aaron.

Well, didn't you? White questions as I hear all the judgement in her voice.

"I guess you failed at that. I can't bring myself to believe I just lost all the colours I once thought could give me a new perspective."

My heart shatters into pieces when a tear slides leisurely over his hardened cheek and tight jaw. I have never seen him cry. Not at the funeral, and not when I left.

To know I caused that. I can't … I can't take it anymore.

With my voice watery, the confession flows out. "I wanted to tell you. Tell you everything that Aaron wanted and that he would give me the answers about Ma and Dad's death. If that wasn't enough, he threatened me with Steven's life. I couldn't think of anything else. There was no time when I didn't curse myself for doing all this. I wanted to tell you—" I halt my spill when he brings out a clear package with evidence of my betrayal.

The USB. The two sheets of names.

"We caught a pawn taking from your letterbox." He throws them behind on the table, unsettling the now completed puzzle. "You were the mole I opened the door widely to. I should've never let anyone in so close that it shut the doors for others. For that, Bianca, I couldn't fucking hate myself more."

He clenches his jaw and leans in with his hands by my sides. His exposed forearms tighten fiercely. "And why should I believe anything you tell me? It could be everything your *beloved Aaron* told you to say. Maybe you're giving him more than what you gave me."

I grit my teeth as each of his words burns a hole in my ears with its toxicity.

The acid in my stomach grows when he speaks again. "Has he gotten into you, made you scream his name, or has he fucked you into an oblivion that you forgot about the rest of the world?"

"Jason! Shut up!" I scream, matching his enlarged and reddened eyes. "Fucking enough! Shut up before I do or say something we both will regret. I will make everything okay, you have to trust me." I sniff, clenching my hands into fists. "I know it's a big ask, but you have to trust our lov—"

"Don't you dare finish that." His calmness returns, but it's nothing to be fooled by. "Don't say it. Don't make this hurt more than it already does." A spark of vulnerability flashes across his face before it returns to the hardness he wears perfectly. "Now I'm even wondering if everything we had was all an act. Was it?"

My breathing becomes unbearable. It's better if I stop altogether. At least that way I won't need to feel the sharp jaws of my own heart ripping it out of its place.

"Jason…" I whisper, swallowing for my dry throat. I search his eyes, hoping to find the enchanting forest I long to explore, but it's not there. The only thing I see is its deforestation, with a haunting emptiness echoing. "Don't you dare insult *our* feelings." I straighten and come nose to nose with him. "There was no moment in my life when I didn't yearn for you—for just a little glimpse of yours. Ever since I met you in the gardens and all the time after, I saw my future in you. Now I see nothing, because you decided to believe a man you don't even know."

I will my eyes to stay strong and not leak tears, and against all my protest they keep spilling and that makes me angrier. "Is this how you fulfill your promises you whispered to me?"

He keeps his lips thinned and eyes dark.

My heart ceases to beat, and I don't think of anything when I push him and face the door with the heart shattering at my feet.

"The night of the fire, I was devastated to lose my parents, but more so to lose *you*. And here I am again," I croak before leaving him and stepping all over my heart.

A fresh wave of tears pierces through my eyes. *This is not the Jason I fell for.* He's not the Jason I love. He's not here. He would've trusted me, even in the slightest, for the sake of what we had.

Maybe there was nothing to start with, Red comments.

Fuck off, will you!

The endless corridors, once a marvel, now seem like walls and floors rushing towards me in a blur. I need to get out. Air—I need air.

This is all my fault. All my fucking fault. I deserve it. I was never meant to be happy. The universe had given me some moments of happiness out of pity, and I am grateful for them, because they've left me with a lifetime of memories.

My hands work to wipe off my tears as they keep streaming. *Why won't they fucking stop!*

"Bianca." A strong grip lands on my arm, halting in place. Dark blue eyes look back at me with knowing sympathy.

"Let me go, Kai," I request with a weak voice.

"Where do you think you're going looking like that?" His voice fills with worry. "What the fuck did he do?"

"Leave me. Please, Kai," I sob. My heart shivers with the comfort my best friend gives me. I may not go to him every time I need something, but Kai has always been there for me.

Kai loosens his grip on my wrist. His jaw twitches, and the usual soft dimples disappear. "Bianca, we're here for you. Things may not be right, but they won't stay like that forever," he promises.

But I've lost all faith in them. Jason's earlier quiet silence taunts me.

I frantically nod, but don't speak—*can't* speak.

He lets go of me and closes his eyes.

You're never going to be happy if you keep running away. White and Red blend to make a shade of pink I want to admire yet can't find any fucks.

I run, letting the night swallow me.

I run to chase away the raw hatred I have in my own flesh.

Tonight, I learned one thing: the embers of that night's fire still glow. The flames of their destruction melt away my dreams and desires with raging vengeance.

Only now they took away my faith in love, too.

CHAPTER 39
Jason

I've had whisky multiple times in my life, but tonight it tastes like nothing. Just another liquid that drains down my throat. Nicholas has a lot to explain with his lowering quality of liquor.

"You did it," Kai says, entering the room, followed by slow claps. It wasn't a question, but a statement.

"It had to be done." My voice is a dangerous whisper in my glass as I take a swig.

"I know. But you didn't need to make it *this* real. She was a crying mess, and I can't see her like that." Kai sits beside me with his bourbon in hand.

"Neither can I. I died just then. I will kill Aaron for this." My rage

quietens as her broken face washes me with terror. "She looked so lost, her fingers shaking and her voice not hers at all. But it had to be done," I mutter under my breath, dropping my head back on the head of the chair. I am trying to convince myself that this is the best way to go. It hurts now, not forever. At least I can hope.

"I've been waiting for years to say this." I can hear the smile in his words before they come. "You're in love, man." Kai shakes my shoulder as he chuckles.

"I am—at the worst time possible," I confess. "I love her like no other man can. I love her with everything I have and with everything I don't. She's the one and always has been." I close my eyes and breathe as I rub the armrest with my fist.

For the world, Bianca is just another woman in their lives. But to me, she is my life. She is the reason I breathe. The reason I continue my clueless journey is because she's the destination. The rainbow behind the curtain of the storm.

She's my other half, completing like no other.

"... *But more so to lose* you. *And here I am again.*"

Silence floats around us like an entity waiting to be released.

"Is all this heartache worth it for someone else? I can't see myself all sober-drunk and contemplating life like you are," Kai says.

We stare up at the clear ceiling. The clouds are in their full glory, and the cheer of the stars is dull.

"Kai, you will go through all sorts of pain for the one you love. Because whoever you love will be worth it for you, and your heart will call it. But one thing I want to wish for you is not to have a love like mine. It's like living in a dream only to wake up knowing she isn't with me, but she will be after the nightmares are over." I gulp down the lump in my throat with another swig of the drink.

He scoffs. "I didn't know you had it in you to speak that. Our wall is more transparent now."

"It's a side effect of love." I lift my glass into the air and swirl the amber liquid.

"To the side effects of love," Kai toasts, touching his glass with mine. "If. *If* I ever fall in love, it will be to save her and give myself a chance for redemption." He hums, and his heartache is palpable. "For the two women in my life. One who is staring down at me right now." He points to the ceiling giving way to the night sky.

It's one thing to lose your mother to cancer, and it's another thing to deal with a living corpse of your father.

He continues with heaviness in his voice, "The second, who will come, and I will cherish her heart like my own."

"Surprising coming from a man who never believed in love but *strong one-night hookups only.*" I try to change the subject.

"I still do. Love isn't something I can afford, and you know it," Kai replies, clearing his hair from his forehead.

"To heart donation, then," I toast. The mood somehow went duller.

Kai huffs a sigh and flicks his eyebrow at the table behind us. "So, the puzzle's complete?"

"Yeah." I nod, then recite the message on the puzzle to him. "Still think it's a trap?"

"Fuck yeah." Kai turns and throws his arm in the air. "We don't know how much we can trust the bastard, but he is our best hit at Pyrosilk." Kai drops back on the sofa.

Just wait for me, Rainbow.

It's another test we have to pass, and we will see the end of the rainbow together.

CHAPTER 40
Bianca

Warmth spreads across my face as softness kisses my cheeks. My heavy, exhausted eyes feel the burden of my body's weight.

I can hear the chirping of birds and silent murmurings of people around me. *Where the hell am I?*

My eyes slowly peel open, my vision getting clearer. So does where I am.

The Botanic Gardens.

And I'm lying utterly spent in the heart of the main garden with the scent of flowers thick in the air. Morning dew on the grass soaks my dress, the dampness chilling me as a silent shiver runs down my spine.

How the hell did I get here? Did I run all the way?

Fuck. Each pulse in my head was like a hammer blow, a dull, heavy thud.

I spent the entire night in the garden. The thought seems bizarre even in my head.

"Are you okay?" a calm voice asks with a comforting hand on my shoulder.

I look up to see an elderly man, his face etched with wrinkles, and a kind smile playing on his lips. He must be in his early sixties, his pristine white hair is styled with precision, while his body, a dense mass of trained muscle, reveals a life of intense physical activity.

"Uh … yeah. Yeah, I'm fine," I croak as I sit up straight. The fabric of my dress bunches at my knees, a chilling wind cutting through the thin material, going straight to my … bare core. Double fuck. I didn't have time to change last night.

Last night. It seems like a million years away, especially the way my lips were smiling. The universe even took that away from me.

I try to get up and immediately slam back down when a jolt of dizziness curses me. My brain buzzes like a hive, and my vision blurs and shakes violently.

"You don't look so all right. Wait, let me get you something," he says and runs off to the nearest cafe. Not long after, he comes back with a cream donut and a bottle of apple juice. He passes the donut, but I shake my head. "For morning energy."

"Sorry, lactose intolerant." I close my eyes and face up at the sky as my eyelids flutter with exhaustion. The sun subtly warms my face as it peppers me with hope to get through just one more day. Though silent, my heart feels like it's fracturing, a slow, cracking sound, and with every beat, hope seeps away like blood.

"Then it's just the apple juice. You need some sugar in your system," he explains, his strong American accent thick with concern. "Or you'll collapse—you can barely keep your eyes open as it is."

I nod and take the juice from him. "Thank you." For a moment, stranger danger clicks in my head but screw it. Life cannot fuck me up anymore.

"I'm a surgeon, if you're wondering. Had my day off from the clinic today and thought a stroll in the garden might help. Maybe I was meant to meet you." He shrugs. "Mind if I join?" He points to the space beside me.

"No." I shake my head and move away a little.

"I'm Marcello, by the way," he introduces.

"Bianca." Turning my head, I see his fair skin, lightly lined with wrinkles around his eyes and mouth, a testament of a life well-lived. "You do look like a doctor. Working for long as one?" I ask.

"Years. Lost count by now. Ever since I was a kid, I wanted to see inside the human body. How all the different individual systems work together so that we can just live. So, being a doctor was the best way to fuel me."

I raise a sceptical eyebrow at his words as I take a small sip of the bland apple juice. My taste buds are still waking up. "That's different. Usually, any doctor would say they became one to help save lives. But good for you, Marcello."

"Not every doctor has the same hunger for the same greed. It's motivation that sets us apart. Whether it's the greed to help or the greed to earn, the only difference is what they will do to get it. I know what I want, and *it is* good for me." He nods.

My spine straightens as he speaks. His tone, once warm, now held a subtle edge, instantly putting me on high alert. My senses sharpen, picking up on the shift.

I don't make a move to shift away. So, we sit in the quiet of the gardens. The only sounds are the birds' songs and the wind whispering through the grass like a ritual to warn me.

"You're not going to ask me why I was lying in the middle of the garden?" I question, getting a strand of grass and wrapping it around my finger.

"Everyone has their secrets." He tilts his head so that his grey eyes are on me. "So do you and I."

"Secrets." I scoff. "They ruin everything you ever make."

"If you're going to learn anything about life, Bianca." Marcello huffs as he stands and wipes his behind. "It's that secrets and promises are never meant to be kept. They will come out one day or another, like a hidden truth. We are just puppets in its play who wait and watch as it reveals itself."

I chuckle, my shoulders shaking. "That's a bit deep for my morning."

"Like the drool on your face," he says, passing me a handkerchief from his pocket.

Using it, I wipe away the streak of drool from the corner of my mouth. "Hey! Should've told me earlier."

"Why tell when you can be surprised? Hope your truth treats you well, Bianca Kennedy." He salutes with his two fingers. "We will meet again." And then he walks off, leaving me stunned.

I sit for some time finishing the juice, and when I examine the handkerchief he left behind, heat leaves my body.

We will meet again, Bianca Kennedy. All of you in the next chapter.

Emblazoned at the bottom of the white fabric is a fox with flames licking at its back in a vibrant pink glow. I snap my head to where he was, but there was no one. *Did I imagine all of that?*

No. I rub my thumb to feel the smooth plastic of the bottle, to feel that it is real and I'm not actually going crazy.

He knew who I was. *But who was he?*

It's been three days since the night at Phoenix. Three nights when I didn't have a safe arm around my waist and three nights since I've cried like I've lost myself all over again.

I've heard nothing from Jason. A small, pathetic part of me wants to hear his voice, even if it's for one last time.

I miss him. Now that I know what a life with him tastes like, I don't know how I'll ever get over him and everything we shared.

My insides tremble, thinking of the haunted look in his eyes. They were dark, yet a spark in them, telling me not to believe everything he said. Jason might not be a man of many words, but his eyes tell a story all their own, conveying emotions and thoughts far beyond what his words can express.

For a fleeting moment, I thought he would come after me and wrap his warm body around me and whisper all those sweet and sexy words in my ears. But he never showed up. Not even his shadow. Maybe he meant every word he said, and I was misreading him.

He isn't coming back.

We're standing at a turn in our lives that's eerily similar to the one who stood at five years ago. Only this time, he rejected my trust, and I now know what he felt back then. Lost and unworthy.

That's why I must do this. I'm staring at my screen with an email typed up for the termination of my contract with the Archers. I've finished my plans and sketches for the floors, with a design palette and proposed equipment to use. Each design is appropriate for their business and branding.

I release a harsh breath and click the send button. A burden lifts from my chest, yet a heavier anchor comes in its place. Working at the Archer Enterprises was a dream. It was truly too good to be true. It's time to wake up.

My phone rings on the table, and slowly, with no motivation, I lift the buzzing device. The breath stuck in my throat leaves me harshly when I see *Steven's* name flashing. He never calls me, and even the text a couple of weeks ago seemed like a fluke.

A lump forms in my throat, and my eyes well with tears. I don't have it in me to pick up the call and not bawl my eyes out. *How does he know I need him?* I just want my big brother to be here with me, so that I can feel him in my hands. It's been *so fucking long*.

We lived in the same state, but it's been over a year since I've seen or heard from him. When our parents died, Steven had it the hardest. At least I cried and cried until I passed out, but Steven kept it all in. Let his grief build up on him until he would disappear for days and sometimes even weeks.

Whenever he returned, he was the same, except he would always have new shoes and shorter hair. It killed me that he didn't share his emotions with me.

I also knew he was doing therapy, at least, that's the story he shared with me. Maybe it was to calm me down.

I pick up the phone on the last ring. "Steven?" I whisper, the sound barely audible above the beating of my heart, unsure if I'm hallucinating.

"That should be the name saved on your phone," he says over the phone. The gentle sound of his voice, like a soft caress, is exactly what I need at the moment.

Emotions take over, and everything clears out. My eyes leak like a faucet left open, hot tears streaming down my face, and my hands tremble uncontrollably.

"How are you?" I ask in my shaking voice.

Steven huffs on the other end. I just know he's holding on. "Just missing you. How are you?"

I smile through my tears as I wipe them away. "The same old. Trying to keep myself together."

"Sorry." There's a heavy pause. "I'm so sorry. I haven't been the brother you deserve in these years, and I want to change that." His own voice trembles.

"Shut up. I fucking love you," I cry, meaning it with every fibre in my being. "Don't you ever say that again. You have been nothing short of the best." I sob.

"I recorded that. If you ever back out, I have the evidence," Steven says. "In all seriousness, I miss my goofy little sister. You are the only person I have, and I don't want to lose you."

"Neither do I. I want my brother in any way you give him to me. You are the only person I can cry with and still kick your ass." I chuckle, finally feeling lighter than I have in a long time. "Wait … that reminds me. You said that you were coming, are you?"

He hums and most likely taps his foot on the floor as he thinks. "I'll see you soon. That's all I can promise right now."

"That's enough."

"I love you, Bianca."

My heart fills with a sudden surge of blood, and everything warms. "Oh, my God. Steven Kennedy just said the L word. Shit, I should've recorded *that*." I gasp.

"Well, you didn't, and I'm not saying it again. Better be a sensible woman when I meet you next. I really can't handle another sunshine in my life."

My eyebrow rises. "Another? Are you dating, Mr *Boring*?" I smile just thinking about it.

"Get your head out of the gutter. If you haven't picked it up, you have a personality of more than one person. I would do anything to get another set of hands to deal with you."

I roll my eyes. "It's a believable lie for anyone who doesn't know you." I laugh.

And just like that, my morning went from shit to more tolerable. Better than that.

After Steven's call yesterday, I thought I would get better. But here I am sitting on my balcony, facing the city.

Somehow the house felt like a place I could hide in—not a home, but something close. The girls and Kai had called. I didn't pick up because I didn't know what to say and still don't. I don't want to hide anything from them, but I don't want to talk about it either.

I tuck my legs farther into my chest as I try to roll into a ball, silently watching the loud crowd. They're bustling with energy as people work like ants going from one place to another. But have they felt pain that pierces their chest like a bullet would? Just letting the blood seep out freely because living without love seems more painful than dying.

That's me right now. I would let myself feel every drop of my blood drip out of me.

"Previously on Bianca's Broadcast!" A chirpy voice echoes around me, very loud and very clear. I stiffen and immediately unfold myself. "She has been underground in her house and hasn't seen the sun straight in days. Her lovely and caring friends have tried to get hold of her and have run out of luck."

I jump to the railing. My warm and sweaty hands nearly sizzle as they meet the frozen railing. When I look down, I see Kiara wearing a backward black hat holding a microphone to Eva's mouth. Sage stands by their side and holds the speaker. They look up at me with blinding smiles.

"What the fuck are you doing?" I ask from the balcony.

"A recap and now open the damn door. I need to go to the toilet," Eva says as she bounces on the spot.

"Unbelievable." I shake my head as I sprint down the stairs and open the door in a rush.

My eyes widen at what I see. The three of them are wearing coordinating shirts of the three monkeys.

Eva's wearing a monkey with its hands over its eyes. Sage's shirt has a monkey with its hands over its mouth. But I raise my eyebrow at Kiara's shirt. The monkey has its hands over its crotch.

"Fuck no evil—very important," Kiara says, reading my mind.

All their shirts have some letters sprawled on them, but they don't make any sense.

"Why am I not surprised?" I chuckle as I roll my eyes.

"This one's for you." Sage holds out a shirt, and it has a monkey swinging on a branch with its tail and hands free. There's also an exclamation mark next to the monkey.

"Free evil," Eva chirps, practically jumping on her feet.

I wince at the screeching sound from the microphone and push my hands to my ears. "I'm right here! Turn it off!"

"Surprise!" deep voices shout from behind them. Kai appears from above Eva's head as Adrian pops in between Sage and Kiara.

"I … What are you all doing here?" I ask, still wrapping my head around what happened in the last minute.

All five of them stand in front of me, and I twist my lips to not laugh. When they stand together, their shirts read out *'The Bitches' Squad.'*

"The Bitches' Squad is offering free therapy with our traditional fairy bread," Kai says, his chin resting on Eva's head.

"And alcoholic and not-so alcoholic beers," Kiara chimes, the clinking of glass bottles filling the air as she shakes two bags in her hand.

"You agreed to this?" I turn to Sage.

"Important times call for important measures. Plus, I would never give away a rehearsal." Sage shrugs as she walks in with the speaker. "They forced me to wear the shirt, though," she whispers in my ear before heading in.

I look around to see the only person missing. And like the past four days, he isn't here.

Eva sprints past us as she rushes for her life and shuts the bathroom door loud enough to be heard from the outside. Everyone enters as I stand by the door, still hoping.

"Let it go. Some things are just not meant to be." Kai's touch on my shoulder is gentle, his dark blue eyes filled with a silent sorrow that mirrors my own.

"Kia! Get your smart ass over here! It's a fairy emergency!" Adrian yells from the kitchen, his voice impatient. Some things drop with a loud crash, followed by colourful curses.

"Coming, my beautiful Adriana," Kai sings, walking away.

Home.

I may not have him, but I have these amazing people who will always be there for me.

A heavy sigh leaves my even heavier heart. "I wish we were meant to be," I murmur to myself as I shut the door.

It turns out the fairy emergency was forgetting the *100s & 1000s* altogether, and instead the bag was full of canned beans. We all groaned but made do with what we had. So instead of sprinkling the rainbow-coloured beads of sugar, we plopped spoonfuls of beans on our buttered bread and a hell load of chilled beer.

"You're cooked, and *I* cooked you, *baby*." Kiara snaps her fingers at Adrian. It's still taking time adjusting to Kiara and Adrian. They're an unexpected match of our group.

"First of all, that doesn't make any sense. And second, I came for moral support. I didn't know I had homework," Adrian says as he puts his hands up in surrender. Kiara towers over him with one foot raised on the sofa, and the other stays strong on the carpet.

"The only support you will be giving is to your poor ego when I crush it. You have nothing to show, so you put a wall of *moral support* in front of it." She squints her eyes. Her cheeks are flushed red, and her stance sways. It's concerning that she can't drive through the day without alcohol.

Adrian pulls Kiara close. Her mahogany hair falls across his chest like a silken waterfall as he says, "We'll see about that, but for now, just sit down and drink this." He reaches to pass her the small bottle of water.

She closes her eyes and sinks into his touch.

"How is she drunk on beer that has Kai's dick-sized alcohol in it?" Eva says from behind the curtain.

We all wince at the picture.

"What did I say about being obsessed with my treasure?" Kai says mockingly.

Here we go again.

"Treasure? I thought it was *Pathetic Mike*," Eva yells over the sound of hangers clinking.

"*Obsessed!*" Kai screams, cupping the sides of his mouth.

Kiara wakes with a jolt and speaks with her finger running down Adrian's jaw. "I'm not obsessed, am I, *baby*?"

"Why is she being so touchy? I've known this girl my entire life and still can't understand her." Sage tsks from my side. She has been fairly quiet today. Well, quiet is her usual game, but whenever I look at her, her eyes trail every move Adrian or Kiara makes.

I don't blame her, we're all still getting used to them.

"Have you seen Eva drunk? She tries to be the boss lady and weeps like a kid the next minute," Kai says from my other side, teasing the one person who always falls for his worded traps.

I'm on the sofa with these two while Adrian and Kiara take the other. We're waiting for Eva to get her collection ready behind the curtains she set up in front of the kitchen. Surprisingly, they all came prepared with everything they needed.

"I heard that, and I *will* fucking pull out every single strand of hair on your perfect head and make a wig out of it!" Eva screams.

Kai and I giggle as Sage sits unaffected.

"You can try—if you can reach it!" Kai responds.

"Stop it." I dig my elbow into his side.

"Ignoring the unwanted presence. May I present the new winter collection! Winter Dreamers!" Eva announces, pushing the curtains. Bright studio light shines from the side, giving extra highlight to the pieces.

The air vibrates with four distinct gasps (except for Adrian), each one followed by the soft thud of hands against mouths followed by a chorus of stunned silence. Stares back at us are sets of puffer jackets and matching pants inspired by the dresses we wore when we—*I*—met for the first time.

"This one is called the *Dream Maker*," Eva says, walking over to the first hanging display of an emerald jacket with strikes of gold with similar pants. "For our beautiful Sage, who has made her dream come true and will, facing everything headstrong."

We all turn to see Sage, and she sits frozen, with no reaction at all. I poke her arm and say, "Hey, you there?"

She shakes her head and nods. "Yeah. It's beautiful." Her chest expands as she breathes and rolls her lips.

From the corner of my eye, I see Adrian's knuckles whiten, clenching his fist and glares in our direction, his jaw tight. I never understood him and his reactions.

"This one is the *Dream Catcher.*" Eva walks over to the next one.

The jacket set is a bright shade of purple with drops of clear beads stitched on it like small diamonds in the studio light.

"Kiara catches her dreams and stores them in small crystals of her photographs." Eva looks over to Kiara and I'm about to burst into tears at the slight glaze in their eyes. "To reveal each one she caught secretly and quietly."

"I love you," Kiara whispers.

Eva smiles and breathes as she walks to the next piece. "This one is *Dream Collector.*" It's a beautiful piece with scattered small, deep-red hearts on a white background. The pants are red with white hearts.

"That's me. I try to collect dreams in my heart, so they live close to me. Sometimes that's the only thing you have when things get hard—the power to dream." Eva smiles, fiddling with her fingers.

"Wow." Kai breathes as he shifts in his place. He clears his throat, his back so straight he comes off the sofa back.

"And now, the final one for the night. The *Dream Purifier,*" Eva introduces as she tugs on the sleeve of the jacket.

It is brilliant cerulean blue, like a cloudless sky mirrored on a clear ocean. The jacket's hem has dark blue flames coming upwards, creating a striking visual effect. The white cloud-like puffs on the neckline balance the intensity of the blue.

"We remember fire as the villain—and it is—but it also purifies us, giving us a new, better life by burning the one we had built. Bianca is the fire that had left us burned, but when she returned, we had ourselves back all the better." A tremor runs through Eva as her voice cracks, a fragile sound like breaking glass, mirroring the tightening knot of emotion in my throat. "She makes dreaming a pure thing."

Kai's muscular arm circles my neck, and his chest becomes a comforting haven as I collapse against him, sobbing now. My body shakes at the effort to keep up with all that's happening around me and to me. I don't know I can handle so much love from them, and hatred from the man I love.

One by one, everyone comes in for a hug around me. To my surprise, Adrian kisses the top of my head, and it felt like I was returning home with everyone here, except Jason.

"We're here for you, Bianca," Adrian quietly murmurs.

I know, but I wish he were here too.

Bianca, he isn't coming. Just let him go. Red solidifies the truth.

CHAPTER 41
Jason

"How is she?" My voice is tired as I drink my third glass of the evening. Not sure how many for the day. I'm at the office, and I've done everything except work. Oscar had cleared my day of any meetings—picking up on my stale mood.

"Lost half her weight and eyes I don't recognise, but okay," Kai says over the phone.

I run my hand through my hair and drain the glass. "Fuck. If Aaron isn't right about this. I will fucking skin him alive."

Kai breathes heavily, choosing the right words to say. "Calm down, princess. There's no point in throwing a tantrum. It's for the best," Kai reminds me.

"Did she…"

"Yeah. She believed you all right. She's looking into tickets. Maybe in the next few days." When the silence from my end gets thicker, Kai adds, "It's for her safety."

"I know," I say, against every nerve in my body that wants to jump up and run to her.

Agreeing to pair with Aaron is a hard game to play. If we are to go by his word, keeping

Bianca away from me and this place is the best for her. I can be everything, but a danger to the one woman I love I cannot be.

In no way will Bianca be bait for them. If they want me, I will face that. But I will not allow them to use her to do that, they will face death before even putting their eyes on her.

I don't consider the agonising cracking in my chest, a sound like dry branches snapping, and the unsettling weakness spreading through my nerves as I sit. Each tick of the clock without her is a hammer blow against my patience.

"What's she doing?" I ask, wanting to see her desperately and hold her. She's mine, and this separation is only fueling me with rage like nothing I've felt. *This is all for her.*

"We just ate canned beans with toast and emptied *many* bottles of beer," Kai tells me as he sighs in frustration.

"Weren't you continuing our tradition with fairy bread?"

"*Were.* By the luck of the devil, the 100s & 1000s turned into canned beans, and I already know which two Satan's heirs did it."

"You can't blame your niece and nephew for your laziness in not checking."

"They are seriously the bane of my fucking existence. I don't know why my cousin even bothered with children. They are another side effect of love I tell you."

I chuckle. "We'll see you saying that when you have your own."

"Not when—they won't happen. They're the biggest inconvenience to have been born on this planet."

I go to argue, but a voice speaks, and it has my heart coming out of my chest. I wish I could just jump through the phone and see her.

"Come on, Kai. Sage is ready," Bianca says, her voice used and tired.

My heart melts, and I've never been so warm from hearing a voice. I fucking hate myself for putting her through this. With the drop on her face when she flicked those blue eyes at me for one last time, I knew I would either kill or die myself. I drowned in the air that poisoned my lungs every time I didn't share it with her.

"Coming," Kai says as he puts a hand on the speaker. "Hey, I'll call you later."

"Enjoy your night." I sigh, looking up at the ceiling. Something I've been doing all day.

"Things will get better," he assures before the line goes dead.

"They will." *And when they are, I will be holding my arrow to the fish's eye.*

Bianca

My flight's in five hours. I didn't want to leave but *needed* to. The ghost of the life I almost had haunts me in Melbourne's streets. Every corner whispers of missed opportunities.

After last night's realisation of what I had, I know I can be anywhere in the world, and I will still have my friends—my family.

The air is thick with the salty tang of the ocean, cooling my skin as the afternoon sun beats down. The wind really is coming from the Antarctic regions down below. That would explain why I'm wearing the purple gloves and beanie with the same dress I came in.

I should be finalising everything back at the house—I couldn't. The urge to come here for one last time was stronger than the dictation of the universe's conspiracies.

St Kilda beach is one place I'm me. Regardless of all the memories I have here, it just brings me comfort like no other.

Because it reminds you of Jason. That's why you're here, White says, and she is right to an extent. But today, it's for me.

A large, wet swipe of tongue licks my arm as I sit down on the wooden bench on the pier. Forcing my eyes away from the easy-flowing water, I see a Doberman standing beside me with its mouth open and tongue out.

Lily. A smile blossoms on my lips, thinking of the last time I met the dog.

"Bianca?" A soft, familiar voice comes from behind me. "What a pleasant surprise."

I look up and squint as the sun comes from behind the short, curvy figure.

"Angel?" Somehow, I recognise the aged hoarseness in her voice.

"Mind I join?" She gestures to the empty space beside me.

I shake my head, still trying to come to terms with the change in the moment. She drops next to me as Lily climbs up to the bench on my other side.

"Don't you look warm and cosy," Angel says as her easy eyes find mine. The weight of the grey matching beanie and gloves feels heavier. "Where's your man? Jason, was it?"

I close my eyes softly at hearing his name. The hole I fell into for his love is drawing me deeper and *deeper.* I should move on from him. Every time I look at my hands, I see his hands in mine, and when I look in my kitchen, all I see is him cooking for me.

I'm fucked, and I know that.

"He's where he is supposed to be," I reply, patting a calm Lily's head.

"No, he's not next to you, is he?"

I drop my head and can't stop a chuckle coming out. "It's not his fault. He's better off without me," I explain, and I can't find any wrong in my words.

"You remind me of Bob." She laughs lightly in her chest. "He was such a darl when he wasn't stuck in his head. From him I learned: sometimes you just need to come out and live for yourself," she says, the quiet strength in her tone both calming and encouraging.

"It's so hard, though. I want him more than anything, but I can't even face myself in the mirror." My voice grows thick. I don't want to cry, and I will not.

"In times like these, you need to hold yourself and see the silver lining amidst all the fog. It's always there."

I shake my head. Somehow the words rush out of me before I can think about them. "No. There's nothing left anymore except the ashes of our burned present. I burned everything."

The wind carries the silence around us as Angel gently smooths a hand on my knee. She nods thoughtfully. "I don't need to know every detail, but the weight of your regret and sadness speaks volumes. It's enough to guide your path to a solution." She turns her head, and her beautiful blue eyes shine with strong empathy.

"Was it the same with Bob?" I whisper.

Angel scoffs lightly and speaks. "Bob was a handful, but I knew that living another day without him I couldn't afford. So, when he lost faith in us, I stepped in for both of us. It was the best decision I made in my life. Since that day and until today—when he is somewhere in his peace—I know until my last breath that there will be only him."

I take her hand and give it a squeeze. My heart breaks for such a wonderful woman to have so much hidden within her. "I'm sorry."

She shakes her head. "It's okay. But before Bob died, he taught me something valuable. We are not human if we don't make mistakes. Some planned, and others just happen. They cause you to drift apart from those you love, but I always believed you must go apart to grow stronger for each other. Just like a tree that stands tall when it loses all its leaves. It doesn't give up, instead waits in the rain, heat and wind for the right season to flourish," she explains. Her face softens with a light smile.

In this moment I feel the one thing I had lost. *Hope.* A ray of silver lining.

We look at the golden horizon, hear the seagulls gawk and the wind's song in the air.

"What is the silver lining for me?" I whisper. My fingers scratch into Lily's hair, and she purrs in appreciation.

"It's something that you know exists. Let yourself a little loose and then see the magic. But to get there, you will face the storm—it's inevitable. Your silver lining is waiting for you to grow and come back powerful for no one but yourself."

"How can I? I don't see the girl I once was when I look in the mirror."

This time her smile awakens something warm—almost like life— in my chest. "Change the mirror then. The mirror of your eyes and the perception of yourself—because to find peace, you need to love yourself before you can love others. Come to accept yourself, with all the good, the bad and in between. It makes you who you are. It's a way to heal."

I close my eyes and let the words wash over me like a warm wave, a feeling more than a sound.

Heal. I don't know when I can fully heal or if I ever will, but I know I want it to be … with *him*. We need to heal together. Nothing is perfect, but we can be for each other.

After long moments of silence and hearing the beachgoers, Angel speaks. "Do you know what Jason's name means?"

I shake my head.

"If I'm right, the only meaning that comes from the name is healer. No matter how stubborn and stern the man with the name becomes, his true nature—a healer who mends both himself and others—always shines through. He will come around." Angel returns with a smile and the same comforting tug on my hands. "It's another test of time you both need to face individually."

What she said isn't wrong. Jason is the only one who invaded me with all his power, giving no mercy to the willowing holes in my existence. But his power didn't aim to crush. It was there to regrow the parts of me I thought I'd lost. The part of me being in the company of another, I didn't feel like a burden. He was there because he wanted to—he wanted *me*.

What the fuck have I done?

"Hope that answers. I'm not a genius and am still learning even at this age. Everything is possible, even if it seems not. Your silver lining is waiting. It will wait until you find it."

Overwhelmed with emotion and epiphany, I take her in a much-needed hug. Finally, I get the right amount of air in me to think past the clouds.

I have enough time. I have my silver lining.

"Thank you. I don't know how, but you truly are my angel without the white wings and floating ring." I laugh through the lump in my chest.

Her aged and well-kept shoulders lift in a shrug. "We come in all shapes and forms. You just need to have the eye to see. If you need me again, you know where to find me. Right here." She winks and runs a soothing thumb over my knuckles. "I won't hold you back longer," Angel encourages, firmly squeezing my shoulders.

Reminder: Go and get him.

"Now?" I ask with my heart racing.

"Yes, now!" she exclaims with a light laugh.

Without thinking much, I push off and straighten my purple dress.

Now or never, Red and White echo in my head.

"Come back to me with him next to you!" Angel screams as I run to my car.

"I will!" I yell back.

A smile plays on my face, and I somehow know everything will be okay.

He can push me back all he wants, but I won't let him kick me out of his life. *You are stuck with me, Jay.* A sense of relief settles, even though I know a fire awaits me.

With urgency, I throw my bag and beanie on the passenger seat of the car I borrowed from Kai, and get my gloved hand to open the driver's side door—

"Argh!" I grunt out of pain as a sharp needle pricks deep into the side of my neck. A strangled cry escapes my lips as I clutch at my throat, the pressure thickening in my throat.

First, my hand slides off my car, and then my knees give out. My lungs gasp for breath. My vision goes blurry as my stance is nothing but a wavering balloon ready to deflate.

"I'm sorry, girl." A sound of a man with too much upbeat for me to forget.

I dig my fingers into my wrist, expecting the familiar weight of the bracelet, but my touch is only met with smooth skin.

I barely make out anything when everything goes black, and my head silent.

CHAPTER 42
Jason

"We got this." Teal rushes in with a small box on the table.

We're in Phoenix's bar and waiting for news of Bianca's safe landing in Canberra. This time I had to nail my feet down not to run off to her—*I had to.*

But the sweat and worry on Teal's face isn't something we are expecting.

She drops a small box on the table in front of me.

"What's this?"

Teal stays quiet.

I reach for the white package, and my steady fingers take out the first object inside.

No.

The golden beads of the bracelet are cool under my touch, but the scratches are enough to tell it wasn't given by choice.

I look back into the box and there's a half-moon pendant on a necklace with a star in the middle. Eva's pendant.

"That's Eva's. I gave that to her on her sixteenth," Kai says in a rush as he jumps out of his seat. "She kept it?" he whispers as he runs his finger, feeling the enamel pendant.

There's a small piece of paper at the bottom. I take it and see the words typed on it. *Come or lose.*

Rage unlike anything I've felt screams within me. "Fuck," I growl, fisting the bracelet in my hand.

"Bianca's not home, and neither is Eva. Not at the boutique or office as well," Adrian says. With intense focus, he watches his laptop screen, his fingers a blur as he types.

Kai stands and fixes his cuff links. "They're taking them to—"

"The Lakes Entrance farmhouse." Aaron completes for him.

The puzzle. We deduced as much but never knew why it held importance until now.

The room goes silent as we take a moment to prepare ourselves. Adrenaline rushes through me, making my blood boil and brain tick the minutes these fuckers have left.

"I'm going to fucking kill you," I say, my demon finally freeing from its cage. My steps are fast as I push Aaron fucking Blackburn with my arm hard on his neck until he hits the wall. "If anything happens to her—*to them*—I will rip out your insides and feed them to you."

His light eyes widen, but they convey nothing. Blank. "Easy, Jason. This is surprising for the both of us." He smiles, showing me the dulling around his mouth. "Now, leave me."

I don't. Instead, press him further into the wall.

"Leave. We have more matters at hand," Steven says from behind us.

War.

Bianca

My head is pounding a relentless rhythm, like it has been dragged on a gravel road and then blown up. Everything in me begs to be relieved of the slow thumping of pain. The heavy weight of my head hangs between my shoulders. Loose strands of my hair stick to my skin from all the sweating.

One side of my neck is stiff and swollen, pulsing with a dull ache that radiates from my neck to my jaw. *What the fuck happened?*

Pins and needles prickle my skin, and I feel the sickening rush of blood as it flows freely from unseen wounds. An odd sense of weakness chokes me, and there's nothing I can do to get my stolen oxygen.

The smell of newly painted walls and something strong, filled with a metallic tang, permeates my surroundings. Although my eyes are closed—blindfolded—I can hear the sound of crashing waves nearby against eroding rocks.

"Bee?" a small shaky voice calls from somewhere in the darkness. I try to open my eyes, but the fabric stops it from happening. The more I try, the harder it becomes as the blindfold glues itself to my lids.

"Is that you, Bianca?" The voice comes again, softer and smoother this time. It's a familiar tone mixed with wariness and confidence I can recognise anywhere.

"Eva?" I ask, unsure whether I verbalised that or if my voice still rings in my head.

"Bianca." This time, it's more certain, and the quietened environment shatters with an ear-piercing sob. Sharp inhales and extra sharp exhales sound in the room. "Where … are we?"

"Please stop crying. It's fine." My voice sounds so weak to my ears I don't trust myself to say the right things when I am fucking terrified. "Breathe for me. It's fine, you're okay," I assure and encourage when she hiccups with empty breaths.

Out of the four of us, Eva was always the careful one, overthinking everything. Now finding herself in this mess, I can only imagine what she's going through.

Aaron is going to be fucking dead meat when I get my hands on him. It was one thing for him to fuck with me, but bringing Eva is just not it.

"I can't … I can't feel anything and … and everything hurts." The sound of her voice is making me tremble. It's breaking with every word, taking my ability to breathe.

"How did you get here?"

"I don't know. I was closing … the… boutique … and … I don't remember." She breaks into another round of sobs.

I try to move towards the sound of her broken vocals, but I couldn't. I *can't*. Thick snakelike ropes bind my arms above me. The same goes for my legs. Stretching me until I can't feel anything.

Cold, unforgiving air whispers through me, and my hands feel solid from hanging, despite the gloves I can still feel on.

Did they do that to Eva as well?

Forget me, I couldn't give more fucks. Not Eva. She has no role to play in these games.

"What's happening?" Her voice calms after the track of sobs.

"I don't know." I give up pulling on the ropes in futile attempts with my weakened strength.

"You guys need to keep it quiet. They don't take it nicely with all the noise." My ears perk up at hearing the strange voice. A woman's voice, used and worn, rasps out, each word like a gravelly echo.

"I second Gail. I got holes in my skin with the number of needles they put in me." Another voice, a boy by the sounds.

"That's nothing compared to being thrown in the middle of an auditorium and being fucked mercilessly." A slightly deeper voice speaks. I can hear the gritting of teeth and the scratching of a chair. Despite his calm tone, the pain in his words is enough to tell how broken he must be.

"Would you guys shut up! This is not a meet and greet," a sturdy woman, much in control, says. "I want to get out of here as much as you do."

My head swims with all the unknown voices I've never heard. "Who are you?" I ask no one in particular.

"People who shouldn't be here," the first female voice speaks. "I just want to get out. I miss my life, family, and my brother."

There's a scoff followed by a laugh. "We don't even know if they remember us anymore. It's been a long time now, I'd lost count by the fourth year. I should've never followed you that day, Levi!" the first boy's voice complains.

"But you did, so shut up your ass, Cooper." The voice of the second boy hisses.

I might be blindfolded, but I can imagine them trying to get to each other's throats.

"Where are we?" Eva asks, her voice fading. At least she can see them—I don't know if that's a blessing for the moment.

"The Waves, at least that's what we call it. They lock us up here until they want us," the sturdy woman's voice replies.

"Shh! They're coming, Isha," the first boy—Cooper—says as his voice trembles.

The door slams open, and collective gasps bounce in the room. Heavy footsteps follow right after, each step heavier than the previous one.

"You're coming with us, pretty girl," a harsh voice commands, and a calloused hand wraps tightly around my wrists. One by one, my feet and hands come undone from whatever they were captive with. My body feels limp and useless as I fall lifelessly onto someone's shoulder. My muscles scream in pain and tiredness, and I'll do anything to get rid of the burn.

"Don't fucking touch me!" I growl through my teeth, trying to let loose from their grip.

The sadist fucking laughs and whispers in my ear. "I love when they resist. It fucking turns me on, especially if you're wearing that tiny as fuck dress." He takes my hand and puts it on something hard as it fucking twitches.

My stomach churns with a bitter mix of nausea and sickness, causing a silent scream to be trapped within me. I squeeze and twist my hand on his crotch to let out my frustration, and it only turns harder. *Fucking hell.*

He chuckles and clicks his tongue. Someone else comes and grabs my other arm, and they walk me out.

"Watch what you do. Our orders were to bring you in one piece, bitch. And that doesn't mean we can't fuck you—*raw.*"

"Take your hands off her, blondie. I don't think you know who you're messing with!" Eva yells, and they stop.

"Couldn't give two fucks. Keep your eyes where they're supposed to be, or we will make you blind for real. The choice is yours," the man on my left says.

A heavy thud vibrates through the floor as the door slams behind us, and an unnerving hush descends. The air is thick with the acrid bite of cigarette smoke and the damp smell of decaying wood, each step echoing with the mournful creak of the ancient floorboards.

I can hear other men speaking among themselves, and the thought of walking into the unknown is eating me.

"Just count your steps. Could be your last," the man on my right says.

Both laugh, a haunting, hollow sound that sends shivers racing down my spine.

The creaking of the floorboard finally stops and gets replaced by solid ground under my feet.

"Here she is, boss," they both say simultaneously.

"Tie her up," a voice of old age instructs, and my hair stands at attention. I get harshly pulled onto a chair, and cold rope-like wrap around my wrists and feet.

I know that voice.

Could it be? White Wings questions.

"Long time no see, honeybee."

Uncle Gareth. That is him. I can't forget the little rasp in his deep voice that reminds of the father I'd lost. The blindfold gets ripped from my eyes, and my last lingering heartbeat stops.

A sudden flash of light hits me, making my vision swim with spots. When it clears, I see him standing tall in his dark suit and hair gelled back, revealing his wrinkled forehead. A duplicate of Dad.

"Uncle Gareth?" I breathe, dropping my tired head while my fingers grip the ends of the chair.

"Oh, I knew I was good at impersonating my brother. Even fooled my daughter. Wait, not mine," he says. His eyes are nothing but a void.

My head hurts from his words. *What does he mean?* He never had a child, never married.

"My brother…"

My eyes go wide at the realisation. No. No. He's lying.

So much has happened in the past hour after I gained consciousness that my brain is hallucinating. The room is dark except for a light bulb hanging over our heads. The open windows rattle violently, responding to the wind's howls and adding to the building dread in my stomach.

He drags a chair across the floor, the screeching metal a painful shriek that makes me cringe.

"I thought you missed me, honeybee?" He looks right in my eyes and smiles sharply as he sits in front of me.

"No, no, no, no…" I chant, frantically shaking my head. My hair falls over my shoulders, shielding me from the man who is lying, and I know it. "No, you're not my *dad*. He … died in the fire."

My scalp burns as a violent jerk pulls my hair, sending a searing pain down my neck, and blurs my vision with tears. I look up into his eyes and I know him.

He leans in close to my lips and spits his words. "I was never your father. But I will be the one who sends you to him," he seethes through his teeth. "I am your *death*."

The first tear rolls down.

CHAPTER 43
Jason

Irony is a nostalgic vice.

Where the gateway to Australia's stunning inland water system provides life to many, it has only given me a reason to believe in what lies beyond life and the ultimate truth of all living beings—death. In an instant, the tranquil waters and the vibrant atmosphere of Lakes Entrance should fill my head, but the only thing it does is fill me with firing rage.

Funnily enough, it has also been the gateway to the many milestones of my life. My first love, first heartbreak and first risk. And now my first death—death if anything happens to any one of them. Especially my rainbow.

No one came back here after the Kennedys' house burned down. We never wanted to relive the memories again. But I couldn't stop myself from bringing both Lina and Oliver's loved lilies to their cemeteries every year. I just couldn't erase them from my life. They were the only light through the inky cloud hovering over me as I missed Bianca.

The familiar texture of my pants offers little comfort as I ball the fabric in my fist. The image of them in danger makes my insides crawl. I can't afford to lose them.

I know deep down Bianca is the only one I will want to see with every sunrise, and she is the one I want to see before I close my eyes. She is my sky that will live on for an eternity. A rainbow to brighten my life of a storm.

Her beaded bracelet, tight in my hand, reminds me of all the time I wanted to remove it from her skin and get her to trust herself to be her own anchor. Now that it's removed, she has nothing to hold on to. This is her own version of salvation and hope. Being closer to Lina and, if anything, Bianca had her life stored in her mother.

Kai sits opposite me, looking equally agitated as he grips his glass of bourbon. A deceptive calm settles over him, more intense than ever before, yet that only masks the simmering rage building within. If history has any play, his bubble of patience will burst with one poke and unleash the monster he hides in the locked parts of himself.

"Prepare for landing," the captain says as the cabin crew busy themselves. The half an hour flight was the longest I've been in. It's all a blur after seeing the message and getting on the plane.

The Smiths stepped in to amp up the security and allow their personnel for extra backup. Luise had her best up for the job after tightening the security at Phoenix, including those trained by the Defence Force. Not only that, but Nick also flew in and has his guards circling the farmhouse and Phoenix as we speak.

"Sage and Kiara are safe," Adrian says, and drops into his seat, the tension lines on his forehead never lessening. "She's safe," he murmurs.

He hasn't left his laptop and is in constant contact with Allie back in Phoenix.

Once we land, the guards have already unloaded and surrounded the property with their guns hoisted on their shoulders, ready for an ambush.

We come out with each step squeaking a death call for all those bastards that are holding their heads on a silver platter.

We're back where it all started. The hope and grief, the connections and separations, the laughs and cries. This is the place where everything came apart only to become a part.

Now we burn for the rebirth. We burn for those we love and for those who deserve to be alive.

What should've been a charred and forgotten field is now a meticulously rebuilt farmhouse, a replica of the original. Even the garden is the same as I remember, with the same fencing, before it was the muddy mess. The house hides in the shadows of the night and possibly in the day, going unnoticed by the many eyes that pass by.

"The bases are set. We can go in from the west," Vincent informs as he comes from behind. He loads his gun in his hands and keeps a finger on the trigger. Turns out Vincent was playing under Aaron's wing, and they seem to have a shared motivation to shake hands.

"I've connected to the closest tower for a better connection and gotten the drone for a look over the property," Adrian begins and gets his team started on the drone. "But I'm coming in."

We nod and look at the house arising from its grave.

"Aaron just texted. They have Bianca alone in the main kitchen area. He's making his way there now, which means Oliver is here. The rest of the Batch are on the property. We can't search just yet. There are guards at every exit and entry," Vincent says.

I don't think when I push Vincent to the side and march towards the backdoor. The same door I used to sneak in to see Bianca before going to sleep.

"Jay, stop …" Kai says from behind me, his voice breathless. "I said fucking stop!" He pushes back on my shoulders, pulling me away.

"What the fuck are you doing?" I grit my teeth, ready to bite if he doesn't budge.

"This isn't the time to do this, Jay. I know what you're feeling. Think before acting, and now is the time to be the most careful. There are people in there we care about—*love*. And others who deserve a better life," Kai blurts, pointing his finger at the house.

Steven comes to stand beside me and puts a hand on my arm. "I agree."

"Got it!" Adrian exclaims, his voice hushed. "The house is one body, but there are smaller sheds to the east for weapons. Look, the guards are coming in and out of there with refills and new guns." He points to the top square on the screen with men wearing all black from head to toe. If it weren't for their silver logo at the back of their uniform, we wouldn't have seen them in the deep night.

"Kai and I can go there and plant the small firecrackers. We can hold that against them and blow it up to lower their resources—on land, at least," Adrian says as he looks around the circle.

"Try not to get eyes on you—they're trained to fight even the largest armies. Better make it quiet," Vincent tells. His body is alert and ready to aim.

"We'll head to the kitchen to be ready for Aaron's signal. Vincent's coming," I suggest. We have no idea what could be waiting for us in there. It could be a massive success or failure. It won't do us any good if I see it as a failure, because it can't be. So many lives depend on this going right, lives that deserve to live and see tomorrow's sun. Even if I don't.

"That sets it. We're ready." I nod.

We begin to pull apart, and head to our positions, but Kai stops us. "Can we do a team call?"

"Really now?" Adrian lifts his eyebrow.

"Yes, now. Come on, everyone." He beckons us back to the circle with his hands. Vincent stays out, and Kai looks at him and closes his eyes. "You too, Vinny boy. I don't trust you, but tonight you're our ally."

When we all come together, we breathe in. "To life and saving," Kai says as he puts his hand in the middle.

Adrian huffs and stacks his hand. Then goes Steven, Vincent, but I look at our hands. We are stronger together. With the thought, I put my hand on theirs. "The Phoenix will rise."

CHAPTER 44
Bianca

The same dark eyes and the charming smile any woman would fall for stare me down—Ma included.

The man in front of me, whoever he is, leans back in his chair and crosses one leg over the other. "I wish things were different, but they're not, and that's why you only have …" He looks down at his watch. "… An hour left of your life."

He pauses to look at me. "You should've died that night at that nightclub, but my pawn disappeared. I wonder where." His familiar, accusing eyes squint at me as if bothered by my existence.

"What…" I gulp through my dry throat. "What the hell are you saying, Da—"

He leaps up from his chair and comes at me. His hands curl around my neck, cutting off all air.

I wheeze, every cell in my body begging for air as they suffocate.

"Don't you fucking call me that! You little prick!" he screams in my face, spit speaking more than any rageful words. "I'm going to say this once and only once. You are not my daughter. Gareth, that fucking bastard, took that away from me, too."

He lets go, pushing me away, and I land with a sickening thud at the back of the chair. This time my spine takes the hit as it goes numb. Any remaining air gets stolen from my lungs as I take the hit not only physically but also from his words.

What is he saying?

"Hold your greed, Oliver. I need my share of the deal before you lose your mind," a deep raspy voice says from behind *Dad*. When he moves to the side, Aaron stands there with a sharp tilt of his smile and somehow, he looks more welcoming than the elderly man claiming everything he's not.

My eyes become blurry as a sheen of wetness coats them. I never knew I would be so happy to see Aaron. He seems like the only person I know when this man in front of me, who I've known as my father all my life, is tilting my axis.

"Aaron! I thought I would have all the fun," Oliver says as he walks towards Aaron and takes him in a hug. Aaron blinks twice. *What?* He always did that when he was emotional or cried in my arms when he needed help.

When they pull apart, the usual darkness returns to his face, and he looks at Oliver, who points at me. "All yours."

Oliver turns around and takes out a crumpled pack of cigarettes from his pocket. He taps one against the side of the pack, then positions it between his lips and strikes a match. Its sulphurous smell briefly overwhelmed the tobacco.

"The Batch is ready to go. Say the word." From the other corner, the door opens, and Max comes in. "Hey girl. Happy to see me?" Max strides in, his hair is put up in a bun, but he isn't the man I saw at work. Maybe it's the look he sees on my face that he says, "Connections happen everywhere. Maybe ask Jason what he's hiding in the basement."

I scoff to myself. Either I'm going crazy in the head and seeing people where they're not supposed to be, or I've just died and am living in my worst nightmare.

"Show me." Oliver faces Max, then turns to Aaron. "Keep your eyes on her, Aaron," he says, blowing a cloud of smoke.

A sickening feeling dawns in the pit of my stomach. Dad never smoked. In fact, he always gave us lectures about its impact on our health.

The world is a wondrous place, and it shows you things you never thought possible.

Oliver and Max leave while Aaron strides towards me. With each step he takes, his gaze intensifies as it takes me in from toe to head. His light eyes move from my bound wrists to my legs, and his jaw ticks. When he gets close, he squats, his gaze unwavering as he looks me in the eye.

He looks over his shoulder once more and then comes back to me. "Are you okay? How are the others?" he whispers.

Out of all the things he could've said, *that* was not it. I tilt my head in question. My shoulders sag out of fear or comfort, I don't know.

"Living my dream." If I could roll my eyes, I would. "Would you tell me what the fuck is happening?" I try to hold back my bite.

My head hurts. *Everything* hurts. The cold wind penetrates my thin dress, and I shiver. With a sigh, I let my head fall forward and shut my eyes.

"Trust me, Bianca. This is the last time you'll see my face. Please, I need you with me." He keeps his voice low.

"Yeah, they're here. I couldn't see them, but they're here," I whisper back.

Aaron shuffles closer and puts both his hands on my thighs. He rubs his hand on my stone-cold skin, the chilling dampness vanishing as his warm touch spreads through me. This feels like old times, when I felt safe around him. My fucking head has had enough of tonight. I want it to end, or I will end myself for real.

"Where?" he urges. His voice shakes as he continues, "Where are they?"

"I don't know exactly. But..." I breathe with a restless sigh. "We took sixty-two steps and there was a right turn, somewhere with a creaking floorboard," I reply, the air leaving my lungs with each word. For the first time, I'm thanking the voices in my head.

"Fuck. You sure?" he asks, as if not believing the words. He lifts my head up, and I see his dark eyes softening.

I nod.

Aaron straightens his back and looks at me with certainty. "Don't worry. We'll get you guys out." Aaron kneels and loosens the ropes holding my feet. "Keep your feet here. You can push them to free yourself. But don't do it yet." He breathes, his hair slick with sweat, each rasping breath exhausted. "I'll loosen your hands as well. Push them to the side, then up."

I slowly nod, confused. Two months ago, he was at my neck to get all the information, and now this. *Helping me out?*

Aaron stands, and in a rush, digs into his pocket, pulling out a small blade. 'Here. Keep this in your hand. If you need to use it, *use it*,' he says, his eyes circles of certainty.

"I'm going to kill you," I mutter under my breath, trying to make sense of everything.

"You do as you wish. I always wanted the best for you, baby. Our paths only collided once, and now we're on different ones." Aaron's eyes search mine as I see the old him returning. "At least I had you once in my arms. But you've got better arms now." Regret plays with sadness in his words, and I don't know if I should cry with him or keep my guard up. For that fraction of a second, my heart breaks for him. "And with all the things you gave me, they never went to Oliver or anyone else. I sent them back to Jason."

What are you, Aaron Blackburn?

I look at him, maybe for the last time. Whatever was between us was a facade, but this moment feels more real than anything we've shared before. "Aaron…" I croak. My head falls on his shoulder. "I'm tired."

"I know, Ice. I know. Just stay tight. We promise you'll be out and safe."

"We?" I ask, not taking my head off his shoulder.

"They are here. Jason and Steven, and the others as well."

As soon as the words leave him, my spine straightens to attention and fresh tears roll out of my eyes.

Steven and Jason are here. *They're here.*

"We don't have time. They drugged you to get you here, you'll need some induced adrenaline," Aaron says as he takes out a syringe with clear liquid inside.

"Bite me," Aaron instructs, and I look blankly at him. "Just do it. Right here." He points to the side of his hand.

I shake my head.

"Just do it," he repeats. His hand brushes my dress higher on my thigh and wipes a small area of my skin.

I sink my teeth into his skin, and at the exact moment he plunges the needle into my stone-cold thighs. Pain explodes as he digs the needle, and the liquid excretes inside me. I scream into his hand, and my bite gets hard.

Tears sting the corners of my eyes, my breaths come heavily as I feel heat rushing to me. My hands tremble, and my head swims.

When my focus clears, there was Aaron's hand, bearing a deep crimson mark, already beginning to swell. Before I could open my mouth, the door bangs open, and Oliver comes in. His aura reformed.

"This will shut you up!" Aaron screams in my face, lightly smacking my head to the side. To Oliver and Max, it would look like a hard slap.

"My little girl's acting up?" Oliver chuckles as he comes from behind Aaron.

"Not so little. Gave me a bloody bite," Aaron complains, shaking his hand as he gets up, wincing from the pain. "So, I jabbed her."

"I don't care. Just needs to be alive enough to hear." Oliver rolls up his sleeves as comes face to face with Aaron.

"All yours," Aaron extends his arm and points at me.

Oliver smirks and pushes Aaron to the side, sitting on the same chair. "Where was I, honeybee?" He tilts his head up and closes his eyes in thought. "Right." Oliver slowly levels his dead gaze on mine, like any human but without a soul.

He looks over his shoulder. "Do you boys want to stay for the gossip?"

"Nah, I'm good. I've heard it enough times to say it by heart," Aaron says as he takes a step back. His eyes connect with mine for a second, and he blinks in assurance.

I don't even know whether I can trust him or not, but my options are limited.

"I know who will," Oliver announces as the far door by the back opens, and Eva rolls on a bed with syringes plugged into her and saline attached. Or I think it is saline. "Evalyn, darling. Lovely to see you again. Hope the blood boosters are doing you well. You're very lucky to have such a unique blood type—many have died in the process of finding it."

Her bed rolls up, so she could see us. Eva's eyes widen in shock. "I wish I could say the same," Eva sneers and spits on the ground.

My limbs shake at her near-lifeless body as she mouths, "*Help.*"

"What the fuck are you doing to her?" I scream.

"Nothing that would kill her. *Yet.*" Oliver laughs, his eyes still lingering on Eva. He turns to focus back on me. "I thought you would like a familiar face when we have the story time. I am still generous, think whatever of me.

"Let's start from the beginning. We met Lina when we were fifteen. Her family moved from Italy because things back home weren't the best. I first saw her at our secret gold mining site in Areum, Bendigo. She was there with her father, who took over the control of the imports and exports of the two sites we oversaw." Oliver's tone is confident as takes another drag and blows the smoke in my face.

I just stare and listen.

"Lina and I met frequently. The charge between us was intense. Anyone around could've sensed it from a kilometre. But then the good twin entered. *Gareth,*" Oliver seethes, his knuckles folding into a fist.

"Anything I had, he took. He looked over the other secret site in Ballarat called Chryses. Lina's mother was a nurse, and her post transferred from Areum to Chryses. That meant Lina went as well. I barely got time off the mine sites, digging and digging for nuggets that were and are invaluable."

Oliver smiles to himself as if remembering everything. "When I turned twenty, I went to visit, and I found fucking Gareth all over her. I confronted Lina about us, and she just replied that we were never a thing. Okay, I get it. We never really went beyond holding hands, and she kept calling me her friend. But for fuck, we were a thing. It was only that Gareth had brainwashed her—like he did our parents. He was their *favourite*." Oliver mockingly rolls his eyes.

My breath is stuck in my throat, afraid to even breathe wrong. I always knew Ma and Dad had been in love long before they got married. Ma said she first saw her love when she was in the hospital helping with errands. *Did she mean Uncle Gareth?*

"I had to do something and fast because our parents made wedding plans for Gareth and Lina. How could I have allowed them to sacrifice my love like that? *Fucking love*," he scoffs and laughs, tipping his head back. "Stupid love. There is no such thing. Only then I was a fucking fool, and kidnapped Gareth, locked him up on *his* wedding day. Then guess who was at the altar waiting for the bride?"

My head lulls, heavy and aching, as I lift my gaze to meet his with the returning blood warming my weak limbs. The shot is working. I can feel the warmth spreading through my muscles, and a surge of energy invigorating me. "What? The second choice?" I smirk. My shoulders shake with laughter, and I look straight into his wrecked soul.

Ouch.

That hit right where it hurt. Oliver springs out of his chair, and his eyes widen at my words. He grits his teeth, grabs my neck and punches my face. The metallic tang of blood floods my mouth, the warm taste far more comforting than this man's unnerving presence.

"I was being lenient with you, girl. You deserve to know why you're getting killed tonight," he blurts. His breath stinks of smoke, and all I think of is the smoke circling me in a chokehold, squeezing the life out of me. Like it did many years ago.

Only now, I remember I died that night. I forgot who I was during these five years. I was the girl who knew herself, but … I lost her amidst these lies and traps. Now, they—*he*—will regret ever pushing me to the corners.

I smile through my bloodied teeth. "You're pathetic. No wonder you weren't the favourite twin. Throwing a tantrum when getting rejected." I spit out the curdling blood in my mouth onto his suit. "I can only imagine what shame Grandpa and Grandma went through."

He lands another hit, letting go of my neck, and my head lulls to the side. Spit and blood fly across to the floor. My lungs burn as I inhale great gulps of air, accepting the deafening ringing to vibrate in my ears.

"Everyone accepted me like their fate." Oliver spits, red hot fury eating him alive.

His eyes are the same, his hands and face. Everything is exactly how I remember. But the person has changed—but again I never knew the real him.

"I joined Pyrosilk soon after we got married, although my father was a member already and Gareth wanted nothing to do with them. Pyrosilk was the one who helped me get Gareth and keep him quiet for weeks afterwards. Not only that, but the jewellery fortune we know as the Kennedy empire is all theirs. Or was." Oliver shakes his head, disappointed. "Your brother turned out like his uncle—stupid and faithful.

"The night of the fire, Gareth couldn't keep his ears to himself and listened to something that got him buried six feet. I did what any loyalist to the Great Leader would: uphold the oath. *Eradicate all those who hear and see us.*"

Oliver circles me as he speaks. His words land on my left ear, then the right. "*I burned them both.*" He breathes. "Your lovely father went crying to Lina about your safety and *their* future child's safety."

My wide eyes find his lazy, dark ones. Questions and horror dance in my head.

"Yes," he hisses. "Lina was pregnant. She told me it was ours. It was a late pregnancy, but we were going to make it work."

Warm tears sting my cheeks. Ma was … pregnant. My brain buzzes with the new information. My empty stomach churns with rage, and sadness consumes me whole. The rotting wood of the armrests, worn and rough, creaks as I clench my fists on them.

A sharp gasp echoes in the room, and Eva jumps up. "You're so sick. Rot in fucking hell!" she screams. Hot tears trace a path down her cheeks, each one a testament to the hollowness in the air.

"I'm sure I will. Only then did I know *it* was never mine, but *Gareth's,*" Oliver hisses. He closes his eyes, his lips turning in a scowl, letting his jaw work.

"Steven is mine—my only child—and the *real* Kennedy blood that will live. *You?*" He pauses, chuckling as he looks at me like a shark smelling fresh blood. "You will melt just like Gareth. Burn from flesh to bone, stink as you melt away. Oh, how satisfying that would be."

My heart thumps with the new information I was better without. My supposed father took five years of my grieving, and for who? A person who didn't even exist—not even in name.

It's fine. We're fine. You can go through this, too. White Wings begins with her useless effort to break through the wall of shattering emotions.

The giver can be the taker.

Replay history, you will find your answers.

Never trust everyone around you, never.

The sentences make an appearance bold and obvious.

This man took away the life I could've had. I couldn't see the signs flashing in my face.

I flick my eyes to him as an unknown force takes hold of me. My lips lift in a weak smirk. "*We* got saved from your filthy DNA. I feel bad for Steven to have you as his biological father. *My brother* is nothing like you and never will be." I heave for the air leaving me. "Kill me all you like. But know one thing: my people are coming for you. Steven, Jason, Kai, Adrian, and my girls. They will shred you to pieces and still not let you die—only to do it all again. *You will die many deaths in one life, Oliver Kennedy,*" I say, leaning back on the chair.

I smile. The blade Aaron gave digs into my palm and sears through my skin. The urge to jump from this chair and cut his throat overwhelms me, but that would be too easy. He needs to live with deaths he never saw.

"That's it. I gave you everything I promised Lina I would before her light went out. She loved you kids so much, like the most lovable mother. The one who would do *anything* to keep you breathing," Oliver says, and puts his hands over my wrists. He pushes them farther down onto the rotting wood. The splinters of the chair scratch my skin as the blade in my hand cuts deeper into me.

His dark eyes hold mine, and I don't lose the challenge in them. "I will erase everything you touched, Bianca *Amante*, with this blade in your hand." He chuckles. "Stupid Aaron thought he was smart. Children these days think so highly of themselves. I was the one who pushed him to be with you because holding his sister over him was his strong vice. It took him two bloody years to get you here. Acted like my puppet all these years, dating you and breaking up with you was never his choice."

Brick upon brick gets stacked with every secret he reveals about my life. They are truths that were hidden behind a series of lies and deceptions.

It's better if I die now. I don't think I can face myself or others with all the pain they went through because of me.

None of this is your fault. Fuck! You didn't even know, Red says.

It was happening to you as well. You are as much a victim as anyone else, White backs.

I don't want to be a victim.

Then work to be a survivor, both answer.

As I register their words, Oliver slips the blade from my hand and runs it along the top of my wrist. A raw guttural scream rips out of me as I lean forward, my eyes pool with tears, just like the blood bubbling from my wrist.

Where are you, Jason? I don't want to die without seeing him. At least the universe can offer me death in his arms. After tonight, all I want to do is sleep forever in his comforting presence.

With loud sobs, Eva scratches her arms, as if trying to tear herself apart. "Leave her!"

"Let her go, please. She doesn't need to see this," I whisper. My throat tightens with each word, and I try not to close my eyes.

White was right. I was better off in the dark. I didn't need to face the darker truth of my existence. Knowledge is not always the answer.

"She is the one who will live to tell the tale. But before I finish you, I need to thank you for all the things you did for us. Distracting Jason was everything I needed to get into their systems. Our world is way darker than they think." Oliver scoffs with a sharp smirk. "Goodbye, *honeybee.*"

Oliver digs the blade in my other hand, circling the top of my wrist. This time it doesn't hurt as much, but everything quietens—Eva's hoarse screams, Red and White fighting me—but I think this *is* my goodbye.

All the times I smiled with everyone come in front of me. The sleepovers, the late-night chats, going to Cornella's. Everything was perfect. We were perfect.

The times with Jason. Every time he held me close to him, every time he kissed me as if I'm his world, every time he gave me new design ideas, every time he called me his rainbow.

Jason. He is perfect.

I may not get the chance to say it to his face and see it for myself.

I love you, Jason. You were *my* rainbow all along, becoming the reason I had the colours. For you, I sought more when I knew I was nothing.

The girl he met sitting under the large tree is happily dying knowing the boy she wished to live for finally loved her—

Oliver steps into me as he captures me between his legs and leans down. "I want to feel your life ending underneath me, exactly like your father's. Right here in the kitchen." He chuckles darkly and wraps his thick hand around my neck.

Reminder: Smile, the truth is here.

CHAPTER 45
Jason

My gun is tight in my hand, and the trigger is ready to pull. We've entered through the west entrance, and luckily for us, it's built the same way. The blueprints of the place were easy to access after connecting to the nearest tower or the dark web. That's for Adrian to know.

Vincent is in front of me, Steven behind, and Teal follows close by in the shadows. She will come only if and when she's needed.

Just hold on, Rainbow.

"I'll take the guards one by one," Vincent reminds me.

"I have Oliver," Steven says.

"Bianca's all mine." My voice is serious as I fix my grip on the gun.

We decide to take the three different doors leading into the kitchen. Vincent's going to take the main. Steven and I will be on either side.

"Brunettes are such a weakness. Sucks they don't last long," a guard says as we approach the doors.

"It was so hot when she had her hand on my cock. Fuck, I'm so hard," another responds.

My fucking blood roars. All I see is red. My feet rush to the voice, but Vincent stops and turns around. "Keep it in your head. I will get them," he says, his eyes wide circles of practice. "You cannot be seen—not yet."

"Guts of a kid like you to talk to me like that. *Stay away,*" I warn. My breathing comes laboured. Bianca is in there, and I'm here losing brain cells with this kid.

Vincent's face hardens, and he tightens his hold on his gun. "I may be young, but I've seen and heard worse things. *This* is only a teaser."

"Let him handle it," Steven murmurs, a hand on my shoulder.

Vincent pastes himself to the wall with the gun on his chest. We do the same as I go on the opposite wall. The room is dimly lit by lamps, their flames casting long, dancing shadows of the guards across the rough walls.

Their voices get louder as they get closer. Vincent looks at both of us and nods. He puts his foot in the doorway, and one guard trips over. Vincent drops immediately to tackle him on the ground, knocking him out with the butt of his gun.

Another loud grunt sounds in the quiet hallway. As it does, I fly to the incoming guard and take him to the wall. "Did she make you hard, fucker?" My voice is tight as I wrap my hand around his neck. "I'll show you what else makes you hard."

A cunning smile lifts on my face as I catch the knife Vincent throws my way. I dig it into his chest, twist it and feel the blood churn against it. He gasps for air as his hand covers mine in retaliation, blood staining my hand crimson before dripping onto the floor.

"You make a good team," Steven says, tilting his head.

"Yeah, right."

"We'll see about that."

Vincent and I say together. Our eyes meet for a second, and then we look away.

We're only a few steps from our door when a bloodcurdling scream, like nails on a chalkboard, pierces the silence. *Bianca.*

Fuck. Fuck!

"I'm going in. Oliver won't do anything to me," Steven says, squaring his shoulder and taking a step to the door. Vincent has already gone through the main door to the kitchen.

I nod. I ignore the burning urge in me to knock this door down to get to Bianca, but I know it will only trigger Oliver, and that we can't afford.

"Teal, stand by," Steven talks into the radio.

"Copy," she immediately responds.

Then Steven enters, and the plan gets into place. Aaron, Adrian, and Kai are making their way to the others and will report as soon as they are on safe ground. Especially Eva. They might not get along with each other in the normal world, but in times like this, they will fight until the end.

After one quick breath, my radio rings. "He knows we're here."

"I'm going in."

I know what my silver lining is. *Love.*

Even when I'm bleeding to death and counting my remaining breaths, all I'm thinking about is how I will walk out of this situation. I *need* to see Jason one last time, even if it's on my deathbed. I will beg life from the universe to steal a minute for us. *He needs to hear how much I love him.*

The past five years had been a dull ache, devoid of life, but the moment I saw him in the airport, amidst the hurried footsteps and echoing announcements, my heart pounded a new beat of rebirth.

Eva's muffled screams intrude my thoughts as I slowly lift my head. Her blurry form struggles against the chains that bind her down on the bed, and the needles that prick her. She's screaming and crying, but I wouldn't be able to make out what for. I smile weakly at her. At least I have my best friend with me, but she doesn't deserve to see me like this. It will haunt her for the rest of her life. I will die, only to leave her with a scar that will never heal.

The grip on my neck loosens, and sharp spikes of air slice through my lungs. I gasp, pumping life into my shrivelling organs and heart. My vision blackens, then agonisingly slowly, returns in a blurry haze.

My head is a wobbling mess of weakness. My hands feel numb, heavy, and unresponsive, as if a blacksmith's anvil were pressing down on them. With some force, I get rid of the ropes from my feet and hands. The only difference is that there is no point anymore. I can't move even if I wanted to.

"I would stay the fuck away from her." My head snaps at the voice. *My brother.* Tears assault my eyes as consciousness blesses me.

With my head still lowered and hair in my eyes, I make through Steven's frame. He's wearing his usual suit, but this time holding a gun at Oliver.

He came for me.

"Son!" Oliver opens his arms like it's a normal reunion. "Come, give your father a hug. It's been some time."

"Father?" Steven scoffs. His eyes, like mine, blaze with a cold, contained fury, a simmering storm threatening to break. "I don't think you even know what it means to be a father, Oliver," Steven says, taking a step forward. His gun still aimed straight.

"That's no way to talk, Steven," Oliver replies. He crosses his arms with mock—unnecessary—disappointment.

"Let them go," Steven orders as he cocks the gun towards me and Eva. "And you can have a less torturous death."

Oliver tips his head back and explodes into manic laughter. "Too bad, if I'm dying, she is too."

The doors and windows explode open, cutting short the conversation and unleashing a torrent of cold, salty wind to howl through the room, raising goosebumps on my arms. Crimson-clad guards enter carrying an arsenal of strange and frightening weapons. The golden logo of a phoenix on their chests is hard to miss.

Jason is here, White says.

A gunshot scars through the air, slicing anything in its path before it goes through a guard's head, dressed in all black. He falls lifelessly with a loud thud to the ground. *When was he there?*

As if the gunshot was a calling, guards dressed in black come forth from the dark corners of the room.

It was silent one minute. Complete silence.

The next.

Chaos. Havoc. Destruction.

I can't tell when the next black guard falls or when the red guards retaliate. It all happens too fast. I don't recognise when I get pulled from my chair.

A woman dressed in red holds me up by my shoulders. My body is dying from the agonising shots of pain eating at my insides.

"Teal?" I ask weakly. We met briefly in Phoenix before Jason dragged me to the forest.

"You're safe now," Teal says, her voice monotonous.

I sigh in relief as she drags my body. "Eva … Get Eva, please," I murmur, not sure if the words are coming out.

"Kai has her. Don't worry, we'll get you out," she assures.

"Jason … Where is Jason? Argh!" I cry out in pain as our bodies collide with another. The force of the impact sends us sprawling onto the ground.

My hands get crushed between us—they feel strangely alien as I finally see them. Blood, thick and dark, paints gruesome streaks like veins of full poisonous ivy on my wrist.

"Take me to Eva. I need to see her," I say as Teal struggles to pick my useless body up. I couldn't lift a feather to save my life.

The world around me is a dizzying blur of motion, bodies colliding with sickening thuds and spurts of blood.

"Give her to me." The voice, a warm sunbeam, melts the ice in my ears, filling me with a vibrant, life-giving energy. His arms wrap around me, lifting me, and my heart flutters at the feeling of his comforting heat to my stone-cold body.

"Jason," I sob when his familiar green eyes welcome me. "You came."

"I will always come for you," he says before caging me to him, charging around the chaos.

"I thought I would never see you again," I mumble through my tears, my forehead resting on his hard chest.

"Remember, where Bianca is, Jason will be close by," he whispers on my forehead. After everything I've done, he came back.

He came back for me.

For us.

We stand in the middle of chaos, but I feel the calmest I've ever been. "I'm sorry, so sorry." The air carries the words as I sink into his neck. In the only place I can find peace, in the only person who completes me.

The loud bangs and clutters don't intrude as I stare up with watery eyes while he manoeuvres through the chaos. His jaw is tense, the creases near his eyes deepen with each step, and silent rage curses his face.

He is my salvation amidst the chaos. My oasis in the desert. My grey.

"Bianca!" Eva's cries break through to me, and I see her on the ground, free from all the tubes and syringes. *My baby.*

Climbing off Jason, I walk, limp, and crawl to her. "Are you okay?" I ask, my hands find her waist drawing her tightly into my arms with their last remaining energy. Her skin, solid as ice, shivers, resisting even the warmth of my body. Her exposed skin screams with torture and pain.

"I don't know," she responds after several minutes. Her voice gets caught in her throat, the shivers and hiccups bringing on a wave of sobs.

I bring her close to my chest and pat her head. "Shh. It's okay. We're here, you'll be fine. You're okay," I chant in her ears.

How did everything get so out of hand that when I recognised it, it was too late to even hold on to a thread to survive?

I glance around to see Kai not far off, his gaze intense and unwavering, the darkness in his eyes a palpable threat. His attention is half divided as he holds a guard down with one hand while also glancing our way.

"I'll be back. Teal is here," Jason informs, loading his gun with a new magazine, and wraps a knife around the tip. For a split second, his eyes drop to my wrists, and his jaw clenches as he inhales sharply. His chest trembles with anger as if he is the one feeling my pain.

Before he could make another move, I stop him with my hand in his. His pulse thunders underneath my touch. The urge to have him near feels desperate, a raw ache words can't express. I shake my head wildly, tears stinging my eyes, breath and words catching in my throat.

"I'll be back," he promises, leaning down, pressing a light kiss on my forehead again, yet this feels different. More like a goodbye.

Then he leaves.

"I knew it." Eva slaps my chest—her voice returning and eyes less pale. "Took you two over a decade." Despite everything, she lets out a laugh.

"Did Sage tell you?"

Eva shakes her head, and a smile creeps onto her lips. "I always knew it would be you and my princess." She coughs, her skin at a loss of colour. "Why do you think I sent him to the airport?"

I look over to *her princess,* who knocks out anyone coming his way as he has his eyes trail to one person.

Oliver is busy being attacked by Steven with his fists. I haven't seen my brother like this before. So enraged, desperate, and *angry.*

Steven's hands slick with congealing blood—his own and Oliver's— make a disturbing tapestry of crimson and scarlet. Deep bruises and ragged cuts mar both men's faces.

Jason puts a light hand on Steven's shoulder, pushing him back with ease and calm that contradict everything about the situation. With a grip on Oliver's collar, Jason lifts him up and pins him to the wall.

Out of the corner of my eye, I see Max getting up with a hand around his stomach. How could I have been so wrong about him? He seemed like any man you would meet at work. Who knew the sweet faces had secrets too.

Max struggles as he crawls to the middle of the room, dodging and ducking bodies as they come at him. A terrifying wave of icy dread takes me hostage as he encircles his fingers on a gun and aims at Jason.

No.

Jason

Death isn't justice. Not for measles like Oliver. They don't have morals and especially no life—they live like they're dead.

Oliver smirks and hits his head on the wall. "I've left nothing for you, Jason, my boy. She's gone," Oliver sings in a whisper. "I took every single shred of light out of her." His eyes dance with sadistic amusement.

With a swift motion, I drive the knife into his arm, causing him to jerk forward with a loud shock on his face.

"That's for killing lives that deserved the air you stole," I say, taking out the knife and putting it back in. "This is for haunting Bianca's life."

Again. "For taking a life that was never born."

Again. "For thinking you will die just once."

Again. "I will kill you slowly every day. You will *watch* your life leaving you."

My chest aches as I force the words out.

Oliver's arm drips with floods of blood, but his smile grows bigger. He opens his mouth, and grunts before pinning on a stern look. "You've grown powerful, boy. But not like I have." His eyes move behind me, and he nods.

A gunshot fires, and a body hits my back, stumbling my balance and digging the blade deeper into his arm.

"No! Bianca!" Steven screams from my side and runs behind me.

Everything goes silent as I look at Oliver. "Stab me again. This time for taking away your *love.*"

The knife trembles out of my hand, and dread chokes me with the scent of cherry blossom.

"No!" I howl as I turn around, and Bianca falls into my lap, taking us both to the ground. My own chest opens like the leaking, gaping wound cursing her chest.

"Get the jet ready … the medical team!" I order, my voice loud and unrecognisable.

Bianca's shot.

My rainbow is shot.

Her shaking hand reaches my jaw and brings me back to her. "Jas … son" Her voice is weak as she gulps to speak. Her beautiful eyes, like the sea of my salvation, weaken and pale.

I hold her tighter against me. "Hold on, Rainbow, please."

"I … love you," she confesses.

Tears sting my eyes. I've been dying to hear those three words, but not like this when I'm losing her. *I need her.* If she stops breathing, and her heartbeat fades from my chest, I'll be lost, with no idea of who I am or what I'll become. She calls me an animal and I will become one. A ruthless creature who hunts down every devil there is.

"I love you so fucking much more. Stay with me," I beg her as I put pressure on her wound with my blazer. It feels like forever when we fought for that exact blazer. "Open your eyes. Look at me. I need you."

She closes her eyes with a smile.

CHAPTER 46
Jason

Her breathing is faint, but a smile on her face.

Her skin is not its usual tan, but a smile on her face. Always smiling.

Bianca, come back, Rainbow.

Her pulse is so low, her heartbeat, which is usually frantic whenever we're together, is now nearly silent.

"Jason…"

This was not your bullet to take. It was for me.

"Jason!" A solid push on my shoulder wakes me back to reality. Kai stands with his arm holding his other bloody arm, and a deathly look on his face. "The doctors are waiting."

With Bianca in my arms, we get off the jet as everyone follows behind me.

All because of me, Bianca is here. *All because of me.*

"You need to clean yourself. We're all here," Adrian says as he sits next to me, passing me a bottle of water.

Fuck, even the water looks like poison to me—everything *feels* like poison. All black and ready to envelop me in a circle of death. If my Bianca doesn't wake up soon, that's where I will end up. Right next to her, holding her hand as I close my eyes forever.

It's been over five hours since they took her to the operation theatre, and the only update we've got so far is that they are trying *their best.*

Their best?

Their *best!*

They need to give it their fucking all and have those blue eyes blink because she needs to. There's no other way around. I don't think anyone wants to know otherwise.

"I'm fine," I mutter, leaning my elbows on my knees as my legs bounce restlessly. We're sitting in the hallway at the Phoenix hospital, waiting for the doctors to come and tell me everything's fine.

Adrian sarcastically laughs. "Trust me, I know. I've been where you are. But you know what kept me on the ground?"

I huff a string of air out of my lungs, already getting agitated by this conversation. But I know well enough what he means.

"Her being safe. You don't need to do what I did, but don't put yourself through hell only to forget what heaven feels like." His voice is quiet in the still hallway of the medical wing.

"When was the last time you felt in heaven?"

Adrian stays quiet for a moment. Then answers, "Heaven isn't something I want." *Or given the choice of wanting.* We all know Adrian will never admit it, but he's been in deep waters ever since he decided everything was on his shoulders. He may not be my favourite person, but that doesn't blur the fact that he is a brother to me—will always be.

Kai and Eva are off in the other room. Eva needed to be given immediate care after the blood boosters they put in her, and Kai was all bandaged up as soon as we landed.

Nick had everything prepared when we arrived. Steven needed a distraction, so he's helping Aaron with the Batch. Sage and Kiara will soon be escorted to Phoenix. We need to keep them safe as well now to avoid a repeat of tonight.

"It takes time, man. Bianca's strong—she'll come for you. We just knew it would be you." Adrian spreads back on the chair with his arms crossed over his head. "Wait? Did you know…" I can hear the smile on his face trying to lighten the situation. "I was actually ready to take Bianca with me after the party. Maybe even a dinner."

I knock him in the ribs with my elbow, and he bends forward lightly laughing. "Like fuck you were. Did *you* know I was planning your murder in my head?" I retort, sitting in the same position, looking down at my bloodied hands. *She's still on me.*

"I knew it!" he whispers, jumping from his seat. "That's why I was surprised by your gentlemanly behaviour. Lady luck changes a man. Never thought it would've been you," he murmurs under his breath, his chin facing the ceiling.

"Not any lady. The one in the room right now—fighting for her life—is the only one who can bring luck to my life."

"Jason." Dr. Moore's voice comes in. Her face is tense as she looks me in the eye.

"What is it? Is she okay? Do you need more doctors? We can arrange that. Tell me what you need." I gather the words out, searching for anything to say.

Adrian stands beside me, also going rigid with the silence. "What's the matter, Doc?"

"Everything is fine. We just need to keep her under observation, but..." Dr. Moore begins explaining.

"We don't have all day." My anger surges hot through my blood.

She straightens her spine, her eyes hard behind her glasses. "There is a possibility we would need to put her in an induced coma. Many injuries besides the gunshot will take time to heal, especially her severely inflamed jaw and the deep cuts on her wrists. That's only physical. There were large amounts of stress hormones released, slowing down recovery."

My heart ceases to beat. I drop my weight down onto the chair with my hands gripping my hair. This can't be fucking happening.

It's been a day since they had to put Bianca out. She's breathing slowly and irregularly, but she is.

I couldn't let her out of my sight once the doctors gave the green light. She could wake up any minute, and I want—need—to be here for her. She deserves so much better than I've given her.

Kai and Adrian had to wrestle me out for a quick change of clothes and shower. Besides that, I'm so overwhelmed by the idea of leaving this room that my mind feels completely paralysed.

The blackout curtains block out the sunlight, and the monitors beat at regular intervals. I spread the curtains wide. The cool hues of the winter morning wake me—like I ever slept. The frost on the window, intricate and lacy, slowly melts with a sigh of frustration.

I take heavy steps, each a harder drag than the previous step, to the chair by the bed. Her soft eyes are closed, and her face shows red, prominent marks, while her chin and jaw are double the size. White bandages wrap her hands, and I feel a faint pulse beneath the fabric where the blade narrowly missed.

"I should never have let you go. I thought I was doing the right thing," I whisper. "Open your eyes, please."

Deep down, I know she can hear me.

"We still need to do the garden and library on the top floor. It's waiting for you," I croak, swallowing the tightness in my throat. I slide her hair from her forehead and kiss it with quivering lips. She loves it when I do that.

I love her.

"Your grey needs his colours. It's all dark without you." I put my forehead on hers. *She is here with me.* Yet the crack in my heart is widening every moment she doesn't open her eyes.

"You need to leave—*now*, Jason. We have this conversation every fucking night." Kai flips his arms in the air.

"Then you already know. I'm not leaving," I say, sitting back on the couch by the corner of the room.

It's been five days now, and still no sign of her waking up. Dr. Moore has assured us that everything will be okay, but with every hour that passes without her, a part of my life gets chipped away.

"Just for a few minutes, go out and breathe. The doctors will be here soon, and they will say the same thing they have been for the past week." Kai's nose tints red and his eyes focus on me. "I love you, man, but…" He pauses and tips his head back as if trying not to cry. "This is not the Jason I grew up knowing. No matter what happened to him, he stayed in his head and took control of the situation. We need you like that, so that when Bianca wakes up, she has *you*. Not a sleepless zombie." His helplessness screams as he gives my shoulder a squeeze. I know he means well.

"I'll stay behind," Steven announces as he comes through the door. "While you drink this down. Turns out Tony supplies his almond white chocolates here as well."

"With cinnamon," Adrian reminds from the other corner of the room as he points to Steven. Kiara smiles from his side.

Sage and Eva are out for Eva's evening walk, which she needs to do to help her recovery process.

"Okay." I sigh, getting up from the couch and taking the cup from the tray. "I'll be back in two minutes. Not any longer," I say from the doorway as I leave the room.

I smell the hot drink, and I feel my heart squeeze, remembering when I last had it.

"Hey, Jason?" Steven calls from behind me.

I look over my shoulder and see him smiling.

"Thank you."

"Don't need to thank me for doing the thing I should've done all this time. Loving her."

He shakes his head, and those familiar blue eyes come to me. "For being the man she needed."

CHAPTER 47

Jason

Two weeks ago.

"We'll see about that," Aaron Blackburn sings, his tone light and expectant. He is wearing a casual black suit with his dark hair neatly styled in what looks like an office.

Kai and Adrian follow behind as they look on the brink of murder. No less than me.

"Great to meet everybody finally. Archer, Jeffords, and Carson, too. No Moretti." He tsks, shaking his head. "Shame. We all know the survival rate of his kind is taking a hit."

"What do you want?" I snap, ignoring his unwanted pleasantries.

"Woah. Someone's eager for a head start. What's the hurry? Let's get to know each other first. I think Vincent hasn't given you a proper introduction."

"Don't think we need one." Kai sits on his chair, the side of his lip quirks in distaste. "A slum dog trying to be a billionaire."

"I'm flattered. But the only thing you need to know about me is that I'm your only hope to get to Pyrosilk," Aaron says. His persona changed to something darker.

"Why would we want *you* for that?" Adrian questions his fingers beating a rhythm on the table.

"I need something from them, and so do you. What's in the middle of all of this is Bianca," Aaron says, and everything in me halts.

"Keep her name away from your dirty mouth," I grit through my clenched teeth. It's a surprise I don't melt the table with the fire rampaging inside me.

Aaron breathes and falls into his chair. "Trust me, my mouth isn't close to dirty." He shakes his head the moment something snaps in his dark eyes. "Bianca isn't safe there," Aaron announces. "Pyrosilk is after her. *Oliver* is after her."

All three of us stare at the screen, a stunned silence hanging in the air as we slowly absorb the new information.

Teal rushes out the door and makes a call. "Get Nick on the line …" Her voice fades as the door shuts.

"Oliver? Steven and Bianca's dad?" Kai asks, recovering first. "But he's dead."

"No." Aaron chuckles darkly, closing his eyes. "Oliver has a history with Pyrosilk. Five years ago, he got promoted to Underboss to handle mining sites and transporting the Batches. On the night of the fire, a batch of four teenagers was being shipped from mainland Melbourne to the ports, and Gareth overheard him. He flew the news to Lina, and

Oliver had to stop them."

The missing pieces finally fit in.

Oliver set the fire.

Lina and Gareth *died.*

Aaron licks his lips and smiles. "What was the difference between the two photos on the USB?"

"Twenty years—the photos were taken twenty years apart," Kai informs. "But how do they link?"

"Gareth and Oliver were the power twins. They were given their own secret land to mine without the government's knowledge.

"Grandpa Kennedy was doing jobs for Pyrosilk. All sorts, weapons, gold, drugs, organs, and even women and children. There was nothing he didn't say no to because money was enough of a motivator."

"Do you know the running head?" I ask, my voice unrecognisable.

"No one lower in the hierarchy does. Only the Primes and Underbosses do. They go by a hierarchical system—from the bottom with the workers up to the two Leaders."

"And you are telling us this out of the kindness of your heart?" Adrian questions. His stance is more rigid, and he keeps the work with his fingers. He can be anything, but faking calmness is his specialty.

Aaron laughs as he tips his head back. "Fuck no. Kindness left me the moment I stepped into this world. I'm only here to help you so that I can find the one person I need."

"Who? Maybe we can help," Kai offers, "only if you let us know what Bianca has to do with all this."

"Good try, Jeffords, but I can help myself. Bianca, though, is Oliver's target. He needs to prove his worth to Pyrosilk to step higher in the hierarchy."

"Why does he need her?" I ask.

"To kill. He doesn't want a failure with his name to live." Aaron takes a deep breath before he continues, "Bianca is not Oliver's daughter, but Gareth's," he announces.

The only sound I hear is the ringing in my ears. The one thing Bianca ever wanted was a loving father, and I see that every time she's with Dad, but the play of time has even taken that away from her.

Aaron hums as he swings in his chair. "Oliver never knew about this until the night of the fire."

"What do you get out of all this?" I say, staring at his figure on the screen, and he just smiles, leans forward with his hands connected under his chin.

"Because believe it or not, I want Bianca safe, but Oliver will not stop until he has her, and that's easier for him as long as she is here. She needs to go back to Canberra because Oliver doesn't have any power in that state," Aaron says. "He already had three minions on her. The rat rotting in your basement and Max—his brother. And me, but I want to change that."

Blinding rage builds in me. How fucking dare he?

"I met Oliver three years ago when I located him. There was nothing I wouldn't do for him because of who he held above me. He asked me to date Bianca and help him kill her. I didn't—couldn't. The moment she gave me her icy glare at Florals & Bells, I knew that woman was a precious jewel meant to be kept. She is."

I close my eyes and try to level my breathing. How I want to thrust his head deep into the ground and fill his mouth with the same dirt.

"Soon the year I promised turned into two, and things weren't the same." His eyes come to me, and I'm dreading what he's about to say. "I loved her only to break up with her because I didn't want Oliver getting the hint. But nothing compared to what I am and was fighting for."

He didn't love her.

If he had, he wouldn't have so easily given up on her. She is the darkness where my demons can live. She is the oxygen every tree begs for. *She is life.*

My knuckles whiten, and my hand shakes with my contained anger. Blood rushes through my body as I feel nothing but the raging liquid.

As if sensing the devil on my head, Adrian puts a hand on my thigh and shakes his head. "Not now," he whispers.

I feel my chest rising and falling with each laboured breath. "Why would we trust you?" I bark.

"Because I do," a familiar voice answers as Steven's face comes to the screen. He stands behind Aaron with his arms crossed over his chest.

"Steven? You're here?" Adrian asks as dumbfounded as the rest of us.

"I need a drink." Kai sighs, sinking in his seat, and runs a hand down his face.

"Let me get to the point," Steven says, and his bright blue eyes find me. "Bianca needs to come back. For her safety, she needs to." His attention shifts to me, and for a moment, something softens in his eyes. "If you love her even in the slightest, let her go," he says.

"She's already so emotionally vulnerable and can't afford to take another hit, especially from me, and you know it." My voice sounds void, and I see nothing but my Bianca.

Steven nods and rests his arms on the back of Aaron's chair. "I do, but Da—Oliver is out for blood. He is running out of time because Pyrosilk only considers members with pure generations, and once they find out that Bianca isn't his, they will erase the mud."

"No. I can protect her here," I say with finality.

"They're too deep-rooted for any of us." Steven passes me a stern look. "Short term loss for long-term gain, and, in many cases, justice is not black and white."

"Grey," I murmur.

I'm her grey.

CHAPTER 48

Present

"Her vitals and pulse are normal."

The ticking in my head beats with the rhythm of the heavy voice. My fingers twitch, barely recognising them as mine.

With a groan, I slowly pry open my eyes, heavy as stones, into a blurry vision of a large room. I blink slowly as I try to make sense of the faces hovering above me. My lips feel swollen and struggle to move in an audible whisper. "Where am I?"

"She's awake! Doctor, she's awake!" Another voice bounces.

"Call Jason!" someone else orders.

Why are they all screaming?

"Oh God, Bianca." I twist my head to the new voice, and a hazy image of Kiara comes into view. She smiles weakly, tears coating her eyes. "Fuck, you scared us."

"Hey." I breathe, letting a weak smile grow on my lips. At least I think it does.

A flicker of recognition, the faces become clear. Everyone but *him*.

"After another few days of observation, she's all yours," Dr. Moore says as she checks something on her clipboard. "You're one strong cookie, Bianca." She smiles at me, her brown skin crinkling with the effort.

"Thank you so much." Steven walks her out as I sit up on my bed.

This room comforts me, as if designed just for me. The colour of the walls is a smooth blue, while the equipment and bedding are shades of light grey. He isn't here, but I can feel him everywhere.

Through the panoramic window, I see the vibrant green forest. The river snaking through it and birds soaring overhead, their calls faintly echoing. It's Jason's Forest, and now mine as well.

"How are you feeling?" Steven asks, sitting down beside me. He takes my hand in his. It hurts, but I want to feel him.

"Better," I say, looking away from him to watch the leaves move with the wind. "Did you know?" I question, not wanting to meet him in the eye.

"Look at me," he orders.

I shake my head as tears well in my eyes. He will try to convince me that this isn't my fault, but it is.

With a hand on my chin, he rotates my head to meet the reflection of my eyes—*Ma's eyes.*

"I knew. Oliver came to me as soon as he transferred the company to my name. He told me about Ma, Uncle Gareth, and everything that had happened. I was furious at how little a man can drop. But I was powerless," Steven murmurs, reflecting the same sorrow swimming in my eyes. "I couldn't do anything—I didn't know what to do. Neither could I tell you because you were already so lost in grief and—"

"So, you took the weight on your shoulders?" I ask in disbelief.

"No." He shakes his head, letting his eyes lower to our hands. "I gave you the peace you deserved, even if it meant putting a bridge between us. You and I, Bianca, are one. If one hurts, the other will know, but this time I didn't want you to hurt. I couldn't bear to see my heart break in front of me. If I'm the body, you're the heart."

I cover my face, my body breaks into tears, as my shoulders shake violently from the onslaught of emotions. "I knew I hadn't lost you. It killed me." I swallow. "Every time you left and lost yourself little by little because I never knew so much was going on in that big head of yours. I had to move away—to give you space to breathe—but the distance only intensified my longing for you."

Sobs crumble out of me, the sound racking my body, until Steven gently traces the bandage over my hand. His scent reminds me of all our cries, laughter and fights. He reminds me of *family*.

Giving myself a moment to sober up, I ask the one lingering question: "Aaron threatened to kill you. Were you involved in this with him?"

"No." His face morphs in disgust. "Since March I had been keeping my eye on him, but he didn't do anything suspicious, so I let him be. That was until three weeks ago when he knew your life was in danger because of him, and I was the best person for you," Steven explains.

I stay stunned, listening to his every word. "God," I whisper.

Steven wraps his warm hands around my wrists. "We have each other, even if everyone leaves," Steven's voice sings like a lullaby in my ear.

I nod, no words giving me mercy to speak.

"I want nothing to do with Oliver. His fate will find him." Steven's eyes harden as he continues, "Our parents don't define us. Whatever they did, it's on them. You and I will *not* live the results of their actions," he says, reading my thoughts.

"It's going to take time to believe that," I murmur, looking up at him and seeing his beautiful eyes glaze with wetness. In this moment, I know things will get better.

Jason

She's back.

I was sitting by the river in our forest with my head resting against the fully blossoming cherry blossom tree, when Sage's angel call woke me from my living nightmare. My feet took flight like an eagle, and all I wanted to do was see her. *Feel her.*

The walls of the library and hallways are a blur as I race to the medical wing. A low hum of conversation fills the air when I come into the corridor. Easy smiles—stark contrast to the days of dejection—spread across everyone's faces as they sit outside.

I look around, all their eyes on me, waiting in anticipation.

"Jason!" Eva exclaims as she comes rushing at me. Her body falls against mine, pressing her face into my chest. "She's okay." Eva's body is weaker and slower than it used to be.

They have all been here since we landed, and not one has left.

Steven stands by the door and smiles at me with a nod. "Go."

The path ahead is dark and misty, like walking into an unknown future, but I sense the promise of a brilliant rainbow beyond this door.

As I enter, the room is quiet. The curtains fly in the wind coming from the open window. Bianca has her eyes closed as her chest moves with a slow rhythm.

Thump, thump, thump sounds my heart in my ears, matching the sounds coming from the equipment in the room. All I can do is stand and admire the miracle lying in front of me. Her eyes are still closed.

My hands fist and a shuddering breath releases from me. "You will live the life you deserve," I whisper, sitting down on the chair.

"Only with you." Bianca's lips move slightly with a tremble. The sound of the same honey tone makes me close my eyes in delight.

She's here, in flesh, and breathing. *Alive.*

"Bianca," I whisper.

"It's me," she says, and slowly opens her eyes. Those blue orbs are looking at me. The epiphany of how truly beautiful they are hits me like never before. "You came." Bianca smiles weakly as her hands shake at her sides.

Heart pounding, I run the back of my hand on her cheek. It's still cold but warming up.

"I never left," I say.

The monitors beep immediately, and Bianca sighs in defeat. "Stupid," she mutters slowly.

"Careful, or I might think you like me," I say and hide how she also makes my heart race too.

"Oh, we wouldn't want that, would we?" She twists her lips, fighting a laugh.

"I would." My eyes find hers, and we instantly melt. "I want you."

"Me too. I'm scared because you really are making it hard to live without you," she mumbles, her eyes slightly droopy. Her speech is slightly unstable as the effects of the medications, and the weeklong coma wear off.

"Thank you for coming back to me," I croak, tears threatening to appear.

"I battled for us. *We* deserve the world," she replies. Her trembling hand holds mine. Her thumb's pulse is calming as she traces it over my palm.

"There is no power strong enough to take you away from me, because even in death, I would follow you," I promise, closing my hand around hers.

I move closer, her breath, warm and rapid, is a gentle current against my cheek, as her eyes remain wide and fixed upon me. Her muted cherry blossom gathers me in a nostalgic hug, bringing me back home. *I'm finally home.* After knocking on every door there was, I found my peace at her doorstep.

"It was your choice to do whatever you had to, but it is my choice to *love* you," I say, wrapping my hand tighter around hers.

"I love you," she replies with the most beautiful smile on her face. "But let me warn you, I have a lot of baggage. Are you sure your legs can handle that?"

I let out a breathy laugh and lightly take her swollen jaw in my fingers. "Give me everything or nothing, I will always return it with our love. Because once I give you everything, you won't be able to see anything but us."

"Only with you," she confesses, and takes my breath away. Her soft smile balances between chaotic and calm. Knowing her, it's going to be both, and now I've become an addict to feel all her shades. Every single one of them.

"You have my life in your hands, so think twice before pulling a stunt like this again," I say as I capture her lips in a slow kiss. This time, I taste what life truly feels like.

"You're stuck with me now," she whispers as her bright blue eyes have me lost in her world.

"I'm glad."

CHAPTER 49
Jason
A month later

The smell of soot and blood stirs in the air as I walk back to the hell we merely escaped. The farmhouse is nothing it used to be. A chilling emptiness fills the stripped hallways and rooms, devoid of our laughter and warmth. It's sad how a place can change so much in meaning so quickly.

Bianca and the girls are staying back at our shared house with Kai and Asher, who will come soon, while Adrian and I finish up closing this chapter of our lives. It's time for a wrecked soul to leave for a better to come.

I've been paying my visits here, telling Bianca that they're business

trips. She doesn't need to know what happens when someone hurts her.

Now Adrian walks by my side, and ants crawl with an angry beat around my body. Vincent and Teal follow behind us.

This isn't just a reunion, but a moment that would mark the unleashing of my beast. The past month has broken the lock I kept putting on the cage to keep him trapped in, but after what happened with Bianca, I don't think I control it now.

"I was wondering when you would come back," Oliver says, his voice a lost cause. He is bound to the chair, with his hands hanging.

"Cherish the moment. It's the last time you would wonder anything," I reply.

Oliver chuckles and throws his head back. His rotting arm hangs loosely by his side, bound only by his dried blood. Fresh and old wounds fester on his skin after all the time I spent with him in these past four weeks. *Four weeks* he dared to breathe.

"You're a thick bastard. I'm surprised it isn't infected yet." Adrian inspects Oliver's arm. My knife carved deep, leaving behind trails of crimson trophies.

"Don't worry about my infections," Oliver rasps, his voice thick with sickness. "The one coming for you is far worse. Would you like me to jog your *memory*?" Oliver's tone is suggestive, and it reaches Adrian.

Adrian snarls and lands a gloved punch on Oliver's face. A sickening crack echoes around us, and my fists clench.

"Say another word, and I'll skip ahead to killing you myself," Adrian warns, his face a mask of untamed anger. "Give me the scanner!" he barks at Vincent.

Vincent—blank as paper—calmly passes the device to scan Oliver's fingerprints and face.

I walk over to Oliver and grab a chair to sit in front of him. "You will die. But let's make it useful. All we need from you is where the

Batch was going?"

The sound of Oliver's laughter vibrates in the air; a wild, uncontrolled burst punctuated by the wet thud of blood hitting the ground. "You think you can fool *them?* You fuckers are more dead in the brain than I thought. Pyrosilk is so deep-rooted, it will take your lifetime and some to dismantle it."

I tilt my head, the tendons in my neck stretching as his incessant chatter grates on my nerves. "The Batch." My voice is calm and heavy with a rope of tension pulling it back.

"Port Kaldr and Ignis. Many say they don't exist, but this is one thing you can trust me on, boy," Oliver says. A warning flared in his dark eyes as they fix on me. "Only step in if you're ready to sacrifice everything you have."

Beside me, Adrian goes still and nearly loses the grip around the device in his hand only to grip it tighter until a crack sounds.

I get my gun ready. "Don't worry about my sacrifices." The first shot fires, and it hits his foot.

Oliver's howl rips through the air, a sound of pure agony as thick-clotted blood flows from his fresh wound, resembling a gruesome river. "Fucker," he hisses.

"You woke the beast in me, and you wish you hadn't. Now it's hungry, do you know for what?" My elbows rest on my knees as I talk with deceptive calm. I still feel the heaviness of Bianca's blood coating a thick layer on me.

Oliver drools. "Fuck off."

"We prey on the first thing we see. Luckily for me, it's *you.*" I swing my hand behind me between Teal and Vincent. "They will live to *tell* the tale of your death. You are the first one in the legacy of the bodies I will lie for ever scarring Bianca and making Eva a witness."

With the second gunshot exploding, the bullet rips through his other leg, the impact sending the chair screeching on the ground.

"You will regret for ever coming near *my* cousin and sister," Adrian says in his ear from behind.

Vincent and Teal come around and go to the intact stove. They twist the knobs, and the sharp, acrid smell of gas instantly fills the air, stinging our noses.

I push myself upright and rest my hands on the sturdy arms of his chair. "She doesn't say it, but because of you, Bianca will live a life with the painful reminder of ever being related to you. She is strong enough to protect herself, but I will give her a hand by burning the biggest monster in her life."

Oliver snickers, failing to hide the flash of worry and fear zapping through his eyes.

We take our steps back and let Oliver struggle in his chair. He screams at us against the restraints. That's the last we see of him, and once we're out and at a distance, I point my gun at the house.

With a deafening bang, the bullet strikes the door, triggering a massive explosion that reduces the house to rubble. The air fills with flecks of burning wood and dust—like the ghost it had become.

We stare at the flames eating away at the memories we once made here. Listening to the wood crackle and sigh, holding a disturbing yet melancholic symphony. Our memories leave for their bittersweet eternal rest.

"That's that, then," Adrian hums by my side.

"Only the beginning, and you're taking the lead from here," I reply.

"I am." He nods, and his chest expands as he breathes. "Not without any of you."

Bianca

My heart eats at my chest as I step onto the soft ground beneath me. The last I was here, I was certain my life had ended in darkness. Now, the cemetery is going to be the place I can finally shed light on my past and try to grow from who I was.

You need this, White and Red remind me.

I do.

In loving memory of
Lina Kennedy
A loved mother and wife

My shoulders drop with a heavy breath. The world is a beautiful place when you have love and affection around you, but Ma—she didn't. She made mistakes and paid for them. Yet, the life she got and the death she was gifted were a bundle of surprises and blending of morals where the right and wrong got lost in the mist of feelings and actions.

Jason gives my hand a firm squeeze and looks at me with a calm in his forest eyes. He and Adrian went to finish up *some business* this morning. He didn't need to say it, but I knew where they went and what they did. It's better we don't speak of it. Leave the dead where they need to be.

"You can do it," he says.

I nod and step forward with the new phrases for the tombstone shaking in my hand.

In life you lived, and in death you're freed
Lina Amante
The lost angel who always believed:
Love the truest

My throat constricts, tears welling, and each swallow is a struggle. Steven holds the stone opposite me, his face etched with grief, and helps me gently place the smooth, grey stone atop her grave.

"We love you," Steven and I say together.

"I'm sorry," I whisper, wiping away the tears with the back of my hand.

Steven hugs me from the side, his fingers leaving a comforting pressure on my arm. "She's still with us, walking beside us on every path."

"I know." I breathe.

Then he steps away from me. "Take your time." He turns me towards the next grave.

In loving memory of
Oliver Kennedy
A loved father and husband

Anger and something ugly bubble inside me at seeing his name. Uncle Gareth—*Dad*—couldn't even have his name on his death, Oliver had to steal that too.

But now is for you, Dad. You were always there for me. Giving me tips on living with lactose intolerance or the winter days when you picked me up from school and took me to Cornella's.

"Here," Jason whispers as he hands me the flat stone. It feels weird even thinking about him as my father. When he was alive, he was the one I would go to when I needed something and cry to when Ma or Oliver got angry at me. Whether I knew it or not, he was always my haven.

The man with a golden heart
Gareth Kennedy
A soul who left selflessly with the love of his life
"To meeting you in the next life, Dad"

I get on my haunches and glide my hand over the grave. The stone feels warm and cold all at once. The wind picks up, rustling the fallen leaves into a swirling vortex of brown and gold, whispering against our ears. It feels like this is a hug of acceptance, a stolen hug from the reaches of the universe—only for me and him to know.

"I love you," I barely confess, the words catching in my throat as a tear slides down my cheek. "I loved you as my uncle, and now you will be the dad I never had. I promise I will love you for all the times you wanted to hug me and tell me I was your daughter. I will love you to make up for all the heartbreaks I gave. I will live with you in my heart."

With a heavy sigh, I put the bouquet of lilies down—his favourite.

"You ready?" Jason asks. He stands by my side, looking at me with everything I could ask for. *My silver lining.*

Reminder: Love is my silver lining.

I nod and take his hand in mine.

Steven brings a smaller tombstone, and my heart crumbles once again. This time, it's real. *You deserve a proper burial, Quest.*

The grey and golden letters on the stone make me want to break through everything and get justice for the sibling who deserved to see the light of day.

A collateral life lost
Quest
Wherever you are, we love you
"We will find our answers in your journey"

My fingers curl around the stone, only for Steven to balance the other half. He looks at me, his blue eyes filled with regret and sorrow reflecting mine. As we place it down, my heart drops, and it hits me now that I will never know who she was, her dislikes and likes, whether we would laugh at the same thing or simply how she would look. She will remain a mystery—*my lifelong quest.*

"I know you were my sister. I always wanted one, Steven would say otherwise," I murmur once we place the stone upright behind the burial site we dug. A sad chuckle leaves me as I mask my inner breakdown.

Steven rolls his eyes. "Don't listen to her. But know one thing,

Quest, we never knew you, but you're a part of us. We hope you have found a peaceful place, better than here."

Breathing becomes the toughest action to do, both from carrying the tombstone, but also from the emotions spilling from Steven's face. He always hid them behind a shield he held too tight, only now there's a slight gap.

I walk up to her grave and put my bracelet in the small hole we dug for her. "Ma and Dad will protect you, and I will live in peace knowing it." A faint smile plays on my lips as tears, warm and heavy, land on the bracelet.

It was Dad's gift to Ma and then came to me. Now it's yours.

To loving you with a true heart.

The sun is out, its rays shine bright through the small litter of clouds. Today is the heaviest of all, and I wish no one goes through it.

Luckily for me, I have my grey with me. He holds me together when I'm breaking apart, filling my cracks with the gold of his silent love. After today, I don't think I can look at life the same way. It feels like I'm grieving all over again, like the past five years never happened. I'm reliving them again, only this time they will be more tolerable.

"All done," Jason announces as he finishes braiding my hair. He turns my head around and inspects his work from the front. "Beautiful," he murmurs against my forehead as he leaves a kiss there. As soon as we sat down on the bench, he began to split my hair, and I was too tired to argue. It felt good, as if he knew I needed a personal touch to the day. He knows everything.

"I love you." My voice is soft as I search for light in his green eyes.

"I live for you."

The wind starts again, and we take in the warming air. My eyes skim his body, but it's the soul I want, just like he consumes mine. The cuffs of his shirt are open and give a hint of something dark on his wrists.

"What's on your wrist?" I ask with a light touch on his arm and stop myself from cringing when my own sleeve lifts and reveals the scars.

He takes a big breath before facing me. His hands, warm and comforting, close around mine, their touch emphasised by the bright, almost electric green of his eyes. "This is for you." His words hit me hard as he lifts his sleeves.

My hands slam onto my mouth. "Oh God, Jay." I breathe.

A tattoo of an infinity symbol intertwined with cherry blossoms adorns his right wrist. But it's the three words that bring fresh waves of tears to my eyes.

My true love.

On his other wrist, with a healed wound the size of a pea by the side, has an inked bracelet like my own, except this one has my name with a small bird flying up his forearm. My hand drops, and I see the difference between my wrist and his.

Mine are a symbol of torture by the hands of the man I thought gave birth to me, and Jason's are … love. Nothing else but pure, unadulterated love. My heart weakens its beating and watches stunned with my eyes.

Jason gets up and kneels in front of me, his own eyes glossy. "I will wear your scars as my bracelet, with your name and our love on them." He clears his throat, running his thumb over my wrist. "Bianca, you're the woman I've sold my soul to. You keep me alive with every breath you take. I don't want to rush anything, but I will have you whole when you're ready to let me in. One day soon, you will be my wife, and every cell in my body will be at your mercy if it isn't already. Until then, I'll live satisfied knowing you're the pulse of my wrists—each one a worship at your altar."

Hearing those exact words from his deep and dark voice wasn't something I ever thought I would hear.

"Jay…." I rush down to him. "I *love* you." And I take his lips in a deep kiss. I want to show him that every cell in my body *is* already his.

"I beat only for you."

The wind swims around us, and birds chirp from above us. A true heaven's calling.

He planted his permanent touch on me with no ink, and the garden he left in me blooms with life only for him.

Epilogue

Bianca

A Month Later.

"Just bring the paint already!" I scream, holding on to the railing of the ladder.

This is the fourth time I've called for him, and there's been no reply—not even a whisper.

"He's coming. The paint tubs are heavy." Sage soothes as she organises our photos in chronological order while Kiara snickers next to her with her mahogany hair tied in loose pigtails.

"And where is Eva? It shouldn't take this long to carry some glasses." Kiara scratches her eyebrow and flicks a bead of sweat.

It's been a month since I moved in with Jason, and it's been nothing short of what he promised—a timeless haven. I needed some help with the room Jason left for me to design. So, I didn't let the opportunity to invite everyone slip over, much to Jason's despair. If it isn't abundantly clear, Jason is a possessive animal, and convincing him to have the others over was like holding a fish fresh out of the water. According to him, I am the only one who can do *my special*

to the room with his help only

It's nothing some batting of eyelashes and a small pout on the lips can't fix. I've grown to know Jason never says no to me. He will never admit it, but I found a dent in his armour—his heart.

"Th e paint on the brush is drying. You try taking that off," I grumble, stroking the last of the grey paint on the wing of the honeyeater. It was the only bird that came to mind when describing our journey and where it has led us—to a place with love and the power to hold on to it in the hard times.

It's a mirror image of the tall, dark pines and vibrant ring of wildflowers by the front of the house. Instead of a flower ring, it's the ring of our time together. Each photo captures our past and present.

Kiara used some of her magic and stirred up all the photographs we ever took. From there it wasn't so much, only needed the paint and some chatting buddies, and voilà.

Tentatively, I take a step down the ladder and another. I feel exhausted already, and it's only afternoon. Th at's me most of the days. My body and brain are still recovering from everything.

Maybe you're just lazy. White rings in my ear, and I can just see her rolling her eyes.

No, White, I'm not.

She and Red have been on a mission to calm my mind, although they are my mind. I've made peace with myself that if I exist, they exist too. Th ey're my normal, and I'm tired of escaping that.

"Ah!" Everything happens in slow motion, my foot slipping from the last step, my hair blocking my vision as the roof gets farther. My eyes screw shut, getting ready to meet with the floor, but it never comes because a strong muscular arm wraps around my waist, hoisting me up.

Cracking one eyelid open, I see the similar sharp jaw and high cheekbones, and the intense green eyes looking right at me. "My love,"

I whisper.

He smiles. A warm and frequent occurrence these days, which makes my heart ache with longing for more.

I grip the collar of his polo shirt and straighten, planting my feet firmly on the ladder's flat rungs.

"You okay?" he asks, putting down the two cans of paint on the floor. Worry dampens his smile as he rakes his glance along my whole body, checking for anything. But it does nothing to reassure him.

"Hmm." I nod, lost for words even when I see his swollen lips move. Before anyone came in, he had me panting his name right in this room, saying, *"Fuck me raw, Rainbow."*

He always gives me access to his body when he craves mine more.

"Fuck me …" I shake my head when the thought comes to my lips. "I mean paint … for the wall …"

Or paint you, Red teases.

Jason smirks at my malfunction. "… Is here," he says, not batting an eyelash away from me.

"Why are *you* holding the paint?" Sage asks from the ground. Our heads snap to where she is on the floor. Between her fingers is a picture of Kai wrestling with a baby Asher and Eva commenting on the match. That was in primary school, maybe when we were ten and Kai fifteen, making Asher close to three.

Flames brew in Eva's eyes as she carries two buckets of paint and clenches her teeth. "Him." She cocks her head back, and Kai appears, balancing the drinks on the tray.

"I thought it would be nice to share responsibilities," Kai explains, placing the tray on the table in the middle of the room.

"Right. Here I was thinking someone had sprained his wrist, so I helped out of the goodness of my heart," Eva mumbles, putting the two cans of paint on the opposite corner.

"I doubt you have a heart at all," Kai half yells and whispers, handing out the glasses.

Orange juice for everyone. The drink we agreed on.

"What did you say?" Eva's eyes squint into slits, anger coming off her in waves.

"Nothing, just saying how beautiful you look today." Kai forces a smile that doesn't reach his eyes as he thrusts a glass towards her. Some of the drink spills on Eva's dress. The poor fragile thing will crush in their heat.

"I know what else will look beautiful. My fist on your perfect jaw." Eva matches eye to eye with Kai as she lifts herself on her toes.

"Aw, you think I'm perfect, Evalyn." Kai smiles and bats his eyelashes.

"Will they ever grow up?" I say, seeing the sparks leaving their eyes.

"Ignore them. What was it about fucking me?" Jason pumps his eyebrow. My sex clenches at his low and demanding tone. I walk on thin ice whenever he opens his mouth between my thighs, and he very much could be doing that now, just by standing and mumbling those words near my face.

"*Painting* the wall." I throw a thumb at the wall, and the bird on the wall also seems to snicker.

I dip my still-damp brush into the pale grey paint, flicking the excess onto Jason's cheek. He grins, unbothered by the playful mess. "Perfect."

He watches me intensely for a second. "I love you," Jason whispers, and leaves a kiss on my shoulder. "So much," he mumbles, his breath warm on my shoulder as he kisses me again while I carefully paint the final details on the wing.

"Juice," I order, adjusting my lips to face him, but still concentrating on the painting.

"Yes, Rainbow," he says and walks over to Kai to get the drink. From the corner of my eye, Jason shakes his head at the two who are still bickering.

Jason places the straw on my lips, and I sip in the delight. To this date, there is no other drink more comforting than freshly juiced oranges with loaded ice.

"Good." I hum. The citric flavour bursts on my taste buds. "Ice," I request, and instantly a spoon laden with ice comes to my lips.

With a satisfying crunch, the ice cube shatters underneath my teeth. Its icy texture numbs my tongue, spreading a pleasant coolness throughout my mouth.

"Sip." I turn my head for the straw to come in, but soft lips meet me instead as the liquid gets poured into my mouth. "*Very* good," I mumble, sipping down the juice. A wave of exhilarating heat washes over me, and I bite down on my lip, barely containing the ache in my pulsing core.

"I love you," he repeats.

"I love you more." I smile and finish with the tip of the wing. It took us three days to decide that grey was the colour of the bird. There were some contradictions from Adrian and Sage, but we listened to them for the furniture. Surprisingly, they agreed to make this a studio for my interior designing. I'm thinking of starting my company, with no influence from the Archers or anyone closely related to them. With that said, I held a heavy heart—very much to Jason's pleasure—when declining McKenzie's offer for the first clients.

Jason steps forward, closing the gap, and brings his lips close to me. "What do you say I give our audience a performance?"

"Hey, lovebirds, keep it in your pants until we leave. Some aren't taking it well, meaning your sister and your brother. Me? I don't mind it. Finding true love is hard in the days of benefits," Kiara interrupts.

It's now that I see Steven and Adrian standing by the door with the rest of the material.

Adrian holds the adhesives and colourful papers to put up the pictures. He stalks slowly towards Sage and places the material next to her while watching her closely. I wanted to ignore it, but the way Sage mirrors his expression, with knowing intensity, is unsettling and disrupts her usual calm. One thing she is good at is minding her own business, saying

"*fuck off*" to everyone else—not him, apparently.

Steven's gaze is gentle and filled with a tenderness I've never seen from him before. He was there for me even when I wasn't. I don't think I can ever make up for all the years he kept the secrets buried within him.

My truth is more bitter than sweet, and my present and future will have their challenges, but if I have my people with me, there's nothing I can't go through. No matter if it kills me from the inside.

"Come out. We're here, but you're not." Jason tucks a strand behind my ear.

"I'm trying," I reply, holding his hand in mine. *My anchor.*

"That's all we need," he says and presses a kiss on my lips.

"I love you," I whisper, getting lost in his forest eyes yet again. He may not have a vast range of vocabulary in his dictionary, but I want to earn all his words. *Mine now and for the rest of time.*

Bianca, you've gone so deep. White Wings begins.

The best deep yet, Red Horns chimes.

I love him more than I can feel.

After a couple of hours and even more laughs, the room is complete. It wasn't as simple as it sounded in theory, but we pulled it out of my imagination and into reality.

A matching set of four-seater sofas and a coffee table is in the corner. A large black glass desk is in the centre near the back wall, with fresh bamboo palms rooted in pots, claiming each corner. On the back wall behind my desk are shelves full of books—the same ones Jason had displayed in the market.

It turns out both of our new offices will have a garden and a library.

The main attraction is the wall and all our memories. Everyone helped put them together and hang them on the wall in a circle.

Kai and Eva had *one* job of putting the unused containers of paint away in *one* piece. But they returned half drenched in paint and water, and their hair standing in spikes.

Kiara and Steven went downstairs to get their hands on dinner.

As usual, Jason stood by my side, admiring my every move.

"This is magical," I murmur, mesmerised by the painted honeyeater soaring with the garland of our memories, a kaleidoscope of emotions swirling within me.

The circle starts with all our baby pictures from when we were toddlers. Then our first days of school, holidays, sleepovers and now as adults.

Jason insisted on getting the puzzle piece I had and put it next to the pictures when I came back. *"You're my missing piece,"* he had muttered before slipping it in my hand.

But my two favourite pictures were the one I took at Queen Victoria Market with the library set up behind us with the soft glow of lights tracing our forms. The other one we took in Cornella's with a grumpy Jason and bubbling girls in the background, with a super happy Kai holding me.

We left the garland incomplete, symbolic of all the memories that are yet to come.

"I'm going down, you guys. I think dinner is ready." Eva half yawns and sniffs as she exits the room, followed by the rest, leaving Jason and me.

"We did it," I say in awe, not necessarily for the room itself.

"We did," he replies, wrapping his arm around my shoulder. Immediately I melt into him and have his mint engrave itself on me.

There's a comfortable moment of silence, and our calm breathing. In the months I've been back, every time we have these moments, the more I crave them. In these moments, I find an escape from my mind, to make one fact clear. That when a storm comes, it blinds us to the calm. But when the calm comes, we understand that fighting in the hail, rain, and gale is the only way to truly find the peace we search for.

"When I asked you to stay behind in this very room, I never thought I would see this day because I did that to push you away. I knew if I pulled you more into me, you would push harder." He pauses, his eyes become heavy with desperation and innocence I only find in him. "And yet I also knew I would still have you even if you weren't here with me."

I'm lost for words. This man takes away my mere ability to speak with the gold that flows out of his mouth. "You were right," I murmur and kiss the pulse on his neck.

"About what?" he asks. The pool of green in his eyes reflects my home.

"I came as Bianca, but I stayed as your rainbow."

He tsks, shaking his head. "You were my rainbow ever since I laid my eyes on you." He leaves a lingering kiss on my forehead before we get lost in the bird of our new beginnings. "You came whole to complete me."

Reminder: Love the truest.

Jason

It's in our gravest state of loss we find the deepest part of our soul. *I found my Bianca.*

The thought floats in my head as the waves of the Lakes Entrance beach kiss the shore. Underneath a flawlessly clear night sky, our thoughts are as open and unburdened. Moonlight shines on the surface of the water, and yet all these things don't give me as much peace as the hand I have in mine.

Bianca has agreed to therapy sessions with Chelsie or Dr. Leon, more professionally. One thing has come into her focus, and Bianca is slowly coming to terms with the potential diagnosis of schizophrenia. Nothing is cemented, but it's a sword hanging above our necks. Whatever it is, she won't be alone. She was never alone.

On the other hand, Eva has rejected any help. I'm concerned that she might isolate herself, making it harder to reach out to her. Every day it seems she's locking the key tighter, and it's just becoming that more difficult to reach her. But if Eva is self-guarded, I'm her brother and no lock can keep me away from her.

"I can't believe you remembered to do the beach date—*day out*—with everyone," Bianca says from beside me.

"The day isn't complete yet," I remind her.

We had a lactose-free picnic on the beach, and it was the most relaxed we've gotten in the past few months. Especially if Dad is here, no one will leave without a smile. I see now what Brandon Archer was trying to pull out of me. He was pushing me towards the only person I needed when I was suffocating myself by distancing us.

"Is it me or I haven't seen another person aside from us today?" she questions, and her hand tightens. Bianca stares at me with the same look that she gave me at the market. "You wouldn't have anything to do with it, would you?"

"Your safety is my priority," is all I say.

"Doesn't answer my question."

She doesn't budge from her place, digging her feet in the sand.

"I hired the beach for the day." My arm wraps around her waist, bringing her closer to me. "And you know why."

All day I just wanted to touch her to make sure she's here with me because life's play is unfair, and I can't imagine living through that week from hell ever again.

Instinctively, I lean down and leave a kiss on the pulse of her neck. "Mine," I growl, and she sucks in a sharp breath. My hand circles her wrist, bringing it to my mouth. "Mine."

We stare at each other, and unspoken words swim between us. There is so much we have to do in so little time. The human time is not enough for me to love my woman. We need to be born in every era and life to find each other in our darkest times.

"Mine." I breathe. My lips touch the pale raised scar on her chest, which sits like a whispered secret. The soft, rhythmic thump of her heart beats beneath my lips.

Her arms circle my neck, and she hugs me like she has every time I kiss her chest. It's a place of vulnerability, a shared scar we both carry, and a painful reminder we wish to erase from memory.

"The bullet was for me," I whisper, my voice barely audible above the frantic beating of her heart.

A tremor runs through her body as emotions threaten to overwhelm. "It wasn't. If you were in my place, you wouldn't waste a second being my human shield. Why would I?" She pulls me up, and her eyes glisten with strength. "This isn't how it goes. If you fight for me, I will fight with you. If you can erase my demons, I will keep yours as mine. You give me something, I will give you everything. Plus, you can't take all the credit." She playfully rolls her eyes, and the lingering teardrop falls on her cheek.

I flick my tongue out and swallow it. "You're my love. The woman who rules over me, and I am nothing without your rule."

She smiles and shakes her head. Her brown hair falls on her face, and her lashes flutter close. "Hey, Jason?"

"Yeah, Rainbow?"

"Shut up and let me kiss you already," she says.

She gets on her toes and presses her lips to mine. I grab her waist and get her as close as she possibly can. All I want is her—all of her. Her tongue dances with mine as our mouths move like they've been starving since the beginning of time. How can I get enough of her?

As we pull away, her forehead rests gently against mine, a silent moment of connection filled with unspoken emotions. She looks up at me, softness coating her smile.

Then, with a furrow of her brows, she straightens. "Who were the others in the room?"

I was wondering when she would ask about the Batch. "They were kidnapped by Pyrosilk. We still know nothing about why and what they were doing, and frankly, their trauma is so deeply rooted that just talking about it has them on the verge of a breakdown." And I very well respect that, because Bianca is also going through the same thing.

She stares at me. The blue eyes I grew to love are not swimming with their usual shine, just still. "Was Aaron's sister one of them?"

Of all the things I would've thought, this was not the one. "Yes. She was fifteen when they abducted her."

"It was her." Bianca sucks in a breath, her grip tightening on my hands. "He always mentioned there was someone waiting for him but never told me who."

I stay silent as Bianca reveals the facts. "He came to me that night in the farmhouse, and I don't know which part of him to trust. The boy I broke up with or the man who helped me."

A burn races through my chest as she even considers thinking about another man, an ex or not. "You are not thinking about him. He had his side of the story, which included you, and that was all I needed to hear from him. Getting to your truth was everything that concerned me. No matter how much it hurts, you deserved to know it."

Silent minutes pass as we walk along the shore. Bianca stops, realisation filtering through her face. "I'm going to kill Kai and Adrian. They helped you with all this, didn't they? Especially Kai when he went all moody and told me to '*let everything go because it was never to be.*'" She puts her fingers for air quotes.

I chuckle. "Anything to make it believable."

"*Really* believable." Bianca scoffs, widening her eyes.

"Those days without you were the darkest I've seen, and when you came back, it was like this," I say, grabbing her hand and walking us into the water. The moment our feet touch the water, the bioluminescent algae come to life. They react, creating a sparkling, otherworldly spectacle as their blue-green light cascades with the current.

Bianca gasps, her mouth opens in awe as a wide smile stretches across her face, threatening to split it in two.

"You colour the dark sea of my head and give way to light."

The fireflies of the sea, tiny sparks of living light, swim in erratic patterns. Their glowing bodies are a warning signal in the night.

"And you with my sky. Being the grey to the colours I've always had," Bianca whispers. Her feet settle in the cool water, and the blue light flashes on. "Let me light you up, my grey." She holds out her other hand.

This is the vulnerability Achilles would've felt when his mortality hid in his heel, as mine hides in the way she gazes up at me. Looking at me like I'm her world, when she has become my universe.

At twelve years old, I saw the girl who would become my friend at the Gardens. At sixteen, I made a joke about her voice because I was nervous talking to her. Nineteen, our hands skimmed for a brief second, and I didn't touch anything with that hand for a week. Twenty-four, I smiled at the rainbow hidden behind a grey cloud, but one I could see clear and colourful. Now, *I'm flying in love.*

We take a step towards each other, and the water underneath us excites the algae. The blue light, vibrant and lively, forms a circle around us, brightening with a mesmerising domino effect.

To living with my colours in a world of fire and rebirth, where the Phoenix will live eternally to give us the reason to wait for the bright future.

It exists, and I found it with my woman.

The woman who I will heal with my love as she does me.

"My life was nothing but a quest to love you," I whisper against her lips.

With my hand in hers on a beach that has become our sacred place of love and healing, we begin the cycle of a lifetime. The sound of the waves bears witness to our promise of a love that echoes through the ages. A love that transcends time itself.

I have returned to my nest.

Only with her.

The End.

Thank you

Thank you so much for reading *Healing Love!* If you have loved reading this book, I would be grateful for you to leave a review on the platforms of your choice.

Your support and reviews are valuable and mean a lot to all authors. Every single one of them.

Love,

Bhumika

Acknowledgements

First of all, this book would be so incomplete if it hadn't been for all the creative inspiration I've had since childhood, much of which followed me to where I am now. So, thank you to all the authors, creators, illustrators and teachers who have become my creative foundation.

There's nothing more important than thanking my family, who subtly pushed me to pursue something I always had in the back of my mind but never had the courage to put forward. This is for all of you.

I'm so grateful to have had the chance to work with Amy Briggs as my editor, and Amy, you were such a guiding light in helping me find my way in writing and the different elements I had learned because of you. And yes, this book would not have been the same if it weren't for you.

The lovely designers at Books and Moods took my breath away with everything they did for me. Especially, being patient with me as I learned the process of self-publishing and got to know the details of the publishing world. Thank you so much for all your hard work and the most beautiful covers, teasers, branding, and formatting.

It would be incomplete for me not to mention the beautiful ladies at Author PR. You guys had taken such an enormous weight off my shoulders with all the videos and posts you made. The release of *Healing Love* would be incomplete without you. Thank you so much.

To all the great early readers and reviewers, thank you so much for making *Healing Love* one to be remembered. My nerves were taking a hit when sending out the early copies or even the early drafts of the manuscript, but your humble and honest reactions made my day in every way and form.

And if you have this book in your hands, you are my favourite person and every author's out there because without you, readers, we are nothing. All readers are such incredible and integral parts of every author's journey, and you guys deserve so much gratitude. Thank you for giving your energy and time to *Healing Love*.

Love,
Bhumika

What's Next

He is the bitter truth…who gave her beautiful lies

Healing Pain

Continue the journey of healing with Sage and Adrian.
Coming 2026

Connect with Bhumika!

Instagram:

instagram.com/authorbbhumika

TikTok:

tittok.com/authorbbhumika

Want a little gossip and just discuss everything reading with like-minded people? Join the Facebook group!

Bhumika's Healers.

If you want sneak peeks and early news, join the newsletter!

All Links:

About the Author

Bhumika lives and breathes stories and the need to tell them. She has grown up with fairy tales, and all things romance, whether they have a dark edge or are action-packed. Her writing takes readers through different tales of the dark and tall morally grey men, strong feminine female leads, and friendships which lead to something truly special.

When she's not writing or reading, she will be found trying her hand at crocheting, painting, and exploring new cafes and loving her favourite ones.